500 Miles

500 Miles

Sometimes distance is only part of the journey

DEBORAH O'FERRY

First published in 2020 by Deborah O'Ferry

A catalogue entry for this book is available from
the National Library of Australia.

ISBN: 978-1-925921-55-7

Project management and text design by Michael Hanrahan Publishing
Cover design by Saffron & Co. Creative

about the author

Deborah O'Ferry is an Australian writer, based on the outskirts of Sydney where she lives with her small family. She embraced writing from a young age and began writing website articles in 2017. Her words have been published on various websites including Kidspot, Panache Bridal Shoes, The Green Elephant, and Channel 9's popular site, The Block Shop. *500 Miles* is her first novel.

You can follow Deborah O'Ferry on Facebook and Instagram.

acknowledgements

Since I could write, I wanted to write books. I hope you enjoy reading my very first, after all these years of talk.

I'm truly honoured that so many people gave me their time over the course of writing and shaping *500 Miles*. I have imagined thanking them on this page for far too long.

To the three Angelas. Green, for lighting the fire in my belly. Haber, for attempting comma education. Lonergan, for your ongoing support and red pen. To my first readers, Shannon, Donna Grant, Sally, Leigh and Gretchen. Your reviews, suggestions and cheers have been the cornerstones of my confidence to publish this book and I can never thank you enough for believing in me.

To my editors, Kate Lo Basso and Kim Smith, for your thoroughness, time and support. To Saffron, for giving me my first break in writing publicly. From blogs to book covers, I am so grateful. To the team at Michael Hanrahan Publishing, thank you for your honesty and expertise. It's been a steep learning curve that I'm so happy to have had.

To my Nay, Tess. For everything in between.

To my husband, Chris. Without ever reading a word, you backed me from the very beginning. You never made fun of my dream or told me it wouldn't happen. You allowed me to invest in something based on your faith in me and I love you so much for that.

Lastly, to April and Owen. I wrote this before you, but I didn't give up on it because of you. I want these pages to show you that whatever you dream to do, it may take time and patience, but there is always a way.

To Chris and Harry.

*My boys who were ignored while
I wrangled a dream.*

Thank you ox

prologue

Perfect. What a word.

Anna grew up idolising the concept, idolising people she thought were perfect—wanting to be perfect just like them. She, like any little girl, wanted it all. She wanted perfect hair that didn't frizz up in the rain or in the heat of a hot day. She wanted perfect handwriting that looped and swirled like a ballerina. She wanted the perfect mark on the perfect school project. But most of all, she wanted the perfect family.

Anna had been the only person in her class with divorced parents. The only one that missed birthday parties because of custody days—the only student teased because her mother didn't live with her dad.

While watching the other parents arrive together for the end-of-year school concert, while hers pointedly sat on opposing sides of the school hall, Anna had made a decision. At the grand age of seven-and-a-half Anna smugly decided that when she was a grown-up, she would never let that happen to her own children. Of course, when Anna was seven-and-a-half, life was very easy to map out and the road was straight to travel. Getting married and having a family was all she wanted, and it would happen as simply as she would find a job—which was going to happen right after she finished school. For Anna, getting the life she had expected was just an eventuality. You lose your front teeth and new ones grow. You finish the second grade, and then go straight on to the third.

In Anna's young mind, getting a job, being happy and getting married were as certain as her feet growing and turning eight on her next birthday.

However, as the years passed and her feet stopped growing, it slowly became apparent to Anna that life was not so straightforward. Jobs, she had to earn. Hair, she needed to tame. Perfect families? They didn't actually exist. And as for marriage, Anna had realised that, ideally, she needed love. But love isn't as certain as a child is led to believe. Love, far above jobs or unruly hair, is the trickiest one of them all. And love, is certainly not perfect.

chapter one

Anna sat in the emergency waiting-room. The seats were of the molded plastic kind, which were certainly not made for comfort. She decided, should she ever find herself with more money than was reasonable, she would donate it to the hospital for the sole purpose of providing cushioned chairs.

Wriggling in her seat, Anna brushed her dark strands of hair off her face with a sigh. She was exhausted, worried, and in pain. She looked down at her finger and winced.

'I have a really bad paper cut from that stupid form,' she complained to Jane, who sat next to her perfectly composed. 'It stings *so* much,' she moaned, before guiltily scanning the company they kept of Melbourne's sick and injured, and then Jane's arm — covered in a blood-stained checkered shirt — and finally at her friend's tired eyes.

'You poor thing, do you think you'll be okay?' Jane mocked as Anna's fingertip sat inside her mouth.

'Sorry,' Anna blushed, removing her finger and trying to ignore the throbbing flesh as she reached for Jane's hand. 'How are you feeling?'

'I'm okay,' Jane sighed, offering a small smile from her pale face and patting Anna's hand. 'Tired.'

It was nearing two a.m. and they had been waiting for almost an hour. They were dressed in what they had planned would be ideal outfits for dancing. 'Ideal' consisting of unbearably high shoes, jeans (too fitted for sitting in hard plastic chairs), tops to keep cool in, that now revealed too much skin for an emergency room full of strange characters, and, in Anna's case, makeup that had now been smudged and sweated out in ways that would put your regular clown to shame—Jane found it annoyingly impossible to not look immaculate.

'Jane Vadam,' a nurse called, her head poking out from behind the swinging doors, her foot keeping one open.

'Thank goodness,' Jane muttered as she rolled her eyes at Anna and stood, securing her slim gold clutch under her uninjured arm and clasping her cardigan between her slender fingers. 'I'm fine to go in on my own.'

'You don't want me to come in with you?' Anna frowned, quietly relieved and wondering why she hadn't let their friend Mel come along after all. Concern aside, Mel was far better with gore. Blood and Anna had had a falling out in the seventh grade when she'd witnessed a hockey stick smack right into her then-best-friend's nose.

Jane declined the offer.

'Oh, ok, if you're sure then,' Anna spoke slowly, feeling useless and a little offended, but mostly thankful, and Jane gave a tired laugh.

'Thanks for the offer Anna, but I'd be too worried you'd pass out. You just sit here and look after yourself and that nasty paper cut of yours.' She winked and walked away, leaving Anna to think about the night that was.

Justin stood at the bar, waiting with waning patience in the Friday night crowd. He was usually a relaxed guy, but certain things grated his patience. Lining up for drinks was one of them, bad phone service was another. Being surrounded by people so drunk they couldn't remember their own name was up there too. How they were managing to take their hourly selfie and post it on Facebook was sheer genius.

He knew he was a hypocrite, he'd been one of them many times before (selfie excluded), but the older Justin grew, the less he could tolerate drunkenness as a sober bystander. The older he became, the more he developed a headache from clubs too. The typical smell of stale vomit, sweat, beer and fake tan was just strong enough to remind him that he didn't really want to be there.

Justin's dislike of the bar scene also stemmed from the fact that he'd witnessed years of drunken bar antics from one of his best mates.

Justin could see Adam through the hazy room now. He was leering unashamedly onto the dance floor, beer in hand, visibly plotting his move on an unsuspecting woman. Adam was simply one of those guys who gave all guys a bad name.

They had met on their first day of high school and the law of opposites attract had fueled the friendship ever since. Admittedly, the times they spent together had decreased in recent years, and tonight was a fair reminder of why.

Justin cringed as Adam danced behind a tall brunette. While Bryan Adams belted out *Summer of '69*, Adam thrust his arms and pelvis towards his prey. *Subtle*, Justin thought, turning his focus back to the bar just as he was cut in on.

'No, no, after you,' he gestured sarcastically to the girl in front of him. She whipped her head around to face him. Her hair jutted out around her face in a halo of poor taste, and she gave him a jagged smile.

'Hi there, sugar,' she slurred, cocking her head to one side. Her slanted eyes darted over his shaven face and dark hair, evidently approving of what she saw. 'Wanna buy me a drink?'

She attempted to flutter her thick false lashes, although Justin thought she may have been blacking out between each flutter. His face made an involuntary wince, but the girl was already distracted by a nearby sparkling top and was calling stretched-out compliments to its owner.

Justin felt out of place. He and Adam had flown down to Melbourne because their friend, Paul, was getting married in two weeks' time. The buck's party was planned for Saturday, but Adam had thought it'd be a great idea to start early and, 'scope out the talent.' Justin was beginning to wonder what exactly Adam's idea of 'talent' was. Justin wasn't single, and he wasn't a pig, so he wasn't looking to find anyone on this excursion to the bar, but if he had been, he would have been disappointed. Luckily for Adam, the surrounding women seemed to have even lower standards than he.

The bartender finally gave him the sought-after nod and Justin yelled out an order. Feeling calmer now that he'd been served, he glanced around at the crowd. The girl with the jagged smile was now requesting the bartender use soy milk in her cocktail, 'Cause I'm on this diet,' she explained. As Justin smirked, he heard someone next to him bellow, 'Is she kidding?' and looked down to find a girl he could only liken to a pixie. Her wholesome rosy face looked like it had come straight from a children's show. Justin smiled widely at her outburst and she shook her head of dark hair towards him, recruiting him as her support.

'Seriously, what kind of an idiot is this girl?' She laughed, her pale eyes reeling at the audacity of the request.

'A health-conscious one?' Justin offered.

'I've been lining up for *forever* and this twit is making us wait longer. Go home!' she yelled at the girl, any casting hope for a children's show fading fast.

The bartender placed Justin's beers on the counter and as Justin paid, the girl with the bad hair turned around, oblivious to the pixie's comments, and spoke to Justin.

'So, you want me number, hon?' she drawled, before proceeding to press her legs up against his. 'Well?'

Justin, surprised being an understatement, replied as quickly as he could. 'Sorry … gay,' he shrugged, feigning regret.

'Your loss, darl,' she drooled through her straw, then pinched his arse before staggering away. Justin stood in a brief time delay of surprise until the bartender's voice dawned upon him.

'Card, mate.'

'Right, sorry. Thanks,' Justin spluttered, his words lost in the noise of the bar, and took his credit card as the bartender served the next grateful patron.

'Wow, what a catch,' he heard at his side again. 'Too bad you're gay.'

With a hint of embarrassment, Justin smiled her way.

'I know, great offer,' he yelled to be heard. 'But what can I do?'

She nodded in agreement. Justin picked up the drinks, smiled a goodbye and squeezed his way back to Adam, who wasn't looking too sober.

'What took you so fucking long?' demanded Adam. 'I dropped my beer ages ago. Almost got kicked out, didn't I? Had to say someone knocked me.' He started laughing hard and a bit of spit took flight and landed on his chin. 'Then they kicked that fool out! Ah mate, it was the funniest thing. You should have seen it.' Justin watched as Adam grabbed a beer and downed it in one go.

'Ah, that's the stuff,' Adam praised as he gave Justin a wide grin. Justin, faux comradely grin in place, tried not to notice he was out with the type of person he couldn't stand.

As Anna nursed her finger she thought of the guy at the bar. There was something about him that had him stuck in her foggy head. She had even noticed over the bar stench that he smelt nice—and in that dump, that was something notable.

The club was not usually a place she or Jane would visit, but for Jane's farewell it had been the most convenient.

After four demanding years of juggling work and study, Jane had finally finished university and was moving back home to Sydney to become a teacher. It was something Anna was certainly dreading and she tried not to think about it, the hospital was depressing enough. She turned her focus back to the guy at the bar. Anna wondered what his name was. She was usually pretty good at guessing names. Could it be Ryan, she thought. Nah. Jonathon? Maybe. Dilbert?

She smiled as she imagined saying passionate things to a Dilbert. Not that she would be getting to see Dilbert again, for the chance to say any passionate things, but he had given Anna some hope that there were half-decent guys out there. Well, more than half-decent in Dilbert's case. She felt mildly embarrassed that she'd let her mouth get the better of her when she had started yelling out at the bar. She had not been so loud intentionally. Sometimes she just didn't think before sending words out—it was a trait Jane often reminded her of. But then Dilbert had turned around; and then he had smiled. He could be a complete arse, Anna mused, but his eyes told her otherwise. He looked just all-round good. He looked like the sort of guy that could hold you when everything was bad and make it nice again. Not a concept that would make feminists proud, thought Anna, but the truth, nonetheless.

Where have all the good Dilberts gone? She pondered, as she waited for Jane.

The music was making Justin's heart thump as he stood at the edge of the dance floor, careful not to cross over to the timber boards. He didn't mind dancing. Not to the point where he'd be found jiggling his legs and feeling the need to *go* dancing. But he was capable of handling himself when a dancing situation arose—though that situation usually involved a forceful request from his girlfriend. Tonight however, Justin was tired and far from tempted to join Adam on the floor. He'd raced from work, to home, to the hospital to visit his sister, home again, and then to the airport. Instead of sleeping on the plane, like he'd planned, he spent the entire flight trying to ignore Adam cracking gum between his teeth as he commentated on the features of the female flight crew.

In truth, besides his claim to exhaustion, Justin was mostly too ashamed to be associated with Adam. In the dark room, Justin could make out Adam moving his hips behind another girl. Her friend was glaring at him with disgust, yet Adam's actual target appeared thrilled to have someone dancing with her.

Justin watched in astonishment as the girl began grinding her back into Adam and giggling into his ear. Justin shook his head. Unsurprisingly, Adam didn't have a girlfriend or any intention of finding one. He truly believed a girlfriend would hinder his lifestyle in a way he was unwilling to succumb to, and that way was monogamy. Adam was so opposed to the concept that he'd openly refused to go to Paul's upcoming nuptials because he thought it was a stupid idea. 'His balls will be permanently locked up in her handbag', he'd declared with all the class that Adam possessed.

Justin's eyes hastily scanned the room in an effort to avoid seeing Adam's tongue in the girl's ear and fell upon a group of women dancing in a circle. The group had piled their bags in the middle and were spending more energy defending them than actually dancing. Two girls, the exception, seemed oblivious to it all — a tall blonde with her hands moving up and down in the air in beat with the music, and in front of her a shorter person whose hands were perfectly synchronised with her friend's. Justin smiled when he realised the shorter girl was the pixie from the bar. This was obviously a song they'd danced to countless times before and had their routine down pat. They paid no attention to the crowds trying to break through the circle and crush their belongings, nor to their friends who hurled abuse at the people that tried. The two friends just kept dancing and were now screaming the words of the song at each other. Noting the song, a Proclaimers hit from the eighties, he smiled as they sung with such intensity. When the song ended, the girls collapsed into each other in laughter, squealing when they recognised the next song. Justin could read the pixie's mouth screaming, 'I love this song.' With her hands on her heart, her not-quite-shoulder-length dark waves bounced as she jumped up and down to the familiar retro beat.

Justin smiled. Her energy was so childlike it reminded him of his nieces; excited, free and impulsive. He considered if that was what he liked about Adam. He turned back to find him, but he'd disappeared from his last place of prey and Justin couldn't place him anywhere on the dance floor.

After spending the next three overplayed songs scrutinising the bouncing bodies for signs of Adam, Justin started to wonder if he had been ditched. It wouldn't be the first time Adam had abandoned him somewhere without warning.

Justin turned to leave, relieved he'd had the good sense to hold on to his hotel room card, when he spotted Adam at the bar lapping up the caged attention of the girls in line. Justin rolled his eyes. Adam was a good-looking guy — Justin's sisters had told him this many times. He was slightly taller than Justin, with sandy hair and a year-round tan. Their soccer attempts back home kept them both reasonably fit, which Adam often flaunted. Justin just couldn't understand how women didn't see straight through him.

Adam eventually headed towards him with two beers, swigging one down on the way, missing most of his mouth in the process and tipping a great deal of it down his shirt. He reached Justin, who went to take the other beer.

'Oi! Wanted one mate did ya? Could have told me,' Adam complained. Justin scowled at him and grabbed the beer on principle more than want.

'How much have you had anyway, Ad?' Justin sipped the beer wishing it were water. 'You missed your mouth back there.' He laughed lightheartedly but it was a sight Justin was tired of.

'Hardly had any,' Adam defended. Justin wasn't so sure, but usually when Adam drank too much his eyes would need to be pried open. Now they looked wide and alert and Justin debated about whether he was telling the truth.

'Did you want to get going mate, it's pretty trashy,' prompted Justin. 'We need to meet the others at ten tomorrow?' They were starting the day at the golf course and Justin was hoping that Adam would remember the reason behind the weekend.

'Ah, bit longer Jay.'

Knowing he'd be called old and boring, Justin relented; suppressing the desire to sleep. Adam had always had the ability to puppet Justin into doing things he didn't want to do. Years ago, he had almost lost his place at university after Adam had convinced him to skip school for a poker game. Justin didn't even play poker, but he went because Adam kept telling him he was a geek and that he'd never get laid. What eighteen-year-old male would take that threat lightly? So, Justin had gone along, and Justin had been caught. The school principal threatened to withdraw his letter of recommendation for his place at university, which was crucial for his application. Telling his parents had been the hardest part for Justin, but he never told the school or his family that Adam was there too. He didn't see the point of them both being punished, and Justin was raised not to pass the blame, and so he didn't. That, and Adam threatened to tell the grade that Justin had genital lice if he did reveal the names of the other poker attendees. Once again, this did little to help Justin's fear of being a virgin forever, so he obeyed. Justin, the school's top student, ended up with an after-school detention plus threats of suspension and ban from their graduation if he didn't smarten up.

Fifteen years later and, against his better judgment, Justin still had little resistance to Adam's poor decisions. He was watching Adam now, whose whole body was jittering about to the booming *YMCA* as he surveyed the room. His eyes locked on to a red-haired woman, and then he was gone.

Justin considered returning to the bar when his eyes fell on the pixie again. Her eyes were now coolly narrowing in on what could best be described as a gorilla. An extremely hairy guy, at least an actual foot taller than her, was not budging as she attempted to push him away with considerable force. A beer swayed in his hand as he bound his arm around her waist to pull her close.

Justin's body straightened as he saw her struggle to keep free. He took a step forward but stopped when two of her friends abandoned their handbag post to rescue her. They peeled the unwanted hands away and gave him a burst of female abuse, ordering him away.

Not responding as wished, the offending gorilla leered at the girls, hovering his face close to them with an arrogant smirk. The dance floor was full and the group were being pushed and pulled in all directions. Y's, M's, C's and A's were flung about enthusiastically, and Justin struggled to follow the scene as the current of the crowd moved it. A bouncer, with arms hanging far from his body due to the induced size of his biceps, approached the situation with pleasure. The gorilla, to the jeering around him, swung around to the challenge.

While the two oversized men sized each other up, the pixie retreated behind their bulk and her friends checked she was okay. For a moment, things seemed under control.

Then the moment passed.

Suddenly the bouncer was pushed by a careless dance move. Mistaken for intent to strike, the gorilla threw his glass at the bouncer, and together they stumbled into the girls. Dancers fell down and a black hole had appeared on the dance floor. Some close enough to the drama, hesitated about continuing their Village People tribute. Most kept dancing.

Another enormous bouncer appeared and together they hauled the resisting drunk away, abandoning the girls on the floor.

As Justin pondered the guy's fate, he watched, waiting for the black hole to rise. The pixie appeared first and when she screamed Justin didn't wait another moment, he started pushing through the crowd. With lights flashing a rainbow of colours onto shiny faces, music so loud, and singing so bad, no-one could hear him as he tried to squeeze past. Finally, Justin made it to the scene of the scream to find the girls kneeling on the floor. People danced, pranced and flung around them in oblivion.

The pixie, held up by the redhead Adam had not long ago preyed on, looked like she was about to cry. Justin followed her gaze to her blonde dancing partner on the floor whose arms were covered in blood. He understood the reason for the chaos — there was a lot of blood.

The group, shrieking and bustling, were failing to actually help the situation. Justin knelt down to the injured girl's side. Blood was smeared on her cheek and she held her injured arm tight.

'Are you okay?' he yelled over the music, instantly frowning at the dumb question.

'I fell on the glass,' she cried frantically.

'Do you think glass is still inside?'

'I don't know,' she cried, shocked at the idea. She was looking at her friend, the pixie, who was refusing to look at her and, even in the retro lights, was becoming paler by the second. She turned to another girl.

'Ioulia, is there glass inside?'

'I don't know,' she yelled. 'Jane, is it hurting?' Jane nodded and her chin threatened with a quiver.

'Why don't we get you to the bathroom and have a closer look?' suggested Justin, who had to yell even louder to be heard.

Jane nodded, closed her eyes as she gulped in a breath, and continued to sit on the dance floor. Justin told her friend, whose name was lost on him already, he'd move Jane and called for her to follow.

He scooped Jane up and almost fell back down again. She was deceptively heavy—or maybe he really needed to work on his fitness regime. He slowly turned her through the crowd, which had become a little more obliging, and walked towards the restrooms. He could feel her body trembling, and her skin felt cool and clammy. He tried to move faster through the crowd; at the same time, he worried he might drop her and look like an absolute moron.

'You're going to be okay, Jane,' he promised.

'Do I know you?' she asked, startled as she acknowledged a stranger was carrying her.

'No,' he said quickly. He couldn't say more, breathe and not drop her.

He found the bathrooms and instantly dismissed using the overly crowded ladies' room. Placing Jane down, Justin nodded towards the men's room and held the door open for them to pass. Faster than the urinal smell could assault their nostrils, two guys at the trough began a bout of indecent proposals and crude gesticulations when they spotted the girls.

'Sorry,' mumbled Jane, whose face was so pale now Justin thought she'd pass out. Her friend on the other hand was blushing quite extraordinarily.

'Jane,' Justin motioned her over to the basin. 'We'll wash your arm and see how bad it is.'

'Do I know you?' she asked again, squinting at his brown eyes.

'No, but I'm Jay. Come over here and we'll wash away the blood, okay?' he said gently, turning the tap. He wasn't sure if Jane was just in shock, if she was very drunk, or if she was just generally a slow person.

'This is,' Jane paused as if to remember, 'Ioulia.'

Ioulia, who had a thin beaded plait hanging by her sturdy face, smiled grimly towards Justin and muttered what Justin guessed she had been muttering her whole life, 'It's Greek.'

Jane folded her arm into the basin and the white sink turned red. Justin could see the wound was deep and worried glass was hidden inside. He was also worried about how much blood she had lost.

'Oh, gross,' Ioulia exclaimed, as she saw the red sink.

'It's pretty deep,' Justin muttered, as he inspected her arm. 'I think you are going to need stitches.'

'Stitches?' Jane slurred. 'No.'

Justin was apologetic. 'Unfortunately, yes. Can you get to a hospital?'

'Hospital?'

'Yeah. Is there one nearby?'

'But … but, I don't want to go to a hospital,' Jane stuttered, then turned to her friend.

'Ioulia, I don't want to go to the hospital.' Tears started to creep down her face.

'Sorry,' said Justin. 'But you really need to have it looked at.'

Justin started unbuttoning his shirt. He'd put a collared shirt on over his t-shirt earlier in the night so he could get into the club. For some reason, management felt a collar would do the trick in keeping the place classy.

He folded the shirt into a bandage and held Jane's arm up from the basin. Tearing off some paper towel from beside the mirror he folded it over the cut and gently wrapped his shirt around her forearm.

'Can you feel something sharp pressing on anything?'

'No. No, it's fine. I can just go home,' she tried.

'Jane.' Justin held her shoulders and looked into her eyes. They were red, but they looked wise, and he decided it was just the shock and the alcohol making her unable to comprehend the seriousness of her situation.

'You have a very deep cut. It's bleeding—a lot. You have to get to a doctor. It's very important that you go. Okay?' Jane stared at her arm and then blankly at her friend before nodding. 'Can you take her?' Justin looked over at Ioulia. 'Or the bar could call an ambulance?'

'I'll call a taxi,' Ioulia rushed, and began searching for her phone in her velvet shoulder bag.

Jane swayed a little and then stumbled. Justin caught her as Ioulia made taxi arrangements over the rush of music and inappropriate remarks coming in and out of the amenities.

'Jane, I think you'll feel better with some fresh air. Let's wait outside.' Ioulia came to Jane's other side and helped her over to the door.

'How far away is the taxi?'

'Ten minutes. I'll get her things and let the others know what's happening.' She went to leave and then hurried back. 'I'm so sorry. Thank you so much for helping us. Are you okay with her while I go back?'

'No problem. I'll meet you outside.'

He turned back to Jane and led her back out into the bar area. On the way he caught sight of Adam, who winked when he noticed Justin with a tall blonde. He then started pumping his arms in his signature thrusting move.

Justin walked Jane out into the icy August air, and helped her to a nearby bench.

'How are you feeling?'

'Yeah, better,' she offered with a wan smile as he sat down too. 'I'm feeling a bit silly now, actually.' Her face reddened.

'Don't. You have one nasty cut. You're lucky you didn't damage an artery.' As Jane paled at such a possibility, Justin quickly regretted the comment. 'You'll be fine,' he promptly added, looking out for her friend or the taxi, hoping the former would show up first.

'I'm going to speak to the bouncer and I'll come right back.' Jane nodded and by the time he was able to ask where the best and nearest hospital was located, the club doors were flung open and Jane's friend (who Justin only knew as the pixie) hurtled out. Her head flicked in all directions looking for her wounded friend. When she spotted Jane, she flew straight over and hugged her protectively. Jane winced and returned the hug with her uninjured arm.

Knowing Jane would be taken care of, and not wanting to intrude, Justin decided to go back inside. He could see Adam and didn't want to lose sight of him again.

Justin looked over at Jane to catch her attention—she caught his eye and he gave a wave goodbye. She returned the wave, mouthing a 'thank you'. Justin walked back inside just as her friend turned her head to see who Jane was motioning to, but he was already gone.

chapter two

'Are you okay?' cried Anna as she hugged Jane, her concern forcing her voice to an unnaturally high pitch.

'Yeah, I think so.' Jane eyed her arm skeptically. 'Are *you* okay? You went a bit funny in there.'

Anna squished her face apologetically. 'Sorry about that. Some friend, huh? One glimpse of blood and I lose my cool.'

'Well, I think you must have lost your cool before that. What was with that meat-axe in there?'

'That guy was a creep,' Anna spat, her anger revived. 'I'm so sorry you got hurt. Ioulia said you have to go to the hospital. The hospital!'

'Yeah, Jason said I'd need stitches,' Jane explained. She felt incredibly tired and her head was spinning. She didn't want to think about having to go to a hospital.

'She told me,' Anna sympathised, frowning supportively. 'Wait, who's Jason?'

'The guy who helped me … actually, maybe his name was Jay.' She turned her head towards the crisp navy sky in thought.

'What guy?' Anna pleaded for Jane's attention, hugging her shivering body as she spoke.

'The guy helping me on the dance floor,' Jane implored, prompting Anna's memory.

'Nope, sorry. Who was he?'

'I don't know. He came out of nowhere and carried me to —'

'He carried you off?' Anna blurted. 'Sounds like a hero. Who is this guy? How did I miss that? Was he single? Did you get his number?'

'Whoa, whoa, whoa,' Jane laughed lightly. 'One question at a time.' She closed her eyes briefly, desperate to rest them, but she could feel herself sway so reopened them.

Anna was staring at her, concerns obvious, when she heard the bouncer inform them their taxi had arrived. Jane thanked him and stood up uneasily. Anna balanced her and led her to the car. When she asked the driver to take them to the hospital, his face fell.

'She isn't about to throw up, is she?' he asked, pointing accusingly at Jane. Clearly, he'd had such luck before. After smelling the cab, Anna wondered if he'd had that luck recently. Her own stomach churned and she forced herself to push the thought away.

'No, she's not! She just cut herself,' she retorted.

He squinted at Jane and, appearing satisfied with the answer, drove off. Jane was asleep before they'd reached the end of the street and Anna let her snore quietly.

Justin walked straight to where he'd seen Adam, slowing as he approached. Adam looked strange. Sweat was dripping off his face and he was bouncing his body around so much that he looked like a frog on a trampoline. Justin worried about how much more alcohol Adam had consumed while he'd been occupied in the bathroom playing doctor.

Justin squeezed Adam's damp shoulder. 'Mate, we need to go.'

'Yo, buddy,' Adam grinned and started laughing, shaking his head in disbelief. 'How awesome is this place? I love it. Love it, love it, love it!'

'Ah, yeah … it's great.' Justin humoured him. He hadn't seen a trashier place since he had taken a load to the tip a year ago.

Justin, deciding to leave Adam to his newfound love, told him he would meet him back at the hotel. He wasn't sure whether Adam understood, his eyes appeared to be darting in all directions, but Adam had managed to call him 'an old fag' enough times for Justin not to care.

Justin squeezed his way back through the crowd. As the hours had passed, the levels of intoxication had naturally increased. The voices were louder and dance moves clumsier. Sweaty skin shimmered throughout. Deodorants had failed. Justin would feel relief when he finally made it back outside.

'Shirt, buddy!' Justin heard someone yell and grab his arm. He turned around to face one of the bouncers from earlier. 'Where's the collar?' he demanded, pointing to Justin's t-shirt. Justin resisted a laugh.

'I'm leaving. Don't worry,' he replied, not bothering to explain. The bouncer led him through the crowd and then he was out. Justin felt like he'd crossed the finishing line. He saw Jane's friend, Ioulia, waiting outside with their other friends. She called out to him and jogged over.

'Hey! Thank you so much for before. That was really nice of you,' she exclaimed.

'No prob—' he started to reply as the other girls began whistling and cheering, 'Go, Ioulia.' She whipped her head around to quiet them.

'Sorry. They're drunk,' she apologised.

'I can see,' he laughed. 'Well, I hope she's okay. I'm sure she'll be fine.' At that, the girls' taxi arrived and they piled in, leaving

Ioulia to take the front seat. Shrieking and giggling, he heard one cry out, 'Where's Jane?' and then, 'Oh, yeah!'

Taking a final look inside before walking back to the hotel, Justin felt frustrated when he spotted Adam. He was just near the entrance and was being dragged out—putting up a fight in the process. Justin watched while he was pushed through the doors and out on to the pavement. Adam, shouting colourful expletives, stumbled, then fell to the ground. He jumped back up, stumbled again, and fell back down.

Justin couldn't think of a moment he'd seen Adam perform worse. He walked over cautiously, and the bouncer questioned if he was with Adam. Justin nodded reluctantly before asking what he had done.

'He's had too much, he has to go. He's just thrown up in there and now he's being a fuckwit,' the bouncer defended, chest puffed further than necessary. Justin frowned down at Adam, who appeared asleep on the sidewalk.

'Okay, thanks. I'll take him.'

'He's all yours,' the bouncer slapped him on the back.

Justin called out to Adam to get up. He remained unmoving on the dirty concrete. Justin prodded him with his foot, but he failed to react to that either. Justin looked at the bouncer, who was quite calm about this, and they knelt down in unison.

'Adam,' Justin called. 'Ad, wake up mate.' To Justin's relief, Adam moaned, but didn't move.

'Think you need to get this one to a hospital, I'm afraid,' the bouncer said quite matter-of-fact, not afraid at all.

'Hospital?' Justin looked at him with wide eyes, and then back at Adam, feeling more empathy for Jane.

'Yep. Probably needs his stomach pumped, or whatever it is they do. Can call the ambos if you want, but it's Friday night. Taxi probably quicker.' The bouncer thought for a second.

'Alfred Hospital. Just don't tell the cabbie he's been sick,' he winked.

When a taxi pulled up the bouncer spoke to the driver, which Justin appreciated. He heaved Adam up and threw his arm over his shoulder. Adam slurred a few words incoherently; which Justin accepted as a good sign. He staggered with Adam into the taxi and fumbled a seatbelt around him, to the cabbie's very vocal insistence.

'He better not vomit! I've had enough of you bloody idiots tonight, vomiting and carrying on.' The driver complained all the way down the road. Justin wasn't sure if the driver wanted a response, but he ignored him either way. By the time they pulled up to the hospital, Adam had come to and his words were making some sense.

Justin paid the fare and helped Adam out and towards the emergency doors. By this stage, Adam was swearing wildly at Justin and he only just managed to duck back to miss Adam's flying fist.

'Mate, what are you doing?'

'Fuck off! Fucker,' Adam slurred like he'd never seen Justin before.

Angry, and tempted not to bother now that Adam was awake, Justin was able to steer him towards the entrance by provoking him to fight. As the automatic doors opened, Adam took another swing. Justin moved again, but not fast enough to avoid the tail end of the blow. Adam hit him square on the cheek bone. Justin was too stunned to feel the pain immediately but knew it would come fiercely later.

A security guard appeared quickly and pinned Adam to the ground. Adam resisted the hold whilst swearing at the entire room. Justin felt an unsettling number of eyes on them. Some people stood up to have a better view, at least one phone capturing the moment. A male nurse jogged over as Adam resisted the guard's hold. Justin tried helping but felt too confused to be of any real use.

'What's he on?' asked the nurse.

'Beer?' replied Justin, disturbed that Adam's feet had started flying towards his head.

'He's not on any other drugs?' the nurse demanded.

'What? No!' exclaimed Justin while simultaneously ducking.

'Right. Can you fill out some paperwork? Name and details?' he asked, raising an eyebrow. He had a no-nonsense face and Justin felt more scared of him than Adam or the huge security guard. Adam had slowed under their weight and Justin stood up to follow the nurse. As he walked away, the guard called out.

'He's out!'

The triage nurse jumped from her seat and hastily moved through to the foyer, the male nurse zipped back and another staff member with a trolley followed a moment after. Justin watched as they heaved Adam onto the bed and rushed him through the double doors.

In a flash he was gone.

Justin was dumbfounded, but before he had a chance to work it all out, another nurse came back with questions.

'What's his name?'

'Adam Blackett.'

'Age?'

'Thirty-three.'

'What's he had?'

'Beer.' With this he received another raised eyebrow.

'How much?'

'Not sure.'

'Any known allergies?'

'No.'

'Any medical conditions?'

'No.'

'Are you a relation?'

'Friend.'

With this he was instructed to wait and was handed paper-work to fill out.

Justin tentatively took a pen from the front desk and sat down on a cold plastic seat in the corner. He filled out the form to the best of his knowledge and handed it in. Returning to his seat, he briefly looked around the busy waiting-room for the first time. The fluorescent lights beamed down on everyone and, at two a.m., was not doing many favours.

There wasn't much of a mix of people inside. Justin could narrow it down to two main groups — people with runny noses and people with bloody noses. He placed his head in his hands. His cheek was burning cruelly and he only just realised. It swelled from under his palm and he considered asking for ice but didn't. He cupped it gently instead and closed his eyes.

Anna sat watching the other people in the room. Most of them were motionless, bar their thumbs, which scrolled over lit-up phone screens. If her own phone's battery wasn't flat, she proba-bly would have been doing the same. Instead she played doctor, mentally prescribing a tissue and a glass of water, and wanting to send half the crowd home to bed; some people had real problems.

She looked down at her paper cut again. She was grateful that at least the sting distracted her from worrying about Jane — and how cold she was. Goosebumps covered her body and she tried to rub them away until a small strangled gurgle distracted her. Her eyes fell on a mother holding her baby. The child's cough was like a dog's bark and Anna felt awful for them both. She wondered how long they'd been waiting for. The mother noticed her looking and Anna was offering a supportive smile when she noticed an increase in conversation around them. People were craning their neck to see out the emergency doors and Anna followed suit. Outside she could see two men fighting and she rolled her eyes.

Then the doors slid open, bringing inside another unwelcome cool rush of air and a familiar face. *Dilbert.*

'Does it hurt?' He heard a concerned voice and looked up. His eyes were bleary, but Justin could see a face he knew and smiled. Jane's pixie friend was sitting two seats over and Justin mentally slapped himself—on the other cheek—for not considering that she and Jane could be there too.

'Hi …' he stopped himself just in time from calling her 'Pixie'. 'You.'

'Hi "you" back,' she smiled. 'Your face must hurt. Are you okay?'

Justin, embarrassed that she'd seen his grand entry into the hospital, felt his other cheek begin to burn.

'Ah, it's okay. Thanks, though. How are you going here?' he asked, her large eyes fixed on his cheek.

'You sure? I can get you some ice? I'll go get you some ice,' and she was gone before he could reply. He was grateful, his face really was hurting. It was making his eyes water and he now had concerns she'd think he was crying.

Returning with a disposable ice-pack and a handful of gauze, she sat one seat closer and he watched as she roughly wrapped the ice-pack and handed it to him. He thanked her and winced as he placed it near his eye. The pack went sliding out and skidding across the floor. Justin leant down to collect it, rewrapped it by neatly folding the gauze around it, and tried again, aware of her eyes on him the entire time.

'I'm Anna. What's your name?' she asked, as if Justin was the new kid at her school.

'Justin.' He held the ice-pack firmly in place, his face appreciating the relief. 'Have you been waiting long?'

'*Forever*,' she drawled out. 'My friend, Jane, got cut at the bar. They took her in about half an hour ago, but we'd been waiting long before that!' She looked like she'd been holding words in for hours and was just rattling them out now. 'So … at least you didn't have to wait for your friend to be seen,' she offered lamely, rubbing her thighs to warm them.

Justin shrugged and smiled in agreement, too tired to tell her he was already aware of her friend's injuries, but glad Jane had followed his advice.

'Is he going to be okay?'

'Adam? He's just drunk. He'll be fine.' Justin looked at her pixie-like face again and took it in under the harsh lights. He thought she may have been the only one in the room that the light didn't make look bad. If anything, it seemed to highlight her features.

'Does he normally do that? You know, go kinda crazy?' Anna asked curiously. He hadn't been able to appreciate her eyes when he'd met them at the bar, but now, as they watched him for an answer, the clarity of their green was striking. He found it hard not to stare, and almost as hard not to comment on them. Fighting the urge, Justin shook his head. Then nodded his head. Then scrunched his face.

'I don't know. I've never really noticed. He's never hit me before, that's for sure. But he does take things too far.' He thought about it some more. 'I guess I'm just used to it.'

'Well, he seems like an arse.' Anna tried to catch the last word with her hands as she was saying it. 'Oh my god, I'm sorry,' she rushed out in a horrified voice. 'I'm sure he's not an arse.'

Justin watched amused as she tried to rectify the situation. Her pleading face stared across at him, searching for forgiveness.

'It's okay.' He smiled to let her know it was. 'He *is* an arse.' Justin sighed a tired sigh. 'Friends, huh?'

'Yeah,' she agreed, her shoulders relaxing. 'Can't trust them to stay outta trouble.' She leaned back into the hard seat with a grin.

'I wonder how long they'll be in there. I didn't think it'd take this long to stitch up an arm. I hope she's okay.'

Anna told Justin she was going to go ask reception and his eyes followed her as she clicked her way over to the front desk. Her heels were high and he marveled at her balancing skills. As she walked back across the waiting-room, she caught him watching her and he cursed himself.

'What'd they say?' he asked, as he changed the position of the ice-pack on his face, hoping it would disguise his staring.

'Well, they said that they had a patient come in that was 'requiring more attention',' she said, making quotations in the air. 'So, Jane is waiting in there.'

'There's a second waiting-area?'

'Seems that way,' she shrugged. 'Looks like you're stuck with me kiddo,' she grinned down at him, sliding back onto the seat.

Justin rolled his smiling eyes. 'What a night.'

'Let's play a game!' she suggested excitedly, ignoring him, and he wondered where she got the energy from. 'We can play Twenty Questions.'

Justin wasn't really up for games at an hour he was meant to be asleep, but relented. He'd hate to disappoint a pixie.

'Me first,' she said, sitting up straighter, and he nodded an okay.

'What is your *full* name?'

'Justin Marcus Owens.' He chuckled as she mouthed *Marcus* with repulsion. 'Now you, full name?'

'Anna Marcus,' she grinned.

He laughed at the coincidence and chose an unoriginal favourite colour question; accepting her answer of 'green' like it was what he expected. Maybe it was because she was wearing a green top that set off her green eyes and he was beginning to love the colour, too. So much so that he told her it was his favourite colour also.

'Oh, twins,' she exclaimed happily. 'Okay. Hmm … job?'

'Yes,' he replied.

'What do you mean "yes"?'

'I mean, yes I have one. You?'

'Yes. But *what* is your job,' she squeaked impatiently.

'Oh, sorry.' He thought for a second. 'Do I have to answer that?'

'Yeah, why?' she leant over and whispered secretively, looking around at the other people in the waiting-room first. 'Are you a secret agent?'

'No!' His big laugh couldn't be unheard in the small space and he dropped his voice when he continued. 'It's just that … and I don't want to be a party pooper …'

'Well good, because *no-one* likes a party pooper,' she advised.

'Once we say what we do for a living, we'll be pigeon-holed. I mean, I love my job but there is more to us than our jobs, right?' he trailed off, looking expectantly at Anna for her reply.

'Intriguing, but too right,' she agreed. 'Okay, no job questions.' She swooshed her hands through the air like a card dealer declaring no more bets.

'What about …' She looked up to the ceiling. 'How much money do you make?' Her blank face attempted to suppress a wicked grin and Justin laughed out loud.

'Not enough. Next.'

All this smiling was putting pressure on his sore face and he slid the ice again to another spot.

'Okay. Where do you live?'

'Depends, are you a stalker?'

'Yeah,' she nodded reluctantly. 'Is that a problem?' His laughter caused people in the waiting-room to look at them in annoyance. Justin pretended not to notice.

'Well, it's good you're talking about it. The first step is talking.' He nodded supportively before breaking into a grin and answering her question. 'I live in Sydney, actually. I flew down today for a buck's weekend.'

'Is that the buck?' she frowned, pointing towards the swing doors where they had taken Adam.

'No!' he exclaimed, appalled at the concept. 'Another friend.'

'Wow, so some night, huh?' she whistled, and he laughed bitterly in agreement.

'It's been interesting.' He shook his head and then looked up at her. 'Hey, are these part of the twenty questions? Where do *you* live?'

'I am from Sydney too actually. Well, originally, but I live in Elwood now.' She saw his confused face. 'It's near St Kilda?' she offered, and he nodded in recognition. 'Okay next question,' she hinted for him to take his turn.

'Brothers and sisters?'

'None,' Anna shook her head. 'You?'

'Two older sisters. One had a baby girl just this week.'

'Name?'

'Bianca,' Justin proudly replied.

'Nice,' Anna smiled. She had tucked her hair behind her ears and Justin noticed they stuck out just a little, only reinforcing the pixie image.

'Yeah. Now, I have another question for you, an important one,' to which Anna sat up, ready. 'What on earth were you doing at that hell-hole tonight?' he demanded.

'Hey!' She became defensive and then thought about it for a moment. 'Okay, fair enough. It was Jane's farewell. She's from Sydney as well, and she's moving back. The bar was easy for everyone. I wouldn't usually go there, I swear!' She held her hands up, pleading her case.

'Okay,' he said, satisfied with her answer, 'your turn.'

'Are you *really* gay?'

'Yes.' He answered looking her straight in the eye. 'Is *that* a problem?'

She laughed, and people gave them more unfriendly looks. She settled into a giggle and hit him on the arm. 'No! But I don't believe you.'

'No, I am. Adam is my partner. Soulmate, actually.' He held his hand to his heart. She laughed louder and the nurse hushed them. Justin put his hand up to apologise and turned back to face Anna.

'Okay, you got me. He's no soulmate. Julia, my girlfriend, would have a problem with that if he was,' he confided. He thought he saw a flicker of disturbance across her features but if he did, it disappeared as quickly as it had appeared.

'What about you? Girlfriend? Boyfriend? Or do you prefer animals?'

'Single,' she laughed. 'But hey, your friend seems to be a good catch. Is he single?' She sat up with wide-eyed hope. It made his stomach do a tiny and unauthorised flip and he promised to pass on her number if she was nice. She agreed and sat up straighter, crossing her leg over her thigh. Her jeans were tight and Justin couldn't help noticing the shape of her legs.

'Okay, next question,' he said, hoping his eyes hadn't wandered too obviously. 'Speaking of animals, do you have any pets?'

'Nope. Do you?'

'Yeah, I do,' he grinned, thinking of his furry friend.

'Goldfish?'

'A dog.'

'Who's looking after it? This girlfriend of yours?'

'My mum and dad actually,' he laughed. 'He's a bit of a grand-dog to them.' Justin knew how pathetic he sounded but still enjoyed her laughter at this.

'What kind of dog is it? No, no, let me guess!' Her brow crumbled in concentration as she started throwing dog breeds at him like they were confetti. He stopped her when she started making them up.

'Give up?' he offered, and she nodded ungratefully, which he thought made her look even more like she belonged in a garden sitting on a mushroom. 'He's a cross-breed, so …'

'Oh man,' she cut him off, slapping her leg. 'No fair. I was never going to get that!'

Justin grinned. 'He's a Schnauzer, crossed with maybe a Labrador or Kelpie.'

'Humph,' she folded her arms across her chest. 'Cheat. You don't even know!' But a smile gave way, 'He sounds kinda ugly.'

Justin laughed at her nerve.

'He's … *different*. He has a beard and a long tail that wags all day long. He's a happy dog. Just different,' he defended.

'You sound like a proud father,' she teased, which, this time, made his face blush.

'You think I'm pathetic, don't you?' She nodded apologetically. 'Don't hold back. Tell me what you really think.'

He waited for her to push for more.

'So, this bearded grand-puppy of yours, where'd you get him? Special breeder?' she asked.

'Actually, I used to work at an animal shelter …'

'Oh, a clue!' Anna whispered. 'Scandalous.'

Justin continued, finding her much more entertaining than his story '… and I was working the day he came in. He was only a pup but was this great big knot of hair and a skinny bag of bones. His owners had neglected him and he cowered around everyone. It was pretty sad. He seemed to take a liking to me though for some reason … I don't know, maybe we smelt the same,' he suggested. Anna had listened quietly for the first time.

He assumed he was boring her and was keen to change the topic of conversation.

'So, you just took him home,' she said, not so much a question but a statement.

'Well, not for a while,' he admitted. 'He was there for a long time and no-one seemed to be interested in adopting him. *Some* people,' he emphasised, 'are just really vain …' he planted a disgusted look on his face, 'and thought he was too ugly to love.' Justin looked over at Anna for her reaction and laughed as she squished her face together in guilty admittance. 'Anyway, it was Christmas time and I couldn't leave him there.'

'That's pretty sweet, I have to say. I can't make fun of you for that.'

'You look disappointed about that.'

'Well yeah, a little,' she nodded, and he gave a small chuckle, her sarcasm amusing him. His girlfriend, Julia, was someone who didn't 'do' sarcasm. It went well and truly over her head and she herself was only ever sarcastic by mistake, as if her mind wasn't tuned into it. When Justin was sarcastic Julia would take his words literally, which could often lead to undesirable situations; Justin having to do things he really didn't want to do. He'd say something like, 'Yeah, I'd *love* to paint your bathroom', and find himself doing just that on his spare weekend; or eating fifty-dollar cucumber sandwiches on his day off, after saying he'd love to go to High Tea. Needless to say, the saying 'I'd love that like a hole in the head,' was one he avoided.

Justin sensed that sarcasm was Anna's crutch. He wondered how that worked out for her, especially when she came across people like Julia.

'So, Justin, *Dog Rescuer Extraordinaire*,' she mocked, 'what is the name of this dog of yours?'

'Hamlet.'

She considered it for a second. 'The beard?'

'Yeah,' he smiled. He'd always had to explain that to anyone else, Julia being no exception.

Anna looked over at him and smiled. She didn't say anything else, just grinned and turned back to the triage window.

They sat there quietly for a little longer. Justin watched Anna fiddle with her finger as he felt the swelling on his face. The coldness of the ice-pack was giving him a headache so he placed it on the ground between his Converse-clad feet. He closed his eyes to rest them briefly but must have drifted into some form of sleep, because the next thing he heard was Anna saying his name as she gently squeezed his shoulder. Startled, he looked up at her and remembered where he was. Her face showed concern and he had to force himself conscious enough to hear what she was saying.

'Is that your friend?' she asked again. He looked around for Adam but couldn't see him. He couldn't see anyone who wasn't there before.

'No, his name. They're calling an Adam Blackett. Is that your friend?' she explained.

'Yeah. Sorry. That's him. What does that mean?'

'You just need to go up to the nurse. Maybe they've finished with him?' she offered gently.

He walked over to the window and gave Adam's name again. The nurse said the doctors wanted to talk to him and then buzzed him through the doors. He moved towards the double doors and turned to see Anna before he stepped through. He gave her a small wave and went in to find Bed Seventeen. So far, she'd been the highlight of his night and as he approached Adam, he was pretty sure she'd hold the title for the weekend.

chapter three

When Anna and Jane reached their apartment that morning the sun was about to rise and they agreed they'd never had a longer night. Grunting at each other, they disappeared into their separate rooms.

Anna peeled off her clothes, pulled a t-shirt over her head, and crawled under the bed covers. However, as exhausted as she was, she was woken by the sun that was in full swing only an hour or so later. Its rays poured through her window shamelessly, her white blinds doing a poor job of keeping them out.

'You're fired,' she mumbled at them in frustration as she hid her head under the pillow and managed a half-hearted sleep for a little longer, before giving up altogether. Growling at the sun, she swung her legs lazily over the edge of the bed, fumbling with the sheets tangled at her feet and straightening her t-shirt that had twisted awkwardly as she'd slept.

Anna padded out to the kitchen and poured herself an orange juice. Her throat felt raw from her singing attempts on the dance floor and she pulled a face at the memory of the night's events. She could only hope that the weekend could redeem itself.

From their small kitchen window Anna dared to look outside, where it was claiming to be a beautiful day, and forgave the sun for waking her. They'd had an abundance of winter sunshine lately and she liked to take full advantage of it. With hope, she looked over at Jane's door for company. There was a pile of boxes stacked neatly beside it marked 'fragile', but the door was firmly shut.

She glanced at the lounge as a second option, plonked herself down, and reached for the remote control. The television switched on to cartoons and sound blasted around the room as one angry cartoon character roared at another. Anna flinched and hastily muted the sound. Whatever happened to *The Flintstones*, she wondered, as she froze to listen for movement from Jane's room, or *The Jetsons*?

The silence disappointed her.

Scrolling through Netflix options, Anna paused to add new options to her list, absently pressing her stinging finger to her lips as she sat mute, unable to commit to any show. She blinked to soothe her dry eyes and told her foggy head it was just sleep deprived. A little part of her admitted it could also have been the wine flooding her blood stream.

Anna stood up to find some food, but while carefully creaking cupboards open, she realised it wasn't the answer. She stared out the window again and watched cars roll by down below, trees sway their leaves about, and runners jog past with too much energy for her liking. It really was a lovely day.

She glanced back to the lounge, chewed her lip and then looked back out to the sunshine. It felt wrong to waste such a nice morning, but it was criminal to not be sleeping-in on a Saturday morning when she had nowhere to be.

She wandered back to her bed, took one look at the brightness and gave her blinds a final glare. Giving in, she showered for an excessively long time before dressing in jeans and a t-shirt and slipped on her sandals — she was hoping for an early summer. Finding her keys on a box marked 'textbooks', she headed to the door.

Outside, the sun felt warm on her skin and like a welcome hug to her weary body. Sliding her sunglasses over her eyes, she turned down the road.

The beach wasn't far and it was her most favourite place to be. The location of their apartment was the prime reason for why they had even agreed to rent it. The apartment itself was quite tiny, the rent more than they were comfortable paying and the road a bit louder than other places they considered. But the beach in walking distance made it a no-brainer for them.

Anna called 'good morning' to an elderly couple and got a 'hey' from a runner. She loved morning people. Everyone seemed so friendly and she made an affirmation to wake up earlier more often. She felt a surge of energy and optimism as she walked past gardens with flowers budding; cafés with food sizzling and mugs tinkering. She thought of Justin, quickly imagining he'd be at one of the tables, before dismissing the idea as irrelevant.

Her energy plunged somewhat once five minutes passed, but she persevered, embracing the challenge. Her optimism took another hit when a lady walking her cruelly short-legged dog refused to return Anna's greeting. Anna huffed under her breath once the lady was well and truly past her and it was clear would not be giving Anna any morning cheer. But by the time the ocean came into view, Anna felt at peace. The different shades of the blue water, the empty horizon … she'd never grow tired of the sight.

Anna had always felt at ease near the sea. Her dad would often take her when she was a child and they had many beach picnics growing up. Her mother didn't share the same passion, often complaining about the sand. But Anna loved it, every bit of it. Even seaweed amused her for some reason. She could see a big clump of it now in her path and she noticed the line of it along the shore. She and her dad used to play with it together. They'd put the salty green grass on their heads like wigs and talk in funny accents; her dad did a mean Martian voice.

Anna smiled a sad smile at the memory. She wondered where her dad was now. Last they had spoken, he was planning on taking on a job offer in Queensland, but she'd never received his new address to be sure. Random text messages from him were the only way she knew he was okay.

He'd left their home when Anna was only six years old. Her parents had sat her down one night and said that they loved her very much and would always love her. They then told her they didn't love each other.

Anna remembered feeling confused and not knowing what that would mean. She told them it was okay but didn't really understand if it was. When her dad left the next morning, Anna still didn't know what it meant. She went to school and boasted very proudly to her teacher, 'My daddy moved out today.' But when she got home and her daddy wasn't there at dinner either, or the following breakfast, she started to worry. She'd asked her mum when he was coming back and when they would be going to the beach. But her mum had just shrugged her shoulders.

Sometimes Anna had caught her mother crying. She'd always say she was watching a sad movie, or a lash had fallen in her eye, but Anna wised up soon enough.

Her dad would pick her up on weekends and they'd go to the movies, or the shops, or make sandcastles at the beach. Most of the time they'd go to a park and she would play while he slept on the grass. She loved her dad, but as the months passed, he started picking her up only every second weekend. Then it became maybe every third. Within a few years, Anna only saw him on holidays or birthdays, if she was lucky.

By the time Anna was finishing high school, she only received brief phone calls from him. He'd be in Brisbane for work, in Malaysia running a course, or traveling through Western Australia. He was also prone to making very random visits that left her mother in tears.

Thinking back now, as she looked nostalgically at the slimy green seaweed, Anna couldn't think of the last time she'd seen him. Her mother was still in Sydney and Anna tried to make an effort to see her, though she knew it wasn't often enough. A part of Anna seemed to harbour resentment towards her, regardless of the strong love she also felt. Anna felt like she'd missed out on so many normalities with her parents and she just didn't understand how people could fall out of love. Maybe, she thought with a sense of embarrassment and regret, because she'd only ever imagined the kind of love people would have to want to get married, she couldn't also grasp people losing it.

In her mind, her heart, the way she believed love to be was that it was so strong and definite, people would do anything to make it work. Anna's real fear in life was that maybe that kind of love just didn't exist at all — that she was waiting for something that wasn't even real.

Anna wandered along the beach until she found a long stretch of sand with little debris. She lay down, nestling herself in the rough grains. The sand was warm from the late winter sunshine and she closed her eyes, enjoying the feeling on her face and on the hint of her belly that was showing. Anna fell sound asleep with the sound of the water lapping in her ears, and only woke when she felt her body shiver. She opened her eyes, frowning at the goose bumps that had sprouted over her entire body. The sky had turned an angry grey and a growing wind was making frothy waves in the water and whipping grains of sand at her skin.

She stood up quickly, brushed the sand off her backside and walked briskly home to Jane.

Bloody Melbourne, she cursed.

chapter four

Justin woke to his mobile ringing. He wasn't sure how long it had rung for but felt irritated that it had interrupted his dream of a girl with a pixie face. His hand went feeling around the side table and when his hand clenched around the phone, his thumb instinctively slid across the screen.

''Ello,' he answered gruffly.

'Justin Owens?' a woman's voice asked crisply.

'Yes. Who's this?' he mumbled at the unfamiliar voice.

'Mr Owens, this is Alfred Hospital. We have you down as the contact for a Mr Adam Blackett.' The name *Blackett* seemed to come from her mouth like she was spitting out something foul.

He leant on to his side and rubbed his eyes. 'Yes. Yes, sorry,' he replied. It all came back, the reminder explaining the knot in his stomach. 'How is he?' he rushed out; the memory of his dream extinguished.

'He'll be fine,' she assured. 'The doctor has approved his release. Will you be collecting him?' she asked, with her voice softening as his attitude did.

'Yes. I'll be there as soon as I can.'

Justin hung up and threw the phone on the other pillow, his head falling not far from it. He took a breath in and risked his eyelids closed, managing a quick glimpse of peace before his phone started singing again.

'Justin Owens,' he answered without looking at the number.

'Mate! You're a bit straight this morning,' a familiar voice bellowed, laughing at Justin's formality. 'Where are you guys?'

Justin looked at his watch, it was already nine-thirty.

'Tom! Shit. Sorry!' he blurted, rubbing his face roughly. 'We've been held up. Long story.' He hoped Tom would let him off the phone without having to explain. Justin didn't know what he could or should say. He wasn't sure what they'd think of Adam's antics, and after last night he wasn't sure how well he knew any of his friends. If he'd missed the fact that Adam was using ecstasy—and God only knows what else—what more had he failed to notice?

'Oh man. Paul's not going to be happy,' Tom warned, but Justin could hear his smile.

'Yeah, I know. Where are you now, anyway?'

'Clubhouse,' he answered proudly, and Justin could hear his friends' voices echo in the background.

'It's nine-thirty!' Beer in the morning was something he was happy to be missing. Justin sensed the day could get as messy as the night before and he was still exhausted from that episode. He heard Tom laugh and someone yell into the phone for him to get his arse to the bar 'stat'. Justin told them he'd do his best and would meet them on the green. He didn't mention that they'd be lucky to meet on the green—he had no idea what state Adam would be in.

Justin rubbed his eyes and let his feet fall to the floor. After a lengthy yawn, he scuffed over to the mirror and inspected his face. It felt tight and his cheek was swollen and slightly purple. Wondering how he'd explain that on the golf course, he reached for his bag that was slumped on the unslept-in bed. He and Adam had booked a budget twin room. The room itself wasn't too bad, although the view was of a brick wall, and the TV screen rivalled an iPad's. The teeny bathroom, however, was a problem.

As he stepped into the shower, he had to be careful not to make any sudden movements. The shower head sat directly on top of his own head, the soap dispenser pressed into his side, the shower curtain stuck to his thigh and the tiles felt loose under his slippery feet. He made a mental note to never book the hotel with Julia, he could only imagine her disgust at the room. Though it did provide an incentive for a quick shower, which was really all he had time for.

Justin was dressed and ready to go within minutes. He grabbed a shirt for Adam, the one from last night didn't have a chance of being clean, but by the time he reached the hospital it was already past ten. They had definitely missed tee-off, but the sun was shining and it lifted Justin's mood. He was feeling apprehensive about having to see Adam. The idea of it had Justin slow his pace as he walked through the emergency doors, without the drama of earlier that morning. There was a whole different line-up of staff and Justin walked up to the nurse on duty and gave Adam's full name before being buzzed through. This time he walked with some direction.

The whole atmosphere of the emergency department had shifted in the hours he had been gone. The mix of people had changed with the staff. While earlier it had been chaos, it now seemed controlled. Justin found Adam sitting up in bed. He was fully dressed, except for his shoes. His eyes were red and he looked like he'd been awake for a week. He was scratching at his arm when he caught sight of Justin approaching.

'Hey mate,' he drawled, unfazed by his location. 'How's it going?'

'Okay.' *You bloody idiot.* 'How are you?'

'The doc says I'm good to go.' Adam swung his legs over the bed and reached for his shoes.

'Don't you need to see the nurse or sign something or … something?' Justin felt confused. He'd never been in this situation before and wasn't sure what the procedure was. He looked around uneasily for hospital staff, hoping someone could tell them what to do. Tell him what to expect. Tell him why his friend had been high on drugs. Tell him how he could make him stop, but there was no-one nearby.

'Adam, what did they say,' Justin stalled, unsure how to ask tactfully and clearly what he wanted to say. 'Are you going to be okay?' he tried.

Adam merely shrugged. 'Sure. I'll be fine. Ready for golf?' he winked at Justin and stood up. His balance faltered, which concerned Justin.

'Can we just speak to someone first?' he stopped him, placing a hand on Adam's shoulder. 'It'd make me feel better about leaving this place.'

Justin sat himself on the bed to tell Adam that he wasn't leaving just yet. Adam looked annoyed, but obliged. He pressed the buzzer by his bed like a pro and Justin knew he'd been amusing himself with it all morning. A nurse hastily arrived by the bed.

'Still here Mr Blackett?'

'Yeah, darl. Me mate's a bit anal. Wants to know the results of my stool sample before I go?' he joked crudely and Justin winced.

'Sorry. I'm here to collect him. Is he alright to go?' Justin asked, feeling like his father and feeling ridiculous for it.

The nurse picked up the chart hooked on the base of the bed and read over the notes. Her eyes scanned the pages and she nodded as she read.

'Ah … yes. All seems okay to go.' She looked up at Adam. 'The doctor explained to you the side effects, I gather?'

'Yeah, yeah. Sure did, love,' Adam said. 'Blah, blah, blah,' he then muttered under his breath, loud enough for both the nurse and Justin to have heard. Embarrassed by Adam's sheer arrogance, Justin looked over at the nurse who stared at Adam with a clear dislike. He assumed her silence was masking an internal battle to remain professional.

Justin didn't know much about drugs—last night was a crash course for him—but what he did know was enough. They'd scared him enough to have never dabbled and the fear he had for Adam was growing.

The nurse left them, and Justin and Adam walked back towards reception. Justin excused himself to use the bathroom but instead went in search for the nurse. He found her at another patient's bed and boldly interrupted. He didn't have the time to be overly polite or patient.

'Excuse me … my friend back there …' he indicated towards the now vacant bed and the nurse nodded.

'I brought him in last night. He was drunk.' The nurse raised her eyebrows and Justin continued. 'They told me he was on ecstasy and I just want to know if he's going to be okay.'

'He's going to be fine,' the nurse said simply, the irritation remaining on her face.

Frustrated, Justin pressed on. 'But … but what now?'

'What do you mean? You take him home.' She began to turn back towards her patient, who was listening intently. With no televisions, entertainment was scarce.

'Listen, I'm sorry if I sound stupid. But are there side effects I need to look out for? Is he addicted? Do I need to do something?' Justin was working hard to keep his voice controlled but he noticed it jump a note with each question.

The nurse blinked at him, unmistakably having little concern. Justin wanted to suggest she rethink her career path.

'He'll be fine,' the nurse maintained. 'He'll probably feel a bit nauseous and tired. But he also had a high blood alcohol level so that, mixed with the drug, won't be doing any of his organs any favours. Think of it like an extreme hangover. Make sure he gets some rest.' Justin didn't dare tell her Adam was on his way to a buck's day.

'Is he addicted? Do I need to get him into rehab or something?' Justin was already picturing an intervention, making lists in his head. But the nurse smiled, finally looking tolerant to Justin's questions.

'He'll be fine,' she assured him. 'Listen, our social worker will have some brochures if you want to know more. Ecstasy isn't actually addictive, not to the body anyway. It isn't safe, don't get me wrong, but it's more common than you may think. I suggest you talk to your friend though; he'll probably have the answers you really want.'

The nurse patted Justin on the arm as she turned back to her patient, who was now sipping on his juice, completely enthralled in the conversation. Justin thought the man looked disappointed when he turned to leave, not relieved to be getting his privacy back.

Justin walked quickly back to reception. His mind was racing through what he'd just been told. He admitted the nurse was right. What Justin really wanted to know, only Adam could tell, but he was quite certain that Adam wouldn't be telling him much.

Justin decided he'd use Google. For now, he'd get Adam out of there and focus on getting him back to Sydney, safe and sober.

'Where'd you get to, Jay?' Adam asked agitated, standing up from the seats in the waiting-area. 'And what the hell happened to your face?'

Justin's brain stumbled upon an answer to the first question, but he was at a complete loss for the second.

'I, ah … got lost. Stupid hospital,' he gestured behind him, looking frustrated.

'That for me?' Adam asked, pointing to the shirt that was still scrunched in Justin's hand. Justin hadn't realised he'd been clenching it all this time. He handed it over, damp from his sweaty hands, but Adam didn't notice. In comparison to his current outfit, anything would have been a blessing.

Adam pulled his shirt off shamelessly and replaced it with the cleaner one as they walked outside. The sun had since disappeared and grey clouds filled the sky; winter, in its final days, was not giving up easily. Justin noticed his mood shift with the weather. He'd been looking forward to this weekend away for weeks. Work had been hectic for months, and Julia had been confusing him so much lately that he had been almost desperate to get away. But so far it had just been hard work, and they hadn't even met the others yet.

He glanced at his watch. The guys would be well and truly into the game by now. A taxi was pulling up to drop a passenger off and Justin looked up at the sky to mouth 'Halleluiah', pushing Adam towards the cab so they wouldn't miss it.

'Watch it mate,' Adam warned, 'or I'll be the one to give you a black eye.' Justin almost laughed at the irony as he climbed into the car, giving the name of their hotel.

'Why we going there?' Adam frowned with irritation at Justin for wasting their time. 'It's golf time.'

Justin stared at him incredulously. 'Don't you want to shower? Change? Sleep?'

'Nah, it'll be right … I'd kill for a Quarter Pounder though.'

Justin shook his head. *He* wanted to shower and sleep, and he hadn't been the one to spend the night in emergency. Not all of the night anyway.

'Ok-ay,' he responded slowly. Adam didn't look like he was going to bring up the events of the previous night. Justin could have been picking him up from the airport for all Adam seemed to care. 'I'm starving too, actually,' he confessed and asked the driver to pull into a drive-through.

As they shoved the food in, Justin's body relished each greasy mouthful. Adam's body had a less than desirable reaction and his face paled noticeably.

'May have to make that hotel stop after all, Jay,' he suggested. The driver looked into his rearview mirror. His face paled too and without saying a word he did some precision driving that Justin found quite impressive, until he made a dicey maneuver around an oncoming tram which took at least three years from Justin's life.

They pulled up in front of the hotel within minutes. Adam leapt out and gulped in the fresh air, holding his side like he'd just run a marathon. His other hand clutched his Coke. Justin, whose heart rate was only just recovering, looked at Adam's seat with frustration, fries and limp lettuce littered the spot. Justin paid the driver, roughly cleaned up the mess, thanked him and jumped out. He slapped Adam on the back to get him to move, but the only thing that moved was a burger, fries and Coke—from Adam's stomach and down onto the footpath in one foul, projectile sweep. Justin gagged and jumped back.

'Whoa, that's better,' Adam moaned as a group of Melbourne's best-dressed walked past in disgust. He straightened up hesitantly, before walking towards the hotel entrance.

'C'mon, let's go,' he told Justin, spitting vomit onto the concrete. The reception staff, having a clear view of Adam, were fairly cringing at what they saw. Their alarm undoubtedly rose when Adam stepped through their doors.

'Can you just leave … that?' Justin queried, gesturing towards the pavement in revulsion. Adam shrugged.

'What do you want me to do, lick it up?'

He was already through the doors and waiting impatiently by the lift. He sipped his drink, pressing the button more times than necessary. Justin gave an awkward glance to the mess and then jogged along inside to catch the lift.

It was almost one o'clock when they reached the others on the tenth hole. Justin and Adam hired a buggy and clubs and once they were surrounded by the others, Justin felt the pressure to babysit Adam subside.

He watched as Adam strode up to Paul, slap the buck's arse, and stick his tongue in his ear. Justin refrained from telling Paul that the same tongue had recently been the exit route for vomit.

'Pauly! How ya going mate?' cried Adam, who flinched at the volume of his own voice. Justin presumed it must have been resonating in his head like a golf ball had been whacked around inside his skull.

'Where've you been?' Paul laughed as he shook Justin's hand.

'Sorry, mate. We got a little tied up,' Justin offered lamely. To his relief they all laughed, shook hands, and asked no more.

The group had split into three and Justin and Adam joined the end of the line of the third. Justin was actually tempted to thank Adam as they walked away from the eighteenth hole, or their eighth. He liked golf in small doses. Like Putt Putt.

It was a warm afternoon, the clouds from earlier having disappeared (again), and against his plan to just enjoy the day, Justin found himself continuously watching over Adam, more than slightly concerned about side effects.

'How you going, Jay?' Justin heard a voice from behind and smiled at the face coming towards him.

'Hey Tom,' Justin smiled, grateful to see him. He'd been playing golf with guys he didn't know, some of whom were undeniably annoying, and Adam. 'How was your game?'

Tom was a golfing enthusiast. They'd met on the soccer field at school, but golf was Tom's first love, at least until a woman came along to replace it, which it did from time to time.

'Okay,' he smiled modestly, removing his gloves.

'You kick their arse?' Justin asked and laughed as Tom shrugged. Tom, squinting at Justin's cheek, went to question the bruise. 'Don't even ask.' Justin roughed up Tom's orangey hair. 'Come on, let's go get a drink.'

The night was long for Justin, but he suspected it may have been longer for others as he observed Adam. Apart from the occasional glance to make sure he was still conscious, Justin stayed well away from him. It wasn't a mature reaction, but Justin felt not only anger towards him, but discomfort. He made a greater effort to get to know the other guys instead, which became a non-issue as the alcohol drowned out all their senses. Even the annoying ones became interesting.

By the early hours of Sunday morning, Justin found himself sitting next to Tom at a strip club in Brunswick. They'd lost sight of Paul through the thick of goggling eyes and skin not normally seen so publicly.

'Julia's good?' Tom asked loudly and Justin nodded, laughing as a dancer briefly bent her butt towards Tom's face.

'You think of Julia *now*?' Justin exclaimed. 'What are you suggesting?'

'She's a girl,' Tom told him and gestured helplessly to the women around them. '*These* are girls.'

'Right.'

'Maybe don't tell her that though,' Tom suggested as an afterthought.

'Wouldn't dare.' Justin slurred as the room swayed around him. Not much more of the night stored in his memory bank. He did have a vague recollection of eating a kebab but wasn't sure when that happened or if he even enjoyed it. He woke in the hotel, fully clothed, with flashes of strange women, golf clubs, steak and boobs.

He groaned and rolled over to see Adam lying butt naked on top of his bed, out cold. Justin didn't appreciate the image but was grateful the room was dark.

Justin lay there until the faint nauseous feeling became a strong nauseous feeling, before he climbed into the shower and was immediately reminded of the bathroom setup. He hit his head on the shower head, fought with the curtain, struggled to find a good water temperature, swore, and got back out again. He walked back out and threw a pillow at Adam, who only moved his lips to swear.

'Get up,' muttered Justin, having too little respect for the guy to care that he wasn't ready to wake. Justin's memory had flashed him an incident from the previous night where a security guard had warned Adam for touching one of the women 'unsolicited'.

'We have to leave by ten,' Justin spoke loudly. A look at the clock told him it was already after ten. 'Mate, get up, we're late.'

'Fuck off,' Adam swore. 'Stop being such a straight-laced fucking-do-gooder,' he mumbled as he rolled over. Justin groaned and shielded his hand towards Adam.

'Put it away, Adam,' he said, referring to his boner, which had risen with the morning sun. 'I'm going to go check out. I'll meet you downstairs.' Justin's phone began to buzz and he sprang to it, thinking it may be Julia. It was Tom.

'You awake?'

'Yeah, just got back from a run.'

'Yeah?'

'No.' Justin relaxed when he heard Adam move towards the shower. 'Where are you?'

Tom was in his own nearby lobby waiting with the others who were flying back to Sydney.

'We'll be over soon.'

By the time they'd reached the airport later that afternoon, after a slow and greasy lunch, the group looked so grave that anyone watching them slouch on to the plane — bags hanging over slumped shoulders, faces drawn, eyes glazed and red — may have thought they had come from a funeral. Four out of the five had to be woken by a stewardess when it came to landing in Sydney. Adam, after swearing at the one who woke him, also went home with her number.

An Uber driver picked them up and they sat in silence during the drive. Justin grunted his thanks when he was dropped off, the final ten-metre leg to his door seeming impossible to achieve. His body's progression throughout the day resembled the reverse progression of primate to man. When he did cross the finish line, he dumped his bag in the entrance, went to say hello to his dog, realised it was at his parents', procrastinated for a full second about whether to go and collect him or call them, and then decided to close his eyes for just five minutes first.

chapter five

'I think a little higher,' Anna kneeled on the lounge calling out instructions. 'No, lower. Perfect!' She smacked her hands together and then held them out to pause Jane.

They were deciding the best length for Ioulia's upcoming haircut. Jane awkwardly held Ioulia's hair over her olive neck. Her lone braid, a remnant from her Bali holiday, had its days numbered — to Jane's obvious relief.

'Now, cut a chunk,' Anna chirped, covering herself with a blanket — their apartment had notoriously bad temperature extremes. Jane frowned at the suggestion, but Ioulia wandered into the kitchen to retrieve the scissors, Jane trailing behind like a bridesmaid holding the bride's veil.

'Are you sure you want to do this Ioulia?' Jane pleaded.

'Sure. It's a great idea,' she nodded and held the scissors out to Anna. Anna smirked smugly at Jane and snipped a rather large chunk of Ioulia's hair in sync with Jane's sharp intake of breath.

'Ta-da!' she grinned at Ioulia as the hair came away in her hands. Jane shook her head at the both of them and let Ioulia's hair fall back to its full length while Anna put the off-cuts in the bin.

'Ladies, aren't you meant to be discussing the big move?'

Anna thought Jane had taken on her teacher alias a little too well, but conceded that she was right. It had been decided Ioulia would become Anna's new roommate when Jane moved back home to Sydney.

Jane had met Ioulia during a yoga class years ago and she and Anna had easily become firm friends. This was even after Anna, drunk and unable to comprehend the Greek name, bestowed the name of Leo on Ioulia—who took to the new name happily. In fairness, Ioulia had a tendency to revert to Greek when drinking, so Anna had merrily accepted many foreign conversations on that fateful night.

Ioulia was moving from an apartment two streets over. She'd been sharing with someone for the last two years, but the guy had fallen head over heels in love—and not with Ioulia, as they'd all predicted—and the new girlfriend was moving in. Anna was actually relieved (as were Ioulia's Greek Orthodox parents) because there was no way she could afford the astronomical rent on her own. It was perfect timing in her eyes and it gave her reason to believe that life really was all mapped out. If only life would catch up with the digital age, she thought, and put those life plans in a navigation unit.

'To happiness, please follow route for another year.'

'This job is a dead end, please turn around.'

'To find love of your life, turn left in one hundred metres.'

Anna woke from her little GPS daydream when she noticed eyes staring down on her.

'What on earth are you grinning about?' Ioulia smirked, and Jane hit her playfully on the arm.

'Don't worry, Ioulia, you'll get used to it,' she laughed and bent to hold Anna's chin in her cool hand. 'You crazy little thing.'

Blushing, Anna pushed Jane's hand away and then spent the next hour with Ioulia going through cupboards, determining what their shortfalls were. Unfortunately, they had two televisions but no table. They had twenty-three odd glasses, but no cutlery. No microwave, but two hair straighteners, three hairdryers, two coffee tables and three ashtrays.

'Well, that's really great guys,' Jane told them from the comfort of the lounge, a Cadbury's block disappearing fast in front of her, 'but neither of you smoke'.

Ignoring her, they made plans to go shopping on the weekend, dividing what they'd each have to buy; Jane donating her cutlery in goodwill.

'Can we watch the movie now?' Jane moaned in boredom. Her arm sported an oversized Band-Aid from the weekend's events and she fiddled with its edges while she waited.

'When do you get your stitches out?' Ioulia asked.

'Next Thursday, they—'

Anna tuned out quickly. Jane's commitment to detail was making her queasy. She eyed off the movies that Jane had pulled out. Hoping *Love Actually*, which lay unsuspecting on the bottom, would be the pick. Romantic comedies were her safe place. Completely unrealistic, but they fed her hopes and were therefore totally excusable. When Jane finished, Anna casually made the suggestion.

'*Love Actually*? Again?' Disappointment resonated in Jane's voice.

'*Love Actually*?' Ioulia repeated. 'I *love* that movie,' cried Ioulia as she fell heavily on to the lounge. Jane cheered with no conviction and told them they belonged together before quickly sitting up straight and grinning meaningfully.

'Hey Ioulia, speaking of belonging together, you just might be saved … Anna met someone.'

'You met someone? Who?'

'I did *not* meet someone.' Jane raised her eyebrow. 'Oh, okay then. I *did* meet someone: someone with a girlfriend, who lives in Sydney, and will never see again.'

'He was hot,' Jane told Ioulia, excited.

'Oh,' Ioulia oh-ed, and leant forward.

'Had an *insane* smile,' Jane added, making quotations in the air.

'*Really*? Do tell.'

'*Girlfriend*,' Anna reminded them both, embarrassed. '*Sydney*.'

'Ri-ght. What about you Jane?' Ioulia winked suggestively. 'Did you get that guy's number the other night? The heart-throb that rescued you?'

'Heart-throb?' Anna asked, dejected. 'You never told me *Hero* was a heart-throb! Why didn't you get his number?'

Jane looked from one to the other, laughing.

'Oh my goodness, you girls are all crazy! Mel rung to ask the same thing. She didn't even see him. Just assumed that someone who could carry me was sufficient for dating.'

'Well?'

'Well? *Well,* besides me moving, it had something to do with blood pouring out of my arm,' she reminded them.

Anna's fingers hovered near her ears, threatening to plug them and drown out any gory details. 'Are you finished talking about it?' she drew out.

Jane threw a cushion at her. 'Agh! You annoy me,' she laughed with exasperation. 'Now are we going to watch the stupid movie or what?'

Anna threw the cushion back, missing Jane by at least two feet, and Ioulia pressed play.

chapter six

Early Saturday morning, Jane watched Anna squeeze another box onto the already full backseat, frowning at the two remaining boxes near her feet. Anna didn't know where Jane expected them to go, but they weren't going in that car.

Moving day had finally come and as the apartment emptied it felt more and more like reality. Jane was really going.

Anna tried being overly positive, frequently reminding Jane about how fantastic it was going to be. But Anna knew she was failing. She'd always been a pretty awful liar; tried hard for the sake of feelings, but Jane could always see through her.

Jane, who didn't feel certain about the move, had missed her family and friends terribly when she first came to Melbourne, especially her sister, Sarah. Her plan had always been to go back home after her studies had finished … and now they had. It was time to go. But as the years had gone by, the missing of home, and her old life, eased. Melbourne had become Jane's home, and Anna her family.

Jane had faced such a dilemma in returning home that she'd applied to schools in both states and decided to let the universe decide—definitely not her usual style. A school not an hour from her parents' place came through first and a class of eight-year-olds were now awaiting the arrival of their new teacher — as soon as she could get the boxes into the car.

'Jane, I don't think this is going to fit.' Anna turned to look at Jane regretfully, hands on her hips, feeling her hair sliding out of their pigtails. 'You should have squeezed more into that van,' she shook her head.

A communal removals van had come to collect Jane's things the day before to deliver them to her parents' place, where she'd be living. Anna had been at work and was glad she didn't have to see the apartment they'd made their home be stripped of half its life.

'They couldn't fit any more either,' Jane sighed. Both girls looked at the car, perplexed.

'Okay …' Anna considered, 'take out a couple of things that aren't a priority and I'll bring them up when I come visit.'

'When are you going to Sydney?' Jane asked surprised.

'Um … tomorrow?' Anna grinned at her. 'Too soon?'

'No, no, that's fine. It's only, what, 500 miles did you say?'

'500 miles,' Anna nodded. She had checked it on Google Maps and made the conversion. 'Easy.'

Jane hung her arm around Anna's shoulders. 'I'm going to miss you An,' she smiled.

'Yeah, ditto,' Anna smiled back. 'Probably not going to miss that pasta bake you always make though,' she cringed and then added, 'or your snoring.'

'Shut up,' Jane laughed. 'Well, I'm not going to miss Grumpy-Morning-Anna, or Long-Painful-Shower-Anna. Or, Missy,' she teased, 'all your hair in the drain!'

'Okay, okay,' Anna held up her hands laughing. 'Even. We're even.'

They looked back to the car. It was time to eliminate.

'I guess I won't be needing these textbooks.' Anna shook her head and Jane wriggled the weighty box back out.

'I'll take them inside,' Anna strained to say after Jane eased it into her outstretched arms. She waddled back up the stairs to the apartment they'd shared for the last three years. They'd been friends for four.

Jane did reception work while she studied and Anna had worked at the same company at the time—and still did. Anna, an IT specialist, or computer hacker as Jane called it, was sent to fix Jane's computer the day that it crashed. Jane had commented on Anna's unassuming brilliance, which Anna took as a compliment, and after that day a morning nod evolved to lengthy conversations. When Jane needed help with a computer course she was struggling with at university, Anna happily obliged. Jane was amused by Anna's randomness and Anna was in awe of Jane's simplicity. Jane was simply Anna's greatest friend, and this move was going to hurt.

Anna worried about how she'd function without Jane. According to her friends (Jane included), serving truths with pizza and wine one night, Anna was forever making rash, sentimental and illogical decisions. She *had* defended this claim but lost the argument.

It was true that Anna would often wander onto roads absently. 'Countless times', Jane had allegedly needed to hold Anna back so a car wouldn't hit her. Anna could only recall two times. Apparently, she depended on her tech skills to operate a GPS because she couldn't and wouldn't follow directions. She'd pull things out of the oven and forget the oven mitt, fish the burnt bread out of the toaster with a knife and blow the circuit, run a bath and forget about it—she couldn't dispute these. They also stated that Anna had terrible intuition when it came to men and was forever picked-up by guys that were simply beneath her. Men whom everyone else was skeptical of, Anna would naively give her full attention to; she would also then wonder why she could never trust males, or why the fireworks never went off. Jane, Mel and Ioulia had discussed in exasperation that when they went out it felt as if they had to babysit; making sure at least one of them had an eye on her, especially after the time she bought a homeless man a pizza and his friend tried to steal her bag in return.

Anna had regretted her attempt at self-defense that night. She had been on the brink of tears when Jane had hugged her and assured her it was also why they loved her so much, as exhausting as it was. That, apparently — and it could have just been her attempt to stop Anna sobbing — she had a spark that was, as Jane's father had once put it, 'endearing'.

Mel had asked if he'd still think her endearing had he heard her curse the delivery guy, as she had done that night, when their pizzas had arrived after nearly two hungry hours of waiting. Jane shushed her, and assured Anna her father believed his daughter was living with a little angel.

Jane could always smooth over her worries and Anna desperately wanted to keep her near.

Anna looked at the time. Jane really had to get a move on if she wanted to avoid driving in the dark. She trotted back downstairs to find Jane making final adjustments. Anna inspected the boot, looked back up at their building, back to the car and then finally to Jane.

'So, is that it?' she asked casually. 'You off now?'

Jane nodded. It looked like a confession.

'I may just run upstairs and double-check.'

Jane had everything, she knew that, and she knew she'd be visiting in no time. But Anna watched as she jogged up the stairs and then followed.

She watched as Jane ran through each room, savoring a last mental picture. Anna was surprised; Jane wasn't usually a sentimental person, though understood. Her life was at a huge turning point and this was a final take of her world before it became something different. Anna watched with a mix of sadness and amusement.

'Are you done?'

Jane stopped in front of Anna. 'Yes,' she smiled determinedly. 'I'm done. I'm going.'

She stepped past Anna and had already started the ignition and was waiting beside the car in the time Anna reached her.

The white paint of their Art Deco building glared at them in the morning sunshine. Jane dropped her sunglasses over her eyes and turned to Anna, who was looking down the street trying to be completely unconcerned.

'Well … goodbye Anna.'

'Goodbye Jane,' Anna replied, looping loose hair behind her ear. They stood looking around each other for a few uncertain moments before Anna threw her arms around Jane's slender neck. Her chin rested over her shoulder and Jane hugged her back reassuringly.

'I'm going to miss you,' she said, and Anna hugged a little tighter. 'I could hate it and be back by Christmas.'

'Yeah. Sure.' Anna forced a smile as they pulled apart. 'Call me whenever you get tired or bored. Don't forget to stop for breaks. Don't speed!' she pointed her finger at Jane sternly, who laughed at the mothering.

'I promise,' Jane said, crossing her fingers over her heart.

'Good. Now get out of here!' Anna said, throwing her hands down and fixing a smile in place. Jane forced a laugh, climbed in the car and pulled the seatbelt across her body; her passenger of boxes also strapped in. Anna stepped back as the car rolled back on to the street.

'Bye,' Jane sung through the open window and Anna blew her a kiss, her rosy cheeks puffed up from her nervous smile.

Jane drove up the street and before turning the corner looked in the rearview mirror to see Anna where she had left her, her arm frantically waving goodbye, her chin determinedly set.

Anna went to work Monday morning with an odd feeling in her belly. After blaming her mood on not being able to find her favourite earrings for a full hour, she begrudgingly admitted that she just didn't want to be at work, regardless of the number of times she had claimed to love it.

She wandered absently to her desk, walking the same path she had walked for almost six years. Anna sometimes felt the carpet had been worn down by her alone. She reached her tiny cubicle and went to put her handbag down only to find a large black binding machine sitting on her desk, obstructing her chances of getting work done.

Anna eyed the binder as her bag slipped down her arm. She looked behind her stupidly and then back at the obstruction, wondering how heavy it was. With her bag dangling from her elbow, Anna bent awkwardly and wriggled a few fingers under the machine's base to try and lift it, confirming its hefty weight.

One of the receptionists, the one Anna liked least, came striding down the corridor that reeked of 1972, and Anna stopped her.

'Hey, do you know what the deal is with this binder?' Indicating her desk, Anna assumed the response would be apologetically helpful. It wasn't.

'We had a temp here on Friday while you were out of the office. No-one else had space on their desk,' she told Anna before attempting to walk off, no doubt in a hurry to make a coffee or fix her lipstick.

'But … now *I* don't have any space,' Anna smiled as she displayed her desk, hinting for a solution. Surely anyone could see that it couldn't stay there. Anna waited for a more helpful reply.

'Maybe one of the guys can help you,' she shrugged before power-walking off, her long hair shimmying across her back. Anna resisted flipping the finger.

'Thanks for your help,' she muttered, turning back to her desk and switching the computer on. She fished her mobile out of her bag, checking it for the tenth time that morning. The day before was Father's Day and though she had tried to call her dad at least three times, each call had been automatically transferred to his voicemail—and she still hadn't heard from him.

She sent Jane a quick text to wish her luck on her first day and then unenthusiastically went through her emails. She had been off-site updating a chain store's database system on the Friday and hadn't been there to check her emails—or prevent large obtrusive items from being deposited on her desk. She turned to give the contraption another glare.

Thirty-eight emails. Great. She frowned and focused on getting through them until she was interrupted by a friendly voice.

'Well, this is a bit offensive isn't it?' Mel laughed. 'Why on earth have you got this here? I thought you were banned from binding.'

Anna had, in fact, been banned from binding after she'd wedged too much paper into the machine and jammed it. As it was the fourth time she'd done it, all in the same week, reception staff had warned her about binding without first checking with them.

'Hi there!' Anna smiled, happy to see a friendly face on a Monday morning. Mel nodded to the binder and raised her eyebrows above her glasses, her red mane of hair framing her face perfectly.

'Apparently, they used my desk while I was out, and they just left it here. I have no space!' complained Anna.

'Just move it,' Mel shrugged, clearly ignorant of its weight. Anna explained her dilemma.

'I'll help,' Mel grinned. 'Hey, maybe we should put it on someone else's desk. Just say, 'Hey, do you mind if we leave this here?' and then walk off.' Her eyes danced wickedly.

'That is so immature,' Anna said, aghast. 'Yet, kinda entertaining. What about that meanie from reception? She refused to help me.'

'Perfect,' Mel purred cunningly.

They grabbed either end and waddled like crabs down the hallway. Their sneaky giggles caused suspicion and a few co-workers watched them with curious glances. No-one stopped them or offered to carry it for them; chivalry was dead in their office.

They heaved it on to the conveniently unattended front reception desk and Anna scrawled the message, 'Mind if I leave this here?' on a post-it and slapped it on the machine. They proudly returned to their desks grinning widely.

'So, how'd the move go?' Mel asked.

The question brought Anna's mood down quickly, like a balloon released. She could envision it spurting around the room, bouncing off walls and making inappropriate noises. She'd spent Saturday night rearranging furniture to fill in the blank gaps left by Jane's move. She'd then spent Sunday shopping, with the crowds of last-minute Father's Day present-buyers, to distract herself.

Two pairs of shoes, some knives and three DVDs later, she went back to her empty flat and wondered if Jane would miss her as much. She felt more childish about missing Jane than she did about leaving a binder on somebody's desk.

'Yeah, it was fine. She got there just after dark. Her mum made her an apple pie and her sister came over. She was happy,' she smiled. Mel nodded before admitting she'd better get back to her waiting workload.

'I'll catch you later,' she called over her shoulder as she stepped away.

Anna sat back at her desk and opened a new email. Just as she did, she heard feet thudding down the hall, followed by a shrill voice.

'Anna!'

Anna spun around and tried to focus on the receptionist's stern face in front of her — pursed lips and perfectly manicured eyebrows arching high.

'Yes?' Anna asked innocently.

'Did you put *that* on my desk?' the receptionist asked, her voice struggling to remain level as she pointed stiffly down the hallway.

'Sorry, put what on your desk?' Anna's face remained blank as she shook her head in confusion for effect, sure it was the best bluff she'd ever performed. She thought she saw the woman's eyes flash with tiny lightning bolts.

'*The. Binder,*' the receptionist spoke slowly through whitened teeth.

'Oh, sorry,' Anna shook her head and chuckled. '*The binder.* Yes, I thought you may need it today.' She tilted her head to the side and smiled sweetly, feeling slightly nervous. She waited for the woman to respond — instead she turned sharply on her heel and stomped back down the hall.

Anna wheeled her chair over so she could watch her walk away and saw another head poke out, red hair hanging near her knees, a big grin on her face. Mel's thumbs went north and Anna mimicked her before their manager came out of his office and they both spun back to their screens.

Anna finished checking her emails, deleting most, and updated her calendar. She had training plans to write up and a software report to fill out before she left that day. She really had no time for binders, receptionists, or thinking about empty flats.

Anna, in a Monday afternoon daze, was typing the date when she felt the urge to slap herself. So caught up in not getting to talk to her dad over the weekend, she'd completely forgotten her mother, and her mother's birthday. She vaguely remembered dismissing the 'organise present' reminder on her phone last week and the faithful Facebook reminder that morning. Her body jerked to and fro, from her phone to the computer. Call, or arrange a present first? Present first, then the call wouldn't be a lie.

She navigated her way through Google with guilt-fuelled speed, then located the address of her mother's office, the website of the nearest florist, and selected an impressive bouquet of flowers. Next Anna tapped out her mother's number and listened for the ring tone. She was still up in the air about how honest to be, but her mother's chilly voice justified her choice.

'Mum! Hi!' Anna exclaimed excitedly. 'Happy Birthday! I'm so sorry I couldn't call earlier. We had a whole system crash. Total nightmare … how's your day been?' she rushed out before giving her mother a chance to respond.

'Thank you, Anna,' her mother replied, ever so curt. 'I was beginning to wonder if you had forgotten.' Anna suspected she was fishing for an ulterior truth.

'What? No! Not at all. It's just been a *crazy* day. Did your present arrived?' she asked innocently.

The lies made Anna's heart beat faster but she persevered, convinced it was for the best. The iciness was already melting and her mother seemed convinced, answering with a hint of anticipation that no, no present had arrived yet.

Anna chatted to her mum about her plans and her day, but her mother apologised that she had to get back to work. Anna hung up with guilt shrouding her mind. She felt horrible, but she figured she probably deserved it. It was times like these she wished she had a sibling, so she didn't carry the sole responsibility of making her parents feel proud and appreciated.

chapter seven

When Justin turned the key in the lock, he felt instant relief. He loved his home, and he loved coming home. When he'd first bought it his friends and family had humored him, but none were very optimistic. His dad, the exception, was the only other person that saw its potential. Now, almost finished, the house finally felt like how he had envisioned his home to be.

He clomped down the hallway in his boots. Work had been hectic. Justin was covering the early shifts that week but his partner, Eric, had gone home violently unwell and Justin had needed to cover all their clients until late.

He threw his keys on the white stone kitchen bench, swung open the fridge and stared at the contents. Yoghurt, beer, carrots, milk. He grabbed the milk and opened it to smell if it was okay. The gagging reflex told him to abort the milk idea — fast. He poured it down the drain, covering his mouth with his hand. Hamlet watched from the back door and his face turned up to the side at the sight of Justin.

'Sorry buddy, I haven't even said hello.' He tossed the carton in the recycling and strode over to the back door. 'Where are my manners?' he asked Hamlet, who replied by jumping up on

Justin affectionately as he pulled the sliding glass door open. Justin patted him roughly on the head.

'Look at you, looking so innocent. Dig any holes today?' Hamlet turned his head up at him again. The puppy-look always made Justin wary. He glanced around the yard and spotted a new excavation, right in the middle of the lawn.

'Good work, Hamlet,' he muttered and shooed him out of the house with his foot. 'Bastard.' Closing the door on Hamlet's face wasn't so hard after he'd done some of his freestyle landscaping.

Justin's stomach grumbled. He looked at the clock. Julia should arrive soon, he could probably wait for dinner, but then his stomach lurched again. There was a staple bowl of oranges on his kitchen table, grown from his yard, and he stared at the over-populated bowl for a full three seconds before deciding he couldn't eat another one. He walked back to the fridge, swung the door open and stared at the contents.

Yoghurt, beer, carrots.

He flung the door shut with a sigh. Magnets and bits of paper flew from the door, making a splat as they hit the wooden floor. He grumbled as he scooped them off the ground, sticking the gas bill back on the door and looked at the other fallen papers. Amongst them were Paul's wedding invitation and a map to the church. The wedding was this coming weekend and he thought that if he packed them now, he couldn't forget them on the Friday night when he knew they'd be running out the door.

He strolled back down the hallway to his bedroom, slid each of his boots off with the help of the other foot, and kicked them into the cupboard. Reaching easily to the top shelf, he slipped the invite inside his bag before questioning the state of his suit. Justin rifled through the wardrobe and rescued the lone suit from the plethora of polo shirts it was cowering with. Hearing Julia unlock the door and click her heels down the hallway, Justin called out from the bedroom and threw the suit over the bed.

'What are you doing?' she frowned as she came into view by the doorway. Justin stepped over to give her a brief kiss. She was still wearing her dark suit. Justin had always thought it made her look drawn—but wisely kept that to himself.

'Just making sure my suit's clean.' He inspected the jacket carefully. 'Do you remember the last time I wore it? If I had it cleaned?' he mused, looking up and down the pant legs. 'It *looks* clean ...'

Julia came and sat on the bed. 'Sorry, can't remember. Was it that wedding on the boat?' she offered.

'No, that was Smitty's,' he said as he thought back. 'It was Tom's brother. In May!' he exclaimed, slapping his leg and pointing at Julia like he'd beaten her to it. They seemed to have had an onslaught of weddings in the last year. They had even met at one themselves. It was like all of his remaining single friends had hit *the* age to settle down. This meant he had been receiving plenty of ribbing about when he would be next to head down the aisle.

'Well, it looks clean. That's the point, isn't it?' Julia spoke, sounding slightly irritated. Justin looked up at her curiously, unsure where the sudden mood change had come from.

'Yeah, it does. Sorry. Are you alright?'

'I'm fine, why?' she questioned, sounding quite normal again, which led Justin to think he must have imagined it. He knew Julia was stressed at work. She'd been snapping more often lately, but maybe he was just overreacting tonight.

'No reason. So, did you buy *another* new dress?' he teased.

Julia looked at him uncomfortably and Justin's body instinctively knew to pay full attention.

'Actually,' she began and paused, deciding on her words. 'I don't think I'm going to go.' She watched for his reaction.

'What? What do you mean you're not going to go?' he laughed lightheartedly, waiting for the joke.

'I don't think I need to go is all.' She sounded so unconcerned, like she was pulling out of a night at the movies. Not a wedding. His friend's wedding—in Melbourne.

'Don't *need* to go? What do you mean? We sent the RSVP. We have accommodation. We have flights booked. How can you say you're not going?' His voice rose gradually with each point.

'It's going to be all your friends. I don't really know them, and it's for a whole weekend. I have other things on too you know.'

She listed her reasons defensively and Justin watched as she became aggravated at *him* for being annoyed.

'You're hardly going to be left alone with them, but maybe you could get to know them better. And it's also a whole weekend *with me*.' He was furious.

'Well, I don't want to go,' she spoke clearly, now standing by his bed, arms folded across her chest.

'But … but what about flights, accommodation? How can you just not go?' He was quieter now, confused and dumbfounded.

'Well, *you're* still going. You'll need to stay somewhere,' she stated. He thought of the hotel package he'd chosen with the spa room and champagne breakfast. He didn't even drink champagne.

'What about your flights?' Julia had said she'd had enough airline points to fly down and would book it herself. Justin didn't understand why she'd throw those away, but when he asked her again, she didn't reply and averted her eyes to the doorway.

'What about your flights, Julia?' he asked, suspiciously this time. Surely she had booked it. They received the invite more than two months ago. They'd known the date for a year.

'It'll be fine,' she looked at him again and shook off his question, but he pushed it further. He needed to know.

'Julia, did you book the flight?' Justin asked her slowly, keeping himself calm. 'When we agreed weeks ago that I'd book mine and you'd book yours, did you book it?' He wanted to make it perfectly clear that that was their plan — that what he needed her to say was yes, she'd booked.

Julia looked him straight in the eye. He held his breath.

'No,' she spoke defiantly. 'I didn't.'

He felt like she had slapped him. How long ago had she decided she wouldn't be going to Melbourne? He didn't understand why she didn't think it was important for her to be there.

'But … why?' he asked, completely baffled.

'I told you, I don't want to go.' She was talking to him like he was a child and he wasn't sure whether to be grateful or offended.

'Why are you telling me this now? I don't understand. The wedding is this weekend. I told them we were both going to be there,' he trailed off. 'I don't understand why you're only telling me this now, Julia.' He looked at her pleadingly, exasperated, and Julia shrugged her shoulders. Justin stared at her. He could feel his temper rise again at her indifference to the situation.

'Tell them I'm sick,' she offered casually. 'They won't even care that I'm not there.'

He looked down at the suit laid out in front of him, surprised by how disturbed he felt.

'I wanted you there,' he said quietly before busying himself with putting the suit back into its bag and hanging it in the wardrobe. He wanted her to leave, or rewind the whole conversation and make it disappear, but she stayed in the room, arms firmly folded.

'I don't think you have to act so immaturely about this,' she threw at him. Justin spun around to face her glaring eyes.

'What?' he cried, stunned at her accusation. 'Me, immature?'

'Yes. You are being a child,' she told him matter-of-factly, flicking a strand of blonde hair from her face.

She looked triumphant, as if now that she had expressed what she thought to be true, he too would come around to her way of thinking. Justin felt bowled over and struggled to reply as he picked his jaw up off the ground. Julia took his lack of words as a sign of his realisation that he was, in fact, a child.

'Listen, I'm hungry. Let's just order dinner.' She walked out of the room and down towards the kitchen. He heard her call out, 'Do you still want Indian because I feel like pizza?'

Justin looked around the room, wanting someone else to verify what had just happened. He saw his boots and his pillows, but nothing with ears. Blood was boiling in his veins and he had energy to burn that wasn't there half an hour ago. He stood looking into his wardrobe and saw an old shirt falling off its hanger. He pulled the shirt he wore off his back and put the old one on. He kicked his work pants off and pulled on shorts.

Justin heard Julia call out again. 'Pick-up or delivery?' and he ignored her.

He found his runners under his bed and hastily pulled on socks and tied the laces. He had to get out of there before he started saying things he might regret. His mobile phone started ringing from his pants on the ground and he kicked them under his bed as he walked out of the room. He reached the front door as Julia walked back into the hall.

'Where are you going?' she demanded, ignorantly perplexed by his behaviour.

'Out,' he managed, before slamming the door behind him.

Justin marched down the garden path and his legs were pounding the pavement before they reached his neighbour's front lawn. He ran the streets, zigzagging through neighbourhoods, trying to clear his brain. Sweat dripped into his eyes and made them burn. His chest hurt from breathing in the icy night air that remained from winter. His face felt uncomfortably hot and his damp shirt was cool against his skin. But he kept running. The houses and trees became a blur. He passed others out walking and barely grunted a hello. He just kept moving, his lungs rasping for breath as he went.

He wasn't sure how long he ran for but after some time he found himself running down a familiar street. Taking in his surroundings, he began to relax and slow down, stopping when he came up to a house he knew well.

Leaning over, with hands on knees to counteract his dwindling stability, Justin sucked in air until it didn't hurt so much, before walking up the driveway; using his t-shirt to wipe the sweat from his face. He felt the muscles in his legs quiver from the spontaneous workout, his mouth parched beyond comfort, and as he reached the door, he took in a controlled breath and knocked.

When the woman answered she looked puzzled, obviously not expecting anyone that late on a Tuesday night. Her fair hair was pinned back loosely and when she recognised his face, her own broke out in a smile.

'Love! What on earth are you doing here? Is it Thursday already?' She leant out to kiss him. 'What a lovely surprise.'

'Hi Mum,' he smiled. 'Sorry, bit sweaty,' he apologised, but she kissed him anyway and then made a disgusted face that made him laugh quietly. She held the door open so he could pass, and they stepped into the lounge room.

'Justin!' bellowed his Scottish dad as he looked up from the news program on the television. 'What brings ye to our neck o' the woods, eh?'

'You guys act like you've never seen me turn up before.'

'Well, usually we know when you're coming is all. And we just saw you—on Sunday. Have you had dinner?' his mother asked, as she headed to the kitchen to make him a plate of food. They would have eaten hours ago, when the sun was still in the sky.

'Ah, no. I'm fine. I was just out for a run and I ended up here,' he explained, loud enough so his mother could hear as she busied herself in the kitchen in the next room—evidently ignoring his refusal of her food. They were right though—he usually only showed up for their Thursday family dinners, a tradition since they became grandparents, and even those he often missed because of work.

'You ran here?' they both responded simultaneously. His dad was sitting in his chair with one eye half-closed, the other focusing on a spot on the ceiling as he tried to calculate the distance.

'Ye ran the main road, no?' he asked, factoring in the difference. Justin laughed at his dad's need for detail.

'To be honest I wasn't concentrating. I was running a bit all over the place.'

'Hmm,' his dad mused, looking his son up and down. 'Aye, ye look like shite.'

Justin's dad sugarcoated the conversations he had with his wife and daughters, but when it came to Justin, he used sheer honesty. He was a firm believer that men should take it like a man.

'Thanks Dad. So do you.' Justin's dad stood up and slapped his son on the back, laughing jollily as they walked to the kitchen where his mother was taking a plate of food from the microwave. Justin took a glass from the cupboard—the same cupboard the glasses had been in his whole life—and filled it at the tap.

'There's cold water in the fridge, love,' his mother fussed.

'This is fine,' he replied, gulping it down and refilling.

'Do you always run this far?' his mother asked. His dad listened in, impressed by his son's efforts and of what his genes were capable of.

'No, no. Just felt like running tonight. I wasn't thinking. I didn't realise I'd run this far.'

'Like that Gump fellow, no?' his dad joked. 'I just kept *running*.' His impersonation of Tom Hanks made Justin and his mum laugh, which was a huge mistake on their part. They'd learned many years ago not to encourage the man.

'How was work?' his mother asked. 'Busy as usual?'

Justin nodded, telling them about how long his days were getting. His parents had always been proud of what he'd achieved and were always interested to know how he was going. He'd once overheard his dad bragging about him to a friend; hearing his dad's pride was one of Justin's most rewarding moments.

'And how's Julia?' his mother pressed on. 'Such a shame she couldn't come on Sunday.' Justin was sitting at the brown kitchen counter, picking at some pasta with a fork. His face must have given him away, or perhaps his mother may have been spending her retirement fine-tuning her senses.

'Good. She's good. I told you she was seeing her own dad on Sunday.' He shovelled some food in to occupy his mouth, hoping that would deter further questions. But what would a mother be if not an infinite source of questions?

'Is she working late tonight?' she queried casually. Justin shook his head, avoiding eye contact. *Must avoid eye contact.*

Justin began to question his own logic in knocking on his parents' door in the first place. Now wasn't the time to talk about life with his parents. He noticed his dad shake his head at his mother and Justin pretended not to notice her as she raised her hands innocently as if to say, 'What?'

Justin stood up suddenly. Pepper, he'd get some pepper. That should slow her down.

'What do you need?' she asked, ready to serve. He always thought his mother would have made a brilliant waitress, not because she wasn't capable of other things but because she had this willingness to feed and please. But then again, she'd have been a great detective too.

'S'alright,' he said, with food in his mouth. 'Just getting some pepper.' Justin forced himself to think of a curve ball to throw at them.

'So … how's Dolly?'

Dolly was his mother's very old, very slow, and very loved Labrador—named after another blonde his mother loved. Justin knew he'd picked a winner when he saw his mother's face change to mush. He almost felt bad using Dolly like that.

'Oh, she's fine. Having trouble on those steps this week, but she's still eating enough to feed a horse so … that's a good sign,' she trailed off.

'Still need her claws clipped?' he offered and then heaped more pasta in. He missed his mother's cooking. He did okay, but he loved food from his mum's kitchen much more. Sheer laziness was probably the reason—he enjoyed the fact he didn't have to do anything to get it.

'Thanks Jay, you're a wee bit better than I,' his dad said with a wink as he opened the fridge and stood staring inside. Justin had mastered the art of paw-clipping when he worked at the animal shelter during his broke student years. It was now his good deed for any friends or family with impossible pets.

'What are you after?' his mother badgered, trying to maintain her patience as the cold air escaped her fridge.

'Dunno,' his dad mumbled as he stared at the shelves. He then swung the door shut and spun around to speak to Justin. 'Are ye about to run back, Jay? Or do ye want a lift?'

Justin hadn't even thought about that. He hadn't the energy to run back. He wasn't even sure where his body had found the energy to run there in the first place. He wondered if an argument with Julia was awaiting him on his return—he definitely didn't have the energy for that either.

'Yeah, sorry, a lift would be great.' He was on early shift again in the morning, and his body groaned at the thought of having to forfeit another decent rest.

They talked about his sisters, Jo in particular. His mum telling him how gorgeous her fourth and newest grandchild was that day—a subject she'd engage in for hours if encouraged. With a big smile, his mother eventually gave in and changed the subject, guiding Justin to Dolly's paws.

The labrador's big brown eyes made Justin sad. They'd brought her home just as he was leaving for university and he could hardly believe how old she was now, mostly because her age emphasised his. He rubbed her legs as his mother handed him clippers and looked on, always concerned he'd cut too far. Dolly offered little resistance and Justin wondered if they knew her days were numbered. Knowing his mother would not accept it, he decided to broach it with his dad on the way home, although did not think he'd take it much better.

Justin patted Dolly on the head before going inside. His dad spun the car keys around his finger and they headed to the car.

'Son, ye stink,' his dad said bluntly as he reversed out of the driveway. Justin just smiled and apologised. They didn't speak again until they were pulling up to Justin's house. Justin decided to leave the Dolly discussion for another time.

'Thanks Dad,' Justin said quietly as he unclipped his seat belt. Julia's car was gone, yet he still felt strangely nervous about going inside.

'Anytime,' his dad said as he watched his son. 'Jay, anytime ye need us, we're here.'

'Thanks Dad,' Justin said again. 'That means a lot.' He jumped out and leaned in the door. 'I'll see you Thursday.'

Justin stood by his gate, giving a small wave as his dad drove off. It was much colder now and Justin rubbed his arms hard to warm them as he headed towards the house and back to his life. Reaching for his key, he swore when he realised he hadn't thought to take one. Walking around the side, he jumped the fence to find Hamlet on guard, threatening to bark. Justin clutched his chest as he spoke to Hamlet.

'Guess I deserved that.'

Justin felt his way around to the back of the house, Hamlet leaning affectionately on his leg as he walked tentatively through the dark yard. He'd hidden a key under a pot, but his eyes hadn't yet adjusted to the dark. He stumbled into what he figured was one of Hamlet's holes and swore again. Finding the key, Justin let himself inside the quiet house. The oven's clock was the only source of light and he used it like a beacon to reach the light switch. In the sudden brightness, he scanned the kitchen for a note from Julia, surprised to find there wasn't one. Curious, he picked up the house phone to check for missed calls. Three. Justin hesitantly pressed the phone to his ear, trying to prepare for Julia's voice to come through.

'Hey mate, Tom here. Just checking you guys can still pick me up to get to the airport Friday. Give us a buzz.' He deleted it and the next message played.

'Hi. Just ringing about next week. Are you still okay to mind the girls? Did you give Samantha soft drink last time? She can't have soft drink Justin.'

He rung off and waited for the next message.

'Jo again. Sorry, that came out wrong. You're not answering your mobile. Give me a call.'

Justin smiled and called his eldest sister back. By the time he was off the phone, after re-telling his mother's theories on good-looking genes, he was officially exhausted. He felt relieved there wasn't a message from Julia, though he hadn't checked his mobile. Instead, he showered—the hot water from the large showerhead turning his skin a deep shade of pink. He sat on the bottom of the shower and let the water fall over his body.

His mind blinked back to a waterfall he'd stood under in Hawaii — a trip he'd made with Julia only last year for her thirtieth birthday. He was trying to imagine that now, not Julia, just the beauty of that moment.

When his fingers were pruned and his long legs couldn't handle being cooped up any longer, Justin relinquished the notion of sleeping in the shower and reluctantly turned the water off. He roughly dried his body, wrapped a towel around his waist and slapped his feet into his room, too lazy to pick them up off the ground. Dropping his towel, he pulled on boxers and climbed under the cool covers. He was fast asleep before his head dented the pillow. He didn't even wake when the messages started coming through on his phone, buzzing aggressively from under the bed.

Justin woke the next morning to the sound of his alarm beeping with an athletic persistence. Reaching for the phone to stop the noise, his body groaned in protest and he groaned outwardly in full support. He hurt.

He wriggled to test for the most suffering muscle group and his hamstrings came out the winners. He grimaced at the tension, and at his brain for letting him run in the first place without considering the consequences.

Meanwhile, the alarm kept beeping, but his phone wasn't in sight. Glancing at the time while he fumbled around for the phone, Justin decoded the numbers on the clock face and bolted upright.

All pain aside, he was late.

'Shit!' he swore as he hobbled out of bed, his muscles briefly collapsing on him. 'Shit, shit, shit!' He was meant to have been at work ten minutes ago.

His phone stopped, much to his annoyance because now he had no idea where it was. He grabbed a polo-shirt and pulled it over his head. Grabbed yesterday's pants from under the bed, where he remembered kicking them, and as he slid them on he felt weight in the pocket.

'Ah huh, so that's where you've been hiding,' he grumbled as he pulled the phone out. It immediately started ringing and he accepted the call with a cringe.

'Sandra?' he asked as he pulled socks on, the phone wedged uncomfortably between his ear and shoulder.

'Justin, where are you?' his receptionist asked curtly, reminding him of his mother.

'I'm sorry, Sandra. Are they there already? I overslept.' He forced his feet into his boots and sprinted pathetically to the kitchen.

'Yes. They are,' she told him, unmistakably annoyed.

'I'm leaving now,' he promised, ending the call as he grabbed his keys and wallet. His alarm began beeping again and he turned it off for good. Heading to the door Justin saw Hamlet panting at the back door, he hastily filled his bowl with kibble and ran to the car.

He sped all the way. When he hit a painfully slow red light just a hundred metres from work, Justin's phone beeped with a new message. He saw that he had seven messages and rolled his eyes when he saw that six of them were from Julia The-Wedding-Piker herself. He threw the phone back on the seat as the lights changed to green, sped into the car park, slammed the door shut and ran inside to a cranky client.

'Good morning Mrs McCoo,' Justin rushed as he emptied his pockets in front of Sandra. 'Morning Sandra,' he winced apologetically and her head of spiky sandy hair nodded in acknowledgment, her short hands passing him a sheet of paper while she glowered up at him so he knew she was not pleased. More so, he suspected, because Mrs McCoo was a royal pain in the arse and Sandra would have needed to sedate her if he'd been another five minutes late.

'Come right in,' he said as he gestured towards the door, trying his very best to control his breathing.

'Good morning,' she spoke briskly, huffing as she stepped into the room. Justin smiled at her politely and once she had passed, rolled his eyes for Sandra to see. Her stern face suppressed a knowing smile as she turned back to her computer screen. He closed the door on reception and turned back to Mrs McCoo.

'I'm so sorry about my lateness,' he apologised, noticing her scan his shabby look. He ran his fingers through his hair and wiped the crusty sleep from the inner corners of his eyes. His breath probably smelt but Mrs McCoo reeked of nicotine, so he wasn't going to apologise if she wasn't.

'How can I help you today?'

By the time Justin found a spare ten minutes in the day, his stomach was staging a rally. Each grumble a blunt outcry for food.

'Have we got anything to eat?' Justin asked Eric, who had thankfully braved work that day.

'Not sure mate. Ask Sandra,' Eric replied as his wiry body rushed off to see another client.

They were flat-out again and both had begun to wonder whether they were really that good at their jobs or if they just had a really awesome logo. It could have been their Facebook page, their 'Likes' were increasing, but it was Sandra's job to write posts and anytime anyone reminded her of this she'd scowl at them and throw her hands in the air, moaning about the good old days.

'Sandra, we have any food?' Justin called out from the office.

'Bread, I think,' she told him, sticking her round face around the door. 'Would you like me to make you something?'

'No. No, thanks, I've got it,' he called over his shoulder as he dug around the tiny kitchen, which was really just a section in the office that had been cleared for a microwave, small fridge and kettle, and found enough bits and pieces to assemble a decent sandwich. He knew he only had about a minute to eat and as tempted as he was to check his phone, he refrained. Until, of course, he heard it ring.

Justin scrambled for it, hoping it wasn't a call from Julia—which he knew it was. He stared at her name for a moment that he didn't have and then reluctantly accepted the call.

'Hel-lo,' he spoke with the most neutral tone he could muster.

'Hi,' replied a stiff-voiced Julia. 'Were you *going* to call me today? Or were you just expecting *me* to?' He actually thought the latter would have been perfectly fair.

'I've been busy Julia,' he told her, eyeing the sandwich in his hand and wondering if he could eat it without her hearing. He bit the corner and swallowed it discreetly.

'Well, it's good to know I'm a priority.'

He wanted to hang up on her. Julia obviously had no intention of being nice, and he didn't have the patience to continue any argument.

'Listen Julia, I have been too busy to read your messages or call you, but I shouldn't have left like that. I'm sorry.'

He felt his masculinity slide but if it cleared the tension, he was willing to live with that. She didn't reply, but he thought he heard her make a satisfied sigh.

'Thank you,' she told him, but he could hear it was through her teeth, knowing he'd caught her off guard. Julia was always up for an argument. Sometimes he even benefitted from them, but he'd much rather she'd just back off or accept that her way was not always what made everyone happy.

'Listen, I need to get back to work. Could I call you later? I think we do need to talk.'

'I'm going to the gym.'

'After the gym.'

'Fine,' she told him, and Justin wondered if he was supposed to be feeling privileged.

He hung up and placed his phone on the table, staring at it while he ate his sandwich. He looked down at his hands when it was gone and realised he hadn't even tasted it.

'Justin?' Eric's voice was loud and serious. 'Can I get your help mate?'

'Coming,' Justin called back. He switched his head back into work mode and tried his best not to think of the person he loved and wanted to spend the rest of his life with. He also tried not to wonder if that were normal.

chapter eight

It was going to be a big night. At the very least, Anna hoped, one with possibility.

She'd seen a sign at a local bar for speed dating and had convinced Mel to come with her.

'It'll be fun,' she'd pleaded.

'Fun? Being analysed in two minutes? No thanks,' Mel shot down the invitation.

'It's five minutes. And anyway,' Anna tried, 'what have we got to lose?'

'Pride. Dignity …'

'I'll love you forever,' Anna sung sweetly, fluttering her lashes.

'Bribery? Nice.'

Anna gave Mel the most desperate look she could muster and was pinched in return.

'Ouch!' she cried, rubbing her arm in alarm. 'What'd you do that for?'

Mel's serious look crumpled in laughter. 'You know why. Because you pull that face and you know I can't say no!'

Anna bounced on her toes. 'So, you'll come?'

'Yes. I'll come.' She didn't sound very enthusiastic, but Anna didn't care, she'd work on that later. For now, she was just happy to have a date to speed date with.

She'd giggled at the thought and Mel gave her an odd look.

Anna showered and approached her wardrobe reluctantly, her movements resembling a standoff from a western movie. *Please give me the perfect outfit.*

On some days Anna was sure her clothes were bewitched. Clothes that made her look amazing in the shops would look downright stupid at home. A pair of jeans she'd wear one week, and look good in, would look absolutely terrible the next.

She closed her eyes, said a little prayer, and swung open the wardrobe doors. Confident she heard little clothes angels sing, Anna reached for her most dependable blue jeans, and a sleeveless white blouse she'd recently bought for the subtle favours it did to her (usually average) cleavage. Tentatively she pulled them on and faced the mirror.

Hallelujah.

Anna did a little dance in thanks and headed to the bathroom. She applied her make-up in relatively good time, grimaced at her ears, shook out her shiny dark hair to cover them, and smiled at herself. She felt positive. She desperately wanted a turn at being in a relationship and was hopeful that tonight she'd meet her man and fall in love—all in under five minutes.

For the final touch, Anna sprayed her favourite perfume before heading out the door.

They had decided to meet at a neighbouring bar and as she neared the first establishment, Anna's confidence remained strong. Then she walked in to find Mel sitting at a table looking like a movie-star and all self-assurance plummeted. She kicked herself for not thinking of this earlier; the tall redhead over her short-arse self. What was she thinking?

'You look amazing!' cried Mel as she took Anna in. 'And what are these?' she gawked, poking Anna's boob with admiration.

'Me? *You* look amazing,' Anna moaned, swiping away Mel's hand. 'I want to hate you.'

'Shut up.' Mel rolled her eyes. 'I think I gained thirty new freckles walking to my letterbox today. Not cute.' Mel held her arm out for Anna to see. 'Now, should we get going?'

Anna nodded solemnly as Mel slid off her barstool, and they headed to the venue where potential true love awaited.

The room was packed with faces too apprehensive to declare anything close to love as Anna and Mel registered their names and numbers, with Anna giving her paper a little kiss for good luck. Their own nervous faces then melded with the others as they stood in line for drinks. Anna hoped the wine would drown the butterflies in her stomach, if the thumping music didn't kill them first.

To their side, a man with a groomed beard climbed up onto the shiny bar top and rang a bell for the crowd's attention. The music was turned down and for a moment there was enough silence that Anna thought she heard a belly gurgle. Hoping it wasn't hers, she tuned in anxiously.

'Welcome everyone,' he bellowed. 'My name is Alex and I'm your host for this evening. The way it's going to work tonight is in groups. Two girls will be at each table and the men will rotate around.'

'Like an orgy!' a guy called out. Some people laughed. Some gave nervous giggles. Most of the women gave him a look of dislike. He really played his cards wrong there, Anna observed. Alex ignored him.

'You have five minutes at each table. At the end of the night you need to write down the names of the people you'd want to

see again. If they write your name too, you'll get their number.'
He looked around the room. 'Any questions?'

Nobody seemed too confused by the process and the girls headed to the tables. Mel pointed one out near a window and she and Anna slid out a chair each, sitting to face the crowd, checking their name tags were showing clearly as Alex rang the bell.

'Here we go,' muttered Mel as potential suitors headed towards them.

Two men took a seat to face them and then hesitated, unsure of where to start. Anna, concerned a fumbled first attempt at speed dating would ruin their chances, extended her hand.

'I'm Anna,' she offered quickly and everyone else followed suit.

'So, Anna, what do you do?' the guy opposite her asked. He had blond hair, blue eyes and a nice smile.

Anna smiled at the question.

'I'm in IT. Actually, we both are,' she pointed between herself and Mel.

'Support, troubleshooting, that kind of thing,' Mel spoke. 'How about you two?'

His friend jumped in. 'Hey! Us too!'

'Oh wow,' Mel exclaimed, and Anna grinned at her. Maybe tonight wouldn't be so bad. But as the five minutes ticked by, Anna found it hard to maneuver away from the computer talk. Their dates were talking companies, software and new systems, and she felt like she was in the lunchroom at work.

The next two were lucky their mothers had let them out for the night, and Anna wondered if it was cat fur she spotted on the one wearing a cardigan.

The night didn't seem to pick up from there, but with more women than men having showed up to the event, there was a five-minute grace period for the girls. Anna was thankful for the break. These men were pushing her optimism out the window with brutal force.

'Will you be my bridesmaid?' Mel asked sarcastically as their latest dates moved on to the next unsuspecting table, 'because *he* was a catch,' she said with stars in her eyes.

'Shush,' Anna giggled. 'Don't be mean.'

'An, I'm not trying to boast, but any of those guys would be lucky to have us.'

Anna waved her hand to shush her again, but thinking back over their six dates so far, she ashamedly admitted Mel was right.

'Okay, so a few clashes, but look, the next ones might be better.' And sure enough, when the bell rang, they were pleasantly surprised.

'Kyle.' Their newest date smiled widely and smoothly offered his hand to them both. His shaving efforts looked neglected, but he seemed otherwise neat and well-groomed. 'And …' he presented the man next to him, who finished his sentence.

'I'm Richie.'

The girls introduced themselves and were surprised by the easy conversation. The two had turned up with an odd number of friends and so were paired together.

'So, if you're computer girls,' asked Richie, 'does that mean you're gamers too?'

The girls shook their heads. 'When I was younger maybe, not now,' admitted Mel.

'Not now?' He started raving about a new game his friend had and Kyle chimed in.

'Oh man, I love that game. Awe-some.' They high-fived each other and Anna noticed Mel flinch, more so when they started to recreate the game with dramatic arm actions.

'Man, we should play online!' Kyle exclaimed and they whipped out their phones. The bell rang and they said goodbye to the girls absently, tapping in each other's numbers as they rotated to the next table.

Mel squeezed Anna's leg. 'Did that just happen? The best guys of the night were more interested in each other?'

'And Playstation,' Anna added, forcing herself to close her gaping mouth.

Four more prospective dates visited and none were worthy of the effort Anna had made to turn up. When 'Orgy Guy' arrived at their table and proceeded to be a rambling buffoon, Anna had to resist leaving. She struggled to listen to anything he was saying as he rudely talked over the other date he had arrived with, who may or may not have been a buffoon. Orgy Guy didn't give them the chance to find out.

Finally, they were saved by the bell.

'Thank God,' Mel muttered when they all turned at the sound.

Alex, with a suggestive wink, told them to get their names in the box, and Mel asked Anna if she was going to put anyone's name down.

'I don't know. Maybe Richie, or Kyle,' Anna said, miserably. 'What about you?'

'Same.' Mel murmured. 'Do you think they'd have time to see us, what with their own relationship to work on?'

'No. But we may as well try. Let's pick one each.'

Mel nodded in agreement and they scrolled their names and the boys' names down, slid them into the box provided, and left quickly.

They walked despondently up the road looking for another bar to sit and chat. Every place Anna pointed out Mel excused for being too loud, busy, expensive, dirty, snobby …

'Melissa Donson!' Anna exclaimed. 'Stop being a pain in the butt.'

'How about that one?' Mel relented, pointing out a smart looking bar across the road. 'It doesn't look too packed,' she shrugged.

They crossed the road and sat at an empty table squished up against the wall. Mel went to the bar, claiming she had the better taste in wine (which was true) and left Anna to scope out the crowd.

Thankfully, there didn't seem to be any faces from the speed dating experience. She did a second scan for familiar faces — friends, bosses, enemies, ex's — and gave the joint a second tick of approval. Finally, she did a search for prospective boyfriends and gave a feeble mental tick. There were some men she judged to have potential but couldn't imagine the girls already holding their hands would be equally impressed.

Her phone beeped an incoming message and Anna frowned when she read it.

Sorry for the delay. All good here. Thanks for your messages. Will call through the week. Dad ox

She'd waited a week to hear from him, calling twice more through the week. She hated the familiarity of the disappointment she felt, though was relieved he was okay. All of the scenes she had imagined and fretted over vanished and she felt herself take a deep breath.

Mel returned with an ice bucket tucked under one arm with a bottle of white nesting inside, two glasses clutched between her fingers, and an eager grin on her face. Anna returned the smile, choosing to accept her dad as her dad, and the toasting began, followed by a dissection of their speed dates.

Without much deliberation, it was decided that overall the men did not fare well, and Anna sunk into a lull.

'What's wrong?' Mel asked compassionately, but Anna could hear the un-said 'now' that hung in the air.

'Why?' she moaned into her drink. 'Why am I always single? What's wrong with me Mel?' She looked up at her friend hopefully. 'Tell me the truth. Am I too fussy? Am I too ugly?'

Mel snorted. They seemed to go through this every few weeks. One or the other would be saying this same thing. It was like a game of tag and tonight Anna was 'it'.

'No. You're not too fussy and you're not ugly,' Mel groaned. 'You *are* too fat though.' Mel nodded regretfully, and Anna's face shot up in alarm. 'I'm joking, An. You are gorgeous and adorable.'

'Then why am I single?' she cried, exasperated.

'Probably because, *even* though you are gorgeous … and adorable, you say *stupid* stuff.'

'What!'

'Don't 'what' me young lady. You know you say stupid stuff. And anyway, you are not the only single one around here.'

'Wait.' Anna thought Mel's consistent stream of relationships made her last point moot. 'When you say, 'stupid stuff' do you mean tha—'

'That you say *stu-pid stuff*,' she spoke slowly. 'You don't think. You just, blah, blah, blah.' Mel's hands made puppet motions and Anna rose in her seat to defend herself. Her mouth opened to speak, then closed. Her body shrunk back.

'But I can't help it,' she wailed, feeling her defeat.

'Well, try. Or …' Mel teased. 'You'll be single forever like me.' Anna scoffed at this, but Mel ignored her. 'We can be spinsters together,' she suggested, flicking her red hair down over her pouting lips.

'No thanks, Mel. Tempting as that is, I'll pass.' Anna took a breath in. 'I just need to change. I'm going to change my whole life, my whole personality, shake things up—make a whole new Anna.'

Mel waited dutifully for Anna's plan as she hung her face over her drink, thinking.

'Maybe I could learn a language?' she suggested meekly. 'Or ride a bike to work.' Mel managed to keep quiet. 'I just want a boyfriend. Preferably an extremely attractive one. Who is of course mad about me …'

Mel raised her eyebrows, 'Well, I'd hope so.'

'A guy who totally sweeps me off my feet; one that tells me all the amazing things I wish were actually true myself …'

'So you want some guy that will carry you off into the sunset, whisper sweet nothings in your ear?' swooned Mel sarcastically.

'No. Yes. So! What's so wrong with that Mel? You want it too. Admit it! And anyway, I never said sunset … just to bed would do fine.' Anna let her voice trail off and they both laughed loudly.

'Oh, how about that guy over there?' Mel pointed to a man, grossly oversized, about seven-foot tall with a seemingly seven-foot wide handlebar moustache. 'He looks strong enough to carry your fat arse,' Mel said, her face smirking at the image. Anna looked over, alarmed.

'Shut up. Why do you have to be so mean? That poor man.'

'What about that guy Jane and Ioulia talk about?' Mel suggested.

'Hero Guy?'

'Yeah. Didn't he carry her off?'

'To the men's room apparently.'

'Romantic. Maybe you too could be so lucky.'

'Well, at least I'd be carried. I've never been carried before.' Anna dreamily imagined she had that memory to look back on. 'Have you ever been carried off?'

'Yes.'

Anna glared at her.

'You asked!' defended Mel.

Anna frowned and ran her finger through the frost on the wine bottle with a sigh. 'I just want someone who makes me feel special. Like the reason why I'm still single is because only *he* could ever get me,' she trailed off again, unashamedly fantasising about her mystery man.

'Okay,' Mel relented. 'So, we need to find you the perfect man. That should be easy enough. Does he do laundry too?'

'Sure.'

'Cook?'

'Why not. I like to eat.'

'Clearly,' Mel eyed Anna's butt and giggled at her friend's sarcastic laugh. 'So, your new life plan is to buy a bike, speak a foreign language, find the ideal man and be carried to bed?'

Anna's face fell while Mel refilled both their glasses. 'Solid plan.'

'Oh, shush. We can't all have the magical powers that you possess.'

'Excuse me? What on earth are you talking about now?' Mel exclaimed, lost in the direction the conversation had now taken.

'You! And your powers,' Anna said, her fingers twinkling in the air mysteriously. 'Mel you just need to walk into a room and some guy falls in love with you.'

'You, my friend, have had too much to drink. Guys do not fall in love with me,' she denied. 'If that were the case, I too would not be single and sitting with my crazy friend on a Saturday night.'

'You blind, blind girl,' Anna shook her head. 'Look, let's see …' Anna started scoping the room. 'Ah, ha! Just over there you have a table of about five guys, and at least two are checking you out. Ha!'

'Where?' Mel humoured her and looked over. Anna was horrified. Having not brought her glasses with her, Mel was squinting quite obviously in the direction of the men Anna had sighted. 'Are you talking about the guys near the ATM? They're all in suits? They're surrounded by girls in dresses?'

Anna adjusted her position to confirm Mel's description of the group. She was trying her best to be inconspicuous after Mel's poor attempt, but she could verify that the group were in fact all in suits, and in addition, that they looked fairly ideal. Mel took great pleasure in the look on her friend's contorted face and sprayed wine out of her mouth.

'Yup. And, they're 'looking at you, kid',' Anna drawled, attempting a very poor Bogart impersonation as Mel started mopping up the table with a coaster.

'Well, if my eyes are not deceiving me, and they very well could be, but from my seat over here Miss Lonely-Hearts, I would say that they are actually looking … at you.'

'What!' Anna laughed and forgetting to look casual, threw her head around to check. The words were already in her mouth to point out how wrong Mel was when she froze. They *were* looking at her. They were looking at *her!* What's more, she knew them. Well, one of them.

'It's Justin.'

Justin begrudgingly agreed to go out afterwards. It was an early wedding, so he had no excuse not to stay out longer, he just wasn't in the mood.

The wedding, of course, was a happy occasion. It was just *so* freaking happy. It made him feel awful and bitter and he resented the bride and groom for most of the day which only made him feel more awful for being such a terrible friend.

Julia had refused to change her mind about coming to the wedding, or Melbourne. He'd tried to convince her, but she was adamant she wouldn't know anyone, wouldn't enjoy herself and wasn't interested.

Justin realised, as he watched the bride walk down the aisle, he had been assuming he had a future with Julia, had felt sure of it. But she didn't seem to be showing those same sentiments. She didn't care enough to get along with his friends or be involved in his life. As Justin questioned what that meant, he started to wonder where his life was really going. He wanted what his parents had—have. Justin simply wanted more.

He was thirty-three years old, and he didn't want the bachelor life Adam had chosen. He wanted to wake up with someone. With Julia—he'd thought. But she wouldn't even consider moving in with him.

When she'd obligingly driven he and Tom to the airport the day before, Tom had asked what she was doing for the weekend (because Justin had led him to believe she had important plans). Julia had replied that she needed to renew the lease on her apartment. She then spent approximately ten minutes telling Tom how great her flat was and how frustrating it was that she could only sign in twelve-month blocks when she'd wanted to secure it for longer. Justin hadn't said anything, but Tom had supported her frustrations and complained that that was the nature of the rental market, suggesting she should buy instead.

Justin had sat there irritated she hadn't considered, or had dismissed, the notion of living with him. He had thought they were in a serious relationship, one that was heading somewhere. One that would involve a shared address at some stage, the possibility of a shared name at another. However, Julia was deciding to miss his friend's wedding so she could sign a contract that would stop her from living with him for yet another year.

The disappointment Justin was feeling was encompassing his every thought as he walked through St Kilda without her.

The clouds had put a blanket on the stars, and the September night was surprisingly mild as the group walked along in their suits and dresses. Couples strolled hand-in-hand around him while his hands swung free in the night.

Justin was still drunk from the reception, where he had been trying to drink himself happy quite unsuccessfully—the alcohol had merely intensified his feelings. *At least I'm not alone*, he thought. He may not have wanted to celebrate, but he wanted to be alone even less.

The group stumbled into a bar they estimated to have the quickest queue to the drinks and the shortest line to the bathroom—criteria requested by those in dresses.

Justin had met some of the group at his designated wedding table but knew others from their school days and the buck's night. Their wives and girlfriends hung off their arms full of adoration and revived love after a romantic day. Justin was grateful Tom, at least, was single.

Packing around a table, jackets and dainty purses were thrown on top, some scattering to the ground. No-one seemed to be bothered and none seemed to notice what a foul mood Justin was in. There was music playing but not so loud that they couldn't hear each other. Tom handed him a beer and asked if he'd spotted any hot women.

'Not exactly looking mate,' Justin replied, as he loosened his tie even more. It hung like a limp noose around his neck.

'Well, you should. Julia's a bitch,' Tom revealed loudly, but was then grabbed from behind by one of the wives and was gone before Justin could comment.

Justin stood stunned. They all liked Julia, didn't they? Tom was just drunk, he assured himself. He didn't know what he was saying. The girls grabbed Justin next and he forgot what he was thinking about. They had another drink and Tom came hopping over towards him again.

'I found one!'

'Found one what?'

'A hot, hot woman, dumb-arse,' Tom scoffed in exasperation. 'Look over there,' he pointed across the bar to two girls sitting on bar stools and leaning on a tiny table. 'See? The redhead?'

Justin looked back over at Tom and smirked.

'What is it with you and red hair, Tommy? You like the brother-sister look?'

Tom looked indignant. 'I'm not a redhead!' Justin scanned Tom's head with a smirk. 'Strawberry blond … maybe,' Tom compromised.

'Did your mum tell you that?' Justin asked.

Tom attempted to look pissed off but cracked. 'Fine. I'm red,' he admitted. 'You happy now? Prick.' Justin shrugged and turned back to the girl Tom had spotted. Tom happily turned back too.

'You want her? I won't tell Julia. If you want to go for it, she's yours,' Tom offered, as if the woman was his to give.

Justin turned to him with a look that was meant to follow with a stern inquisition on why he was suddenly so against Julia, when something caught his eye and he did a double-take.

'No mate,' he declined vaguely instead, and slowly assured Tom, 'She's all yours.' It was her friend he was looking at.

It was Anna.

chapter nine

Justin's spirits lifted at the sight of her, her easy smile clearing his jadedness. He told his feet to move towards her but then questioned if he should.

He didn't realise he was staring at her so intently while he decided, or that Tom was still by his side with his tongue hanging out of his mouth at the sight of Anna's friend. At least, he didn't realise until she looked over suddenly and then he felt like a deer caught in headlights. And he couldn't look away.

'Uh, oh. Busted,' Tom laughed as he smacked Justin in the chest. 'Come on bud, let's go.'

Mesmerised, Justin followed Tom over, drink in hand, stepping around the other groups out enjoying the night. Anna watched as he approached.

'Hi,' he smiled uncertainly, doubting his decision to follow Tom over—his fingertips shouldn't be tingling the way that they were. He advised himself not to drink any more as a precaution. 'How are you?'

'Hi, Justin! What are you doing here?' Anna's smile grew wider with every word and her hands flung out in excitement, freezing in wait for his answer. Her eyes were prettier than he remembered.

Tom stared between them. 'You two know each other?' Confused, he looked at Justin as though he'd been holding out on him.

'Um, yeah,' Justin said as he tore his eyes away from Anna to look at his friend. 'Tom, this is Anna. We met on the buck's weekend.' He looked back to Anna for validation.

'Hi Tom,' Anna smiled at Tom and then back at Justin.

'I'm Mel,' Mel cut in, looking at Anna with interest. 'Nice to meet you both.' She shook both their hands and Tom took the opportunity to start up a conversation with her. Justin noticed Tom stand taller. He'd have laughed, but he was too aware of Anna looking at him and taking him in. Seeing her scan his body so obviously made Justin feel self-conscious and it took away any of the questions he was about to ask her.

'So, wedding this weekend? Or are you just trying harder?'

He felt himself relax for the first time that day and pressed his palm to his skewed tie. 'Yes. Wedding,' he agreed.

'Any good?' she asked, adding dreamingly, 'I love weddings.'

'Sure.'

She laughed at his poor attempt of a polite answer.

'Not a wedding person I gather,' she smiled, eyeing his crooked tie.

'Ah, it's not that. I like weddings.' Anna's head dropped to the side, weighed down by doubt. 'Really, I do,' he laughed. 'I just wasn't in the mood I guess.' Justin was thankful when she didn't press the issue.

'Hey, how's your friend … Adam?' Anna asked.

Justin rolled his eyes. 'How's Jane?'

'That good, huh?' she grinned. 'Jane's good. She says she's adjusting to Sydney. I think she's glad to be away from the AFL and grey skies,' Anna laughed lightly, her cheeks glowing as she did. 'She is kinda proud of her scar though … thinks guys will think she's more interesting now.'

'Ah, come on. I'm sure she did fine without the scar.'

Anna nodded in agreement. 'Well, you've never met her, but you are right, Jane is pretty great.'

Justin considered correcting her but couldn't seem to string a response together that didn't make him sound like an egotistical hero.

'So, how are you? It's nice to see you've improved your standards since last time,' he spoke indicating the bar.

Anna laughed and explained her night with Mel. She pointed across the table to her friend whose ear was now very close to Tom's mouth. Anna raised an eyebrow towards Justin and protectively asked if Tom was anything like Adam or the losers she and Mel had already met that night. Justin shook his head.

'No, he's safe,' he laughed. 'You have my word.'

'Good.'

'Hey, Doc,' called Tom, and Justin obediently looked over at him. 'Don't you think Mel looks like that girl in that show?' Justin agreed wholeheartedly, having no idea which girl or what show he was referring to.

'Doc?' Anna queried, looking between both the boys.

'It's his name. He's a bloody brain!' Tom explained loudly as he slapped Justin on the back, harder than Justin would have liked and had to try hard not to show it hurt.

'Nickname,' Justin butted in, waving his hand to dismiss it. 'We all seem to have one or two.'

'What's yours?' purred Mel, tapping Tom's beer with her glass.

'Donkey,' replied a straight-faced Justin on his behalf.

'Donkey?' Mel scrunched her face. 'Why?'

Anna smirked. 'Let me guess. As in, 'hung like a …'?' she trailed off. Justin shrugged modestly. Mel's face lit up with intrigue and Tom gave Justin a grateful wink. Anna giggled and Justin smiled at her pixie face.

'Do you have one?' he asked her.

'Donkey? No.'

'A nickname. Smart-arse.'

'No. Not really ... just An.'

'They call you An? That's it? You've never had a problem with that?'

'Never had a problem,' she assured him, sipping her wine.

'Bit lame.'

'What?' Anna frowned. 'What would you suggest then?'

'Annie.' Anna shrugged at the name. 'Tony?'

'Tony?' Anna shook her head. 'Genius. No wonder they call you Doc.'

'Thanks,' Justin mused. She laughed again and he found it infectious.

'Want a drink?' he asked, nodding to the bar.

'Sure. I'll come with you.' She bounced off the bar stool and grabbed his hand, dragging him through the crowds.

'What are you having?' he asked, forgetting his recent decision to not have another drink.

'I'll just have what you're having.'

'What if you don't like what I'm having?'

'I'll deal with it,' she assured him, patting his arm. He looked down at her hand on his arm. Her eyes followed his and she removed it quickly.

'What will Mel have?' he asked, ignoring the momentary distraction of her touch.

'Mel? Same,' she replied simply.

'What if she doesn't like it?'

'She'll get over it.'

'Okay ...' he shrugged and turned back to the patient bartender. 'Can I please have four Long Island Iced Teas?'

'Agh!' he heard her exclaim. 'That's mean!'

'What?' he faced her innocently.

'Nothing,' she grumbled with a smirk.

He laughed inwardly and, as soon as the most potent drink he could think of was prepared, Anna took two of the glasses and Justin carried the others back to the table. He was surprised upon their return to find it was Mel who had Tom cornered. The two parted slightly to accept the drinks, revealing their flushed faces. Anna and Justin exchanged looks.

'What is this?' demanded Mel after one sip.

'Long Island Iced Tea,' Tom told her, frowning as he tasted his own. 'Mate, what were you thinking? This is poison.'

'I like it,' Justin lied as he sipped his drink, trying to take in as little as possible.

'It's gross. Do I have to drink it?' complained Mel.

'Well, Anna here said you wouldn't mind,' Justin claimed innocently. Anna shook her head at him.

'Smart-arse,' she smirked. 'Mel, it's okay. If Justin likes it so much, let *him* drink it.' Her face was pure glee as she plonked the glass down in front of him and he couldn't help but laugh with her.

Tom and Mel reverted to focusing on each other and Justin watched as Anna scrolled through his phone, after a random, yet educating, conversation about Apps.

She looked up at him suddenly, commending his collection, and caught Justin off guard. She was staring intently at his eyes and it was starting to make him feel awkward, as though she could see all his thoughts, all his secrets.

Up so close, Justin saw light freckles on her nose and cheeks and thought it made her look even cuter. He felt an impulse to touch her nose—another to feel her cheeks. If he was being completely honest with himself, he'd also admit he was fighting the desire to run his fingers along her lips. He was enthralled by her. He had a fleeting thought of Julia and guiltily looked away.

He wondered what Anna was thinking and whether he should say something.

'Have you ever plucked your eyebrows?' she asked, her eyes holding his face.

'What? No!' *That's what she was thinking about?*

'Why not?'

'Because I'm a guy.'

'So?'

'What's wrong with my eyebrows?' he demanded. They'd never had a mention before. She shrugged her shoulders at him. 'Now I'm going to have an eyebrow complex. Thanks,' he said.

'No problem,' Anna smiled, looking quite smug, and continued playing with his phone. She'd opened the camera feature and was happily entertained.

She took photos of Mel and Tom, one of Justin, and then one of herself. She squished her cheek to his and took some more, pulling different faces for each shot. Content with her efforts, she scrolled back through them.

Justin watched her, his head thoroughly spinning as the second iced tea travelled through his body, successfully numbing each cell in its path. His legs felt uneasy and he tried to move his feet to balance but seemed to be stuck to the sticky floor. He didn't think that could be a good sign but forgot about it as Anna laughed at the photos she'd taken. He watched her in a slight haze as she giggled at each frame—though the moment her smile faltered, he saw clearly.

Justin leant over, her waves of hair smooth against his face, and saw she was looking at older photos on the phone. She'd already scrolled slowly past the short series of the day's bride and groom, and he watched as she then saw a little ballerina, then two little ballerinas, a middle-aged woman holding a baby, Justin and a little girl wearing hats backwards, Justin with a blonde woman, the blonde woman smiling, then frowning.

Justin's head on a pillow, blonde woman's head on a pillow, Justin and blonde woman laughing on the pillow.

'Is this your girlfriend?' she asked casually, and he felt a rush of feelings he couldn't place.

'Um, yeah.'

'Pretty. What's her name again?' Anna's eyes remained fixed on the last photo, but Justin was watching her closely.

'Julia. Her name's Julia.'

Tom, having overheard the name, untactfully cried, 'Julia? Julia's a bitch.'

Justin stared at him, he'd momentarily forgotten Tom was even there, and felt lost for words. Anna looked on uncomfortably.

'Tom, how can you say that?' he was astounded. 'She's never been anything but nice to you.'

'Well, where is she now?' Tom asked, holding his hands out. Mel chorused him and asked where she was, claiming she wanted to meet her.

Justin felt confused and embarrassed. He was angry at Julia for not coming, he didn't deny that, but that didn't mean he wouldn't defend her. At the same time, Anna, with her pixie face, was looking up at him. Her face had seemed to fall with each picture she'd seen of Julia. She looked so much more sober and sombre than only moments ago and he didn't know what his head was doing, or why. His straight life felt like it was warping.

'You're a jerk,' he told Tom with a forced laugh, who held his hands up in defense.

Conversation continued between the three of them, but Justin became a spectator, laughing when expected. He shouldn't be here, he thought, and pushed away the remains of his drink.

'Hey, I'm going to get going.'

'Don't go, Doc,' Tom jeered. 'I'm sorry, I didn't mean it. Julia is great. She's hot.' Mel pinched him and Anna's face fell a little more, even though her mouth still smiled.

'It's all good mate, I'm just tired.'

'Actually, I was thinking we could go too,' Anna said quietly to Mel.

'What? No!' she looked pleadingly at Anna, eyed Tom and mouthed, 'please'.

'You're welcome to come sit with the gang over there,' Tom pointed out their friends still happily chatting on the other side of the bar. Mel looked at Anna, who shrugged her approval. The girls collected their bags and Mel and Tom stood side by side.

Together the four of them crossed the room to the wedding after-party. Justin shook hands and kissed cheeks and told them he'd see them at breakfast. Anna hugged Mel and they whispered quietly into each other's ear. Anna kissed Tom on the cheek and warned him to look after her friend. Justin watched as Tom laughed at this, and then seeing her steely glance assured Anna that Mel was in good hands.

Justin and Anna walked to the exit together. He didn't notice the others question who he was leaving with. He never considered what it might look like—he just wanted to go.

When they reached the street, a cold breeze blew, reminding them it was a long way from summer. They turned to face each other, shy again, and Justin spoke first—head still spinning, fingers still tingling.

'It was nice to see you again.' He wasn't sure how loud his voice was, every sound seemed to be amplified now they were outside.

'Yeah. You too ... *Doc*,' she teased, a mischievous smile painted across her face. Justin detected her sway while trying to stand still, as if the crowd had been holding her up and now she had to readjust.

'What way are you?' he asked as his thumb pointed in different directions up and down the busy road.

'Oh, I'm that way,' she pointed. 'But I was going to get a taxi. You?'

'I think I'm going to wander actually. Fresh air and all,' he explained. He didn't really want to say goodbye now or be alone after all. He was trying to think of how he could stall her leaving.

'Can I join you?' Anna asked, and Justin marvelled at his luck as he nodded at the unexpected offer.

chapter ten

Justin and Anna walked down the road, concentrating hard not to stumble. The streets were crowded and they zigzagged around others whose own feet and directional skills seemed to have failed. Laughter echoed in the wind and colours blurred around them. A brightly lit tram rocked by, and souped-up cars cruised the main road; music thumping out. Justin commented on the drivers and Anna responded in hysterics. He doubted she would have thought him so funny in a more sober situation. She was laughing so much that she almost missed the moment a group of guys gave her a wolf whistle. Her mouth gaped and she gawked at Justin with shock, right before she high-fived him — almost missing his hand.

Justin wasn't sure why she was so surprised and had enough of a lack of inhibition to tell her so.

'What do you mean? People don't whistle at *me!*' she cried with a slap to her chest. Her cheeks glowed from the cool air and she shook her hair as she spoke. 'They don't look at me. They look at Mel, or Jane. Not me,' she stated, with an air of general knowledge.

'I'm pretty sure they do Anna,' he laughed at her genuine naivety. Anna shooed him away and ambled on.

Justin stopped his feet in his shiny black shoes and watched as she continued along up the street, her balance considerably better than his own and much improved from where they'd first begun. She was oblivious she walked alone.

Justin drew his lips to cover his teeth and blew the loudest wolf whistle he could manage. It earned the attention of those around him, including a nearby busker. They stopped to follow his gaze to see who he'd whistled at; to see who had deserved such attention.

Anna stopped too (the sound piercing her tranquility), noticed Justin was no longer by her side, and looked back to find him. When she spotted him standing in the middle of the footpath with a wide smile on his face, he gave her another loud, appreciative whistle.

A younger man out with his girlfriend, and sporting the tightest jeans Justin had ever seen, gave Justin a thumbs-up and called approvingly, 'Too right mate. She's hot'. His girlfriend slapped his arm loudly. Justin chuckled and jogged up next to Anna, who stood with blushing cheeks pushed high by a wide grin.

'Three whistles in one night? Whoa. I'm impressed,' he told her, and gave her a smaller whistle for good measure.

Anna walked along with Justin. They passed restaurants and bars and drooled at bakery windows. She was still smiling at Justin's whistle. The big ones were funny, but the soft, low one he'd given her had sent a thrill through her body. She had to remind herself he had a girlfriend, a Julia, and that even if he didn't, he was not in the same league as her. Or state.

Jane had told Anna once, and then many times afterwards, that she dated low-lives. This was much to Anna's distress of course, because she'd actually liked those guys. They were never the most attractive guys, like those Jane would see; they weren't the smartest or most interesting, but they were (generally) nice enough to her, and that's what mattered.

In some sick way, Anna figured that if they weren't too ideal a man then they wouldn't leave her for someone better—she'd watched her mum sit through too many years of heartache to want to do that to herself. The problem was that they seemed to bore her, disgust her, or lie to her eventually and she'd ask them to move on. She didn't think she was breaking any hearts though—she'd never seen tears shed.

Justin though, he seemed different, and maybe it was simply because he would never be hers to lose, but he made her imagination soar with 'what ifs?' His eyes, besides being a shade of brown that looked almost amber, told her he was clever. He could keep up with her rambling tongue. And there was no doubt he was amazing to watch, especially in his suit. She didn't want to part with him. Maybe he had another single friend, a twin possibly.

Her face flinched when Adam sprung to mind. She was curious about their friendship, though Tom was the friend she was concerned about for now.

'So ... Tom?' she fished, watching Justin's face for clues.

'So ... Tom,' he copied, not giving anything away. 'What'd you think?'

'He seemed nice enough,' she chewed and watched as he nodded—not being helpful in the slightest. 'What does he do?' she asked casually, shaking her hair out of her eyes as the breeze blew it there.

'I am not at liberty to say,' he told her as he pretended to zip his mouth closed and throw away the key.

'Ah, that's right. Special Agent Justin Owens doesn't answer that question,' she recalled. 'What if I guess? What if I guess his job, or *your* job for that matter ... you'll tell me?'

He thought about it for a second. A sports car sped past and his eyes followed it.

'Agreed. But me first.' He looked at her seriously. 'Are you a butcher?' She flexed her small arms, enjoying his smile. 'Is Mel?'

'No and no. But we do have the same job,' she hinted. 'Are you an accountant?'

'No. Do I look like an accountant?' he seemed concerned and she thought about teasing him with it but forgot before she could.

'Is Tom an accountant?'

'Yes,' he laughed. He had such a warm laugh it made her want to laugh along with him.

'Wow, I'm good,' she praised.

'And modest,' Justin added.

'So … Tom,' she looked up at him mischievously. 'Is he really hung like a donkey?'

'How would I know?' he cried as he side-stepped a bunch of teenage girls. He didn't seem to notice their eyes following his every move, but Anna did. She felt a sense of pride walking down the road with him. Totally unauthorised pride, as he was some other girl's guy, but in Tom's words, where was Julia now?

'We don't exactly stand there checking each other out.'

She giggled at his indignation but the more he shook his head, the funnier she found it; so he scoffed at her some more, and 'hee-hawed' like a donkey. She held her sides as she cried for him to stop between her fits of laughter.

'You know it wasn't that funny, right?' he quizzed once she'd calmed. Anna nodded, forcing herself not to start again.

He said nothing for a while, and she enjoyed the silence between them. It was an easy silence.

They'd strolled away from the Saturday night traffic of people and arrived at Luna Park, its giant clown face guarding the fun park's entrance. Anna and Justin could hear the water lapping on the shore not far away, the smell of the sea strong in the air. They strolled past the clown face and Anna made a comment about it looking scary and hungry; she truly believed the face was behind many childhood clown fears.

They walked a little further and came to the steps that led towards the beach. She looked up at him for approval and with a nod, he followed her down. Her balance faltered with the change of direction and she grabbed the cool steel banister to brace herself, giggling as she gingerly descended the remaining steps to the road below. Justin chuckled at her poor balance, then checked for cars and grabbed her hand to pull her across the road as though she were a child. Anna went to protest and remind him of her age, but she looked at her hand lost in his and lost every other thought. She was so absorbed by her hand being in his that she almost tripped on the gutter.

'Are you alright?'

She nodded, embarrassed. *Not your guy Anna.*

They reached the sand and she watched the width of Justin's back as he leant over to take off his shoes. She kicked her heels off too and scooped them up, dangling them from her finger.

It was much cooler on the sand and her skin became cold once it was hit by the breeze off the water. Justin saw her hug herself and without words, took his jacket off and draped it over her shoulders. She thought it was the most chivalrous thing anyone had ever done for her and didn't reject the gesture. The satin on the jacket lining was smooth and warm against her body. She could smell his aftershave on it and wondered what he wore. It made her remember when she'd first met him at Jane's farewell.

They strolled along the water's edge, talking intermittently, before Anna confessed her exhaustion and they sat down on the soft sand. She was grateful not to have to walk anymore but the cold became more obvious to her senses once her body was still.

While attempting to ignore the goosebumps, she wondered what he was thinking about.

'Are you a teacher?' he asked, and she felt happy it was her in his thoughts.

'No.' She turned away, so her grin didn't blind him in the dark.

'Podiatrist?'

'Not even close. Are you an astronaut?'

He chuckled as he shook his head. 'Oh, I know. Are you and Mel dancers?'

'Ah, no … but when I was little, I did *want* to be a dancer.'

'Didn't we all, Anna? Didn't we all …' he trailed off, impressively maintaining a straight face.

'Are you like your friend Adam?' she enquired deviously.

'What? No!' she'd caught him off guard, but he relaxed and continued softly. 'No. I'm definitely not,' he assured her.

'Shame because he seems *delightful*.'

'Doesn't he just?'

'You know, they say you can tell a lot about a person by the company they keep?' she joked. He didn't reply and she had no idea it was an opinion that would stick with him.

'What's his deal anyway?' Anna knew she'd only seen the drunken Adam but from what she saw, she wouldn't have picked the pair as friends.

'I'm not sure to be honest,' Justin answered thoughtfully. Anna assumed he was going to end it there but he went on, telling her about how he and Adam had met and the things they'd done together.

'He just seems to have changed a bit now. Intensified, I guess.'

Anna pressed for more. He looked across at her and she waited for him to tell her to back off. His arms rested on his knees and he hung his head lower.

'That night at the hospital? When they called me in?' she nodded to her memory of it. She remembered thinking he looked so troubled and she'd wanted to hug him. 'They asked me how much he'd had and *what* he'd had.' He shook his head and looked out to the water. 'I'm just so naive sometimes.'

'What do you mean?' Anna shook her head, confused.

'I told them he'd had beer. Then they handed me this little plastic bag.' He looked at her, embarrassed. 'I had no idea what it was and when they told me it was ecstasy, I was … shocked, to say the least.'

'Oooh,' Anna drew out. 'And you had no idea?' Justin shook his head.

'Wow,' she said quietly. 'That must have been a bit of a shock for you.' He looked so distressed and she didn't know what to say.

'Yeah. It was some night,' he sighed. 'I don't know much about drugs like that. I know they're around and people use them, but I guess I felt …' he stopped to search for the right word, 'duped. Lied to. I felt pretty stupid holding that bag with the doctor looking at me like *I* should have known better.' He looked across at her and she could see the frustration on his face, his jaw set firmly.

'I'm sure they realised it had nothing to do with you,' she reassured him. 'What did he say about it?'

Justin shook his head and laughed ironically. 'That's the other part. He didn't say anything. We went to the buck's day and he continued drinking like nothing had happened.'

Anna felt her mouth hang. 'Seriously?'

'Seriously.' Justin almost smiled. 'I picked him up the next morning and when I tried to broach the subject, he just shrugged it off.'

'And he hasn't brought it up since?' Anna was amazed. If one of her friends had put her through that she would have forced them to spill the beans immediately. Justin just shook his head.

'What did Julia say?' she blurted out.

'Nothing. I, ah …' he stopped and Anna cut in before he could continue.

'You didn't tell her?' she exclaimed involuntarily, pulling his jacket tighter to her body as a shiver ran through her.

'No. I didn't,' he admitted.

'But … why? Did you tell anyone?'

'Well, I didn't want her to judge him. I didn't want anyone to judge him. And I didn't know his story to be able to defend him.' He looked across at her and when she said nothing, he kept talking. She could tell he was trying to justify his decision, but she was surprised by his secretiveness, or maybe it was his loyalty.

'It wasn't my place to tell people his business. I've looked into it a bit, and I don't know, maybe I'm just getting old and uptight.'

Anna mulled over their conversation thoughtfully.

'You are not too old, and you can never be too old to worry about people anyway. Especially friends,' she confirmed. 'And, sure it's his business, but Justin, his business affected you! He hit you for crying out loud.'

He sat quietly, without rebuttal.

'Now, I'm not saying I am a drug expert — by no means. I'm a bit of a scaredy-cat with those kinds of things, even my stupidity with alcohol scares me sometimes, but that's not to say some of my friends feel the same. I've been told they are harmless …'

'That's what I read!' Justin cut in, relieved someone else had heard it too; no doubt hoping that maybe it was true. But Anna extinguished that hope straight away.

'Harmless my arse!' she exclaimed. 'It's a drug, and drugs kill people. It's that simple.'

He didn't respond, and she softened.

'Listen, you have every right to say something. To him, but you have every right to talk about it with whoever you need, surely.' If it were her, it would have been eating her alive. Maybe it was a Y chromosome thing.

'Thanks Anna,' he said softly. Hearing him say her name gave her a new and sudden appreciation for it. 'I don't think I'd tell Julia though. Don't think it'd sit well.' He laughed awkwardly.

'So … you haven't told anyone.' She wanted to firmly establish, and he agreed. 'So, why now? Why me?' She looked intently at him, wanting to know, but from her observation it seemed he didn't know himself.

'I have no idea,' he laughed. 'I guess no-one else was there. It didn't come up. You were there?' he seemed to be asking her rather than answering her. 'You asked.'

She gave a slight smile, letting it slide.

'Maybe you really are a secret agent. You're very good at keeping things under your belt. Speaking of which, are you a builder?' The change of subject surprised him, and he laughed loudly, shaking his head, the sound breaking the quiet on the empty beach.

'No. Not a builder or a secret agent. What about you? You love your questions … are you a detective?' he grinned and she wanted to crash tackle him to the sand.

'Ha, ha. No. You're way off my little friend,' she replied and enjoyed hearing his laughter again. 'So, tell me more about this girlfriend of yours,' she pried, too tired to care how nosy she was being.

'What would you like to know?' he asked her cooperatively.

'Well, what she does of course, but I know that's a big no-no,' she mocked, and he nodded regretfully. 'Do you love her?' she asked instead and noticed him shift uncomfortably in the sand.

'Yeah. I think so.'

She sensed his awkwardness but pressed on.

'You going to marry her?' she asked bravely, mildly hopeful he'd say, 'No, I prefer short brunettes.'

'Um, I don't know. Maybe … we've talked about it,' he admitted carefully.

'Really?' she wasn't sure if she was impressed or disappointed. 'Is she waiting for her diamond?' she ridiculed, wanting to be mean to the tall, beautiful woman that had nabbed him. He laughed lightly and Anna sensed a trace of bitterness.

'Ah, no. Not really,' he looked down at the sand again and dug his toes into the rough grains. He wouldn't look at Anna and she wasn't going to push this time, letting him sit quiet in his own thoughts.

'How's your sister and baby?' she eventually asked, remembering the baby's face from his phone.

'Baby Bianca …' he smiled, pleased in the change of topic, '… is good. My sister says she's never known a baby to be so sleepy and is pretty happy to be getting sleep herself.'

'Was that her photo on your phone?'

'Yeah. Bit of a cutey.'

Anna smiled and played with the sand, pouring handfuls from her cupped palms. 'Do you think about having kids one day?'

'Would you think me unmanly if I said yes?'

'No.' She was confused. 'More so, actually.'

'Then yes,' he smiled. 'I get the impression that guys aren't meant to want kids.'

'How'd you mean?' she asked curiously. She thought of her dad. Maybe he'd just never wanted her. Was it a guy thing?

'It just seems like it's always the guy having to be convinced to have kids. The guy who can't handle it. The guy complaining about his life.' He thought about what he'd said. 'I just made my whole gender look really bad.' She nodded in agreement. He nudged her with his elbow. 'What about you? Do you want kids?'

'You mean, another kid?' she corrected and watched his face for a reaction. 'Joking. Joking. Man, you're easy.' She took a breath in and thought. 'Would you think I'm a typical female if I said yes?'

'No,' he chuckled. 'Not at all.'

'Then, yes. I think about it all the time actually.' Anna scrunched her face. 'Was that too much?'

'What do you mean?' he laughed. 'What's so wrong with wanting that? It's a natural want.'

'Then why doesn't everyone want it?' she said, more to herself as she thought about her dad again. She sensed Justin looking at her closely. He seemed puzzled by her — he probably thought she was a nutter.

'Why do you think about it so much?'

'I don't know.' She looked at him and considered shutting herself up, but her tongue was on a role. 'I just want to love them, you know? I want to teach them things. I want to make someone happy. I'm worried that I'll never get to.'

She'd never really said that out loud before and felt embarrassed that she'd shared it with a stranger. Not that he felt like a stranger. He felt like a friend; an old friend. Still, she became worried he thought her weird for sharing such personal thoughts.

'I know what you mean,' he said quietly, and Anna relaxed.

'What about Julia? Does she want kids?' Anna regretted it before she'd even finished saying it. She knew it was the wrong thing to say. He looked at her and his body slumped. She'd definitely stepped into rocky terrain.

'She says one day she might,' he said blankly. Anna didn't know what to say but could tell it was a sore point. He must really love her, she thought, if he was willing to sacrifice what he wanted. She sighed. This Julia was lucky.

'Oh well, at the rate I'm going kids should be the last thing on my mind,' Anna stepped in. 'That Mary chick may have been onto something with the whole 'immaculate conception' thing. Not sure if my mum would buy it though.'

Justin chuckled lightly. 'You never know, maybe some lucky guy will call you after the speed date.'

He was mocking her, but she thought that maybe he was right. It *was* a possibility and she brightened at the idea.

'Yeah, maybe.'

They sat in silence again. She could hear the traffic die down on the road behind them. The sound of water smacking the shore was making Anna feel drowsy. Her arms were hugging her knees, his sleeves keeping them warm; her head rested on top.

She looked over at Justin leaning back on his arms, his shirt sleeves rolled up to show his forearms, his tie still hanging loosely around his neck.

'*Do* they call you Annie?'

'Sometimes,' she smiled lazily. 'Are you really a brain?' He shook his head and they shared another silence.

'You have big feet,' she commented.

'Thanks, I grew them myself,' he said coolly and changed position to mirror hers. Leaning on his arms and looking across at her. She stared at his face.

'What's wrong with my eyebrows,' he demanded quietly. 'You could give someone a complex you know.'

She gave a hint of a smile. 'Nothing.'

'So why would you say I needed to pluck them?'

'I never.' She denied his claim calmly and corrected him. 'I asked *if* you plucked them.'

He raised his head up and rubbed his fingers over the hairs, so they stood up at odd angles. 'What's wrong with them?' he demanded again.

Grinning, she leant over the space between them and used her fingers to straighten them back into place. His smile fell at her touch. Hers faded too as she gently traced his brow.

'Nothing,' she said in a very quiet voice. 'They're perfect.'

Justin looked into her eyes, but she kept hers on his eyebrows. Her finger vaguely drew a line from his brow, along his cheek bone and down onto his lip.

He was staring at her but didn't stop her, didn't move. She leaned forward a little further and put her lips where her finger was, as if it were saving the spot. Her finger continued lightly over his chin and onto his warm neck.

She kissed his bottom lip briefly and stopped. She could hear his breathing in her ear and feel his pulse racing under her fingertip. She didn't know if she was completely intoxicated or completely sober.

'Sorry,' she whispered. 'I … I didn't mean for that … to do that.'

She bravely looked at his face and thought it looked sad. It looked sad even as it came closer, even when his lips gently touched hers. She wasn't so sure after that.

Her eyes were closed as he softly kissed her. Small, sweet kisses, that tasted like bourbon. They slowly grew firmer, and she felt her head spin until she lost her balance. Her elbow thoughtlessly collapsed from under her and she fell from his lips, breaking the moment. She composed herself and sat back up.

Anna instantly felt the worry on her face, nervous about how Justin would respond. But he just looked at her sadly.

'I'm sorry too,' he murmured. His eyes locked on hers. She could glimpse the regret in his eyes. She wanted to cry. Tears were at the ready and she panicked.

Please don't cry, please don't cry. Pull yourself together woman.

What was she thinking?

He has a girlfriend. A beautiful girlfriend. He wanted to marry her and have kids with her. He was unbelievable. She didn't get to have him.

You idiot.

'We should get out of here,' she suggested quickly, wishing she could blink and be in her bed hiding under the covers.

'Right. Yeah, you're right,' he agreed hastily. She could feel her face flush with embarrassment. They stood up and dusted the sand off themselves, picked up their shoes and headed back towards the road. Justin had to hurry to keep up with her. Anna was fighting the urge to run home. She'd raced up the stairs and was hailing a taxi before Justin could even finish putting his shoes back on. She shook off his jacket and half hugged, half patted him, goodbye. He offered to call her, but she'd already jumped in the taxi, and was gone.

Justin stood on a footpath somewhere in St Kilda. He looked around and saw the big clown face laughing at him and he wondered if anyone else was as he crossed the road and wandered back to his hotel, alone.

chapter eleven

Anna lay in bed, motionless. Through narrow eyes she could see it was a gloomy morning and she was glad. It was exactly how she felt.

Last night with Justin had been perfect. They were having a good time. It was nice, *he* was nice. And then she went and kissed him. Why did she do that? She wanted to kick herself. She felt incredibly, horrifically, embarrassed and just wanted to take it back … almost. It *was* an amazing kiss. Just remembering it made her stomach flip. It was perfect. He was perfect.

He has a girlfriend, she reminded her foolish self. *He lives in Sydney. He lives in Sydney with his girlfriend that he loves and wants to marry and have babies with.*

She rolled over and groaned.

Her head hurt, along with her pride, and she made the executive decision to never leave her bed again. She would become a bed hermit. She'd lie there in her own filth and embarrassment until the police came. It was the only practical thing to do.

She lay staring at her blinds. They were slightly ajar and the clouds could be seen hanging sullenly in the sky. Her feet scraped against each other because they were still sandy from the beach and she was thinking of how the newspaper article would read when they found her stinking dead body inside the apartment: *Sand gives clue to the Hermit 'Crab' corpse mystery.*

But nature erased any potential embarrassing headline when her bladder forced her out of bed. She never could commit to the rules she placed on herself. However, the broken rule of kissing another girl's guy *was* an isolated incident.

Her feet hit the bathroom tiles and her feet performed an involuntary jig at their coldness. Her head was thumping and the sudden movement made her brain sulk. Bracing her head with her hand, she wished someone else was home to give her sympathy. Prying her eyelashes apart, she looked at her reflection in the mirror.

'Ewe,' she groaned. The makeup around her eyes had joined forces and had invaded areas of her face where it did not belong and was not welcome. She looked like she'd crawled out of the Underworld. Her lips were dry and pale, and her hair would have been an eighties' success story. Anna quickly changed her mind about wishing someone else was there, to being eternally grateful no-one could witness her appearance at that moment.

She splashed water on her face and felt a short relief at its coolness on her skin. She considered going back to bed but decided instead just to confine herself to her flat. A hermit had to have its comforts after all, and TV would be hers.

Anna flicked through Netflix and decided on a classic. Pressing play, she settled in to watch *Bridget Jones's Diary.* It usually made her feel happy and would remind her that her single life could be worse, but by the time she was singing along to an already badly sung version of *All by Myself,* she felt envious of Bridget for at least having greater European shopping options. Anna was in a far much worse position and her cruel mind kept going back to Justin.

Briefly she wondered if he would actually call, remembering saving her number in his phone. She wished Jane lived closer so they could analyse it together. Jane could always make her feel better after she'd done something stupid.

Anna picked up the phone to call her but dialed Mel's number instead—she had to stop relying on Jane. But the phone rang out.

Anna felt bad. It *was* Sunday. Mel was probably trying to sleep in. Anna cringed as she recounted how much they'd had to drink at the bar and calculated that Mel wouldn't be up until lunch time. Anna considered calling Jane after all but refrained. Feeling a loss at what to do next, Anna sat with folded arms and legs. She was staring at a freeze frame of Hugh Grant, but she didn't want to press play, she just wanted to hide somewhere far away, where she couldn't find herself.

Justin had lain in bed, wide awake, for hours. He'd stared straight up at the ceiling wishing himself asleep. His body was exhausted and his eyes burned, but still, his brain was buzzing.

He had arrived back at his hotel room in a daze. He'd watched his reflection as he brushed his teeth, not seeming to recognise the man staring back. He had shed the suit from his body and hung it in its bag; absentmindedly washed his feet in the empty spa and patted them dry. He had gone through the motions feeling confused. His body told him to go to sleep, promising it would all make sense in the morning; but as he folded into bed, and slid under the crisp white sheets, his brain refused to cooperate.

He couldn't stop thinking about Anna.

Without explanation, she fascinated him like few people had. He felt he could have talked to her all night—he could have sat next to her in silence as well. When she asked him a question, she actually listened with interest. When she spoke, she spoke honestly. And Justin thought that when she kissed, it was much the same.

She made him feel happy and she made him feel sad.

He pictured Julia. Her bored face shrugging off his day when he tried to tell her about it. He imagined her new lease contract too. Both tempting him to justify his actions.

But then Justin thought of himself and Julia laughing; of them cooking dinner together. He thought of him telling her that he loved her. He thought of the trust they both shared, and he felt disgusted that he had just broken it.

He eventually drifted off to sleep and when he woke the hotel room was dark, but Justin was surprised to find it was almost ten in the morning. Check-out was in a little over an hour and he was meant to have met the others for breakfast at ten.

For a brief moment he considered jumping in the shower and rushing down to meet them but, with relief, realised he couldn't be bothered.

Instead, Justin switched on the TV and found an episode of *Seinfeld*, the car park one. He stayed in bed for another half-hour, forcing laughs in an attempt to clear his conscience, but it did nothing to erase his guilt. He had done the wrong thing and now he had to live with it.

chapter twelve

'I have a date.'

It was a quarter to eleven on Wednesday morning. Anna sat at her desk at This is IT, mindlessly typing out a case report. She was in no mood to be there, and the sun, shining through the yellowed venetian blinds, boasting about the blue sky that it was putting on show, was of no help.

She missed Jane and, until Ioulia moved in, Jane's share of the heartbreakingly-high rent. Anna's self-esteem had sunk to an all-time low (her bank balance and hopes of buying her own home threatening to follow) and to make matters worse, she still couldn't find her favourite earrings. They were shiny and pretty and made her feel good, unlike this phone conversation, which was of no help to her situation.

'Mel?'

'Ah, y-e-e-s. Anna I have a date!' she shrilled down the line. Anna could hear Mel's voice echoing from down the hallway.

'That's fantastic,' she smiled, hoping that would make it sound more believable, and then chastised herself for her lack of support. 'Who with?'

'That guy Kyle, from speed dating? He just called to ask me out.'

Anna, hearing her friend's excitement (and slight trepidation), fought the urge to ask if they were going to play PlayStation for their first date. Or maybe Kyle had an old Donkey Kong he whipped out for special occasions. *Stop it*, she warned herself. It was only a five-minute meeting she was basing the guy on.

'Oh, that's great,' Anna crooned, hearing her falseness, regardless of her own warning. 'When?' She hoped she'd regained her composure in the question and disguised the fact she was moody and not yet equally excited.

'Friday night.' Quickly adding, 'I know, I know. We had movie plans. I'm really sorry, but …' she trailed off innocently, 'would it be okay if we cancelled?'

Anna had forgotten they'd had plans. It must have happened over the bottle of wine.

'Sure. You'll just have to give a full report.' Like who wins *Tomb Raider*. 'Which one was Kyle again?'

'The blond one, you wrote down Richie, the one with the brown hair. Hey, has *he* called?' Mel asked suddenly, excited at the prospect of them both having dates. Anna had completely forgotten (on top of their movie plans) that they had chosen *any* names, but now that Mel had reminded her, Anna chewed her lip trying to picture the two dates whose names they had written. She thought Richie was the blond guy, which meant … she had written the wrong name down. Anna felt her stomach tighten.

She considered telling Mel, but she was so eager, and Anna didn't want to dampen her mood. She assured herself that he, Kyle, probably wouldn't have written her name down as well and even if he did, he wouldn't ask both friends out on a date.

Accepting that she had just forfeited her chances of any dates, Anna saw one of their managers approaching and hastily ended the call, hanging up just as he reached her desk.

'Anna, how are you today?' John smiled.

John Chan, computer genius, was one of the big bosses from the Sydney office and was also rumored to be the brainchild behind their company name. This is IT had branches all over the country and Melbourne had the second largest. How he knew everyone Anna would never know, but always admired.

'Hi, John. Great thanks.' She eyed him skeptically, wondering what he wanted. 'How was your flight?'

He rolled his dark eyes up to the ceiling. 'Early. To say the least,' and she laughed politely.

'Anna, we've had some great feedback from our clients about your work,' he praised. She was certainly not expecting a rap and felt pleasantly surprised. She wanted to cry, 'Really! For me?' but managed to keep herself composed—wanting to disprove Mel's recent comments about speaking before thinking. Instead, Anna modestly raised her eyebrows and let an 'oh' escape.

'Yes. Yes,' John said thoughtfully as he placed his whole hand on the side of his face. 'Great feedback indeed. You know we could do with some brains like you up in head office,' he smiled down at her.

'In Sydney?' she asked carefully, not knowing exactly what he was getting at—whether he was joking or actually suggesting.

'Yes, yes. Sydney. Do you think that is something you would consider?'

Anna wanted to spin around in her chair and confirm that it was in fact her that he was speaking to. She had always received positive praise from her clients and from the company, but she'd thought they were just being polite, that everyone was treated similarly. Computers just came second nature to her. She didn't think she was working too hard nor doing anything too testing. She actually found her job quite fun most of the time. The case reports were a bit dull, but apart from that …

'Anna?' she heard John chime in and Anna shook herself from her thoughts.

'Sorry, John,' she said. 'I've never thought about it to be honest.'

He smiled at her again and for an awkward moment she thought he was going to pat her on the head.

'Well, Anna,' he said. 'Think about it.' John glanced over her desk, taking in the assorted bits of life she'd decorated it with: photos, motivational quotes, a teeny succulent, post-it notes of calls to make, codes she needed. John rocked forward on his toes and made a little satisfied noise with his throat, then walked on into the boardroom.

Anna's eyes followed him, glanced briefly at her desk, looked back at the boardroom doors as they closed, and then looked around to see if anyone else had witnessed their conversation. Once confirmed that not a soul was in sight, she turned back to her screen, gave her head a shake and went back to work.

Within minutes her mobile phone began to ring. When she didn't recognise the number her stomach made a little flip, as it had done the past three days, each and every time it had buzzed with an unexpected call. *Justin?*

She ran her hand over her hair, rolled her shoulders back and quickly answered before it annoyed anyone.

'Hello,' she spoke ultra-casually into the receiver.

'Hi. Is this Anna?' a male's voice asked smoothly, and her heart began beating wildly. Act cool, she told herself.

'Yes, it is. Who is this?' she asked sweetly, hoping it conveyed that she was nice, sexy, interesting, fun, relaxed and amazing all at once.

'Hi Anna, sorry,' he said. His voice sounded different, she thought … higher. 'This is Kyle. We met at speed dating the other night.' He went on, saying something about how he hoped she remembered him, but her ears were still trying to catch up, her brain frantically sending messages and connecting the dots. When there was silence on the line, she realised it was her turn to speak.

'Kyle,' she stalled. 'Hi.'

So, you want to date me *and* my friend? Real clever … dumb-arse.

'Um, so, apparently we both put each other's name down,' he began, playing the coy card well. She felt bad for the other guy, Richie, but realised it was her turn to speak again.

'Oh, um … great,' she offered lamely.

'So, I was wondering if you were still keen to meet up?' he battled on undeterred, and she would have given him credit for that, if his audacity to ask had not taken it away.

'Sure, how about Friday?' she asked mischievously, impressed at her own nerve. There was no way she was seeing this guy.

'Oh, I'm … ah … actually busy that night,' he stumbled his way through, careful not to admit he had a date for that night already.

'Are you free Saturday?'

'Sorry, I have a date,' Anna lied flatly.

'Right …' he said, and she could hear the hesitation in his voice. 'How about through the week?'

'Pretty busy,' she said, being difficult. She actually felt a yawn coming on and didn't even bother to fight it, but he showed sheer determination.

'Next Saturday night?' he offered.

She reminded herself that not only had he already asked Mel out, but that he had asked her out first; Anna was a mere second choice.

'Sure,' she agreed, with every intention to cancel the same day, and Kyle wrapped up the call with an air of relief. She wondered what version she was going to tell Mel when they met for their daily lunch date, and then she wondered if Justin would call.

'Anna, hurry up.' Mel eyed the man queuing behind Anna at their favourite cafe.

'But I just got here,' she whispered, indicating her spot in front of the cashier.

'Just order *something*,' Mel hissed.

'Relax,' Anna reassured her, inspecting the man waiting behind her to make sure he looked happy enough. Mel had already ordered her sandwich but Anna was never very good at decisions. She could get the chicken, but then maybe she should get the tuna. They say you're meant to eat at least three serves of fish a week and Anna couldn't remember the last time she had eaten any.

'Just order already,' Mel begged quietly, breaking into Anna's thoughts.

'Stop distracting me,' Anna shooed her friend, turning back to the board, and then it hit her. Wednesday! She'd had salmon on Wednesday.

'Anna!'

'I'm trying!' She continued to focus on her options, frustrated with the constant interruptions. Mel looked uncomfortably between the man waiting and Anna. Her brow furrowed and she shifted her weight from foot to foot. Anna wondered if Mel actually just needed to pee.

'Get the chicken,' Mel urged, and Anna crinkled her nose. 'She'll have the chicken,' Mel said to the waitress. Anna looked at her appalled.

'What if I didn't want the chicken?'

'Anna, honey, be reasonable. Eat the freaking chicken sandwich and shut up before I ask them to wedge your cute little face between two bits of bread, and me and this guy ...' She indicated the man who was still waiting, somewhat patiently to order, 'will eat *you* for lunch.' Mel smiled at Anna, daring her to argue back.

'Okay,' Anna moped, 'I'll have the chicken,' and she handed the woman her card.

'Would you like that on white or wholemeal bread?' the woman asked, bored. Anna went to speak—but paused.

'White,' Mel piped up for her, and this time Anna was grateful. They chose a seat outside and basked in the sunshine until their lunch arrived.

'What should I wear on my date,' Mel asked, her eyes dancing with anticipation. Anna gulped. She'd been itching to tell Mel how Kyle had called her as well. She'd envisioned Mel and herself deliberating the nerve of the guy, but Mel looked so happy and Anna couldn't ruin that. Mel hadn't been her usual vibrant self during the past few days. Anna thought it was just her imagination at first, because she hadn't been that chipper herself! But when one of the other girls in the office asked Anna if Mel was okay, Anna had begun to suspect it was something more. She hadn't even mentioned Justin's friend, Tom, and her night of shameless flirting. Anna wondered if Tom had a girlfriend too.

Under normal circumstances, Anna would have just asked what had happened, but it would involve mentioning Justin and she didn't want to risk his name in a conversation in case she blurted out her own story and Mel told her what a fool she was. Anna knew she was a fool; she just wasn't ready to hear it out loud.

Mel looked on expectantly, smiling, and Anna felt the guilt swirl in her hungry belly. The whole phone call would just have to remain a secret, and Anna hoped that if it came to a wedding, Kyle didn't remember Mel's bridesmaid as the one who stood him up.

'How about that blue top you love?' Anna suggested, wondering if her deceit was showing on her face.

Mel pondered on the shirt until their lunch arrived and then halted all discussion to eat.

Anna frowned at her sandwich. 'I should have picked the tuna,' she complained, ducking as a serviette ball was hurled towards her.

chapter thirteen

It hadn't even been two weeks of living back with her parents, but Jane had cracked. Anna held the phone, patiently listening to Jane claim that she couldn't stand it any longer: that their disregard for housework was 'killing her', that their incessant questions, including the 'what time will you be home?' classic, was costing her an extra twenty minutes to her preparation time, to do anything, and that her father's heavy snoring was halving her sleep.

'It's worse than it ever was,' moaned Jane. 'If the bacteria doesn't get me first, the sleep deprivation will. It's ridiculous and I'm getting out,' she proclaimed. Anna laughed as she reached for the box of Cheezels in the cupboard and sat on the lumpy lounge, asking what her plan was.

'What do you mean?'

'Well, where do you want to live? What can you afford? Who do you want to live with? Can you move in with your sister and her husband?' she rattled off, sliding the cheesy rings over her fingertips and then crunching them off in Jane's silence.

'Jane?'

'I'm here,' she moaned.

'Well, did you think of any of that?'

'No.' She sounded deflated. 'I didn't. Well, except Sarah. But I can't do that to them.'

Anna could have heard crickets during Jane's next silence and filled it by rustling in the Cheezels box again.

'Jane? It's okay. We'll work it out now. Let's make a list.'

Anna could hear as Jane rustled around for some paper and muttered something about stupid pens not working in stupid Sydney, and then, 'Uh huh! Found one!' Anna chuckled. She really missed Jane, so she had her own incentive to help. Once Jane had a new place, she could go visit. She'd have driven the distance already, happily, if it weren't for the accommodation situation. Seeing her mum would be a bonus, but both of them staying with their parents would annul any re-creation of their usual conversation comfort, which is what Anna craved.

Together they went through the criteria and came to the conclusion that on Jane's starting pay she should find something cheap (but not 'crack-house' cheap), basic and closer to work, the hour drive was also killing her. Finally, they decided Jane had to rule out living by herself, at least until she had a permanent job or a pay rise.

With a plan and hope for her freedom, Jane bid Anna farewell so she could scour the rental sites. Anna hung up feeling as though she had done something good and noble—and therefore needn't feel guilty about the now near-empty Cheezels box in front of her.

Justin was turning the sign on the door over to 'Closed', when he heard his phone beep from the front desk. He was about to do a final check on the building before he left for the night; too late to eat with his family.

He picked up his phone and read the message, frowning at Julia's words.

R u home yet? We need 2 talk.

No kiss, hug or smiley face. No 'love'.

His immediate reaction was one of guilt. He'd been feeling it all week. His conscience had been in a constant state of argument with itself; one half reasoning he hadn't done anything too wrong, that it was just a kiss, the other half chiming in with a counter argument.

Realistically, Justin knew he had nothing to fear. There was no way Julia could ever possibly find out. No-one knew he had kissed Anna except himself and Anna.

But Justin knew what Julia wanted to talk about and he could see no way around it.

He locked up and while driving the short trip home he thought back to Saturday night. He'd gone over it a million times. It was almost sadistic the way he was punishing himself, but he just couldn't shake Anna from his mind. The kiss, sure, but Anna herself was stuck inside his head. He was constantly wondering what Anna was doing—what she was thinking. He'd considered calling her numerous times. Not to be deceitful, not to be unfaithful to Julia, but just to talk about what had happened. To say sorry; to make sure she arrived home safely. There had even been a few times when he had just wanted to call because of something he'd found amusing that he was sure she'd find funny as well.

But he hadn't. Actually, that was only partially true. He'd pressed 'call' numerous times but had hung up before it had even begun to ring. He wondered if she'd even want to talk to him.

Justin pulled into his driveway. Julia's red car was already parked out the front. He could see the house lit up inside and the journey towards it was a reluctant one, as though his feet were braking in front of him and tearing up the path. He took a deep breath, preparing for battle, and unlocked the front door.

Julia was talking to someone and he headed towards the sound of her voice wondering who else was there; who had saved him from confrontation. But as he saw her, one arm folded across her waist, the other holding her phone to her ear, he realised it was only the two of them in the house and he was surely approaching the frontline.

She wore her usual black suit, her hair taut in a bun. She looked serious, prepared—more so than usual—and it made his stomach tighten.

'He's here now,' she told the person on the phone grimly. 'I better go.' Julia snapped her finger on the screen to end the call.

'Hi,' she said crossly and tossed her phone onto the bench. It was almost like a direction from a script. He watched as the phone slid to the other side of the bench and placed his own phone, wallet and keys next to its landing spot.

'Hi,' he returned, his face quizzing hers.

'What took you so long?'

'I closed up,' he explained, noticing Hamlet scratching at the door. 'Did you feed him?' he asked her as he walked to the door to unlock it.

'No. It's *your* dog,' she told him coldly. 'Why don't *you* feed him?'

Both her arms were now firmly folded across her body, which remained unbudged from her place behind the kitchen counter.

Justin looked at her in disbelief. There was no need to take it out on Hamlet. He dished out some food and gave him a scratch on the head.

'Gee Jules, something on your mind?'

'Don't. Call. Me. Jules,' she warned.

'Fine. What would you like to talk about then, Julia?' he asked with sarcasm, locking the door behind him.

'Monday night,' she told him. 'To start with.'

The awkward memory of Monday night was still fresh in his mind. Justin had been cooking dinner and Julia had asked to see pictures of the wedding. Surprised she was even interested, he remembered he'd taken a few photos on his phone. Without thinking, weary from the weekend, he'd found the pictures and passed Julia his phone. She started going through the shots, asking a few questions about the dresses. He didn't have many to ask about, but he heard her pause and glanced over to see her puzzled face.

'Who's this?' she'd asked, her head tilting to the side. She didn't hold the phone up but kept flicking between the photos of the faces she didn't recognise. Justin knew exactly who she meant the moment she'd asked. His head shot up and his first thought was simple — *shit*.

'Who's who?' he had asked casually, and she held the frame up for him to see.

'Oh, that was this girl Tom met. Melissa, I think her name was,' he had said vaguely, throwing in a chuckle for good measure. He'd then gone straight back to the carrots in front of him.

'And this is?' she had asked holding up the photo of him and Anna. His immediate response to the picture had been to smile, but he then quickly replaced it with a dismissive look.

'Oh, that was Melissa's friend,' he'd told her.

'Were they at the wedding?' Though he knew they were all fair questions, he had felt like she was grilling him, and he'd begun to feel very hot, very quickly.

'Ah … no,' he'd stumbled, opening the window. 'We went to a bar afterwards. They were there.' His back was to her, but he'd felt her eyes glaring.

'You didn't tell me you went out afterwards,' she'd said quietly, sounding hurt.

'We went out afterwards,' he'd told her blankly, starting to get angry. So what if he'd gone out. Didn't she trust him? The thought was ironic, he knew that, but still, she had no reason not to trust him. To Justin, the fact that he *had* done the wrong thing was not the point.

'Did you get drunk?' Julia asked; her chin high, her question pointed.

'I had a few drinks,' he had replied, knowing it was an understatement and that he would never have a Long Island Iced Tea ever again.

'Is that why you didn't call me that night, because you were out drinking with a bunch of girls?'

What?

'Julia, I didn't call you because I was pissed off with you.'

Placing the knife down, he had turned to face her.

'For what?'

'Are you serious? For not coming to the wedding!' *For not moving in with me.*

'Oh, grow up Justin. We've been through this,' she'd said with a dismissive shake of her head. Justin had fumed at her arrogance and her ability to brush him off. He'd gone to speak but couldn't find words that his mother wouldn't cringe at. He'd settled on the most gentlemanly option.

'Fuck you.'

She'd given him a poisonous look. It wasn't something he'd ever said to her.

'You wish,' she'd told him slowly and spitefully as she picked up her bag. 'I'm going.'

He had gladly let her go, and that had been their last contact until her message tonight.

'Monday night?' he asked. 'Oh, you mean the night you told me to grow up?'

'You got it *babe*,' she said sharply.

'What would you like to talk about?' he asked, suddenly very drained. He couldn't be bothered going through this again.

'I want to ask about the girls in the photo. What were their names again?'

'Anna and Mel,' he answered without thinking. He didn't even stop to remember their names and he watched Julia as she raised an eyebrow, like a gauntlet going up.

'Anna?' she repeated nastily, and he knew he may have just stepped in a big heap of steaming metaphorical dog shit. He didn't say anything, just nodded, hoping to brush it all off with vagueness.

'Well, I ran into Daniel and his wife today,' she boasted, and Justin wondered where this was going, 'and they asked how you were. She said they'd missed you at breakfast on Sunday.'

'I didn't have breakfast. So what?' he cut in.

She glared at him and began again.

'She said that they had missed you at breakfast and that the last they had seen of you had been when you were staggering off with some girl.' Julia's hands rested on her hips—her face expressionless. Justin thought she seemed very calm for what she was insinuating.

'I did not stagger off,' he defended. At least he didn't think he had. 'And we just left at the same time.'

'Did you sleep with her?' she asked with a level voice.

'What!'

'Did. You. Sleep. With. Her?' she asked again, her head changing angles with each word like one of those annoying bobble-heads that people stick on their dashboards.

'No! What the hell, Julia?'

She stood staring at him. Sizing him up, studying him for any evidence that he was lying.

'I would never do that to you. To anyone. You know that.'

'Do I?' she asked coldly.

'Julia, have you ever known me to do anything remotely unfaithful?'

'Did you leave with her?' she pushed, completely ignoring his question. He felt like he needed a back-up character reference.

'Julia —'

'Did you?' she asked again, and he couldn't lie.

'Yes,' he said. He felt like Hamlet looked when his tail went between his legs after digging a hole, but this was a hole Justin knew no way out of. He could only see it getting deeper.

'Did she go to your room?' Julia asked.

'No,' he shook his head at her in frustration.

'Where did you go? An alley?' she threw in cruelly, crudely.

'What? Julia, no. We just walked. We sat on the beach.' He wished he could rewind. Press pause. Think about his answers better. But he was tired. He knew her questions would lead her to what she was searching for. He knew he'd lost already — he didn't need to wait for Julia to tally the scoreboard. He couldn't lie. He wouldn't lie. He'd just hope she'd forgive him.

'You sat on the beach?' she thought about that for a moment, 'And nothing happened?' she confirmed. He felt some air come into his lungs.

'Nothing happened,' he assured her, realising he could lie after all.

'You didn't kiss her?'

He stalled and Julia glared at him.

'Well. Wha — ah ...'

'Justin, did you kiss her?' Julia looked as startled as he felt.

'It didn't mean anything,' he eventually said. He was right the first time, he couldn't lie.

Julia stared at him in disbelief. He thought she would cry, but she just gaped at him, almost smiling even. She picked up Justin's phone and he assumed she was going to find the photo of Anna. He didn't ask. He didn't stop her. He was curious what the next scene would be, watching as she flicked through his phone.

'Have you spoken to her since?' she asked quietly, looking him in the eye so sharply he felt his face flinch.

'No,' he murmured. 'Julia, listen it—' but she silenced him with her hand.

'Justin, this is all I need to know,' and she placed his phone in front of him. He looked down expecting to see the photo of him and Anna, but it wasn't. It was his call list. It was a long line of 'Anna', with a few others dotted in between. He went to explain, but as he looked up, he saw the last glimpse of Julia's black suit as she marched down the hallway, out of his house and, presumably, out of his life.

'It didn't mean anything,' he muttered.

But even he didn't believe it.

chapter fourteen

Saturday morning, Anna lay in bed. The sun was hibernating behind the clouds and she was grateful for it. Having now decided that she despised Justin (The Snake) for having a girl-friend, being an amazing kisser, and not calling, she'd opted for a chilled Friday night, and went to see a movie with Ioulia. They had seen the stupidest, most unromantic movie playing and changed the ratio of their blood sugar levels through the consumption of chocolate. Both felt totally within their rights to be pigs seeing as they'd agreed to wake up early Saturday morning to exercise. Ioulia declared it would be good for their chakras. Anna, having no idea what a chakra was, hoped it came in the form of milk chocolate and vowed to exercise early in the morning. Naturally, upon approaching consciousness Anna thought maybe she could exercise Sunday instead, and stayed under the covers for a while longer. She'd definitely go to the gym on Sunday … or Monday, when the week would really begin. Definitely Monday.

She hazily watched the morning gradually brighten her room, while gently tracing the pattern on the small pillow by her head with her finger. It had an outline of a green bird that made her think calm thoughts. She'd bought it at the St Kilda markets for some exorbitant price, but its quaintness justified the expense. Eyeing it now, she thought wistfully of the day Jane had tried to throw it out during one of her cleaning rampages. The memory eased her missing of Jane.

Anna lay peacefully until she heard the knock at her front door. She let it go, hoping it was her neighbour's door, but its quiet persistence forced her to listen a little closer and accepted grumpily that it was, in fact, her door that needed answering. In a huff, questioning who on earth would turn up at this ungodly hour, she checked the clock to see it read 9:42 a.m. Not so ungodly after all.

She slunk out of bed and begrudgingly walked to the door. The feeble knock grew louder and she heard a little voice sing, 'An-na,' making her smile—even at this ungodly hour, or not so ungodly. She couldn't remember what she'd decided.

'Mel? Is that you?' she asked, looking, and frowning, at her state in the mirror by the front door. Mascara smudged under her eyes, lines from her pillow on her forehead; hair, manic and punk-like.

'It is. I bear presents if you let me in.'

Anna liked the sound of that. It wasn't even her birthday. She unlocked the door and opened it enough so Mel could step through, but not enough so any neighbours that happened to be walking by would see how brief her pajama shorts were. People could be very judgmental, she scowled.

'What are you frowning at?' Mel asked as Anna realised she'd taken her pajama defense against a nonexistent bystander way too far.

'Nothing. Just being woken up by some redhead that comes to my door at the crack of dawn on a Saturday morning.'

'It's almost ten!' Mel defended. 'You kids these days, you waste the best part of the day,' she scolded as she made her way to the lounge, placing a white box on the coffee table.

'Thanks Nanna,' Anna replied. 'Where's my present?'

'And don't even get me started on your manners,' Mel shook her head and Anna jumped on the lounge next to her, her hands stretched out. Mel laughed tiredly and opened the box she'd left on the table. Inside was an array—a drooling array—of desserts. Anna's mouth hung open and her hands went to her heart.

'For me?' her eyes locked on the chocolate éclair.

'Well,' Mel shrugged and smiled. 'For us.'

'Occasion?' Anna asked skeptically.

'Us again, I'm afraid.'

'Something I don't know?' Anna enquired as she reached for the éclair.

'To celebrate our lives together.' Anna frowned, confused. 'As spinsters,' Mel finished.

'Oh,' Anna said slowly and winced. 'Bad date?' Mel nodded sadly, her usual spark thoroughly tarnished.

'He was nice enough, I guess, but just …' She trailed off trying to find the right words to explain herself. 'Wrong.'

'Wrong as in Vegemite and Jam wrong, or wrong like me playing trivia?'

'Jam and Vegemite,' Mel said sadly as she reached for a piece of baklava.

'Oh, sorry Mel,' Anna replied, genuinely. Anna considered telling her about Kyle's phone call, momentarily thinking it would help, but was quickly convinced that the insult would do more damage than good.

'Hey, I took a photo of him. Long story, but, let me show you and you tell me the first thing that comes to your head.' Mel whipped on her glasses and reached for her phone.

'Um, okay,' Anna agreed as she wiped the remaining chocolate from her face. Mel flicked through one or two shots and then nodded in approval when she found the image she was after.

'Okay An,' Mel took a big breath, 'tell me honestly what you think.' Anna accepted Mel's task and her phone.

'Oh my. Were they there before?'

'That's what I said!' shrilled Mel.

'Did you really?' Anna gawked.

'Yes. No. Well … in my head.'

Anna nodded understandingly and shook her head again at the photo. 'He needs some advice about the length of those sideburns.'

'Ah huh,' agreed Mel, clearly distressed by the excessive fur on this guy's face. It definitely had not been there at their last meeting. Anna recalled him needing a shave, but in the week gone, while he had managed a shave, he had also provided his sideburns with more growth and nurturing than was advisable.

'Who does he think he is? Mr Darcy? Luke Perry?' exclaimed Anna, who was starting to wonder if sideburns were coming back. This could add years to her singleness.

'Elvis, maybe?' Mel suggested through the extravagant frown on her face.

'Wolverine?'

'They weren't there before, were they? Surely I would have remembered them …' Her eyes strayed to the ceiling as she sent her mind back to their initial date.

'No. We'd both have to have been blind to miss those babies,' Anna assured her. 'Now, apart from this excessive hair,' *and the fact that he called me too*, 'was there anything else wrong with him? Because the sideburns are quite easy to fix—the mindset to have grown them I'm not so sure about, but one slip of a razor and you could have your potential soulmate right here … right?' Anna slapped the phone, hoping to put a positive spin on Mel's heavy heart. But Mel continued to sit glumly, visibly resigning herself from the whole dating game before Anna's very eyes.

'No. He was fine. Really, he was,' she sighed, putting her glasses away again. 'I guess.'

'You guess?' Anna probed some more. She had been sitting cross legged on the lounge but unslumped herself to look at Mel straight on. 'What do you mean 'you guess'? Did he talk computer games? Get you to remove the virus on his PC? Challenge you to Wii tennis? Honk your boob, fart at dinner, pick his nose?'

Mel looked at her, alarmed. She had syrup on her face and Anna refrained from telling her so, firstly because she didn't want to distract Mel from answering her question, and secondly because it was quite funny to look at.

'No, he was fine,' Mel replied vaguely. Anna found an extra inch in her spine and sat up even higher.

'Come on!' she hit the cushion, laughing. 'You have to have more than that to say. What made it such a bad date, apart from the facial fur?'

'He, just … I don't know,' she waved her hand absently.

'Well, neither do I, so …' Anna was about to threaten her with eating all the pastries, but Mel was staring at the desserts not looking remotely tempted, just sad.

'Hey, Mel, what's really up?' Anna frowned. 'It was just a stupid date.'

Mel avoided looking at her, but when she eventually turned to address Anna's persistent stare, she fixed a trying smile on her face. It lasted all of a moment before it crashed.

'He just wasn't right. I–I guess he was perfectly fine, just not the person for me.'

'Ri-ight,' Anna said slowly, leaning over and wiping the syrup from her friend's face, deciding Mel didn't need that on her plate as well as single-dom depression.

'Mel, it's okay. It was just a bad date,' she soothed, knowing the disappointment all too well.

'But it wasn't even bad. Do you think I'm being too fussy?' she frowned, and Anna shook her head adamantly.

'No way. Mel, you can't just settle for someone. You can't, I can't, and no-one should. If you don't meet someone who isn't right, it doesn't mean you're fussy. You deserve to be happy, to be loved and all that gooey stuff. You are being too hard on yourself. So wise up, kiddo,' she smiled firmly.

'Right, you're right. I know,' Mel nodded as she reached for a custard tart, which Anna thought was a good sign.

'Too right I am,' Anna announced. Though Anna had to wonder if she'd just lied to a friend—she'd never once seen a sign of the relationship she had just described to Mel and claimed she deserved.

Anna reached for an unidentified slice, hanging it over her mouth as she tried to eat it as neatly as possible, catching the crumbs with her gaping mouth.

'Classy,' Mel drawled. 'Anna, I have a confes—' she paused midsentence to scan the flat, then waited for Anna to finish her bite before continuing. 'Anna … Hon?' Confusion tweaking Mel's mouth. 'What's that smell?'

'Could be the bin,' she told her, unconcerned, before taking another dramatic bite of the slice.

'That's coming from your bin! Are you joking?' Mel asked in alarm, her body trying to edge as far away from the kitchen as she could.

'It's not *that* bad,' Anna told her, licking the crumbs off her fingers one digit at a time. Mel guffawed.

'And I thought I had problems. Anna, it is terrible,' placing way too much emphasis on the last word for Anna's liking. 'Why haven't you emptied it?' she asked, aghast.

'It was Jane's job,' Anna reminded her.

'Anna, Jane doesn't live here anymore. She's hardly going to drive down every week to empty your bin, is she?'

'Well … I don't like emptying the bin,' Anna huffed, emulating a child who didn't want to do their homework. 'I'm five-foot-one. Do you know how steep those stairs are for me?'

'An, I get that. I really do. Stairs suck. It's dirty work. But, *no-one* likes it. If you don't empty your bin then I'm pretty certain that bin is going to grow legs, come drag you off this very lounge one day when you least expect it, and throw *you* out! Now stop being gross or you really will be single forever.'

Anna began to wish she'd left the syrup on Mel's face. She glared at Mel in annoyance and Mel returned the stare.

'Now.' Mel pointed to the bin in question, sitting at the edge of the kitchen. Anna crossed her arms firmly. Mel raised an eyebrow and pulled a warning face that concerned Anna.

'Fine,' she groaned, storming over to the bin. She'd begun to tie the bag when Mel waved the empty dessert box in the air and smiled sweetly. Anna stood up straight and frowned at her, hands on hips. Mel smirked at Anna's behaviour, which infuriated Anna even more as she snatched the box out of Mel's hands and then stomped back to squish it into the bin. Anna tied the bag and thumped out the door and down the stairs—in her short, short pajamas. By the time she'd re-entered the flat, Mel was sitting, awaiting her arrival and smiling widely, her previous misery a distant memory. Anna pounded her feet back to the lounge and heaved herself back down. Mel rose a fraction when Anna landed.

'Happy now?'

'Very.' Mel responded with a smile. 'Are you?'

'No.' Anna threw a cushion at Mel's face, cracking a smile. 'I don't like you anymore,' Anna told her meekly as she let her head fall on Mel's shoulder. Mel patted her head.

'Now, now, don't be like that … I'm your Plan B.'

chapter fifteen

Justin woke at midday. He was curious if he could have slept the whole day but didn't see where finding out would have gotten him. Julia wasn't taking any of his calls. It had been over a week—ten days to be exact—and he was at a loss of what to do next. Apart from sleeping, his only other idea was to run. Justin was pathetically reminded of past teenage angst.

He rolled onto his side, stared at the door for a minute, moaned, and then rolled out and onto his feet. His face was unshaven and it prickled his palms as he rubbed it. He had no intention of shaving either, he had to reason with himself just to put deodorant on, which he did, and then pulled on clothes.

Walking into the yard, runners on, the sun blared onto his face and he shielded his eyes in annoyance. Hamlet had stirred, and as if reading Justin's mind, refrained from jumping. Instead he sat innocently and watched his master, wagging his tail ever so slightly. Justin ruffled his ears and leashed him.

Together, they ran to a local oval and ran laps—going around and around the field, mimicking the thoughts in Justin's head. He was due to play a soccer game there the next day and he wished the game was on now, so he could really run his frustrations out.

By the time they returned home, and Hamlet was drowning his gums in his water bowl, Justin felt it was time for bed again—guilt was exhausting.

He showered, hearing the phone ring as he towelled himself down. He almost considered answering it, but it wasn't Julia calling—that, he was sure of—and there wasn't anyone else he wanted to speak to.

He was an idiot. He knew this now. He'd suspected it many times before, but now it was a certainty. He'd had a great woman and he'd stuffed up. He'd had a great woman and he went and met another—another that he couldn't stop thinking about even though he kept trying to convince himself it was Julia he was thinking of. And he *was* thinking about her … mostly. Justin rationalised that he was only thinking about Anna because she was the instigating factor in his breakup.

He was an idiot.

He pulled on some shorts and fell onto his unmade bed. Sleep was the only place to be.

A series of heavy knocks brought Justin to consciousness.

'Jay! Mate! Open up!' banged a familiar voice.

Justin lay willing the noise to stop. But then the banging began to gain a melody, a bad melody, but a definite tune that was not going to ease up any time soon.

'Jaaaaayy!' sung Adam, and Justin unwillingly stomped to the door and opened it. 'Justin, mate,' he said as he slapped Justin on his bare back and strolled past into the house.

'What are you doing here?' Justin grumbled, holding the door open and hoping Adam would walk straight back out as easily as he had waltzed in.

'Came to rescue you,' he declared. 'Tommo's rounded up the fellas and we are hitting the town.'

Adam stood tall, proudly waiting for Justin's gratitude.

'I don't want to hit the town,' Justin told him straight out, door remaining open. Adam scowled and shook his head.

'Too bad. You are. Jules is gone, bud. It's time to have some fun.'

Adam clapped his hands together and walked himself further into the house and towards the fridge.

'Got any beer?'

Justin stood frowning and reluctantly closed the door. Adam stuck his head back down the hallway, holding a bottle out in offer. Justin walked towards it and considered drinking as another possible solution he hadn't been tapping into. Maybe Adam did know a thing or two.

By nightfall, after giving into the notion of hitting the town, Justin was struggling not to fall off his bar stool. He was sure it had become more a case of the town hitting him.

He hadn't drunk much, he was sure of it, but he hadn't eaten either, and figured that was why he felt so awful. He wanted to go outside. He was so hot he couldn't concentrate, but the group (collected from their soccer team and almost positively securing their defeat for the next day's game—which was not the best game plan coming into finals) wouldn't give up their view of the TV.

'Another drink, Doc?' Tom shouted.

'Just water,' Justin called back, louder than he needed to, but Tom seemed too far away to hear. Tom rolled his eyes and stumbled to the bar. Justin felt his heart race while he waited. He really wanted to leave, but his feet kept slipping on the rungs of the stool, and he wasn't sure how he'd go driving, or where his car even was. Originally, he'd planned to leave it and pick it up in the morning, but now he wasn't so sure, he'd only had a few beers, and he wanted out.

'You hot?' he asked Shane, who was downing bourbons.

'Yeah mate, just ask the *ladies*,' he grinned and Adam high-fived him.

'Jay, mate, you need another drink,' declared Adam when he noticed an empty glass in front of Justin. 'Let's do shots. We gotta loosen you up!'

'I'm fine, mate. Tom's getting me a drink.' He could see Tom yelling across to the bartender. 'Hey Ad, where's my car?'

Justin had insisted on driving because he feared for his life any time Adam drove.

'Why? You're not going mate,' Adam said, his face growing serious.

'I left my dog,' Justin told him, seriously.

'Your dog? Mate, the dog didn't make the cut.' Adam laughed hard and Shane joined in. Justin squinted in confusion.

'What? What dog? Where's the car?'

Justin saw Adam wink at Shane, who snickered like an arse-hole. Justin had never liked the guy.

'It's across the road. It's fine. The dog's fine, you're fine, we're all fine. Now go get another fucking drink.'

Tom returned just as Adam flung a coaster at Justin.

'Water for the weak,' Tom laughed as he sat a whole jug of water in front of Justin and floated a black bendy straw on top for laughs.

'Water for the lady, more like it.' Adam chugged the remains of his beer and sauntered off to the bar for another.

Justin held the jug with two hands and poured as much water down his throat as he could stand. Some ran down his throat and shirt, but it brought relief to his rising temperature. Tom laughed and slapped him on the back.

'Mate, should I get you another? You look a little thirsty.'

Justin tried to smile back, unsure if it was water dripping off him, or sweat. 'Tommy, I think I'm going to head off.'

'Already? Jay we're all here for you!' Tom laughed and Justin smiled dismissively.

'I think they'll be okay,' he said hazily as he watched the team drinking themselves into oblivion.

'Are you right to drive?' Tom asked, unsure and gaining control of his own senses.

'Yeah. I've only had a few. I'm fine,' he assured him as he slumped off his stool. 'I'll catch you tomorrow at the game. Don't drink too much,' Justin warned as he regained his balance. The words seemed to have swum out of his mouth. He felt foggy and wondered if he was actually getting sick.

'Sure thing,' Tom grinned and looked around at the others slyly before whispering loudly. 'Go, go, go!' and pointed him to the exit.

Adam was still at the bar; Shane was ogling some poor girl, and the others were ogling the sports channel. Justin took the opportunity for an easy escape.

Outside, the cool air embraced him like an old friend and it brought his senses some clarity. He gulped in the air like he'd drunk the water. His black SUV sat across the road just as Adam had said, and he turned the air conditioner up as soon as the engine was running.

The roads were empty and Justin cranked the stereo up as he cruised through the streets. His heart thumped with the music, egging him on. The steering wheel felt smooth under his palms and now that he was alone, he didn't feel in such a great hurry to get home. Instead, he took a detour and drove a longer way.

The drive was settling his nerves and he felt clear and in control. He swerved past the other vehicles with precision and felt as though he could drive all night. Justin came to a long stretch of road and praised the green light he was granted so he could zip right on through. He wasn't far from Julia's flat and he toyed with the idea of going there. He wondered if she'd take him back if he said sorry again. If she took him back, he wouldn't feel like such a bad guy. People wouldn't think he was such a bad guy if she forgave him. They could get married—they'd be happy then.

He glided through the next intersection as a set of bright headlights turned towards him and Justin's mind couldn't keep up with what his eyes witnessed. His hands couldn't move the steering wheel with such short notice and his arms locked as the headlights became a red car that slammed into the front corner of Justin's vehicle. Hard.

The impact sent his car spinning and his head rolling. The airbag exploded in his chest like a punch and his brow hit the side window. The sudden blow sent pain soaring through his head just as his car came to a complete stop.

Justin's palms felt his body, concerned he was dead. Once confident he was still alive, and swaying slightly against the deflating airbag, he slowly unclipped his seat belt. The door opened after heavy force and Justin awkwardly stumbled out of the car and onto the road. His car was now on the roadside, facing the other way. The front end of his car was rearranged in an ugly fashion and he cringed at its sudden death.

Justin spun around, remembering another car was involved and searched the road for it.

His heart stopped when he found it. Beat. Paused, then went into overdrive.

Justin ran to the car. He could make out the driver slumped in the seat, hanging over the seat belt. The car had stopped directly under the streetlight it had smashed in to. Part of the car was well lit, and Justin could see the front end had become a mash of red metal, similar to his own car but worse. It was too crumpled to work out how many were inside, but Justin pulled at the door and yelled at the driver. When she didn't respond he grabbed at the handle with both hands, shaking it furiously—but it wouldn't budge. He tried the back door, which was also locked.

Frowning in frustration, Justin took a step back and tried to kick the window with his foot. His unsuccessful attempt forced him to bounce back—landing on his side, gravel splitting the skin on the palms of his hands. Clumsily, he stood back up and sized up the window, feeling defeated. Then, in a moment of clarity he thought of the boot. It opened easily and he lifted its base to feel for the wheel jack. He hurried back to the window, glanced at the motionless woman in the front seat, and used the jack and sheer adrenaline to smash through the glass. Justin hastily leant through and fumbled with the lock. The door opened at last and he reached around to unlock the front door. Yanking it open, Justin carefully pressed the woman's body back on to the seat and rested her bloody head on the head rest. Vague first aid training faded in and out of his consciousness and he did well to remain calm.

'Wake up! Hello!' he called to no avail.

He felt for the pulse in her neck and was convinced he felt a faint beat. He squeezed her shoulders and called to her again. This time she moaned ever so slightly. Justin felt a brief relief and planned to wait by her side, but the heat coming through the dashboard urged him to try and move her.

Justin unclipped the seat belt and tried to pull the woman from the car. Her moans became deeper and her eyes fluttered. Justin looked down at her legs and could see they were wedged, the car impacting upon them at an awkward angle. With gentle force he freed them and, as smoothly as possible, eased her out of the car and carried her away from the scene as far as he could. He heard a voice coming towards him as he placed her on the ground. Headlights glared into his eyes once more and he shielded them as the voice produced a face.

'Are you okay?' called a man with long hair.

Justin could offer only a grunt and a nod. He knelt next to the woman and squeezed her shoulders again, aware of the man phoning for help. To Justin's distress, the woman made barely a sound this time. Blood covered her face and legs, and even in the dim light Justin could tell her arm lay at an odd angle.

'You're going to be okay,' he soothed. 'What's your name?'

She murmured a sound that was indistinguishable. Her breathing sounding laboured, and he felt her pulse again.

'Mate, what can I do?' asked the long-haired guy, as he awkwardly scattered to the woman's side.

'See if her wallet is in the car. Find her name,' Justin suggested as he had a flash of brainpower. Long-haired Guy shuffled off, grateful for a task, and ran back with a sagging handbag. He shuffled through it to find a wallet, bits and pieces falling out as he searched.

'Her name is Bernadette O'Donnell,' he said in a shaky voice as he knelt next to the woman again. Together by her side, the two men called Bernadette's name. Her eyes fluttered open briefly and she looked at them both vaguely before closing them again. Justin felt relief when he heard sirens approach — flames had begun to engulf Bernadette's car. His helper announced the police arrival, like Justin was both deaf and blind.

Whilst pulling on a fluro vest, one officer ran towards them. He knelt by the woman and slid on blue latex gloves as an ambulance pulled up. Justin watched the flashing lights, trance-like, feeling thankful to have help.

'Hey, you alright?' the officer looked up at Justin and Long-haired Guy with concern, his face changing colour from red to blue under the flashing lights. Justin nodded, while Long-haired Guy anxiously explained he had only stopped to help, and then stared, hypnotised by Bernadette's injuries.

'Her name is Bernadette O'Donnell,' Justin told the officer, who nodded and called her name, although she gave zero response this time.

The second police officer, an older woman in a matching bright vest, arrived by her partner's side and a moment later the ambulance officers joined them.

'Anything you can tell me?' one paramedic asked Justin as he stared at Justin's forehead, which Justin could now feel stinging, the skin around his eye feeling tight.

'I found her over the steering wheel. I tried to get her out but her legs were stuck. She did open her eyes at one point …' He struggled to get the words out, his tongue felt like it had lost all coordination. The female officer looked at him strangely and stood up. Her short blonde hair was pulled tight behind her head, her eyes were hard.

'Are you hurt?' she asked, and he shook his head. 'You have a gash on your head,' she told him sternly and Justin reached up to feel something sticky there.

'I'm Constable Fields, this is Constable Hodge,' she said pointing to her partner. 'Before you speak sir, this conversation is being recorded. Can you tell me what caused the accident?'

The male officer came to her side, leaving the ambulance officers to tend to Bernadette. Justin saw another police vehicle and ambulance arrive. Long-haired Guy had also stepped back and Constable Fields looked over at him.

'I'll need to speak to you too if you don't mind,' she told him, and he obediently hung back near his car, watching as the fire crew arrived and tended to the flames. Everyone was moving so quickly that it all felt like a blur to Justin, who was now incredibly thirsty again and wondered if he could get a drink.

'Can you tell us what happened, sir?'

'I was driving,' Justin said and pointed his arm lazily in the direction he was travelling, 'and this car came out of nowhere and crashed into me.'

'O-kay.' Constable Fields noted down their conversation in a small flip book, and then looked up at him again. 'Sir, have you had anything to drink this evening?'

Justin's heart sank, before his defenses emerged. 'Yes, but not much,' he swore, holding up his grazed hands.

'We'll have to do a breath test nonetheless,' Constable Hodge told him and went to the car to retrieve the device. Justin watched as he spoke briefly to the other two officers.

Constable Fields looked at the now smouldering car and then to Bernadette on the ground. She let out a sigh and even in the shadows Justin could see the clear look of dislike on her face. Other cars drove past slowly to scope the scene, their lights briefly taking away the darkness before they continued on through to their lives.

Constable Hodge returned and held out a Breathalyser. Justin heard him mutter something to his partner and Justin was given no other choice but to listen.

'These guys just heard on the radio there's been another DUI on the highway,' he shook his young head and Fields responded bitterly.

'I've had enough of these idiots,' she spat. Justin arched his back, wanting to defend what she had obviously suspected him of. Constable Hodge didn't respond to the comment but moved the Breathalyser in front of Justin to gain his attention.

'Just count to five, mate,' he told him, and Justin obeyed nervously. Hodge looked at the reading and raised his eyebrows. He held it out for Constable Fields to see and she frowned.

She looked at Justin, intensely studying his face. Hodge muttered something in her ear and walked back to the car. Justin didn't know if he was over the limit or under.

'Can I see your licence please?' she demanded, no politeness in her words.

'Ah, sure.' His eyes darted between the two officers as he pulled his wallet out of his back pocket and slid his licence out. She read it slowly and held on to it.

'You came in just under the legal amount for driving, Mr Owens,' she said suspiciously. 'Have you used any other substances tonight?' she asked bluntly, expectantly.

'Substances?'

'Drugs? Have you been using any other drugs?' she spoke curtly.

'No,' he shook his head at the absurdity of the idea. He looked past her to see Bernadette being lifted onto a trolley and wheeled into the first ambulance, a brace around her neck, oxygen mask over her face.

'Mr Owens,' Fields spoke as the other officer returned with something in hand. 'We have reason to believe you are under the influence of drugs. This here is an oral fluid test. All you need to do is hold your tongue to this section here,' she said as she indicated the strip. 'It will allow us to test you for other substances.' She handed it to Justin, who accepted it, and looked at them blankly.

'But I haven't used anything,' he told them, confused, unsure why he couldn't just go home. He wondered if Long-haired Guy could give him a lift seeing as good old Bernie had totalled his car.

'Great, then you won't mind doing the test,' she said dryly, watching the ambulance leave swiftly. 'We'll also do another breath test in ten minutes, to verify.'

Justin looked at the male officer, who nodded his encouragement to Justin. Justin licked the strip and handed it back feeling overpowered.

'This will take about five minutes. Constable Hodge will get a paramedic to clean you up,' she told him, and then crunched her way over to the guy with the hair. Justin could faintly hear what they were saying but everything seemed hazy to him. Constable Hodge steered him to the ambulance, where a paramedic tended to Justin's head and asked more questions than he was capable of answering. Justin cringed as the alcohol swab stung his flesh. The officer apologised, but continued to inflict the same sting to his grazed hands.

He could see Officer Hard-arse Fields taking more notes as she spoke to Long-haired Guy and he wondered vaguely what they were discussing. She then returned to where Justin sat and Long-haired Guy left. Justin, feeling smug that he was about to prove the officers wrong, was questioning if he could ask them for a lift home. They spoke in a huddle before turning back to face him and Justin thought nothing of their grave faces.

'Mr Owens, the test shows you to be positive for a prohibited substance,' Officer Hodge informed him, not looking surprised. 'We will need to conduct another test to confirm it, but that one will need to be analysed by a lab. Looking at the seriousness of the accident and your own injuries, we will be taking you to a hospital for the test. Did you want to say anything? I will remind you that anything you say is being recorded.'

They looked at Justin with complete disregard, and confusion overwhelmed him. None of what they were saying was making any sense. Justin looked from one face to the other and shook his head.

'I-I don't understand. I only had three beers,' he pleaded.

'Mate, let's just go do the second test and we'll go from there, okay,' Hodge advised and led a limp Justin to the back seat of the police car.

Justin watched as they spoke to the fire crew and the tow truck drivers who had arrived to clear the scene. He saw them hook up his mangled car and watched on with uncertainty.

Another police car had arrived at some stage and Justin hadn't even noticed until now. All he could see were flashing lights, it looked like Christmas, though the feeling in his stomach was not so festive.

They drove him towards the hospital and Justin resisted the urge to vomit. The lights faded away into the distance as his reality came in to focus.

chapter sixteen

Initially, Anna had intended to stand Kyle up. She had no respect for the guy due to the fact that he'd chosen to date a pair of friends that he'd met simultaneously, *and* because he made her his Plan B. Anna didn't even know how many dates he had squeezed out of the night—she could actually have been his Plan F for all she knew! But after Mel's date had gone so unsuccessfully, and because she was very much feeling as Mel was—that she would be single forever; Anna's negative opinions of the guy had loosened. Maybe Kyle hadn't realised she and Mel were friends. It was possible. And he was already three up on any other guy she was interested in, being that he called, lived locally, and (she presumed) was single.

Anna wasn't actually expecting the night to go well, and if it did, she'd come up with a story for Mel then. For now, sitting at home on a Saturday night and feeling sorry for herself was not an option. If she was going to complain, she had to at least give herself something to complain about. Not exactly the positive attitude one should have when preparing for a date, but at least she was trying.

When Anna pulled her silver Mazda into the restaurant's car park, her insides did a turn. An awkward hello was only minutes away and she saw no way around it, other than to boycott the date entirely.

She took a look in her rearview mirror and checked her mascara hadn't flecked on her eyelids, that her lips were shiny and that she had no unsightly bits clinging inside her nostrils. It was all clear. She took a big breath, let it out, and stepped her high-heeled feet out onto the bitumen.

Walking towards the entrance, Anna considered the possibility that Kyle hadn't arrived yet, or worse, that he'd stand *her* up.

God, she hated dating.

Why couldn't she just be happily married already? Why read children fairytales and build their little hopes and dreams up when life wasn't really that sweet? Snow White could go choke on her apple for all Anna cared. At this stage in her life, the dawning stage of thirty, she thought Prince Charming had better arrive with a good excuse for taking his sweet-arse time.

Please don't stand me up.

Pushing the restaurant door open, she breathed in the strong smells of Thai cuisine and her stomach grumbled loudly, which she had to admit was much nicer than it turning and threatening to vomit.

'Hi. Booking for Kyle?' she asked the tiny girl behind the front desk in hope. On cue, Kyle walked through the door behind her.

'Hi,' he smiled cautiously at Anna as he not-so-subtly checked her out. Anna wasn't sure how she felt about this but seeing as she was doing the same to him, she considered his lack of discretion a non-issue, just this once.

'Hi,' she smiled back. He looked fairly wonderful. She obviously hadn't been paying enough attention the night they had met.

He looked over to the hostess and gave his name, and she bobbed and nodded her head of shiny hair several times before leading them to their table. Kyle smiled and extended his long arm, indicating for Anna to go first.

Manners, nice, Anna thought as she walked through the restaurant. She swore she felt his eyes on her behind and walked conscious of her every move. She also prayed not to slide on the very shiny floors in her very high heels. She couldn't imagine that being a drawcard.

The hostess pulled out Anna's chair, removing any chance for Kyle to prove just how much of a gentleman he really was, and Anna thanked her politely. When they both sat down, the hostess shuffled back to her post.

'Hi,' Anna said again as she explored his face. He had blond spiky hair, a little too much product, but then—she quickly realised—no sideburns. Not unfortunate ones at least. She almost wondered if it was the same guy Mel had dated.

'Hi.' He smiled again and Anna began to question if this would be the extent of their conversation. Maybe she could start saying it in different languages, but then she only knew 'aloha', and that meant hello *and* goodbye—she didn't want to confuse the guy.

'Have you eaten here before?' she asked, hoping to ignite conversation as well as everlasting love.

He nodded with enthusiasm. 'Yeah, I work not far from here actually, we come here often. Have you?' He smiled, and it was a nice smile. Anna gave him a bonus point for that.

'No, but it smells amazing.'

She thumbed the menu and wondered how un-ladylike it would be to ask to order straightaway. She hadn't eaten much all day out of nervousness.

'What do you do for work?' she asked, purposely disregarding another's opinion of the generic question.

'I'm an architect.'

Get out of here, she wanted to say, feeling impressed but not sure why. She knew very little about architecture.

'Well, that's impressive,' she responded against her will. *Way to act cool,* she told herself, although Kyle and his ego seemed quite happy and the conversation took off from there. They ordered food and the plates arrived with an assortment of colour and flavour. While she happily picked at her meal, Kyle did most of the talking and Anna learnt he was into computers. She had figured this from their first meeting, but now realised his interest extended past computer games. He'd set up web pages and, for an amateur, he seemed to know his stuff. She also discovered they had travelled to similar places. She heard his stories about the people he'd met and places he'd been and mentally compared them to her own. She also discovered they lived ten minutes from each other. Admittedly most of her jokes seemed to go over his head, but when he did catch one, he slapped his leg and laughed hard. It made her laugh too and by the end of the meal, when not one more ounce of food could possibly fit into the space between her ribs, Anna realised that she was having a good night. What's more, Kyle seemed just as happy.

Not wanting the night to end, Anna slowed down the rate at which she was drinking her wine. Little sips so as to prolong the night—holding her glass and putting it down again, to stretch it out a little further. When she noticed Kyle's drink was also remaining full, Anna wondered if he was doing the same, or if it was just a bad wine.

'So …' he said as the waitress collected the bill and his credit card from the table, 'there's a pretty good bar across the road. We could get a drink if you are, um … if you didn't need to get going.'

His awkwardness was sweet, and Anna wondered again why Mel hadn't rated Kyle higher. Had the sideburns totally disrupted her view of the guy beneath?

'Sure, that sounds great,' she beamed and swallowed the rest of her wine.

They crossed the road and entered the bar, Kyle's hand gently guiding Anna from the small of her back. Her lips pulled an unstoppable smile as they squeezed through the crowded bar to find a quieter beer garden at the rear of the building. While Kyle went to the bar to get her another wine, Anna fantasised about having a real-live boyfriend. When the current leading man in her fantasy returned, she ignored the white socks she spotted under his dark jeans, shaking it off as a small fault that could be easily rectified. He sat down and (socks mostly forgotten) they became deep in conversation about jobs they'd had and what made them fun.

'Just recently we had this competition at work to see who could grow the biggest sideburns,' he started.

'Did you win?' She laughed, thinking about how Mel had it so wrong.

'No, came fourth,' he shook his head. 'I work with some very hairy men it turns out, but I tried. I guess it's stupid stuff like that that makes work fun.'

Anna nodded in agreement, thinking of her own shenanigans with the binder.

'I had a date actually, while this competition was going,' he told her bashfully. Anna didn't know whether she should tell him what she knew—remind him that Mel and she were friends. Clearly, he didn't realise, or had forgotten; or possibly dated too many people to recall. Surely he wouldn't have referred to the sideburn story if he knew Mel was her friend. This realisation consoled Anna's doubts about him and she felt herself officially relax—choosing to ignore the possibility that he'd had too many recent dates.

'What did she say about the sideburns?'

'Ah … not much. She wasn't impressed, that's for sure. She was looking at them the whole night as though I was part Wookie. She even took a photo,' he laughed.

'Did you tell her about the little competition you had going?' Anna asked, deciding to play dumb.

'Well, I went to, but she seemed pretty uninterested in me anyway. She was a bit of a snob. I figured that if she was going to judge me based on facial hair then maybe it wasn't worth telling her the story.' He shrugged, and Anna agreed, even though it was Mel he was talking about. Then she felt bad for judging him on his white socks, maybe he was behind on laundry. She really had to be less critical.

They sat and chatted, with only minimal lulls in conversation. Anna found herself listening to his university stories with a forced smile that hurt her face, but apart from that, she was having a good time. When she began to yawn she checked her watch and was surprised to find it was almost midnight. Kyle had just gone to the bar for fresh drinks—by now Anna had succumbed to water—and Anna wondered how long she had before her eyelids started looking lazy and deranged.

Smiling politely as Kyle returned to their table, Anna felt her phone vibrate in her bag and fished it out from amongst the random things it had to cohabitate with. Smiling apologetically, she quizzed the number on the screen. She didn't recognise it and considered letting it go, but it was a Sydney number and Anna thought it might be Jane. Jane would only call so late if she really needed to, so Anna accepted the call.

'Hello?' she called, turning away and pressing a finger to her free ear so as to hear better.

'Hello. Is this Anna Marcus?'

'Yes. Who's this?' she asked politely. It definitely wasn't Jane and she felt in a hurry to get off the phone and back to her date.

'Anna, I'm calling from Westmead Hospital.' Anna remained silent—confused and silent as the woman continued carefully. 'We have your mother here.'

The words echoed in her head. Her eyes darted for a path to a quieter spot but couldn't find one. Kyle turned his head politely away, so he didn't appear to be eavesdropping. People at the table behind them had started talking to him about the night's football scores and Anna was relieved she didn't have any of his attention.

'My mother? Is she okay?' Anna asked slowly, as if she were waking up—her heart on standby.

'She's been in a car accident Ms Marcus. She is in a critical condition.'

'What?' Anna said quietly.

'I'm very sorry. Your mother's emergency contact, a …' Anna heard her flick paper and continue gently, 'Brian Hill. He told us you are in Melbourne.'

'Brian Hill?'

'Yes, her partner I believe. Anna, she has endured severe injuries. She'll be moved to ICU and we recommend family come if they are able …' the voice continued but Anna didn't hear anything. Words were spinning in her head as though someone had just opened a window and blew her life all around her.

'I'm in Melbourne,' Anna said, more to herself, as the distance between her and her mother dawned on her.

'Yes, I know dear.'

'I need to get to Sydney,' she murmured.

'Okay Anna, how about you call us tomorrow, after you get your affairs in order. My name is Tracey, but anyone here can help you.'

Anna was numb. 'Okay. Thank you,' she whispered and hung up. She thought she may have heard the woman continue to speak but she didn't want to hear any more, she just had to get to her mother.

She put the phone back in her bag slowly and looked over at Kyle; he was turning back from the group he was befriending to face her. Anna coaxed herself to keep calm until she was home. Then she could have license to react.

'Kyle, I'm sorry but I need to go,' she told him, placing her hand just near his arm sincerely.

'Oh, right. Okay then,' he gave her a tight-lipped smile.

'I'm really sorry. That was um … my mother's had an … accident. I need to go,' she told him calmly and amazed herself with how neutral she sounded.

'Yup, right. Sure thing,' he said after a long pause.

'I'll … um, call you,' she told him, standing to leave. Kyle stayed where he was. The group behind him watched on, making the situation even more awkward.

'Sure. See ya,' he said, looking at her impassively.

Anna didn't know what to do. Her body made a strange jerky movement, one move towards the exit, and one towards Kyle. She gave him a pathetic, hasty little wave and left, looking over her shoulder once to see him turn to the group he'd been talking to.

A section of her brain, the one that desperately wanted to be madly in love and be loved and cared for, wanted to sit and analyse Kyle's actions. The rest of her body was fighting to keep itself together and not interpret the information she had just been given on the phone. She let her mind settle on nothing more serious than the objects in front of her. She crossed the road and focused on the colours of the cars. She walked behind the restaurant they'd eaten at and thought of their meal. She saw her car and let her mind dwell on how badly it needed to be cleaned.

Anna climbed in her car, started the engine, and used all her brain power to operate the vehicle. By the time she'd pulled up to her apartment block, her ability to not think was wavering dramatically. Anna could barely keep the words 'ICU' and 'critical' from her brain. She floated up the stairs, removing her heels as she did, tripping up a couple of steps in the process. Her keys were drawn, ready to unlock her front door. Once in, heels dropped, bag down, keys clattering to the floor, she curled on the lounge and cried. Quiet sobs of the emotions that were overflowing in her mind. Her body shook and she hugged herself, crying harder, gasping for breath.

She wanted so many things that were completely intangible to her. She wanted someone to take care of everything that she now had to do to get to Sydney; but she had to accept that there was no-one. It was her job alone.

Anna tentatively stood up and wiped her face. She located her iPad, swiped it on and started a flight search. Watching the site match her request was a slow process and she wanted to throw the tablet at a wall. She breathed and counted to ten, watching as her options lazily appeared.

'It's all going to be okay,' she said to no-one. 'It'll be okay.'

Within the hour Anna had booked a one-way flight to Sydney for six-forty the next morning. She'd organised a taxi to pick her up at five, packed a carry-on bag, and even hired a car. It was close to three a.m. by the time she was finished, and Anna sat numbly on the edge of her bed. She was beyond exhaustion, but adrenaline pumped through her veins and denied her the option of sleep. She sat in a trance. Everything felt surreal. Everything felt hollow. Anna watched as her dark room altered in focus, as the tears came and went with her fears.

At 4:30 a.m. she heard her phone's alarm beep from her bedside table. She stretched across to turn it off, straightened her bed impulsively, and walked zombie-like to the shower. She peeled her carefully selected date-clothes to the floor and stood under the hot bursts of water. Practicalities began to set in. She had no idea when she'd be back. Ioulia was set to officially move in that week. She had a training course at work to complete. Her car insurance was due Monday. The thought of who would empty her bins plagued her mind more than usual, and she kicked herself for not being better organised. She'd sat dwindling the hours away with useless sentimental thoughts, when she could have been easing her own burdens.

Rushing, she left notes on her neighbour's door about where she was going, who was moving in and that her bins were full. She could only hope they'd feel obliging.

She was waiting on the curb when the taxi pulled up. The driver, not so chirpy at five in the morning, suited Anna just fine.

'Tullamarine Airport was it?' confirmed the white-haired man.

'Yes. Please,' she told him as she settled into the back seat to watch the empty streets on a dark Sunday morning.

chapter seventeen

Her entire trip was smooth, but Anna was too focused on where she had to be to even appreciate it. Thankful for Google Maps, the little hire car took her to the hospital where her mother lay. As she walked through the multilevel car park towards the entrance, the sheer size of the building intimidated her. She entered wishing she weren't alone or that bravery didn't feel so distant.

The ICU nurse had given Anna the harrowing update that her mother's lung had collapsed and that she had slipped into a coma. Any assurance that this was the body's way of coping was useless in Anna's tiny world that consisted of just her and her mother. There was no room for a coma in that world.

The pale blue hospital unit had a matching slip-free floor. It was a space that could essentially be hosed down if required. It wasn't a space that came up and welcomed with warm assuring arms and Anna braced herself with the knowledge it would be the same case with her mother. The curtain to Bed Five loomed in front of her and Anna approached the blue sheath slowly. She could hear the beep of monitors, the sucking in of breath, machines breathing, careful footsteps and hushed voices. Anna felt like she was standing on heaven's doormat and she looked behind her absently, half expecting Saint Peter to say hello.

She stood on the safe side of the curtain for a moment longer, biding her time while her brain accepted that the situation was a real one and she had to face it. Behind her the nurse busied herself at a computer screen, while another filled paperwork with a furrowed brow. A doctor was talking quietly to an older couple nearby and Anna wondered if they were receiving bad news; if they too were looking for the Pearly Gates.

Looking straight ahead, she took in a sharp breath of sterile air and slid the curtain aside to step through. Anna noticed the thick bandage on her mother's leg first; recognising the thin toes poking out like they were her own. However, looking along the body in front of her, that was as far as the recognition went; her mother's name, scrolled in bold capital letters above the bed, was the only other source of familiarity.

Her mother's eyes were taped with gauze, the red skin bulged through from underneath. Her swollen face was decorated with small red scratches and a breathing tube was wedged in her mouth, her pale lips camouflaging with her dry and lifeless skin. Anna noticed a fleshy row of stitches on her mother's chin and a part of her hair had been shaved just above her forehead to show another raw gash. The slow and constant beep of the heart monitor was disheartening background music as Anna saw through the carnage to see that it was her mother in front of her, and she watched the room blur as her tears came.

'Mum?'

There was no reply, and Anna couldn't help but wonder if there ever would be.

Justin woke to the sounds of a dog barking, loudly. His head was pounding furiously, and his tongue had dried to the roof of his mouth. With an aching jaw he frowned at Hamlet's barking before realising it wasn't Hamlet's bark at all. Justin opened his eyes warily. He was in a single bed and felt his feet hang generously over its edges; his body covered by a fairy bedspread. When he tried to sit up the memory hit him with a firm right jab, followed by a hook, and he collapsed back onto the pillow.

He felt sick instantly.

He stumbled to the bathroom of his parents' house and made it just in time to miss his mother's carpet. Justin was grateful his mother was a cleaning enthusiast as he pulled his head out of her toilet bowl. Not that he felt any better off. The feeling it left in him was dirty and grey.

He looked at his raw palms, which had stung as they'd clutched the porcelain edge, and felt his heavy head hang. He thought a shower would rid the feelings from his mind, but as he stepped under the steaming water, he realised it didn't make an ounce of difference. He could scrub his body until his skin peeled off, but it wouldn't take away the feeling he had inside. He felt hopeless to it and revolted by it, and he couldn't settle on the words that justified what was happening inside his head. He was trapped in a world that didn't feel real.

How could this happen? He asked himself again and again. How could this happen *to me?*

Justin walked down the stairs slowly. His hip ached, and he suspected it was bruised from his seatbelt. Holding it tentatively, he found his dad at the dining table and his mother at the sink. They looked up at him. His dad put down the thick Sunday paper and removed his glasses. His mother took her hands away from the dishes and placed her pink rubber-gloved fingers on the edge of the sink.

Even Dolly, their dog, stood to attention by the door, her legs buckling behind her but determined to hold out.

Justin felt his stomach churn again but swallowed the acidic taste down.

'Hello,' he said, not knowing what else to say. He hoped they would take it from there; throw rocks at him, push him in a hole, tell him it was a dream — do *something*. They only offered him grim faces, a thin-lipped smile from his mother and a questioning stare from his dad. Justin was reminded of his younger years and he felt ridiculous standing a head taller than his mother and feeling four feet shorter.

'I'm sorry,' he told them, the shame making his face burn. 'Thanks for getting me, Dad … and for letting me crash.' He frowned at his choice of words and noticed they all had.

'Justin, what happened?' implored his mother. His father had asked him the same question the night before when he'd collected Justin from the police station, but he didn't know then either.

'You're bleeding,' she fussed, before he could speak. She was pointing to his forehead and he raised his fingers to the skin above his brow. There had been a butterfly patch on it before the shower. He pulled his fingers away and saw red.

'You're lucky that's all ye got,' his father told him gruffly. His dad was right. Justin's mind flashed back to his car, he had a vague memory of its mashed frame.

'Ye could have been killed,' his father continued.

Justin and his mother turned to face him. His mother looked as though she was about to cry and Justin felt like passing out. He could have died. He really could have. But so could have Bernadette.

Justin's mother tended to his cut. She busied herself by replacing the butterfly patch with a band aid and he wondered if she could feel his body shaking.

'Mate, what happened?' his dad asked this time.

Justin looked from one parent to the other. He clenched his hand and then stretched it out, the graze from hitting the gravel stung with a sharp reminder. He didn't want to speak, he didn't want to disappoint them, but he didn't see how he could avoid that — even though he didn't know the answer.

'I don't know,' he began. He stood with one hand fidget-ing with his wrist, he felt unsteady, and sick again. His mother seemed to sense this and handed him a glass of water. He took it gratefully and then took a seat at the head of the table.

'Start at the beginning,' his father suggested, not exactly patiently. Justin looked at him. His dad hadn't spoken to him with that tone in years, and his body seemed to shrink even more.

'I'd gone to the pub. We had some drinks,' he admitted, and as he did, he saw his mother shake her head. His father laid his arms on the table and hung his head. Justin swallowed quietly and kept talking. 'I only had a few drinks. I felt funny, and decided to leave and—'

'But you'd been drinking Justin!' his mother cried. He went to defend himself but then thought against it.

'On my way home a car came out of nowhere, and I hit it. They did a breath test and I was under the limit. They thought I looked suspicious I guess, and they did a drug test … it came back positive,' he admitted, and his mother's eyes opened wide in alarm. She looked at his father, who nodded silently.

'They took me to the hospital for another test. The official test comes back today, tomorrow maybe, but they suspect it will come back positive for MDMA,' Justin said.

'M, D, M, A?' his mother asked, trying to recall each letter.

'Ecstasy,' he told her. 'They think I had taken ecstasy, which means I was driving under the influence of drugs,' he ended, to the distress of both his parents.

'Justin!' cried his mother, appalled. Tears came to her eyes.

'Mum, I didn't take anything. I just don't do that, and if I did, I wouldn't have been stupid enough to drive,' he swore to them both.

'Then how do ye explain *this*?' his father demanded, not knowing what to call the situation.

Justin shook his head as he hung it in his hands. He found it hard to move his tongue.

'I don't know.'

'What happens now?' his mother asked, after blowing her nose, unsure whether to believe her only son who had only ever made them proud. Mostly.

'It depends on the official test results. I'll have a court hearing soon.'

'What can happen?' his father asked.

'Will you go to jail?' cried his mother, her hand flying to her mouth.

'It depends on what happens to the other driver,' he told them reluctantly, not wanting to say what he knew to be the possible penalties and feeling absolutely terrified.

'You mean,' his mother swallowed, 'if she, dies?'

'Then it's manslaughter,' Justin said in his lowest voice.

No-one spoke. They all remained silent as the information echoed through the room. Justin didn't want to think about it—any of it. He wanted to be where he was yesterday. He should have stayed in bed.

Sleep was the only safe place to be.

The doctor had warned that her mother's body had had a huge shock. The staff spoke to her gravely and Anna had felt like a child. The nicer they were, the more it terrified her. The small smiles they gave her only made her expect the worse was still to come. Anna wanted them to be brash and disrespectful. She wanted to feel like the staff thought she was being paranoid and dramatic. But they were calm, and they were patient. When Anna didn't understand something, they spoke slower and simplified things to where her head was at. When she cried, they handed her a tissue and offered her as much time as she needed.

They had told Anna the night of the accident that her mother was critical, now that she was also in a coma, Anna didn't understand the chance that she'd come out of it. Seeing her mother lying motionless, Anna understood that everything could change. Life could change.

Anna stayed at the hospital all day. When doctors or nurses came in, she'd often walk out. She didn't want to be near anyone and feared the concept of having to hold a conversation. Every conversation brought more truths.

Earlier the doctor had come to explain that, as well as her mother's leg being dislocated and severely fractured, her mother's back had absorbed a lot of impact from the accident and they'd found considerable swelling. They wanted to wait until she was conscious or in a less delicate state before they could determine just how much damage this impact had done. He couldn't tell Anna if there was nerve damage but let her know that due to her mother's age, there was every chance her bones would be weak, that her spine could be damaged too. Anna had put the information together like a puzzle and asked the question she couldn't believe she had to ask.

'Are you saying she won't be able to walk?' Anna didn't see the point of them bothering to put her leg in a big white cast if she couldn't even use the leg.

'We don't know. It will take some time. Like I said, it may very well just be swelling. We just have to wait.'

He said 'we' like they were in this together. But if her mother couldn't walk, Anna very much doubted that the doctor would be around for the next thirty years to wheel her mother to the bathroom. He'd left the room and Anna listened to the sound of breath whistling through an empty tube.

She'd been avoiding the doctors since.

As the hours passed, she reached for her phone spasmodically. She went to call Jane out of habit, she almost called Mel, and had started dialing her dad; but each time she looked at her phone's screen, she remembered that to call them she'd have to also speak, and she didn't think she could. By dark, no-one was any the wiser that Anna was no longer in Melbourne. Even her own mother, whose bedside she had sat by for hours on end, had any idea.

A nurse came in between the closed curtains and Anna exited the space. She wasn't supposed to be there for more than two hours at a time anyway. Her legs had been wasted as she'd sat staring at her mother's broken body and they, at least, revelled in the movement. She wandered corridors, in a vain attempt to console her pain through other people's miseries. But as she strolled past doorways and saw the faces, the families, the doubt, the harsh reality of life, she realised they were doing nothing for her confidence or faith. In this part of the hospital, death was on everyone's tail.

She retreated back to her mother and the same nurse intercepted her.

'I know this is hard,' she smiled apologetically. 'How about you get some rest. Will you be staying at your mother's?' Anna could hear the suggestion in her question and looked from her mother and back to the nurse. She hadn't thought that far ahead. She hadn't planned on leaving—didn't know she had to.

'I-I, um, I don't even have a key,' she realised aloud. The nurse patted her arm and reminded Anna that they would be in her mother's belongings which she had handed Anna earlier, sealed in plastic. Anna had accepted them, put them on the side table, and hadn't thought of them since.

The nurse walked back to the desk as the phone tweeted and Anna slowly tore at the plastic and fumbled through her mother's belongings. She pulled out her handbag first and then found the keys in a separate zip-lock bag. Putting them aside, she found a smaller bag with her mother's phone inside, and another with the necklace and earrings she always wore. Anna tossed them all into the handbag without a thought. Reaching for the keys again, Anna took them out of the plastic and held them reluctantly in her hand, feeling their coolness like it was her mother's touch. She placed them gently in her own bag, kissed her mother's soft and lifeless cheek as gently as she could, not wanting to jeopardise her comfort, and left.

The nurse gave an encouraging smile as Anna passed and made her way back to the car park. It felt like years since she'd parked there that morning. Remembering the day before felt even further away and Anna wished for the ignorance of Saturday as she drove to her mother's empty home.

When Anna turned the front lock and swung open the door, she simultaneously opened the vault to some very distant memories. The house wasn't where Anna grew up, but the smells were the same; the feel was the same. Before she even flicked the light switch she was having visions of her old life. With the lights on, she stood in the entrance, which doubled as the lounge room, and looked around. She dropped the keys on the cane coffee table, a steadfast piece of furniture from her childhood. The sofa was the same one she'd sat on while studying for her high school exams. The only modern item was the television Anna had given for Christmas the previous year. Her mum had never had much money and, looking around, Anna felt guilty that her own living standards far outweighed those of her own mother. The woman had given all she'd had to raise her daughter, and Anna had packed up and moved on, making inconsistent calls or visits; living a lifestyle much grander than … this.

Anna frowned as she walked through her mother's cramped home. It was an attached unit, not far off a main road. Downstairs, Anna glanced over the kitchen, its cupboards a chipped brown laminate. Mugs and cutlery rested on the stainless-steel sink; plates stacked by the side. It was as her mother had left it the day before, the day of the accident.

There was a laundry room off to the side and the back door opened up to a small courtyard that her mother had filled with plants—potted plants that she'd move around to entertain her creative side. She had them hanging off the fence palings, clinging to the bricks, and swinging from the gutters. It looked like a jungle and Anna smiled at the mess they seemed to create. Jane would never have approved.

In the eerily still house she wandered slowly back to the entrance where the stairs led up to the remaining rooms. Anna's fingertips trailed against the wall as she floated up the steps. Along the walls were the same pictures her mother had always hung—a painting of a lofty gum tree and an old shabby house, photos of Anna through the ages. There were ones where she was a baby, through to missing teeth and being covered in acne; to the most recent of Anna at her high school formal. She was standing next to her mother wearing a long blue dress with impressively puffy shoulders. Her hair was fixed firmly in large barrel curls and her makeup resembled the standard of a child beauty pageant. Anna cringed at the photo but smiled at the memory of that night. Her fingers traced over her mother's younger face and the sadness that had been lingering in her took its toll. Tears slid down her face as a mix of nostalgia, fear and anger swept through her. Calming herself, she reached the top of the stairs and switched on more lights. Her mother's room, the bed neatly made like she always had done; a characteristic that Anna was programmed to share. She looked into the spare room that her mother had filled with an old sewing machine, and a single bed for when Anna graced her with a visit. It was the bed she had slept in as a teenager, stickers that she'd collected from bubblegum wrappers and teen magazines stuck to its aged frame. From outside, the streetlights blared through the open blinds. Anna stepped through and closed them, shunning the world from their life. Lastly, Anna stood in the bathroom. She remembered that recent water damage had forced her mother's landlord to re-tile it. Looking at it now, Anna thought how its contemporary look clashed with the rest of her mother's home and décor — it was the nicest room in the house. Glimpsing her weary reflection in the vanity mirror, Anna frowned. The unexpected trip had left her feeling like she'd run a marathon, and it showed.

Anna stepped back down the stairs to get her bag out of the car. On opening the front door, she heard a shrill cry and looked down to find her mother's cat.

'Claude!' she exclaimed, horrified with herself for forgetting him. Her mother let him roam outside through the day, but he had always stayed inside at night.

Claude cried loudly, winding in and around her ankles desperately. Anna scooped him up and hugged him fiercely — he dug his claws in in response and leapt from her embrace towards the kitchen.

'Nice to see you too,' she muttered, remembering the history of his name as she dabbed at her scratched forearm, and brushed at the grey fur he'd left on her shirt. She searched through cupboards for food and, once found, he ate it like he'd been neglected for months.

'It's only been a day, you spoiled brat,' she scolded him, stroking his fur while he ate. He hissed at her and she took the hint to go to the car.

Once home, Justin was sure he'd aged ten years. He looked in the mirror to confirm, gingerly feeling his swollen eyebrow that was now touching on purple, as his phone buzzed in his pocket. Tom. He'd had two missed calls from him already and let this one go too. Justin had phoned that morning and gave a very short version of what had happened after he had left the bar. There was also a text from Adam informing Justin he was a prick for not turning up to the game. Justin looked at the clock and realised he was meant to have played a game of soccer an hour ago. Leading into finals, no-one was going to be happy with him. Justin sighed in resignation, ignoring the message, and the feeling he should call Tom. He contemplated showering again, but he knew that the stench that seemed to be following him was nothing but guilt, anger, and a whole lot of fear. He despised what was pulsing through his veins, hated he could do nothing to get it out; hated the thought of how it came to be there. The previous night had been going over and over in his head, and if he wasn't confused, he was suspicious.

He considered lying down but knew sleep would not be granted to him. What he really wanted was Julia. He wanted her to tell him it was going to be okay. He needed someone who wasn't going to judge him, but listen, help … work magic.

Justin reached for his keys before realising that he didn't have a car—even if he could drive. He felt bound, his freedom taken.

Julia lived too far away to walk so Justin wheeled out his bike, feeling like a child under the circumstances, and rode to her apartment. On arrival, and to his relief, Julia's car was in its usual spot.

Locking up the bike, he wiped sweat from his face and pressed hard on his temples, before climbing the single flight of stairs to Julia's door. Justin knocked twice and waited. Music and laughter echoed from inside and the noise sounded inappropriate in his head; fun couldn't apply to him right now. Julia opened the door holding her phone to her ear. The smile that was spread across her face sagged instantly. She excused herself from the conversation by telling them, with an air of repugnance, who was at the door.

'Hi.'

'Hi,' she returned stiffly, her body blocking the entrance.

'Can I come in?'

'Why?'

He took a sharp breath in. 'I need to talk. We need to talk,' he began. 'Listen Julia, I'm sorry about the whole Melbourne thing. It just happened. I was drunk. I'm unbelievably sorry and it will never happen again … I love you,' he pleaded.

Julia crossed her arms and sneered at his words.

'Julia, please? I've had the most awful night and I … I just want to be with you,' he begged, searching her face for sympathy.

'Yes, I heard,' she told him and seemed to revel in his confusion. 'Suzanne rang me,' she told him. 'You told Tom? He told 'The Boys'. They told their girlfriends. The girlfriends called me.'

Justin stared at her waiting for more. Waiting for her to tell him that she stopped the gossip. Waiting for her to tell him it would all be okay.

'You know Justin, I never took you for an idiot, but then again I hadn't taken you for a cheat either.' With her casually folded arms, all Justin could do was gape at her.

'Oh wait, I have something for you.' Julia retreated back inside the flat, leaving Justin lost at her front door, and returned with a plastic bag.

'These are yours,' she told him, shoving the bag towards him. He looked down at it stupidly and only accepted it when she began to jiggle it at him impatiently. 'Goodbye Justin.'

The door closed in his face and Justin stood feeling, not just ten years older, but also ten years old.

He didn't know what to do next. But after five minutes of standing at her door, he backed away.

Hanging the bag, which boldly advertised a woman's clothing store, around the handlebars, Justin climbed on his bike. He rode in a daze, his brain leaping from one bad thought only to land on another. He had no place to hide from them and no idea what to do.

chapter eighteen

Anna spent almost the entire week by her mother's side. The beep of the monitors had almost become pleasant. The nurses and doctors almost seemed like old friends. The seats were almost comfortable. Almost; but far from it.

Each day had been as long as a normal week, and each night spent in her mother's home seemed to take a lifetime to end. Lifetimes of looking up at the ceiling thinking the same thoughts over and over again. Each morning she'd dress from her limited choices and tread into the ICU to continue her vigil.

On the Monday, her second day in Sydney, Anna had called her boss and gingerly told him her mother's story. He was sympathetic and allowed her all the time she needed. When he asked the token question of 'Is there anything I can do?' she uncharacteristically accepted by asking him to tell Mel. She wasn't ready to talk to her just yet. She hadn't even felt brave enough to call Jane, who was only half an hour away. The truth being that, though Jane was so close geographically, Anna felt much further away and in a whole other realm.

When Anna had reached her mother's open curtains on that second day, someone else had already taken the seat beside her.

Anna froze mid-step. The male visitor was no-one that Anna recognised. She hesitated, not wanting to interrupt the stranger or make conversation, and walked to the nurse's station instead for an update on her mum's condition. The nurse, a different one to the day before, spoke softly.

'She's still stable, but hasn't gained consciousness yet. Her heart rate has increased though, so that's a really positive sign. Her lungs could be … better,' the nurse told her, smiling reassurance across the desk.

'What about her back?' Anna braved.

'You're best talking to the doctor. I can get them to speak to you when they are in.'

Anna nodded her thanks, not sure how thankful she actually felt, and walked back towards the bed. The man was now holding her mother's wilted hand. Anna felt protective, defensive and shy all at once. She cleared her throat lightly and the man turned to face her. His sad eyes seemed to recognise Anna, yet she remained none the wiser as to who he was.

'Hello,' he smiled uneasily. 'You must be Anna.'

He looked back at her mother and brushed her hand gently with his before leaving it by her side to stand up. Anna watched as he approached her and held out his hand.

'I'm Brian. Your mother has told me a lot about you.'

Anna looked from Brian's face to his hand and felt taken aback. She remembered his name from the nurse. It was a curiosity which she had chosen not to attend to until now. This man was her mother's emergency contact. This man was her mother's.

'Hi,' she managed as she weakly shook his hand, not able to create a smile. She had nothing else to say because her mother had told her nothing about him. She felt strangely deceived. A part of her brain told her to grow up, but the part that was simply her mother's daughter, felt protective. The part that was her father's child, felt defensive.

They both looked to her mother, lying motionless and oblivious to the awkwardness that hung in the air.

'Would you like the seat,' he offered, gesturing the spot he had occupied only moments before. 'I can find another.'

She shook her head, but when he left to retrieve an unused chair, she relented and sat down. Anna studied her mother, who looked the same as the day before. Battered, bruised and limp. It seemed Anna's sense of uselessness would unwittingly prevail for another day.

Brian returned, chair in hand, and sat on the opposite side of the bed. He frowned across at Anna after taking in the woman in front of him for another moment.

'They say she's stable,' he said.

'I know.'

'Oh. Right,' he looked back to her mother as if she could suggest another conversation point.

'I'm sorry,' she told him with embarrassment. 'But my mother never mentioned,' she waved her hand limply between the two of them, 'this'.

'Oh. Right,' he replied again, even more uncomfortably than the first time. He looked hurt and Anna felt a sudden sense of empathy for him. 'I was under the impression you knew,' Brian apologised, looking at her mother as if for an explanation. Anna mirrored him.

'How long have you been together?' she asked gently, wanting to assure him her mother would have had her reasons, whatever they may have been.

Without moving his eyes, Brian told Anna that he and her mother had been dating for nearly a year and that they'd recently made plans for her to move into his home.

A wave of guilt hit Anna—hard. For not knowing and for not having visited all year to have even found out. Her calls had been almost as rare, and emails didn't really allow for mother-daughter bonding. She made a vain attempt at justi-fying that her mother's contact had been minimal also; neither of them had encouraged the other to make more of an effort. Whether it was directly or indirectly intended, Anna didn't really know, but it did nothing to lessen the guilt that she now felt or the reality before her.

Anna sat looking at her mother. Her boyfriend, partner, or whatever she'd called him, was holding her hand, and Anna realised she didn't know her mother at all. She'd assumed for so many years that she knew her mother's life. She honestly had hoped she would move on from her father one day. But now that it had happened, without Anna knowing, she didn't know how she felt about it. Anna wondered what else she didn't know, and if her mother had been feeling the same.

Anna excused herself, claiming the need for some fresh air, and hastily left the room. Brian met her at the door upon her return and suggested they get a coffee. After a reluctant nod, they silently walked through the hospital. Anna felt nerves grow in her belly, she wondered if her mother would be okay with them talking to each other without her approval.

As if sensing her thoughts, Brian eventually spoke.

'I'm sure your mum would be happy if we got to know one another.'

Anna looked at him, not completely convinced, and he gave a small chuckle which Anna didn't quite understand.

Lining up in the hospital's café, Brian ordered a large coffee for himself before turning to Anna with raised eyebrows. Anna spoke to the woman behind the counter and asked for a hot chocolate.

'I'm not really a coffee drinker,' she explained, granting fleet-ing eye contact.

'Unlike your mother,' he smiled briefly before the bleak look of worry clouded his features once more.

They found a spare table near a buzzing Coke machine. Anna looked over at another table, faking interest in the other patrons as an excuse not to look at Brian.

'When did you arrive in Sydney?' Brian tried, fishing for a conversation starter.

'Yesterday. I was on the first plane out,' she told him with another small glance in his direction. It hardly seemed that Sunday was only the day before. Time could be so cruel, Anna thought. Why bad moments in life could seem to linger for so long and happy ones should flit by so quickly, she could never accept.

'How long will you be staying for?' he asked kindly.

'I-I don't really know. I haven't any plans, I guess. I'm waiting to know more. I want to talk to her,' Anna told him, gingerly feeling the scratch on her arm left by Claude the night before. She felt tears begin to prick her eyes and he handed her the serviette that was in front of him. Anna took it gratefully and dabbed her eyes whilst looking to the table, biting her lip in an attempt to distract herself from the fear that was threatening to show. When she did look up again, she noticed Brian's eyes were also red. They smiled helplessly at each other, and their drinks arrived to fill another silence.

'You look so much like her,' Brian commented, speaking softly. Anna nodded, she had heard this before. Her own reflection was a daily reminder that she should call her mother more often.

'Different eyes,' he added as an afterthought and she nodded again. She'd inherited her green eyes from her father.

'Do you live far?' Anna asked after a moment, learning he lived further north of Sydney, in Berowra, because he loved the trees. Between work and home, her mother and he must have been clocking up the kilometres to see each other. No wonder she was going to move in, thought Anna. Anna also learnt he had two children and was a grandfather. She wondered if they had met her mother but wasn't comfortable asking.

Feeling safe hugging the warm cup in her palms, Anna felt relieved there was someone to share her grief with. Together they spent the day by her mother's side, forming a friendship based on solidarity, and Anna left the hospital that night feeling brave enough to call Jane.

When her friend answered the call, Anna managed to get through most of the events of the last two days without too many pauses for composure. Jane, who had remained silent for the duration of the call, simply asked for the address, told Anna she was on her way, and within forty minutes of hanging up was at her mother's door. Anna cried like a child in Jane's arms and she would never have thought she'd be so glad that Jane had moved to Sydney.

By the Thursday that week, the weary Anna and Brian had good news. Her mother had woken through the night. She wasn't altogether sure of her surroundings, but she was conscious, and Anna felt delirious. When they stroked her hand, she reacted, and this was good news for everyone. Seeing Brian simply besotted by her mother's open eyes convinced Anna that her mother had been looked after during her absence.

By Friday, her mother was speaking.

It was almost too much happiness for them and when Brian arrived that day to Anna's news, they hugged each other willingly. Her mother looked on somewhat dazed but with a definite comprehension and relief as she dragged her breaths in by herself.

'This. Is. Anna,' she managed slowly, her voice raspy and dry—her lung having a lot to recover from. Her head, stabilized by a neck brace, couldn't move to see them clearly. Brian practically leapt to her side to kiss her cracked lips.

'Yes love,' he told her and smiled up at Anna. 'We've met.'

Friday afternoon came, and the good news brought bad news. Now she had woken, her mother had been scheduled for more tests. Terms like MRI and CT scan made Anna's heart quicken and she hoped the fear didn't show on her face. Results, she was told by the neurologist, could take days and they needed to compare them to her original tests from her admission the night of the accident. They had few answers for them but what the staff did know was that due to the extent of her mother's injuries, she could be in hospital for weeks. In that time, her internal organs would be monitored for fear of complications from the stress of the accident; her left lung a huge priority.

With every new bit of harm Anna learnt about her mother, she hated the person who caused it even more, which she had thought was impossible. Yet as she sat listening to the doctor, holding her mother's weak hand, her feelings were glowing red and punching through her veins. Her mother smiled at her reassuringly as the doctor spoke and Anna realised she had been squeezing her hand too tightly, and guiltily loosened her grip.

Knowing that her mother would be hospital-bound for weeks, needing support, treatment, and rehabilitation; Anna accepted that the time had come for her to make some bigger decisions. She spoke with her mother, whose weak protests to her leaving, told her she was making the right choice. She'd found Brian in the hallway and told him her plans as well. He tried to talk her out of it, but she knew her decision was for the best. She called Jane that night as she packed her few belongings and gave her mother's home a quick clean. She knew Jane would support her decision and she was thankful when she did. Anna was booked on the 6.35 plane from Sydney to Melbourne the next night.

Every part of her ached for Melbourne and she couldn't wait to put the last week behind her.

chapter nineteen

Justin sat at the communal desk. He had a small mountain of paperwork in front of him that he looked at with resentment. This wasn't his work. This was papers handed to him from the court after the morning's proceedings. The Unforgettable Moments montage still played in his head. The forms dictated his responsibilities now that he was found guilty. Part of him felt sick just staring at it. He'd felt sick all week. He couldn't shake the memory of the accident from his mind and he wanted to take a break, from paperwork—from everything. A knock at the door brought him a brief escape.

'Come in,' he called quietly.

Sandra, his receptionist, stepped through the door that was usually open to her, and looked at him with concern.

'Justin, how you holding up love?'

She'd worked there for almost ten years and she could remember when Justin, or Jay, as she liked to call him, first walked in the door. She smiled despite herself at the memory of saying to her friends at tennis that night, 'If only I were twenty years younger.' Of course, she'd said it to Justin too, and his bashfulness made him even more charming.

'Hi Sandra. I'm fine.' He sighed quietly and made a poor attempt at a smile.

'Honey, you don't look fine. What have you got there?'

'It's from the court. I need to return them.'

'Justin,' she began, not really knowing how to finish. 'I'm sorry it's all turned out this way. Is there anything I can do?'

'No. No, it's okay. Thanks though. You should be out of here.' He looked at the clock and his heart sank even further. Eight-forty-five. 'You should have been out of here over an hour ago.'

She smiled sympathetically at Justin, she really did feel for him, but she also had to get home to her own family. 'Okay hon. I'll see you Monday. Do you need a lift?'

'No, it's okay,' he lied. 'See you then.'

She walked back to the door and stalled. 'Justin,' she stopped to decide what was best to say. 'It'll be okay. I'm sure of it.'

He smiled a weak, yet grateful smile as she closed the door behind her. He looked at the forms again and felt that familiar sick feeling he'd had so much lately. He wasn't certain if this was the worst day he'd ever had, or the Saturday the week before. What he did know, was that he was going to be sick. And with that realisation he jumped to the sink.

Today, he thought bitterly as he spat vomit out of his mouth. At least a week ago he still had hope on his side.

The police had charged him with driving under the influence of substances and causing grievous bodily harm. They'd informed him that the case would be put before a magistrate within twenty-one days, in which case he would need to make a plea. By the Monday afternoon he'd had a court date for that Friday. He'd never known the government to be so efficient. Justin wasn't sure if he was glad it would be over so quickly, rather than delaying his fate. But it was irrelevant—Friday it was.

He had turned up in his only suit. When he'd taken it out of the wardrobe, he was reminded of the last time he had worn it. Having since been dry cleaned, it couldn't possibly still smell of the bar, the beach, or Anna. But Justin was doused with the memories of the night in Melbourne as he put it on.

He'd never had to go to court before and hated that he had to stand within its walls, alongside its sketchy characters. He wasn't the only DUI case presenting that day. Amongst many things, Justin was disturbed by how ordinary the offence was.

As he faced the magistrate, Justin felt the dark-haired man observing the raw cut over his eye, the bruising now yellow but just as obvious. Justin managed to ignore the look of contempt the magistrate gave him and focused on maintaining a level voice. He felt it falter a few times, but he made it through the hearing without looking like a complete idiot, hoping the sweat through his shirt wasn't too noticeable, or his trembling hands, as he stood at the microphone.

Justin had pleaded guilty to the offences laid against him, because his blood test results showed no other option. His solicitor had warned that the court may have no sympathy for Justin's belief that his drink had been tampered with. They had no evidence, and a deposition from Sandra stating his good character did nothing to prove his innocence. Not to say his lawyer didn't try and state Justin's version of the truth, but it was done without gain. When the magistrate eventually read his conviction, Justin felt rage and disappointment resonate within him. He had a hefty fine to pay, which exceeded his lawyer's expectations. The magistrate had also ordered Justin to attend a traffic offenders 'intervention' program. Seven weeks of learning why it was unsafe to drive under high-risk situations. Topping it off was a criminal record—dangerous driving, causing grievous bodily harm, and a good behaviour bond. There was one minor reprieve, due to his driving record the magistrate reduced his license suspension from the standard three years, to the manda-tory minimum of twelve months.

The magistrate had held the piece of paper with two over-sized hands. Justin tried to focus on the obscene amount of hair on them instead of the anger inside of him. He'd been asked if he had any questions, but all Justin could do was jerk his head. The magistrate — hairy handed, yet remarkably self-righteous — lowered the sheet and looked him square in the eye. He reminded Justin that in the circumstance of his case, if the health of the victim deteriorated his charges could be upgraded. Justin almost smirked at the term 'upgraded'. It made it sound like a bonus, as if he'd be getting extra fries with his fine. But he didn't smirk. His lawyer had already warned him about the conditions of his case, and Justin understood that if Bernadette O'Donnell was to die, or *deteriorate*, as the magistrate phrased it, he would be facing more than a seven-week program about road safety.

He thanked the magistrate with great force and left, while another man took his place in front of the bench. Justin heard him stutter over his own name and couldn't help but feel pity for him.

Leaving his suit hanging in the office, Justin filled his backpack and prepared to go home. He could have accepted the lift off Sandra, but he needed to walk off his frustrations. Apart from the court hearing, it was the people in his life that weighed on Justin's mind. He had been avoiding his friends and family as best he could; feeling too ashamed and angry to know what to say to them. He hadn't seen or heard from Julia since she had closed her door in his face — and it was she that spread the word on that fact. Tom had called several times to make sure he was okay and, when Justin didn't respond, followed through with frequent texts, which Justin appreciated, though still mostly ignored. Justin had not heard from Adam, but was fine with that, because Justin only had one theory which explained his positive blood test. The theory plagued his mind constantly, because it made too much sense. Justin had considered confronting Adam and asking if he had slipped him the ecstasy the night of the accident but didn't think he could handle hearing that he was right.

When it came to his family, Justin simply felt guilty. Amongst all their own problems and responsibilities, they wanted to support him, but Justin didn't want their time. His new niece wasn't behaving like the other babies had and it had become evident that it was a real concern. What he wanted was to be able to support *them*. But he just couldn't. He needed to be selfish. He needed to mope in his self-pity without feeling petty; because though he knew his family had their own problems, that didn't mean his went away. His were still there, regardless of the fact that it could be worse. The only way he knew how to do that was to keep his head down and do what he had to do to make each day pass. He had no capacity to deal with more than that. So, if he had to be selfish, he regrettably would, at least until the anger subsided.

His walk home broke into a run and he pulled his pack straps tighter to his back. He made promises as he ran—as if that would make him a better person. As if being a better person would make life better.

I'll be fitter
I'll be a better son
I'll be a better brother
I'll work harder
I'll read more
I'll sponsor a child in Africa
I'll drink less
I'll save more
I'll eat better

He'd run out of promises by the time he'd reached his front door.

He'd run out energy by the time he reached his bed.

But he hadn't run out of thoughts as his head reached his pillow. He lay on his back, his front, his side — images of the day, the week, the month, the year, flicking through his head. The thoughts he had, making him a stranger in his own bed. Hours passed before he finally fell asleep, granting him a few hours peace before the sun would wake him to his miserable self again.

chapter twenty

Anna wheeled her bag into the terminal and felt her face contort as she processed the length of the line snaking back and forth in front of her. Thanking technology, and her meagre luggage, she hurried towards a self-check-in kiosk; waiting her turn as another passenger squinted at her own flight details. She turned around to face Anna, who smiled hastily.

'Don't you just hate computers?' the woman sighed.

'Yes,' Anna lied supportively, women-in-arms style, offering to help.

'Where are you off to?' the woman cooed, watching as Anna finalised the check-in on her behalf.

'Melbourne,' she replied reluctantly, passing her the ticket which had effortlessly zipped out of the machine.

'Oh, thank you!' she gushed. 'Melbourne, that's lovely dear. That's where I'm off to!' And with that, the woman, intent on becoming Anna's friend, continued to stand by Anna as she typed in her own details. Anna, speechless by the lady's comfort in her personal space, nodded to the continual talk in hope the lady would respect her wish to be alone soon enough.

She didn't. But when the woman was held up at security by the forgotten nail file she'd had in her handbag, Anna gave a polite wave and took the opportunity to wheel her own bag quickly away to wander aimlessly around the airport, where her convenient carry-on bag became somewhat of a hindrance and her smugness fast deteriorated.

Wheeling in and out of shops, the clothes didn't warrant her attention and the music felt too lively. She glanced at magazine covers; the gossip of the stars splattered across the pages. But any interest in the glamour was nonexistent; her own life made all the needless reports more trivial than usual. Even the rows of chocolate didn't tempt her. Frowning, she wheeled her way to the departure gate. Boarding was not far away so she sat and watched the large crowd that had gathered, quickly accepting that the luxury spare seat she'd envisioned next to her was not going to happen.

As time dragged, Anna watched the businessmen read their papers or cram in another call. She saw the odd parent chasing their children or negotiate snacks. Other lone travellers like herself dotted the seats, but it was the couples she enjoyed watching the most. Some sat making no physical contact or exchange of words and Anna prayed she'd never be like them — she'd rather be single. One couple sitting close to her, sat with their arms entwined, the man's hand squeezing his wife's leg. Anna thought it was sweet, until she overheard the husband comment on his wife's thighs. Anna had to resist throwing her shoe at him. Then she spotted the two that sat talking quietly to each other, the woman giggling at what was said into her ear, the man soaking up every ray of her smile. It made Anna swoon. She wondered if she'd ever have that, and then she thought of Kyle.

She hadn't spoken to him since she ran out on their date. She had texted him the day before, but to no reply. In his defense, she had waited five days before contacting him. But maybe *he* was her guy. She sat, hand lazily on her bag, and dreamt of the possibilities that lay between her and Kyle. Anna was so lost in her thoughts that she failed to notice the couples stand. She was completely oblivious to the businessmen who rolled their bags away and didn't even realise that the noise of a shrieking child had faded. When an elderly woman struggled to walk past Anna's bag, Anna tuned back in to see that it was boarding time.

She exhaled sharply, leapt to her feet, and resigned herself to the back of the line — so far at the rear she was almost in the boarding line for the adjacent flight. Looking down at her bag, she felt a sense of panic stir inside of her. Once directed to her seat, Anna offered the stewardess a sweet smile, hoping that would make all the difference in getting home safe and finding room for her bag.

Shuffling down the aisle, the click of closing compartments made her steps quicken. When she came to her seat Anna saw that both seats either side of hers were already taken and fully occupied. On one side, by a woman whose arm had already claimed the armrest, her newspaper the airspace; on the other was a man holding a baby.

Anna opened the overhead compartment to see that it too was fully occupied, and her stomach tightened. After reaching up onto the very tips of her toes to close it, she breathed a sigh of relief when the next compartment had space. The remaining passengers trailed down the aisle towards her and Anna hastily heaved the bag up into place. The man sitting in the seat under her winced, clearly not trusting Anna's ability, which was fair, because the bag didn't fit. She stood in the aisle, holding up the line of people, pushing on her luggage with her fingertips and inwardly begging it to move. But it didn't, and Anna wanted to cry. Had it not been for the knight that offered her help, she would have. He easily flipped the bag around, slid it in place, and slammed the compartment shut. Anna gushed her thanks as he sat back down and she wedged her way politely to her seat, grateful for an hour to do nothing. But with one arm pinned so her elbow was pressed firmly into her liver and the other constantly retrieving a dropped dummy, teddy bear, or rusk with a carefree smile spread across her face—constantly assuring that it was no problem, it wasn't the restful trip she'd hoped for.

By the time the plane landed in Melbourne, she felt desperate to get off, but the woman next to her remained steadfast in her seat as the crowd unlinked their seatbelts and fought for belongings. Anna sat patiently and smiled her best unfazed smile, which she'd practiced for the entire journey. When eventually freed and she went to retrieve her bag, it was stuck. Sighing—instead of swearing like she absolutely wanted to—she struggled to free it when her knight appeared again.

'Thank you!' she rushed as he placed it on the ground at her feet. He shooed her thanks, and she wheeled her way off the plane and on to home.

Mel had refused to let her catch a bus home and Anna was now especially grateful. Pulling on her jacket, she stood outside in the pickup area with wobbly legs and slanting eyes. A car gave a toot in front of her and she looked up with annoyance to see that it was Mel. Her frown broke into a grin and she leapt for the car, pulling her bag behind her.

'Hi, hon,' Mel smiled encouragingly as Anna climbed in, assembling her bag onto the back seat. 'Good flight?'

'I don't want to talk about it,' she huffed as she clicked her seatbelt in place and went on to tell Mel the blow-by-blow of her entire trip home.

'So, glad to be back, I gather?'

'Like you wouldn't believe,' Anna admitted. 'It's not going to be for long enough though.'

Mel looked at her in confusion and the look reminded Anna that she hadn't yet shared her plans.

'I'm driving back to Sydney as soon as I can,' she explained warily.

'When? For how long?' Mel exclaimed. Anna felt too exhausted to be talking about it but didn't know any other way to update Mel.

'Um,' she stalled, bracing herself for Mel's response. 'Indefinitely.'

Mel didn't respond. Her mouth opened for a moment, and then closed. Her eyes stayed steadfast on the traffic in front of her and she beeped her horn loudly at a car that barely cut her off. Anna didn't think it was completely necessary, but figured it was as good as any verbal response from Mel.

'But,' she stammered. 'What about work?'

'I've spoken to John already. He'd spoken of transferring to Sydney recently and he was more than happy to find space for me up there.'

Mel's mouth opened and closed again like she was a Koi fish at feeding time.

'Mel, Mum's really bad.' Anna explained. 'She's conscious now, but she's badly hurt. There are so many risks associated with her injuries, and they don't even know how long she'll be in hospital for. I just have to be there. She's all I have,' she told Mel helplessly.

'But what about that guy you said she's seeing?' Mel threw in defensively.

'It's my mum Mel,' she reminded her gently. 'She may not even be able to walk'. Hearing the words come out of her own mouth, about her own mother, was a strong dose of reality.

Mel understood. Anna knew that she would, but she also knew that Mel didn't need to be losing another friend right now.

'Freaking Sydney,' Mel muttered and smiled at Anna. Anna, on the verge of sleep, smiled and settled into her seat. She'd just sunk into a hazy doze when she felt the car stop. Forcing one eyelid open, she saw her building, the white bricks grey in the night.

'Home,' Mel smiled across at her. 'Want me to come in?' Anna shook her head, too tired for company. 'Call me in the morning then.'

Anna climbed out feeling heavier than she had that morning. She yanked her bag out; sure her knight wouldn't be turning up again anytime soon, and waved Mel off. Climbing the stairs, lugging her bag awkwardly, she had a fleeting wish for stronger muscles, but replaced it in a nanosecond with a wish for a man with muscles, only to replace that wish to simply just be in bed asleep already, blissfully ignorant of having neither.

Arriving at her front door with dull triumph, Anna saw light around its rim and heard music from inside; louder, was the voice singing along. She knocked with determination to be heard, the impact on her knuckles making her frown.

'Leo!' she called, and a moment later a breathless Ioulia opened the door, jumped out, and hugged her before Anna could even say hello.

'Anna! You're home! How are you? How's your mum? How was the flight?' Ioulia felt like a boa constrictor as she wrapped her arms around Anna's ribs.

'Can I come in first?' she laughed between sharp breaths. Ioulia released her and stepped back, allowing Anna to enter. Anna noticed the flat already smelt of Ioulia's candles.

'Tell me everything,' Ioulia exclaimed gravely. 'Everything.' Anna's insides grimaced along with her face.

'Tomorrow then,' Ioulia smiled.

'Tomorrow,' Anna agreed. Maybe it wouldn't all seem so hard then. 'Did you move everything in okay?'

'Yup. All good. I am glad you're back though, even if it's only for a little while.' Anna had told Ioulia that she'd be living on her own for a while over a text conversation that morning.

'Yeah, me too.' Anna admitted. 'I'm going to bed.'

She swaggered off to her room, leaving her bag in the middle of the floor, and put her head to the pillow. 'I missed you,' she muttered into the familiar softness before falling asleep until noon the next day. Even the sun and its sneaky ways couldn't disrupt her.

Anna spent Sunday down at the beach making lists. Her feet braved the flat water, but it was far too cold to extend the invite to the rest of her body.

Ioulia joined her, claiming the need for fresh air, but Anna knew the walk would allow her to be the counsellor that Ioulia always was. Ioulia had a knack for asking the right questions in the right way. While Jane was known for her efficiency and Mel for being direct, Ioulia was famous for her ability to listen and be their mediator with the world.

Down on the gritty sand, Anna told Ioulia about the past week in detail. By the time Anna had reached the part in the story which brought them to where they were, she felt lighter. It didn't make it all okay or less scary, but it felt strangely manageable.

Once Ioulia was clear on Anna's agenda, they set to work. Originally Anna would have preferred to do this alone, but now she was grateful for the help.

'Okay, tell me what I've forgotten,' Anna told her. Kids played nearby and Anna was momentarily distracted by their carefree demeanor. They didn't care if sand stuck in their hair or if the water splashed their shorts. They weren't worried about feeling sticky or salty or frizzy, they just played. She felt a pang of jealousy before reading her list of things to do.

'Shoot,' replied Ioulia, leaning her elbows into the sand.

'Organise meeting with boss. Email clients. Put gym membership on hold. Pack. Pick up microwave—again, I'm so sorry I didn't do that before. How did you survive a week without a microwave?'

'Take-away. Mum's moussaka.' Ioulia shrugged and grinned. 'It was a great excuse.'

'What about the oven?' suggested Anna with a smirk and Ioulia looked at her aghast.

'Okay, where was I?' Anna scanned her list. 'Pick up microwave,' she muttered. 'Pay car insurance. Laundry. I think that's it for now.' Anna looked at Ioulia for confirmation.

'Are all your other bills sorted?'

'All online,' she explained unconcerned. 'You'll forward any mail?' Ioulia nodded at her task.

'I think that's it then. When do you think you'll head back?'

Anna looked at her list to calculate her answer. Assuming her boss could meet on Monday, Anna could be Sydney-bound again by Tuesday. She yearned to be there already; yet facing it all again by Tuesday felt so abrupt. She wanted her beach, her home and her friends. She knew she'd cope so much better if she had all those things nearby.

Together they stood to head back home, and Anna noticed a familiar-looking man jogging nearby. He stopped to stretch, and his blond spiky hair reminded her of someone.

'Kyle!'

Ioulia stopped at the exclamation and looked around.

'What? Who?'

'I forgot. I need to call Kyle. Let me write that down.' She fished the paper out of her pocket. She needed to apologise for running out on him.

'Who's Kyle?' Ioulia asked confused, looking from jogger to Anna. Anna filled her in, realising her earlier story hadn't started earlier enough. The man broke into a jog and came closer.

'We should take up running Leo.'

They admired him run past in a steady beat before walking back home, finding Mel on their step, phone to her ear.

'Where have you been?' she demanded, throwing the phone in her bag. 'I've been calling you for ages.'

'Oh, sorry. My phone's upstairs,' Anna apologised.

'Mine is—' Ioulia checked her pocket, 'flat. Sorry,' she scrunched her face in apology.

Mel looked huffily at them. 'Your hair cut looks good,' she told Ioulia grudgingly, defrosting. Reaching for Anna, she squeezed her arm. 'How you going, An?'

Ioulia played with her hair, basking in the compliment, while Anna felt bad for not even noticing.

'Yeah, it really does. Sorry.' She looked back at Mel. 'I'm okay. What are you doing?'

'Seeing if you were free. Thought we could get dinner. Hang out before you leave.'

Anna beamed at the offer and an hour later they wandered down the road towards St Kilda, searching for a place to eat.

'Sushi?'

'Nah. Pizza?'

'Oh! Gelato!'

'No!' dismissed Ioulia and Mel in unison.

They strolled some more and approached a pub they had frequented in their drinking hay-days; the beer garden tempting them towards it, their hangover memories repelling them away. People sat out front and in an unspoken agreement they headed to the entrance until Mel slowed.

'Oh, ah, there's someone over there I don't want to see. Quick, let's cross,' she said as she checked the road for cars.

'Who? Where?' asked Ioulia, searching the street for a face she knew and continued walking towards the pub.

Anna too had been searching for a familiar face, but unlike Ioulia, she found one. Ten feet away at the forefront of the beer garden, in prime position to see and be seen, sat Kyle.

She instantly smiled, and then stopped, remembering that she'd never told Mel about her date.

'It's that guy I had that horrible date with,' Mel muttered to Anna and discreetly pointed her head in his direction.

Anna wasn't sure what to do. She wanted to talk to him, but the spotting had happened too quickly for Anna to even register that Kyle wasn't alone — nor crowded.

He looked up just as Mel, Anna and Ioulia stood staring at him and his date, whose friendly hand was lingering high on his thigh.

They were all close enough to hear each other and Anna felt her face warm.

'Anna,' he nodded, before noticing Mel with surprise. 'Mel!'

His date looked at him and then back to the three girls gawking at them, her hand rising shamelessly higher on his leg.

Ioulia looked amongst them all, obviously confused.

'Hi Kyle,' Anna and Mel both staggered and then looked at each other. Anna's embarrassment turned to anger. She'd only been gone a week, and she had thought their date had gone well. Was she that forgettable?

Anna, glancing at the girl, could have sworn she remembered her face from the group at the pub the week before. Her anger went up another notch to fury. Kyle seemed to see her anger — granted it probably wasn't that mistakable — and became amused by it.

'How's your *mother*?' he asked, sarcasm clear in his voice as he ignored Mel altogether. His date snickered and Anna looked on in shock. Mel appeared even more confused. Ioulia looked like she was ready to deck the first person in her life.

'In hospital,' Anna informed him through her clenched teeth. He looked momentarily taken aback, then — the guy who only the day before she'd dreamily thought could be her *one*—shrugged, turned back to his date, and gave Ioulia a slight wink in the space between.

'Prick,' muttered Ioulia, and pulled two flabbergasted girls away. Neither spoke until Ioulia led them both into a nearby Mexican restaurant. She organised a table and they sat down in silence, even ignoring the waitress when she welcomed them with a loud 'Hola'. It was Mel who eventually spoke.

'What was that?' she demanded from Anna.

'Um, well, it's a funny story actually,' Anna tried, but Mel shook her head confused, showing it was no time for vagueness. 'I put the wrong name down,' Anna began, and then rushed out the rest of the story that had brought her and Kyle on a date together (she left out the part where she'd fantasised about falling in love with him).

'Huh,' Mel huffed. '*Not* so funny.'

'You didn't even like him,' Anna implored desperately. Ioulia watched on like she was at the tennis, her head flipping from face to face, trying to work the parts of the story out that she didn't already know.

'So,' Mel sulked stubbornly.

'So, does it really matter?' Ioulia asked, and Mel threw her a firm look.

'I just feel like you lied to me,' she said gruffly. Anna, feeling incredibly sensitive, was trying very hard not to cry, and bit her lip.

'I'm sorry. I wasn't. I was going to stand him up. That was the plan. But I felt so *single* that day, and I went. We actually got on great,' she admitted the irony, throwing her hands up. She explained how the date ended, and their nonexistent contact in the last week.

'What a prick!' Mel cried, now forgiving Anna, but disliking Kyle even more. 'I want to go back and give him a piece of my mind!'

Anna shooed her away. 'Leave it. Really, it's for the best, isn't it? I really am a terrible judge of character.' The others nodded solemnly, and Anna's self-confidence took another plunge.

'Who wants a drink?' shouted Ioulia, bringing Anna back to St Kilda. She smiled weakly, pushing bad thoughts to the bottom of her brain.

'Me.'

'Me too!' agreed Mel. All was forgiven. However, the realisation that Anna was back to Square One on the single status floated back to her. She forced it away with a sequence of margaritas which they'd all regret early Monday morning when they had to get up and face the world again.

The meeting with her manager went quickly and easily. The fact that Anna had been with the company for so long and was one of their key technicians—something she was only new to finding out—meant that they were incredibly flexible with her options. The company had already organised a temp to replace her while she worked in Sydney, simply requesting that after twelve months they look at alternative or more permanent arrangements. Anna almost cried with gratitude and assured them that she hoped to be back much, much sooner than that.

John, who managed the Sydney office, had already lined Anna up with a position as a senior IT technician. She had already been accommodated into their shifts and projects and Anna couldn't have been more appreciative. She already knew a handful of people in her new office whom she'd met over the years, and John informed her they were excited about her arrival. The simplicity of it all gave her the break she needed and the relief it brought was welcome.

Anna headed to her desk. The office was low-staffed that day and the corridors were quiet; even Mel was working offsite. She craved happy sounds to pierce through her emotions but made do with the consistent rhythm of typing from a neighbouring desk.

Finding an empty box, she began to clear her desk of personal items. She didn't know how long she would be gone and was sure her replacement would appreciate not having her things around. Then, with a strangely vacant workspace, Anna checked her emails and crossed tasks off the list that she and Ioulia had made the day before. As she ran out of reasons to be at work, and regardless of the fact that the move was temporary, the lingering sadness which had been building in Anna intensified.

Everything had happened so quickly that most people didn't even know about her transfer. She wouldn't get the chance to say goodbye the way she wanted to. No party, no card. No hugs, no speech. Just an empty desk and heavy heart. Illogically, it felt like people didn't care. She thought back to when other staff had left and wondered if she'd lavished them with best wishes, or if she gave a fleeting goodbye in a rushed afternoon. Goodbyes take on a whole new meaning when it's your goodbye, she realised forlornly.

When Anna finally allowed herself to leave, she tread past Mel's neat desk. Pens lay horizontally, paper filed accordingly, and framed photos were perfectly lined. Anna smiled. She continued to walk towards the exit. Passing another colleague, she waved goodbye.

'Hope everything will be okay, Anna?' Bill Lobasco, their oldest and most experienced technician, called.

'Thanks, Bill. Me too.' She gave him a quick hug. 'Take care.'

She held her smile as she walked into the reception area. Anna was determined to say goodbye to the administration girls properly and leave on good terms. She was concerned that if she had annoyed the receptionists, they could make her life hell across all the offices — these women talked daily, and Anna wanted a good reputation. However, when she reached the front desk it was empty, and Anna cursed them. She was considering writing a note when she noticed the binder sitting nearby. Pausing for a moment, she dropped her bag and went back to Bill's desk.

'Could you give me a hand with something, Bill?'

chapter twenty-one

Mel turned up to work Tuesday morning, brazenly strutting down the hallway feeling quite content. She'd spent almost the whole night on the phone, sharing a conversation that made her feel like life had a lot more colour to it. Flicking her long hair, she reached her desk, stopped suddenly, and almost tripped over the heels that she had decided to wear that day in respect of her great mood.

Now frowning, Mel reached for the yellow post-it note stuck to the big black binder balancing on her chair.

'Morning Mel, Mind if I leave this here? A.' She read the words under her breath. 'Bitch,' she muttered and laughed, before heading back to reception to find some helping hands to clear her seat.

It was a sunny day and Anna thought the fields looked rather lovely and endearing as she drove by. Tiny canola flowers bloomed for spring, the long grass swayed in the paddocks that she passed on the empty stretch of road, and it seemed to all happen in tune with the Coldplay album blaring from the speakers.

She heard her mobile phone beep over the guitar riff and glanced at the screen.

U r a child. Enjoy the drive.

Anna chuckled at Mel's message, having completely forgotten her prank. It made her feel good for another ten minutes or so, before her thoughts darkened against the blue sky yet again. The last four hours of her drive had been that way, and since she was alone for the journey, she did her best to embrace her feelings. Ioulia had encouraged her to, and Anna agreed to try. She refused to burn the incense Ioulia had given her, and seeing as she had barely suggested reiki, Anna felt obliged to at least do part of what her friend had urged of her.

In some ways the drive felt therapeutic, in others, her own company was simply irritating. Her eyes had misted over many times and not always about her mother. At times she thought she needed her window wipers inside her sunglasses rather than outside her windscreen, because almost anything was making her teary. A love song would make her feel so desperate and lonely that she'd weep. A huge bug hitting her windscreen sent her reeling with worry that its family would never see it again. Elton's *Tiny Dancer* came on and she had to pull over. When she drove through a McDonalds and they informed her that there were no more hash browns—she was nothing short of devastated. It all seemed to accumulate and break her down. She didn't see how it could possibly be a good thing, but Ioulia would assure her it was, so she tried to let it be.

Justin was eating lunch when Sandra called out his name.

'Lesley's on the phone, Jay.'

He took the call in their office, continuing to chew his salad sandwich.

'Hi, what's happening?' he smiled, pushing the bread to the side of his mouth. Another week had passed since his court hearing and he had forced himself to function again. Bitterness aside, he did have a life to live, and there were other things he needed to be together for, family being one of them — lack of money another. He really had to think of a way to save more.

'Hi. I was just out shopping,' his sister drew out. 'You?'

'Well, you called me at work, so …'

'Right. Of course,' she muttered, sounding distracted.

'What's happened?' he asked, hearing the trepidation in her voice and her son, Joshua, give a short cry in the background. Justin stopped chewing, fearing the worst. A hundred bad scenarios flickered through his mind.

'Um, nothing actually. I'll call you later,' she decided — about to say goodbye.

'No. Wait. Tell me. What is it?' he encouraged her. His curiosity would have scratched at his brain all afternoon.

'Um,' she stammered again. 'I just saw Julia.'

'Right,' he tried to sound nonplussed, the simple mention of her name brought a sense of frustration and sentimental longing.

'And … I just saw Adam.'

'Ri-ght.' He realised that hearing either name made him nauseous.

'Um … they were both at the shops.'

'Stranger things have happened Lesley.' Justin tried to swallow his bite to fit in another.

'Ah, sure.' She rushed, sounding distracted herself. 'They were in the food court actually.'

'O-kay,' he said slowly trying to encourage her to get to her point, distracted by the tomato that had slipped out of his sandwich and splattered on the plate like a scene from *Cliff Hanger*.

'Did you know?' she asked meekly. There was a lot of noise around him and Justin was finding it hard to concentrate as he tried to reassemble his sandwich.

'Well, now that you've told me, I do. Why would I know that?' He picked up his lunch again and chewed off another large bite. He was curious but didn't want to admit it. He wanted to know if she looked miserable. It irritated him that he didn't know how to ask without sounding conceited. Furthermore, Adam was just a prick. Or a potential one, he conceded.

'Justin!' she said exasperated just as Sandra called out the same.

'Oh hey, listen, can I call you back? I think they need me out there.' He muffled with a full mouth and hung up on his sister. Wiping his hands on his pants, he went back into the clinic with the full intention of calling Lesley back later.

By midday, Anna was well and truly over the long drive to Sydney. Her mind was firmly mulling over one topic when a call from Mel came through. Anna grinned broadly.

'Hi Mel!' Anna yelped, thrilled by the distraction.

'Just calling to see how you are?' Mel laughed at Anna's keenness. 'Where are you now?'

'Oh, I'm just *peachy*. I'm at Gundagai. A few more hours to go yet.'

'You sound tired,' Mel said sympathetically.

'That's probably because I am!' Anna laughed. 'How's your day been?'

Mel groaned. 'You mean apart from a certain binder being left on my chair?' Anna could hear the smile in Mel's voice but also heard when it went away. 'I forgot to put deodorant on this morning and I had a client be awful to me.'

'Are these two things related?'

'No. Two separate whines.' Anna heard the mouthpiece muffle before Mel spoke again. 'An, sorry, I've got to go. I'll call you later.'

Anna hung up the phone feeling positive and her thoughts turned back to the catalyst of her previous contemplations. Brian Hill.

The man seemed nice. Caring, concerned, supportive—had neat hair. But Anna felt confused by the fact that her mother had never brought him up in conversation. She wondered if this man would become her stepdad, and if this would be weird at the age of twenty-nine. Then a whole other situation dawned on Anna; getting siblings at twenty-nine. Could she be getting the family she had craved as a child? The idea brought a whole new perspective to her drive, and it occupied her all the way to Sydney.

Her mother looked more like her mum on Anna's arrival. The swelling in her face had almost completely gone and with the stitches removed, leaving only a red scar, she looked less unnerving; as did her hospital room. She was stable enough to be transferred out of the eerie ICU and into a standard ward, complete with three other patients.

'Hi Mum,' Anna said softly as she reached her side. She squeezed her thin hand and her mother returned it with a much gentler squeeze.

'You're back,' she smiled slowly. Anna nodded and spoke of her drive up and everyone that had passed on their best wishes. The space was decorated with cards and flowers, and Anna felt relief that more people had spent time with her mum while she had been away. Her mother gave her a stilted version of what the doctors had said and once she drifted off to sleep Anna received a more in-depth account from the hospital staff. The good news was that the swelling on her spine had reduced and the doctors could now determine that her vertebrae were bruised but not fractured. On hearing this news, Anna felt her first real breath in days. Now that her spine was deemed safe, the doctor wanted to operate on her mother's severely fractured leg. Pins would be surgically placed in her bone and her leg placed in traction. Hearing the procedure made Anna want to pass out and she had to ask for a seat before the doctor could finish explaining.

They couldn't tell how long her leg would be immobilised for, only that 'time would tell'. An expression Anna was loathing. But they were sure that her mother would recover well, though slowly.

While her mother slept heavily, Anna also learnt that the police had been to question her. It gave Anna a familiar chill of resentment that the police were involved. She'd wanted to know what they'd asked and, while Brian was not there, Anna had also wanted to ask her mother about him, but she had to accept it was for another day.

As she left the hospital, she tried calling her dad, feeling like he should know what had happened to his once-wife. After the number rung out, and frustrated by the lack of communication, Anna left the news in a voice message and made the final leg of her day's journey to her mother's home.

chapter twenty-two

Anna had another few days off before her roster began at the Sydney office. She wished she didn't need to fit work around her days, but she just wasn't in that position. Grateful for the time she did have, Anna spent it organising her mother's affairs: rent, leave from work, insurance for her totalled car.

On the Friday night, Jane came by to see how she was getting along.

'How's the house hunting going?' Anna asked, wanting some normal, less intense conversation. Jane's face crumpled—to her that *was* an intense conversation.

'It. Is. Awful. Everything is too small, too old, too expensive, too … wrong. I hate it. One place was okay. And the girl seemed perfectly nice …' she trailed off. Having now thrown herself on the lounge, Jane was busy fishing out the remote controls that had become lost under her.

'But?'

'*But* it had an ugly old brown kitchen. Can I live with a brown kitchen?' Jane propped herself up on her elbow and looked at Anna expectantly for advice. Anna pointed to the aged brown cupboards of her mother's kitchen.

'*I'm* living with an ugly old brown kitchen!' she laughed. 'It's not desirable, but perfectly do-able, especially if it's at a good price,' Anna reasoned.

'Yeah, yeah,' Jane shrugged and fell back to the lounge. 'Hey, I'm heading out again to look this weekend. Do you want to come with me? I could do with your opinion, and it may be good to get out of the hospital for a bit,' she suggested cautiously.

Jane had met Anna at the hospital the day before to visit her mother, who had been overwhelmed by the gesture. But on leaving Jane had asked Anna how she was coping being in the building, let alone the room — knowing her tolerance for blood and needles. But Anna didn't feel she really had the choice, or right, to complain. After all, at the end of the day she could leave, and pee without a tube. Her mother, branded to the bed, heavily medicated to manage the pain after her leg operation, and at risk of complications and infection, had to remain within the confinements of the sterile hospital. Anna wasn't going to complain about her own visits but agreed that doing something different would feel good.

Late Sunday morning, Jane picked Anna up sporting a whole new outfit.

'What's this?' Anna grinned, as Jane justified her purchases as a job requirement. Anna 'oohed' and 'awed', but her enthusiasm was a performance for Jane's benefit only. Anna was starting work the next day and the nerves of the impending morning, as well as the guilt of not being at the hospital, were making her anxious. Meanwhile, Jane (who had been at work all of four weeks) had been on school holidays for the last week and was feeling sufficiently relaxed — Anna didn't care how Jane defended the holidays, it was unfair.

'Okay, so there are only four places to look at?' Anna confirmed. If there were only four, she could still get to the hospital at a reasonable time.

'Maybe five … plus lunch,' Jane added. But since Jane ate like a bird, and Anna had lost her appetite, she figured lunch wouldn't take long and she'd get back to her mother before dark.

After seeing three terrible properties, they turned into the street for Jane's fourth next possible address. Right away, Anna could sense it was a good neighbourhood. Quiet, but not too far from anything Jane would need. There was a large green park at the far end of the street and leafy jacaranda branches hung over much of the road, creating a canopy of leaves. Anna could imagine their purple flowers sprouting in an already beautiful scene.

Jane pulled up near the house, parking two driveways down so they could inspect it casually. Shielding their faces from the hot afternoon sun, they took in the home and smiled widely at each other. It was definitely the best place they had seen so far—cheap, stylish and, almost as important, close to good shopping.

Before them stood a cladded grey house with white trims and wide steps leading up to a decked front porch. Three large windows filled the front of the home and the garden was neatly kept. A small hedge grew along the paved walkway and Anna saw a wooden birdhouse hanging from the blossom tree that had begun to litter the ground in white petals. She smiled. It was exactly the sort of place she'd love to own one day, and she felt a little bout of envy grow inside her. Forget Jane, she thought, I want to live here.

'Come on,' Jane said nervously. 'Let's see if it's this good on the inside.' She smiled hopefully and stepped through the gate and up the path to knock on the charcoal grey door.

Anna followed and together they waited. They could just manage to hear laughter from the back. Jane knocked again and they heard the laughter die down, followed by heavy footsteps.

'Coming!' a voice called. 'Sorry … I didn't hear you,' they continued, unlocking the door as they spoke, their body distorted through the glass panel. When the door opened, Anna and Jane were greeted with a wide smile, before its owner's face fell.

'Jason.'

'Justin!'

Jane and Anna spoke simultaneously. One voice horrified, one pleasantly surprised.

'Justin?'

'Jason?'

They spoke in unison again. Turning this time, and questioning each other in confusion, now much quieter.

'*Justin* Justin?'

'*Hero* Jason?'

Meanwhile Justin, holding the door open, stood frozen. When the women turned back to him, he spoke, stunned.

'Hi.'

'Hello,' Anna replied through gritted teeth.

'Um, hi,' Jane said hesitantly. 'We were here about the room … I thought your name was Jason? Your text just said 'J'…' she trailed off while looking from Anna to Justin, utterly confused. Anna watched Justin as his face and neck began to redden. She felt both angry and embarrassed at the sight of him. He went to say something, when a yelp from the backyard made him turn.

'He's out! He's out!' they heard a young girl shriek with delight. Suddenly, something resembling a big wet mop came scattering down the hallway and shot out the front door between Anna and Jane.

'Oh, crap. Sorry!' Justin called, as he bolted barefoot out the front door after it. Anna and Jane turned to watch. Only Jane was amused.

Justin called out to what they now saw was a dog, to sit. When it finally obeyed, he scooped it up and held it like a baby. The furry face looked quite pleased with the escape, and as if to confirm it, the panting tongue looked like a big fat grin. Carrying him back up the path Justin muttered to the dog, explaining what it had done wrong. Anna heard Jane laugh quietly and shot her a warning look.

A little girl came sloshing down the hall, followed by another, and ran straight past Anna and Jane and down the steps. They stopped at Justin's side, their clothes dripping puddles on the ground. Giggling, they tried to pat the mop of a dog with a scruffy-looking beard.

'Uncle Jay! Uncle Jay! Do it again,' they cried. 'That was so funny.'

They bounced around him with excitement, their blonde hair flying around them — their size making Justin look giant-like. A fit giant, Anna thought, as she tried not to stare at Justin's arms, which were flexed from holding the weight of the dog. She heard Jane mutter, 'Jay. Not Jason,' and smiled apologetically at Anna. 'Small world, huh?'

'Not now, Olivia. We have company,' Justin said softly, and with his hands full, pointed towards the two women on his doorstep with a nod of his head. The two little girls looked up at the two bigger girls and grinned, noticing them for the first time. Their uncle looked at them too, considerably puzzled.

'Come on, let's take Hamlet back,' he spoke to the girls and then looked back up at Anna and Jane. 'You're more than welcome to come in and see the place if you're still interested.'

'Yes, of course!' Jane said instantly, as Anna gave her another look, which Justin caught.

Anna watched as the girls ran inside and as Justin waddled down the hall with Hamlet trying to lick his face, as if to apologise for running away. She grudgingly acknowledged how gentle he was with his nieces and wondered how a jerk who didn't call, and who'd kiss someone else when they already had a girlfriend, could seem so nice at the same time. She felt like an idiot and wanted to get in the car and go. Jane did not pick up on this vibe and followed the crowd down the hallway and into the cool house before Anna could insist that they leave. Anna could feel her heart beating faster and noticed her hands were undeniably trembling. She wasn't liking the effect he had on her.

As they approached the back of the house Anna could see that the cottage charm of its exterior was modernised on the interior. With the exception of a trail of wet paw and footprints, the wooden floor was shiny and smooth, with lines that ran perfectly down the hall. Hanging on one otherwise bare wall were three matching timbered frames. They housed a bright child's painting of a dog, an old black and white photo of three kids hugging, and an older wedding photo hung in the final frame. Anna slowed to look more closely at the final photo and thought without a doubt that it was Justin's parents and grandparents. The groom had Justin's tall build and dark hair, and the bride, boasting a beehive up-do, shared his smile. Not that Justin was smiling now, observed Anna. Good, make him squirm, she thought with conviction.

They passed the lounge room and Justin apologised for it being in the process of being renovated. A sheet was half draped over a grey lounge, and paint tins decorated the floor space. At the very back of the house, where Justin had led them, was the kitchen. It was a bright new kitchen, with nothing cottage-like about its spotless white cupboards. Stainless steel appliances were fitted into place with a white stone benchtop gleaming up at them. Adjacent was a dining area with a large round table and a low hanging light.

While Justin was putting his dog outside, Jane briefly traced her finger along the kitchen's smooth bench and turned to face Anna. 'I love it,' she whispered, almost pleading.

Anna folded her arms across her chest and huffed, but before she could voice her opinion, Jane spotted the air-conditioner wall control, and held her heart—making Anna's case even tougher. As she went to try, Jane moved away to look out at the yard. Anna, not wanting to be overheard through the open back door, managed to keep her mouth shut.

They could see Justin placing Hamlet into a kiddy pool that the two little girls were splashing about in. He was wearing board shorts and t-shirt and Anna's mind was having trouble deciding whether he looked better in the suit. She stopped herself immediately once she realised her internal debate.

Outside, but too quiet for her to hear perfectly, she could see Justin speak to the girls carefully. She watched as Justin stepped out of the pool and instructed the dog to stay. He then muttered something to himself, making the two little girls gasp.

Anna, amused by their cuteness, watched as they covered their mouths giggling.

'Um ah! You said the *F* word,' the eldest cried up at him. Saying 'F' in a hushed voice, like she too was swearing just by uttering the offensive letter.

'No, I didn't.'

'Yes you did! Yes you did!' she disagreed loudly and, with her little sister mimicking, started chanting, 'Uncle Jay swore, Uncle Jay's in trouble.'

Justin's face almost gave way to a smile, but he composed it, and Anna strained her ears to hear him warn that if they told their mum they wouldn't be allowed to come over and play anymore. With the look of desolation on their faces, Justin could have just told them that Santa Claus was a hoax. Anna looked over at Jane, also eavesdropping, and saw her trying not to laugh by averting her eyes from the scene and covering her mouth. Anna suppressed her own giggle just as Justin approached.

He closed the screen door on his nieces, who were now close to silent as they played, and turned to face the women in his house. Anna noticed a red scar that split his eyebrow that she knew wasn't there before. He looked slimmer than she remembered and his eyes, shining almost yellow in the afternoon light, appeared more serious than they had in Melbourne.

'Sorry about that,' Justin offered shyly. 'I promise it's not normally this hectic.'

His shirt was wet in patches and the fabric half clung to his body, revealing his shape. It wasn't helping Anna to be angry at him.

'Do the girls live here?' Jane interrupted Anna's thoughts, showing obvious concern the pair came with the lease agreement. Working with them was one thing, but living with someone else's kids was a whole other conversation; no matter how nice the house was.

'Oh! No!' Justin exclaimed, seeing how it must look to a prospective tenant. 'I'm just baby-sitting. Doesn't normally happen, but their mum—my sister—had her hands full,' he explained hastily. He'd looked at Anna as if to make sure she knew the kids were not his. Anna, who hadn't even considered the possibility, was simply thinking about how good he was with the girls and how sweet it was to help his sister. She was surprised if he didn't do it often. Then, realising she was giving Justin credit for something, she cursed him for being an unhelpful brother the rest of the time.

Jerk.

She looked over at Jane for justification, but the doe-eyed Jane had an uncharacteristically dopey grin on her face and was only looking at Justin. Baffled by her friend's antics, Anna wanted to cry out, 'This is *Justin*. Lying, cheating, Justin!'

'That's really nice,' Jane cooed, and Anna rolled her eyes at her naivety.

'Um, no. Just doing what anyone would, I guess. Oh, but Hamlet—my dog—he lives here. Is that a problem?' he asked as an afterthought.

'No, I like dogs.' Jane assured him. 'Hamlet? Are you a Shakespeare fan?'

Anna rolled her eyes again, and before Justin could reply she sighed at Jane and spoke, forgetting she'd made a promise to herself not to speak. 'The beard,' she said bluntly, remembering the conversation she'd had with Justin at the hospital all those weeks ago. Justin looked at Anna, confused by her tone, then turned back to Jane and nodded that Anna was right.

'Oh yeah. Cool name.'

'Um, did you want to see the rest of the house?' he offered awkwardly. Anna sensed that he too was keen to end the meeting. After all, if he couldn't handle a phone call, she imagined that her presence in his home couldn't be that desirable either.

'No,' Anna muttered.

Jane gave her a sharp look and replied pointedly to Justin, while eyeing Anna. 'Yes, thanks.'

Jane continued to ignore Anna as Justin gave them the tour. He glanced at Anna and attempted to give her a smile, but she would have none of it. He continued on, showing Jane the room for rent, which was bare but for the neatly made double bed. It was a reasonable size, with an even more reasonably sized wardrobe. The large window looked out into the yard and onto a fruit-filled orange tree. The ceiling was high like in the rest of the house, and on the picture rail hung a large mirror. It was elegant and light … just Jane's style.

Anna frowned. This would only make it harder to convince Jane that she couldn't live there.

Justin showed them the bathroom next; it too was renovated beautifully and had a large, modern, freestanding bath that Anna could almost feel herself sinking into with a glass of wine in hand. She gave a silent sigh and avoided Jane's excited eyes.

Moving on, he opened the door to another spare room, promising he could make more space if needed. Anna noted a wetsuit and two sports bags amongst a stack of wire cages. It took her an enormous amount of self-control not to ask what they were for and she silently commended herself on her success.

Justin walked on to show the lounge room properly, casually acknowledging his own bedroom as he passed it. The door was ajar more than enough for Anna to get a preview inside the room of a guy who doesn't call. With its white shutters open, the large front window made it a bright room. The grey cover on his bed looked hastily thrown over and complimented the various shades of sample paint that had been rolled on the wall. She glimpsed a stack of books on his nightstand, a bold lamp and a laundry basket full of clothes on the floor. Overall, Anna admitted that the guy had style. Though, remembering that she didn't like him one bit, Anna convinced herself that he probably hadn't changed his sheets in months.

'So, that's it,' Justin smiled at them as they found themselves back in the kitchen. He kept looking Anna's way and she fought to keep a passive expression.

'It's great,' Jane enthused.

Anna kept her eyes fixed on the back doors, watching the girls. They really were very cute. She felt Justin's eyes on her and, embarrassed about him knowing her want for children, she hastily looked back at Jane. Anna didn't want him to see her vulnerabilities. He didn't have the right to know her any more than he already did.

She was trying to send a telepathic message to Jane, 'must leave now'. But before Jane received it, there was a knock at the front door which startled them all. When Justin excused himself, Anna took the brief opportunity to give Jane a pleading look, but Jane wasn't paying her any attention.

'Sorry I'm late,' they heard, as footsteps headed down the hall towards them. 'I didn't mean to—' the tall woman with dark hair stopped when she realised Justin had company. 'Oh, sorry!' she exclaimed, looking at Justin for an introduction.

'Potential tenant,' he explained, and understanding showed on her face. 'Jo, this is Jane,' he said, extending his arm to her. 'And this is Anna.'

Jo greeted them both warmly and Anna saw the exhaustion in her eyes.

'Jay is my little brother,' she explained with exasperation at Justin. Jo then crumpled her brow in thought. 'Sorry, do I know you already?'

There was an obvious awkward pause in the room, and Jo looked on with curious interest, her eyes twinkling the same way Anna remembered Justin's being capable of.

'Um, yeah,' Justin said, trying to sound laidback. 'We all met in Melbourne actually. I may have mentioned them.'

'But this here—' he pointed between them all quickly, 'is sheer coincidence.' Anna saw Justin's face redden again as he looked anxiously at his sister.

'Oh,' Jo nodded, realisation growing on her features as she visibly remembered something of significance. Justin looked as if *he* was trying to send a telepathic message of his own and Anna wished she could intercept it and know what it was. Jo smirked at Justin, then turned to Anna. 'It's nice to meet you face-to-face then,' she said happily. Justin's head dropped and Anna thought she saw him flinch.

'The girls are out the back.' Justin pointed out his nieces suggestively, quite obviously trying to get Jo out of the equation by subtracting her from the room.

'Okay,' Jo smirked again, putting her bag down on the table. 'I'll go get them. Are you all nearly finished up here?' she said pointing to all three of them with a swirl of her finger. When Justin nodded, Anna fought the urge to hug Jo with gratitude for giving them the opening they needed to leave.

Jo stepped outside, leaving the three remaining in the room to say an awkward goodbye. When Jane said she'd call Justin, Anna added that Jane had more places to see first and ignored the look that both Jane and Justin gave her. After he had closed the door on them, and they had safely reached the letterbox, Jane looked across at Anna, mortified.

'What has got into you?' she demanded. 'You were so rude.'

'I'm rude?' she exclaimed, thumping her finger to her chest. 'He's the one who didn't call! He's the one who cheats on his girlfriend!' It was an open and shut case.

'He seemed pretty nice Anna. Let's not forget he was the one who swooped me off the floor and looked after me, while *others* freaked out, rendering themselves useless. You didn't have to act like that.' Jane shook her head and Anna thought she was overreacting. She hadn't been *that* bad.

'It's an act,' Anna explained slowly, like Jane was in fact very stupid. 'He's a jerk.'

'Ri-ght,' Jane agreed slowly, and Anna felt momentarily relieved. 'Anna, did you ever consider that he had a good reason not to call you? Like the fact that he has a girlfriend?'

Anna's body tensed again. 'I thought you were on my side. You're meant to be on my side,' she huffed, as she climbed into the car and took a final look at the house. It really was a lovely house. She thought about her rented flat back in Melbourne, the one with no air conditioning and a tiny kitchen — he never said he had a lovely house.

'All I'm saying is that you think he's a jerk because he didn't call, right?' she watched Anna for confirmation and Anna nodded.

'And because he cheated on his girlfriend,' Anna added, almost triumphantly.

'Okay,' chewed Jane. 'So, did he even say he was going to call?'

'Maybe. I don't know. No … he kissed me!' Anna said, stung, fuming at Jane's insubstantial point.

'You kissed him first,' Jane reminded her, but raised her hands to pause Anna, who was about to retaliate. 'Okay, okay. He kissed you. But say that he did call you, and he has a girlfriend, what would that make him?' Anna sat quiet. 'A jerk, right?' Jane answered for her, as Anna gave a small stubborn nod.

'Anna, either way you'd think bad of him. I'm sorry to say it, but he probably thought he was doing the right thing.'

Anna said nothing for a moment, busy scanning her brain for a response. 'He still could have called,' she sulked, not wanting to lose and hating that what hurt was he probably only kissed her because he was drunk — not because he was mesmerised by her uniqueness and beauty. 'We could have been friends. Now he's a just a big fat jerk.'

'Oh wow, bringing out the big insults now are we?' Jane laughed at her friend. 'Actually, I didn't think he looked fat at all,' she winked and a grin spread across her face. 'No wonder you're cut, how could I have forgotten how good looking he was? Was I that out of it?' she questioned, feeling her scar absently.

'He's not that good looking,' Anna scoffed. He was way too tall for starters. 'And I'm not cut. I just think he was rude is all.'

Ignoring Jane's gawk, Anna fixed her stare straight ahead and they drove on in silence to the last house on the list.

chapter twenty-three

Justin closed the door on Anna and Jane and walked back down the hallway. He felt dizzy. His heart was thumping like he'd been running, and he had the thirst to match it.

Seeing Anna—and Jane—felt so surreal that he had to wonder if it had really happened. He was tempted to go back and open the front door, just to check if it was in fact the two girls from Melbourne that were out there.

He met Jo, and her curious face, in the kitchen.

'So …' she began, 'was that *the* Anna?' her expression one of amusement and disbelief.

'Yup,' he smacked his lips together and reached for a glass from the top cupboard and gestured to it to offer Jo a drink.

'Coffee,' she replied instead, before continuing. 'Wow.'

'I don't know how this happened.' He felt dumbfounded as he leant his forearms on the cool counter.

'Coffee,' she reminded him, and he jumped up and hastily flicked the kettle on.

'You wanted a roommate. She found out. Simple.' Jo watched the kettle as she spoke, relaxing when it reached boiling point.

Simple, he scoffed. How can life flip everything around on him and it just come down to 'simple'?

'Right. Simple,' he frowned as he made her drink, pouring in her requisite half-milk ratio. 'Here, take your stinking coffee,' he huffed.

Jo smelt it and shook her face. 'What is this? Mud?'

'I don't know, I don't drink the stuff,' he protested. 'It's whatever Julia drinks … drank.' Jo sniffed at it again, its smell not stopping her from downing it like a shot of tequila.

'Needed that I gather?' he laughed, and she stood and busied herself making another. 'It mustn't have been that bad then.'

'No,' she shook her head, as if to remove the taste from her mouth. 'It was bad. But I'll never make it through to bath-time otherwise,' she reasoned, looking at the clock and feeling her breasts absently.

'Are you ready for me to ask how it went today?' Justin asked carefully, but Jo waved her hand at the question, requesting a break from her life. Her baby girl was sick, and no-one could confidently tell them why. What they thought was a sleepy baby with jaundice, was now thought to be something more. Jo and Dave had been at the hospital all weekend, waiting, while Bianca's little body was poked and prodded to find the answer.

'Later.' Fresh tears coated his sister's eyes but refused to fall or be acknowledged. 'Now, was I right to notice a bit of a chill in the room when I arrived?' she grinned lamely, subject officially changed back again.

'A chill would be an understatement. I was tempted to get a fire going,' he smiled bitterly, dutifully ignoring Jo's agony. He told Jo about Anna and Jane's arrival, Hamlet getting out, the filthy looks Anna had given him and everything else right up until they'd left. Justin then looked at Jo for a female analysis of it all.

'She hates you,' she told him, very matter of fact. 'Maybe you're a bad kisser.'

'You're not helping you know.' Leaning on the bench again, he placed his head in his hands. 'She's really nice Jo,' he muttered towards the benchtop. 'I don't need someone else hating me right now. I should have called her. Or texted.'

'You hardly know her,' she dismissed him. 'And she was a bitch to you.'

'No, she wasn't,' he straightened up. 'Okay, she was. But she's not normally.'

'Normally Jay? You hardly know her. She could be a piece of work like Julia.'

'What? You liked Julia!' he was astonished.

'No I didn't,' she confided. 'Complete cow. The girls were scared of her.'

'What? I was going to marry her.'

'You were not.' Jo shook her head at him, like she had more information on this then he did.

'Well … I could have,' he trailed off, feeling somewhat beaten.

'No. You couldn't. Mum would have stopped you before you had the chance.' She said the words with such certainty that Justin felt the need to confirm what she was implying.

'Mum? Jo, Mum loved Julia. She almost cried when I told her it was over.'

'Well, she felt bad for you, but they were tears of joy. Mum even had a scotch that night,' she nodded, as if the scotch was the clarification.

His mind was whirling. He didn't want to believe that Jo was being truthful. First Tom, and now his family, hadn't approved of his girlfriend? Justin questioned how he had been oblivious to this and wondered what else they hadn't told him. 'You have vomit on your shirt,' he grunted.

'What about that Jane girl? She seemed sweet,' Jo suggested, ignoring his pettiness. 'Beautiful too.'

'Yeah, she's nice.'

'And beautiful,' Jo pushed. 'And you have her number …'
Justin stood up straight, realising where Jo was heading.

'What? No! Jo, Jane seems great, don't get me wrong, but I'm not interested. I'm not looking for a new girlfriend. I just don't want people hating me.'

'Yeah, well, Julia and Anna do hate you. So get over it,' Jo said, as she slowly sipped her second coffee. A look of disgust planted on her face through the duration of the task. 'Do you have any biscuits?'

Justin looked at her, hurt.

'Just Mum's shortbread.' He hated that Jo was right.

'No choc-chip?'

'No.'

'Fine, they'll do,' she frowned with disappointment as he handed her their mother's biscuits.

Justin wondered if Jane would take the room. The awkwardness made him half hope that she would decline. Then again, if she did take the room, Anna would be around, and he could make it up to her. He had thought of her a lot since she'd ran off that night on the beach. It was hard not to when Julia, spitefully, mentioned her in every contact they'd had. Yet even with the consequences it brought to his relationship with Julia, that night on the beach was his best memory from a long time. Thinking of Anna's pixie face made him smile. Even after Julia walked out, after the court handed him his papers, and even after they suspended his licence; Anna, and things she had said, continued to amuse him. But now was not the time in Justin's life to be thinking about women or relationships — past ones maybe, but not daydreaming of future ones. He was beginning the Traffic Offenders course that week, and he was still trying to move on from Julia. He hadn't expected his life to turn like it had, but it did, and now he had a new way of living to adapt to. Anna — she was just confusing.

He had told himself again, and again, that she was only on his mind because she was the catalyst for all the recent changes in his life; that it had nothing to do with the fact that she was the lone choc-chip cookie in a jar of bland shortbread.

What was she even doing here?

His nieces came running inside. Justin picked them both up easily and swung them up onto his shoulders. Spinning them around, they giggled with delight and cried for him to stop. He put them back down and they shrieked for more.

'Come on then,' Jo hurried them along. He tousled their hair and left to collect their scattered belongings from the lounge room, as Jo picked up shoes and socks that had been thrown randomly in the backyard. She looked exhausted and Justin worried she wasn't finding enough time to look after herself, while she tried so hard to look after her girls. He wondered how her day had really gone. How his youngest niece was faring.

'I'll see you two soon,' he told Olivia and Samantha affectionately.

'Will those girls be here next time?' asked an excited Olivia.

'Probably not,' he laughed. 'Just me and Hamlet I'm afraid.'

Jo hugged him goodbye and promised she would call if he could do anything to help. After they'd driven off, he was left to his still house. Smudged footprints and paw marks traced the floors. Cups were stacked in the sink and outside he could see Hamlet collapsed on the lawn. Justin followed suit on the lounge.

chapter twenty-four

As the sun began to set, it filled the room with a yellow haze. Mel lay on her bed with her feet in the air, deep in conversation.

'So, did you give — Jane was it? — my mate's number?' Tom asked over the phone.

'Yeah, she said she'd ring him,' Mel yawned. 'I'm not sure if she did though.'

'Hey, is she single?' he asked suddenly, and she felt more than a bit put out.

'Why, are you looking for a date?' she snipped, not really meaning for it to come out as harshly as it did, and not knowing how to recover from it.

'No,' he chuckled. 'But *Justin* is,' he emphasised.

Mel's eyes had been drifting closed on and off, but the mention of 'Justin' brought them wide and anxious. The name had been heard cursed too many times for her to forget. Anna's only mention of that night at the pub was to curse all men named Justin. Mel, not wanting to dwell too much on the evening in case her feelings for Tom were realised, didn't argue with Anna's decision.

'Justin?' she cried, hoping she'd heard wrong. 'You gave me *Justin's* number? You said Jay!'

'Yeah, Jay,' he agreed. 'Jay, Justin, Doc—same thing. Oh hey, that's right, you *met* Jay,' Tom laughed.

Mel wondered if she should hang up and call Jane to let her know the awkward trap she could be entering into. But then she'd have to explain Tom, and she wasn't ready to. Maybe Jane wouldn't call him. Mel convinced herself of this and relaxed into her pillow again.

'Yeah, I did meet him,' she said reluctantly. 'You just didn't tell me it was him.'

'The one and only,' Tom said, and it sounded to Mel like he was throwing a ball up against a wall.

'But … doesn't he have a girlfriend?' Mel was curious.

'Did.' Tom corrected.

'Not now?'

'Nope. Actually, your friend was the reason they broke up,' Tom revealed.

'What! No, it wasn't,' she cried, like a bullet from a gun. All Anna did was have a drink with the guy.

''Fraid so. His girlfriend found out what happened, and it was all over. Hey, have you tried that new Macca's burger?' Tom jumped ahead while Mel was still three steps behind and trying to catch up.

'What? No! What do you mean?' Mel became instantly frustrated.

'It's really good, is all.'

'No, I mean about Anna and Justin. What happened?' demanded an exasperated Mel.

'Some friends told his girlfriend that he'd left with some girl—'

'So what!' she defended, cutting him off.

'Well, if you'd let me finish,' he joked. 'When Julia asked him about it, Justin admitted they'd ended up at the beach and—'

'The beach? Anna never told me that!' Mel's voice rose with each piece of news.

'Hey, easy Songbird, you're gonna pop an eardrum.' His inability to get to the point had her sitting up, anxiously listening. '*Anyway.* Apparently, they'd kissed or something. Julia found out, and she ended it,' he concluded, leaving Mel speechless at last.

She had thought Anna had gone home after she'd left the bar that night. Mel had been so caught up with Tom that when she woke the next day, in his hotel room, with missed calls from Anna, she'd ignored them — not wanting to explain her whereabouts or dampen her perfect night with any reality. Then she'd been so depressed afterwards, Mel now realised that she hadn't allowed Anna to do much talking at all — just the odd curse. She had never prodded for more.

Poor Anna. Maybe. She did just supposedly cause the end of a relationship. Mel didn't know enough to know whether she should be so hasty with her sympathy.

Mel wondered if Anna even knew. Then she wondered if she should tell her. She definitely didn't want to be the bearer of that news. Knowing Anna, the guilt would turn her friend inside out.

'Are you sure that is how it happened?' She knew that boys, historically, were not well skilled in the art of gossip.

'Yup. It completely messed him up, that break up,' he said bitterly. Mel remembered Tom giving Justin's girlfriend a hard time the night they'd met. He, clearly, didn't like her to begin with, so she wasn't sure how fair he was being.

'Wow,' she murmured thoughtfully. It did explain why Anna failed to elaborate much on the night in question. Mel had simply thought Anna didn't like Justin — or Tom. She hadn't realised, until now, that she'd never asked why. 'Wow,' she said again, feeling like a terrible friend.

'Yeah,' Tom agreed softly. 'Anyway …'

They talked for a little longer about nothing, simply happy to just hear the other speak. Mel cursed the distance between them and pined for something more. While she tried to figure out a way to voice that, without seeming suffocating, Tom admitted he had a week's worth of ironing to get to and had better go. He sounded regretful, but Mel wasn't completely sure.

Justin was woken by a persistent ring. He blinked his eyes in the dark room, saw his phone glowing from the kitchen bench, and staggered to it.

'Hello,' he breathed out, switching on the kitchen light.

'Hi. Justin? It's Jane,' a female voice asked tentatively. Justin glanced at the clock; it was almost seven.

'Oh … hi.'

'Bit quieter there now?' she joked uneasily, the discomfort in her voice.

'Yeah, it is,' he laughed quietly, looking around at his silent house.

'So, I'm just calling to let you know about the room.' She seemed hesitant to speak and Justin sensed that she was about to turn the room down. When she did, he congratulated himself on his perceptiveness and was about to end the call, when his sleepiness allowed his curiosity to be tended to.

'Is this anything to do with Anna?'

Hearing the words, their sound still lingering in the room, Justin regretted that he sounded so vain.

'Ah, no. No. Um …' Jane stumbled over choices of answers. 'It was just a bit further away from work is all.'

'Right. Sure,' he said kindly, not believing her for a moment.

'How's the move been anyway?' he asked, doing Jane the courtesy of changing the topic.

'Good. Thanks,' Jane replied, the conversation halting suddenly.

'How is Anna?' he braved.

'She's … good.'

'Coping without you?'

'I hope so,' she laughed. 'No-one stopping her from bringing home chocolate or lost kittens. But she has Leo now, so I think she'll have to behave,' she joked, easing up a bit more.

Justin felt his face frown, trying to piece together more of Anna's character and life. Part of him was curious for more, part was happier not knowing. A much smaller part told him it was all irrelevant. He feigned a lie, telling Jane someone was at the door, so he could hang up. Jane herself seemed relieved.

'Okay. Well, thanks for today and thank you so much —again—for helping me that night,' Jane said, indicating the incident in Melbourne.

'Oh, please, not at all,' he dismissed her. 'Take care. Good luck with the house hunt.'

They rung off and Justin put the phone down with a sense of resignation. He wasn't surprised by Jane's call, but disappointed. He wasn't too concerned about finding another housemate or that it wouldn't be Jane. If he were honest, he didn't think he could handle a housemate right now—he just needed the extra money. What disappointed him was that Jane's reason to reject the room had to do with Anna's opinion of him. He must have really pissed her off, he thought, annoyed at himself again for not having called her.

Justin looked around at his home again. Spotting the footprints and mud, he smiled a sigh, and began to clean his house.

Anna's visit to the hospital that evening was a difficult one. She had been helping her mother practicse the breathing exercises prescribed for her lungs and Anna found herself easily irritated.

She'd remained calm by focusing on the flowers in the room, commenting on the newest and most extravagant arrangement.

'Hmm,' her mother, whose responses and memory were somewhat delayed, rolled her eyes as Anna stepped closer to read the card perched amongst the stems. 'Those are from your father.'

'What?' Anna snapped out the card and read it quickly, not that she needed long. 'That's it? *Hope you're doing OK ox.* Did you tell him about the accident?'

'No,' her mother replied, standoffish, and Anna momentarily questioned herself about whether she had done the right thing by letting him know.

'So, he did get my message … nice of him to call.' Anna actually wanted to cry; she felt so disappointed that her dad hadn't grasped from her message that she needed him. It wasn't like the time someone stole her purse, or when her car wouldn't start … her mum was broken.

Anna put the card back, gently touching a large white lily before turning back to her mother; working her irritation out through questions. When pushed, her mother had spoken briefly of the police visiting her, but to add further strain on Anna's mood, was uninterested to discuss it in any depth—and Anna wanted details. Between exercises, Anna tried to steer the conversation back, but her mother consistently closed up before she eventually fell asleep. Frustrated, Anna's personal vendetta towards the driver intensified. Where she didn't have hard facts, she made assumptions, and those assumptions fed the anger that raged through her body. It brought her bad mood to its height.

When her mother began her soft snores, Anna went home to prepare for work. Her anxiety for her new workplace was increasing the closer Monday loomed, and her frustrations towards Justin—and then Jane, for not validating them—wasn't helping. It only added to the resentment she was clinging to for the driver who had hit her mother's car. Additionally, because her mother showed no apparent hard feelings towards the driver, Anna felt resentment on behalf of her as well. She would wonder at what age that kind of forgiveness set in, if she weren't too angry to care, because, if Anna was being honest, she liked the feeling. It drove her.

Anna was relying on her anger like it was a human need and so it was one fortunate fact that it was in no short supply. That anger put her feet on the ground each morning and that feeling let her walk into her mother's hospital room each day and tolerate her pain. That feeling let her resent Justin for the excuse of a man that he was.

Anna didn't want to see the back of it anytime soon.

chapter twenty-five

Where is your dustpan?

Anna received Ioulia's text message early Monday morning. It had woken her up, and she frowned at the lame reason for the text.

She replied and hid the phone under her pillow to enjoy a few more glorious moments of shut eye. She was easily drifting back to sleep when her phone alerted her again. Like a well pro-grammed droid, she read the message obligingly.

Found it!

Anna groaned. Cleaning was the least of her concerns right now. This time she hid her head under the pillow and when her phone beeped the receipt of another new message, she ignored it. She didn't care. She couldn't care less. She sealed her eyes closed with fierce determination to relax, but it was useless. Throwing the pillow away from her head, she grabbed the phone, read the message and frowned.

IOU a vase ... sorry ox

Anna only owned one vase to be broken. It was a gift from an ex-boyfriend. She wasn't sentimental about it, but knew it was expensive, knew it was nice, and knew Ioulia would never remember she'd broken it long enough to actually replace it. It just wasn't in her disposition.

With a sigh of resignation, she tossed her phone away and stared up at the ceiling. She noticed, and not for the first time, the paint beginning to flake off. Anna thought with longing of her neat flat down in Melbourne — the one with the broken vase.

She allowed herself one last minute and slid out of bed.

Her outfit was laid out ready to go, thanks to Jane, who'd coordinated her clothes before she'd left the day before. This gave a grateful Anna a full hour to stress about her hair and whether her teeth were the cleanest they could possibly be. By eight, she was as ready as she could be. Knowing a few faces would make her first day easier, but butterflies flapped about in her belly nonetheless. Anna felt painfully nervous about being the 'new-kid' again. Each freckle, every octave of her voice, she was paranoid of. Plus, Jane reminding her not to say anything stupid didn't help. Mel texting the same advice late the night before however, simply gave her a complex.

Anna drove to work, accidently cutting off several cars as she struggled to be in the correct lane at the right time. What Google maps told her would be a forty-minute journey across the city was a straight-up lie. Admittedly, had she been able to keep up with the GPS instructions, she may have arrived at the North Sydney office earlier. When Anna eventually pulled up to the building, This is IT boldly scrolled on the front, she felt like the effort in getting there was a day's work in itself.

'Hello, I'm Anna Marcus,' she told the receptionist, mustering up the sweetest of her smiles and praying that no bad reputation preceded her. 'I'm here to see John Chan.'

Anna took in the bright office. It was more modern and spacious than the Melbourne office, and much more fitting for an IT company.

John showed his dependably happy face an instant later, and Anna could have hugged him. He asked about her mother and assured Anna she'd be fine—the perfunctory line that she'd been hearing of late. In all honestly, Anna was tiring of people telling her how 'fine' everything was going to be. She knew they meant well, but they didn't know. She was quickly learning that people didn't know what else to say in these situations. She had probably been guilty of it countless times herself, but it didn't stop her from squirming every time someone uttered it to her.

'Your desk is just over here. There's an arrival for you already.' John gestured his hand toward a desk that was taken over by an oversized box of flowers.

Anna stared from the beautiful bright arrangement, to John, who seemed to sense her uncertainty.

'They arrived for you a little earlier,' he explained, confirming they were in fact for her.

Anna, not sure why she'd have flowers, wanted to reach for the card instantly, but convinced her curious fingers to resist.

'I'll leave you to it and come back in a few minutes,' John smiled and retreated to his office. Anna's fingers plucked out the mini envelope that was tucked between two budding roses, tore it open and slid out the yellow card. The words brought a chuckle from her throat and a shine to her eyes.

Mind if we leave these here? We'll miss you! From the Melbourne Team.

Anna looked down at the flowers with her widest smile.

They cared.

chapter twenty-six

Justin waited for the ATM to spit out his receipt and when he read the figures, he had to read them again to confirm. Blinking, in hope the numbers would transform and pierce the feeling of worry that they gave him, Justin read them for a third and futile time, but the numbers remained unchanged. He was broke.

Between mortgage payments, inconceivable legal fees, the fine, repairs to his broken car, and Uber rides (that had been increasing as his motivation to walk waned); his savings were fast declining. He really needed to do something about his financial situation—hence the reason he had beautiful girls turning up to his house to tease him about moving in. He'd had no other interest from the ad he'd posted online over two weeks ago. He still couldn't believe the coincidence of Anna and Jane being the sole people to find it. He made a mental note to check the listing and then, joining the masses, Justin wished he was rich.

He folded the ATM stub and slid it into his back pocket. His brain was searching for a positive spin on his situation, but he began the Traffic Offenders Program in less than an hour, so his mood was unhelpfully sour and nervous. With hunched shoulders, he put his earphones in and pressed play on his *Run* playlist, hoping the beat would lift him. He noticed a missed call from his dad but decided to call him back after the class. In short, Justin felt like a loser and he didn't want to talk to anyone.

The course was held at a local college he'd driven past hundreds of times and he now walked with trepidation to the bus stop that would take him to its door. A kebab in his hand, Justin planned to eat it before the bus arrived. His stomach grumbled as he walked, competing for attention from his back, which ached annoyingly from his backpack—housing what would traditionally have been found on his backseat, and mostly less than notable items like emergency muesli bars and bruised apples.

The bus arrived late and Justin boarded as he chewed the last bite of food, stressed from the delay. He couldn't imagine that being late on the first night would set a very good example of his character.

Feeling unusually flustered, he arrived to a half-empty classroom. A man sporting a rather large mustache stood at the front of the room. 'Traffic Offenders?' the mustache called, as if he was offering a beer, and Justin nodded—albeit, not as willingly.

'Take a seat,' the man smiled, throwing Justin off. He was anticipating a night of scornful looks and finger pointing, like the ones he'd received from the police the night of the accident.

When he eventually left that night, Justin was relieved to be wrong. The first session was a general outline of what the following weeks would bring and what the 'Offenders' had to do to be signed off for the courts. Justin had already read and agreed to this information, so it wasn't anything new. New, however, was being around other people charged with the same or similar crimes. The group was also not quite what Justin had expected. Twelve of them sat in the room, more than he'd anticipated. There were more young people, but older people were represented too. A man with a neat pinstriped tie sat not far from

Justin. A much older woman sat with a hung head. Another woman, who looked about his own age, sat looking as stressed as he felt; frown lines cutting deep into her forehead. Justin couldn't help but feel relieved that he wasn't the only person in the room over the age of twenty-one, like he had suspected he would be. Foolishness, it seemed, had no age restrictions.

The group had each introduced themselves to begin. Each person gave their name, but nothing else. In the short break they were given, Justin joined a small congregation of the class and learnt that three of them had been charged on the same night. Craig, the man with the tie, was one; the other, a skittish, eyeline-wearing teenage delinquent, who struggled to make eye contact. He had a plaster cast wrapped around his arm and confessed with arrogant pride to being high even then. Justin tried not to react to this like every part of him wanted to. Craig, remaining quiet, looked on in surprise.

Scratching his chin, Justin looked at the young guy with sincerity and spoke carefully.

'Is that the best move, mate?' he asked, trying to relate to him big brother style.

'Fuck off,' the teenager replied and slumped off, scuffing his feet as he went; his dirty jeans hanging ridiculously low.

'Right,' Justin nodded, as he watched him slouch back to his seat. Craig chuckled to the ground beneath him.

'I think that there is the difference between stupid choices, and just plain stupid,' he muttered towards Justin, who shook his head and agreed, hoping he knew which category he was in.

When he left later in the night, he felt his body notably relax. *One down, six to go.*

Justin waited outside on the cool aluminum seat for a bus and remembered he needed to call his dad. The street looked deserted as he listened to the ringing tone. After brief greetings,

Justin's relief from leaving the college fell back on him swiftly once his dad announced the reason for his call.

'It's wee Bianca, son.'

Justin swallowed. He didn't think the results would be back this soon and he wasn't prepared.

'What did they find?' he asked tensely, instinctively dreading what he was about to hear, what the doctors found.

'Well, it's her liver,' he sighed, and Justin's heart beat faster. 'It's turning on itself. They think it's some disease I can't pronounce son, Biliary or something? Jo said it's to do with bile ducts. They don't know yet how progressed it is … but it's causing her liver to fail.' Justin heard his dad's voice falter and felt his face spasm trying to control his own reaction. If his dad lost it, he wasn't sure that he could control his own emotions. He could barely get out his question about her prognosis and while he waited for an answer, Justin focused on the concrete; the grey, dirty concrete. Gum had deteriorated on its surface, leaving black marks. Someone had sketched a love heart in it, with initials scrawled inside. Justin didn't want to know what his dad would say next. He'd much rather critique the ground below him. *J.M. 4 R.B.*

'They, eh,' his father hesitated, and it gave Justin enough warning that what he was about to hear was not going to be good. 'They are talking about surgery for now—there is a procedure that has been successful. But they suspect a transplant is a possibility down the line … if that doesn't work.' He heard his father's thick voice struggle to get the words out.

The word 'transplant' fell on Justin's ears with a heavy thud; its weight being felt all the way to his heart. His whole life, Justin had been told that 'Men don't cry'. *Owen men* don't cry. His father, an Owen, had never shed a tear in Justin's memory. Nevertheless, Justin could swear that the rule was being challenged. He nodded to the ground and stood up to give his body something else to concentrate on, his throat making some kind of sound to acknowledge that he'd heard, but actual words took a little longer to compose.

'They've increased her medication,' his father added during his son's absence of speech.

'Is she still at home?' Sound came to Justin at last.

'Yes … for now.'

'When are they going to operate?'

'Soon. They want to confirm all the options first. Find out how severe it is and what type it is. More bloody tests.' Justin could hear the frustration in his father's voice.

'How are they?'

'Jo and Dave? Upset, naturally. Quiet. They're having tests too, to see if their livers are compatible … just in case. They won't know for sure for another week or so.'

They both stayed on the line, quiet themselves. Nothing was left to be said. A bus rounded the corner and drove towards Justin, its bright lights blaring into his stinging eyes. He stepped forward for the bus to stop.

'Dad, I need to go. I'll call you tomorrow.'

'Right mate, take care.'

Justin sat on the bus, feeling his whole body move at each turn. His whole body jump over each bump. He almost missed his stop. He was in a trance, feeling ambushed by life, mesmerised by its cruelty.

She's only seven weeks old, he kept saying in his head. *She's only a baby.*

chapter twenty-seven

On her second day working in Sydney, John had recommended that Anna get counselling. His wife had been hospitalised suddenly three years ago, and he was incredibly empathetic to Anna's situation. John handed her a business card and told her it was the one the company referred when their employees had issues.

Issues. Anna had frowned at the simplicity of the word used to describe her life (and apparently crazed head).

When Anna had told Jane about it, laughing at the notion, Jane's concerned silence convinced her to go.

'I don't need counselling!' Anna pleaded over the phone.

'Well, then it won't hurt to say hello once then, will it?'

Anna grudgingly promised to attend and as she sat awkwardly waiting for her assigned counsellor just the next day, she wished she wasn't so obliging. That morning, a client had yelled at her over the phone when their computer crashed. She'd tried to explain the problem, but it did nothing to curb the expletives that they spat at her. Anna, usually tolerant of such clients, had hidden in the bathroom, crying big ugly sobs for a solid ten minutes before she could bring herself to walk back to her desk. The new junior technician, Sally, was then assigned to Anna for the day. The team thought it made sense to match the two new recruits together. Anna privately disagreed, not feeling herself to be a very good role model and was almost glad to leave for counselling that afternoon.

As she toyed with the seat's cushion a young girl walked in, her shirt tight across her chest. A flicker of concern sparked in Anna. With each fraction of a moment that the girl remained in the room, more clues allowed this concern to grow. Anna reasoned with the universe not to make this child her counsellor but, regardless of any negotiations, the girl in front of her sat down, her shiny pink lips smiling.

'Hi,' Anna said, her lips forming a thin, tight line.

'Hello, Anna. I'm Jessica,' Jessica spoke sweetly.

'My … counsellor?' Maybe this girl was just confused with a group session.

'That's right.' Jessica's smile was steadfast.

'You don't look like a counsellor,' Anna remarked defiantly.

'Well, Anna,' she spoke sincerely, 'we come in all shapes and sizes. Shall we begin?'

Anna nodded unenthusiastically. Unsure if she was willing to impart personal information to this girl, who may or may not have been taller than her—unable to convince herself that it wasn't the point.

John had given Anna the time to see Jessica in her work hours; that part, Anna was grateful for. It meant that she could get to the hospital at a reasonable time, get home earlier, and eat properly. She had kept reminding herself of these perks as she resisted giving in to Jessica. But Jessica was right, counsellors came in all shapes and sizes, and by the end of her session Anna's eyes glowed red, her head pounded from crying and thinking; but her heart felt considerably unclenched. It didn't make every-thing okay—that wasn't possible—but it made her feel okay about not feeling okay. For now, that was the best Anna could ask for and she thanked Jessica sincerely as she walked out the door to visit her mum.

By the time Anna reached home that night, she felt like she'd lived a week in a day. If work and her appointment with Jessica hadn't already exhausted her, her mother did. She had seemed more agitated than the day before and Anna had spent the afternoon trying to calm and reassure her that she would get to go home soon enough. She tried to sympathise with her, but having never experienced bed sores, catheters, sponge baths or metal rods in her bones, Anna knew her attempts were feeble. She had rationalised that at least she was out of the worst of it. Her bones were showing improvement and ICU was a distant memory; Anna had told her this brightly, hiding the feeling she was failing. She'd wished that Brian could have been there, he was much better at calming her, but he worked so far away that he couldn't always make the journey in time.

Anna left at dark. Her stomach grumbled and her eyelids felt heavier than the rest of her body. Parking next to the neighbour's car, Anna slumped out of her own and heard Claude cry frantically.

'Hi buddy,' she crooned, unlocking the front door. She felt him slide past her legs as she switched on the light. Throwing her bag on the lounge, Anna, noticing Claude's lack of speed, watched him carefully. With alarm, she saw that his ear was mangled and caked with dry blood, one eye was swollen closed and he wasn't using his front leg at all.

'Claude!' She yelped, but he skitted under the table, looking at her accusingly as she crept towards him. 'Oh Claude, you poor thing,' she whispered, with panic setting in.

Anna jumped to her bag and rummaged for her phone with shaking hands. Finding its smooth case, she quickly hit Google to search 'vet' and frantically scrolled through the ads for one that seemed like a location she knew. Making her choice, and taking an ineffective calming breath, she saw Claude looking at her bleakly from his empty bowl. She filled it hastily, and he limped away after one sniff, flopping onto the carpet instead. Anna frowned. Taking another breath, she dialed the vet while trying to coax Claude to water.

'Hello, Hills Veterinary Clinic,' sung a friendly voice.

'Oh, hi,' Anna said breathlessly. 'I have a cat.' *Breathe.* 'He's,' *Breathe.* 'He's limping and has blood …' she trailed off and felt herself starting to cry. 'I think he's been in a fight,' she eventually bawled, too exhausted to care how dramatic she may have sounded.

'Hey, hey,' soothed the woman on the line. 'Calm down, love. Listen, bring him down, and we'll take a look,' she said gently.

Anna, feeling incredibly stupid, cried harder.

'I'm sorry. I'm sorry. It's my mother's cat. I, um …' she sucked in a strangled breath and swiped tears from her face. 'I don't even know how far you are. What time do you close?'

'It's okay. It's okay,' she repeated, her voice remaining kind. 'We're open till eight tonight. We are just near the primary school on Gilbert Road. Do you know where that is?'

Anna knew the school. It was in the suburb where her mother used to live and she had a vague memory of the small group of shops behind it. She looked at her watch and checked it really was okay to come down.

'Honey, it's fine. It's pretty quiet here tonight. Just bring him down.' Anna could hear the smile in the woman's voice and relaxed again.

She hung her bag back over her shoulder and scooped Claude affectionately into her arms.

'C'mon, Claude,' she crooned, disgusted by his ear. Anna placed him delicately on the back seat, cautious of hurting him, and slid behind the wheel. She took each turn carefully, while trying hard to remember where to go.

When she pulled up into the small car park, she panicked again. The idea of her mother knowing her precious cat was hurt upset her and she fanned her eyes before getting out of the car. She'd anticipated that catching Claude in the car would prove difficult, but he had lain miserably still the entire way.

Walking into the reception, the woman behind the front counter instantly supposed Anna to be the same frantic person who had recently called. Anna felt her face heat up, knowing the stress showed so clearly on her face, but was at a loss to contain it.

'Hi love,' the woman smiled motherly and her kind voice almost broke Anna.

'Hi, I rang earlier,' Anna managed, albeit in a shaky voice, as she and Claude approached the counter. 'This is Claude.'

'Yes dear, of course. I'll just get his details,' she smiled up at her from the screen and Anna nodded obediently, answering questions absently as she tried to ignore the gory blood on the cat in her arms while the receptionist hit the keys.

'Here, follow me through,' she eventually said, tapping in the final client detail with a warm smile. 'The doc will be over in a moment,' she stood and led her into the examining room, giving Anna's arm a reassuring rub before she walked out.

Ignoring the chair provided, Anna chose to remain standing, hugging her mother's cat like it was her mother herself. She heard a voice approach, mid-conversation with someone else. The door swung open, and Anna stood up straighter, expectantly. Then it swung shut, without anyone appearing. Her shoulders slumped back down. Then the door swung open again and the vet appeared.

'Sorry about that,' he apologised, idly arranging a stethoscope around his neck. He was reading a piece of paper as he came in and Anna found herself standing very straight. Claude's claw dug in a little to her movement and she winced.

The vet looked up at Claude with a relaxed smile and greeted the cat before Anna. Then his brown eyes, that Anna thought looked almost amber, met hers.

Her throat dried and it took her a seemingly long and stagnant beat to find her voice.

'Vet.'

Justin nodded uneasily. 'Vet.'

chapter twenty-eight

Justin stood stunned. He wondered where this woman could have been hiding all this time to suddenly be reappearing and letting loose in his life now. With Bianca's health so prominent in his thoughts, he'd already been overly distracted that day, but another Anna appearance felt even more unexpected and random for his mind to comprehend. Assessing Anna's face, he decided she felt the same.

'How are you, Anna?' he finally asked, when his brain caught up with the situation. The whites of her eyes were pink, and he suspected she had been crying. She blinked at him and Justin wondered if she was about to cry now, as she sniffed softly.

'Bu-wha-how,' she stuttered, her eyes becoming shinier and her expression reaching panic. Justin made the decision to ignore the awkwardness for the moment and focus on the cat.

'Let me have a look at Claude,' he suggested, lifting him gently from her arms. His claw was hooked on her blouse and Anna watched on helplessly as Justin easily freed him. He could see Claude cared much less about the situation than Anna. His ear had been torn, but the blood made it look worse than it was. A claw had also been ripped out and Justin frowned as he turned the paw over, Claude looking on indifferently.

'Has he been eating?' he queried Anna, while feeling the other paws. When she didn't reply he looked up at her. 'Anna? Has he been leaving his food?' He waited while she watched blankly, thin lipped and rigid.

'Anna?' he pressed gently, and she shook her head and shrugged a shoulder.

'I … I don't know. I guess so.'

'Well, have you noticed his eating change?'

'I don't know,' she replied again, leaving him confused. 'It's my mother's cat,' she shook her head, as if confessing a crime. 'She's in hospital, I came home, and I think he's been in a fight. I don't know if he's eating more or less, because I don't know how much I'm meant to be feeding him. He just seems to sit there. I just don't know.'

She blurted it all out so quickly that if she didn't look so distressed, he would have smiled at her speed.

'Sorry,' she added quietly, looking down and discreetly brushing new tears from her eyes.

'Hey, it's okay,' he spoke gently, wanting to hug her. She looked so fragile, the hard Anna he'd met at his house was nowhere in sight. She ran her fingers through her hair and smiled stiffly, her eyes eventually meeting his more confidently and he smiled reassuringly.

'Is your mum going to be okay?' he asked carefully, thinking of Bianca, and hoping he wasn't being too intrusive.

'She's … improving,' Anna nodded and quietly changed the subject. 'How about Claude here?' she thumbed the fur on his neck and he purred briefly in response.

Justin looked at her, carefully considering whether to push the subject of her mother and deciding against it. At least he knew why Anna was in Sydney. His attention was brought back to a restless Claude and Justin resumed his vet role.

He listened to Claude's slow heart rate and then reached for a thermometer. Justin typed the information into Claude's blank file and then met Anna's anxious stare. She'd said nothing in the time he'd examined Claude and he wondered if it was because she was still mad at him, and if so, he was curious to know just how mad. Looking into her eyes now, he did a quick calculation — pretty mad. But also, Justin acknowledged, pretty eyes. Man, were they pretty eyes. They made his hopeless heart shrink down to his stomach and then leap back again; it was still recovering from reverberating bounces when he spoke again.

'Okay, Claude here should be fine,' he promised her and saw her shoulders drop in relief. 'He'll need some stitches on his ear to stop it from opening and becoming infected. His paw should be fine, but I'd like to splint it, so it heals better. He'll just need to stay inside until we take the stitches out. Is that possible?' he asked her, emanating calm, and she nodded unquestioningly.

'Now, he seems anxious. Would you agree, or does he seem his normal self to you?'

Anna gave it some thought and Justin took the opportunity to update his memory of her face. The way her nose wiggled to the side, her pixie-ears, the freckle that sat right above her lip like a tiny beauty spot. Her brown hair that fell in short waves like she'd just been at the beach; and then those eyes, so pale and green and big, he could stare at them all day …

'I guess he has been acting differently. I've just been so busy. I wasn't paying attention.' She looked ashamed and embarrassed to admit it. 'I didn't mean to neglect him,' she rushed as an afterthought, and he laughed.

'It's okay Anna, I'm not judging you. It's not your fault. When a pet misses its owner, they will often act like this,' he told her. 'It is definitely not your fault,' he repeated firmly, holding her gaze. Justin felt confident when she didn't break it and was paying full attention as she began to speak, when a knock sounded at the door and Sandra walked in.

'Sorry to interrupt,' she apologised to Anna, whose cheeks were turning a pinkish colour. Sandra hid a smirk as she looked across at Justin. He wasn't entirely sure what the smirk meant, but resented Sandra at that moment; not a lot, but definitely a little.

'Jay, the Hendersons are on the phone. They have a question for you that 'can't wait',' she rolled her eyes. The Hendersons bred Labradors and were waiting on a litter. He'd been enduring their phone calls for four days, and he couldn't wait for the pups' arrival.

'Oh, right. Thanks Sandra.' He looked back at Anna. 'Can you excuse me for a moment?' he asked, taking his hand off Claude, who glared at Justin and began to lick the spot clean.

'Of course,' Anna said softly, as he walked back out, past Sandra, who gave Anna a friendly wink before closing the door.

As Justin hung up the phone, Sandra was by his side.

'Puppies?' she asked hopefully.

'Nope. None,' he spoke unconvincingly blasé, and Sandra chuckled at his attempt of professionalism.

She cocked her head to the examining room. 'Everything okay in there?' she whispered, so the nurse out the back of the clinic couldn't overhear.

'Fine. Why?'

'No reason, *Doc*,' she smiled innocently, turning back to her computer. Justin gave her a look that her oddness justified and went back to Anna.

'Okay, Anna,' he said as he came back into the room. She jumped at his unexpected return, and he hated that she felt so anxious around him. He really wanted them to be friends.

'I'd like to keep Claude overnight. Are you alright to get him tomorrow?'

'Um, sure,' she said hesitantly.

'Are you?' he checked.

'Yeah. Yes, that's fine. Just, um …' she paused, her eyes darting to the walls behind him, that shade of pink hitting her cheeks again. 'Um, just wondering how much it's going to cost?' her awkwardness unmistakable.

'No cost,' he said firmly, and she turned her head up to meet his eyes.

'No cost?' She was alarmed and uncomfortable. 'Of course there is.'

He smiled at her kindly. 'Anna, no cost for Claude …' he lingered a moment. 'But there is a catch.' She looked at him warily and waited.

'You let me help Claude …' She nodded, prompting the next line, 'and you forgive me for what happened in Melbourne.'

He noticed her face pause, and then turn from pink to red.

'Forgive you for what?' she asked casually, quickly knitting her brows together while looking back at the cat. 'There's nothing to forgive.'

She was a terrible liar. Justin wanted to laugh at her, but his jaw hung instead.

'Oh really? So, what was with the nasty Anna at my house?' he remarked, folding his arms across his chest. Her behaviour had stung him on Sunday, but made him want to laugh now.

'Nasty Anna? What are you talking about? I wasn't nasty,' she denied. He went to refute but thought against it. He'd play along.

'Oh, okay. Sorry. My mistake,' he held his hands up. 'Then if you have nothing to forgive me for, then we're friends, right?' he asked brazenly, enjoying the suspicion on her face. He pushed on while her tongue was tied. After all, if life was going to make her keep turning up, who was he to stop it?

'So …' he mused thoughtfully. 'Claude is no charge, but *you* can take me out to dinner in return,' he decided out loud, smiling with certainty. 'What night is good for you?'

Her face said it all, but she spoke it anyway. 'Wh-what!'

'Dinner,' he beamed. 'You eat, right?'

'But …'

'But what? If we're friends, then let me help you, and …' he added, 'you can help me. I'm starving,' he put his hand on his stomach. He really was starving.

'What? Now?'

'Hey, why not? I can finish up with Claude in say … twenty minutes?' he calculated innocently. 'You have plans?'

'Yes!' she cried, a little too quickly.

'I don't believe you,' he told her, shaking his head. 'You know, I wouldn't have taken you for a liar, Anna.' With that he broke her, the reluctant smile on her face giving her away.

'You're a piece of work.'

He smiled encouragingly. 'C'mon, what do you say?' She stood with her hand on her hip, the other fiddling with Claude's collar. 'You have obviously had a bad day. I've had a bad … month. Let's go douse our problems with food and take our minds off things.'

'Okay. Fine,' she nodded begrudgingly. 'We'll eat.'

'Really?'

'Really,' Anna signed and confessed. 'I am pretty hungry.'

'Great! Hey … one more thing?'

'What's that, you want me to pick you up too? Buy you flowers?'

'Yeah, how did you know?' He enjoyed hearing the giggle that unwillingly escaped her but didn't know how to word the truth. 'No seriously, I, um … I don't have a car right now.'

Almost two hours later and Justin remained in the company of Anna. The funny pixie he'd met in Melbourne had returned and the angry Anna was a mere blur in his otherwise perfect memory of her.

He'd chosen a nearby Chinese restaurant for its proximity and speed, because by the time Justin had tended to Claude's wounds and closed up, both of them were too hungry to be waiting long.

While he worked, Justin had left Anna in the care of Sandra. Anna, reminding him of her queasy stomach, had chosen to pass on being a temporary vet-nurse. Apart from Anna inviting Sandra out for dinner—who had declined the offer in favour of her husband's company—Justin wasn't completely sure what Sandra and Anna had talked about in his absence. He did over-hear snippets of an animated conversation and returned to them laughing over a shared joke. Feeling self-conscious as they'd turned to face him, he hoped that he wasn't the topic of any of their discussions.

He looked at Anna now, hopelessly trying to use her chop-sticks after eyeing them off for the last hour.

She laughed lightly as she successfully picked up a diced carrot, cheering prematurely as it slipped back onto the plate. Justin grinned slowly, enjoying her momentary delight.

'Do you come here often?' Anna asked while she attempted to pick up a piece of broccoli, wriggling her eyebrows sugges-tively at her choice of words.

'Yeah,' he nodded. 'It's where I practice picking up,' he grinned proudly as he clicked his chopsticks together like a pro. Anna rolled her eyes, and Justin, adamant it was clever (though certainly not his best), couldn't shake the memory of her mouth on his.

He looked around the restaurant to diffuse his thoughts. It was cheap and nasty. The pink walls, with flaking shards revealing the green paint hiding underneath, were decorated with a series of faded polyester flower arrangements. On the wall behind Anna were separate pictures of star signs with outrageous mockup meanings. He'd read them often over the years, but he didn't think Anna had noticed them yet.

'Hey, what's your star sign?' he asked as he took a sip of his flat Coke, enjoying the retreat from his life as he sat in the haven of Ling's Golden Wheel Restaurant.

'Taurus,' she told him suspiciously. 'Why?'

'Taurus,' he tutted as he read from the wall. 'Hmm, says here that you are prone to lying and can't be trusted. You're a possible pyromaniac and that you enjoy group sex.' He looked back at her with wide eyes. 'Something that could have been brought to my attention earlier.'

'What!' she cried as she spun around to see the wall behind her and spun back to face him.

Justin leant across the fried rice on his plate. 'Is this true Anna?' he asked. 'I mean, it's fine. I'd just like to know.'

Anna had turned to read them for herself, confirming she had heard him right.

'What is this? Isn't this a family restaurant?'

'It's your horoscope,' he informed her, and she chuckled at its ridiculousness. She had relaxed since their earlier encounter that evening and even he was the most relaxed he'd been in weeks.

'Okay then, what's *your* star sign?' she demanded.

'Well, as a bit of a coincidence Anna, I too, am a Taurus.' Anna's lips twisted with doubt, unsure whether he was telling the truth—which he was. 'You know what that means?'

'No,' she laughed. 'But please, do tell.' she amused him, holding her chop sticks mid-air as she waited.

'It means that *we* are only one Taurean away from group sex,' he grinned wickedly and revelled in her laughter.

'Lucky us,' she laughed. 'Best not use candles though,' she pulled a face, visualising the outcome of three pyromaniacs.

'My thoughts exactly,' he confessed. 'Maybe we can read minds too,' he rubbed his temples as if getting a message. 'Did you hear that?'

'No, I must have missed it. But I get poor reception when I'm sitting near idiots,' she apologised.

'So, *I'm* the idiot?' he queried, pressing his finger to his chest.

'Yes. Now are you done with your little bit here or are the voices still trying to get through?'

'I'm done,' he grinned, scooping more honey chicken onto his plate and then Anna's. While she protested, a woman about to take a seat caught his eye. Justin's breath briefly caught in his chest before realising it wasn't who he thought he'd seen. Turning back to his plate, he put a big mouthful of food in before he noticed Anna watching him with a curious smile.

'What just happened there? You turned a little pale. Ex-girlfriend of yours is it?' she asked, indicating the older woman taking a seat.

'No,' Justin said a little distractedly. 'I, ah, thought it was a patient, or patient's owner I should say,' he tried to explain vaguely.

'And do you often cower from your clients?'

'I wasn't cowering,' he denied. 'You don't understand.' He brushed her off and ate another mouthful. His sisters hated his ability to eat three times as much as them and not get fat. Or fat *yet*, as his father reminded him.

But Anna was now leaning back in her seat expectantly. 'Oh really, I don't understand? So, make me,' she dared, her teeth gleaming at him. Justin considered whether he should impart this information to her. After all, she was a Taurus and they couldn't be trusted—but he conceded.

'Okay, just as long as you promise not to laugh.'

'No,' she smiled at his terms.

'No?'

'I can't promise that.'

'Well then, no deal.'

'Well … I didn't really want to know anyway,' she told him petulantly.

'How old are *you*?' he laughed.

'Is that a rhetorical question?' she checked.

'No. Yes … Both.'

'How old are you?' she challenged him.

'I asked you first.' Geez, how old *was* he?

'I'm twenty-nine,' she confessed, and he felt his eyebrows rise.

'Really?'

'Really. Now, how old are you?' Anna pressed.

'I thought you were younger.'

'Thanks, I guess I should be flattered,' she pondered. 'Maybe you need glasses though. Any headaches? Scalpel slip-ups?'

He shook his head, unable to stop a laugh from escaping.

'It may have just been your maturity level that threw me off,' he offered apologetically.

'Nice. Right then, your turn. Older or younger?'

'Older. Obviously.'

'Well, I didn't want to make you feel bad. Especially after you just told me I had amazing and youthful skin—I read between the lines,' she added to his raised eyebrows. 'Now … birth date. In full. Are you in fact a Taurus?'

'Third of May.'

'Me too!' she cried, and the other four patrons looked over.

'Really?'

'Nah.' He wanted to shake her. 'Age?'

He shook his head at her. 'You know, no-one likes a smart-arse.'

'Age.' She pressed on, ignoring him.

'Thirty-three,' he gave in.

'Huh,' she frowned. 'I could have sworn you were older.' Justin let her enjoy her moment before replying. She sat smiling, waiting.

'Well, that's an easy mistake. Once again, like me, you were probably just put off by my maturity and wisdom.'

'Ha! Now, tell me about this scary customer of yours. Would you like me to sort them out?' She looked at him like she was dealing with a child.

'I'm not scared of her,' he persisted. 'I just don't … *enjoy* her.' Anna's eyebrows frowned with curiosity, but before she could badger him for the story, he gave in. 'I have this client who seems to be a bit too fond of me. Don't laugh,' he warned as Anna had begun to. She lowered her hand over her face and presented him with seriousness.

'She has this old Maltese and more money than sense. She'll bring him in at any given chance and insists on seeing me. Sandra thinks it's hilarious,' he frowned. 'She'll come in and side-up right next to me. She wears these *very* tight shirts. She found me on Facebook and invited me over to her place. I had to change my profile. It's … awkward.'

'She invited you over!' Anna exclaimed, and Justin was grateful she wasn't still laughing at him. 'Why don't you just get the other staff to deal with her or talk about Julia the whole time?'

'Well, for starters, Eric—the other vet—referred her to me as a joke, and it's only me that is put out. What can I say? I'm too nice. And I think she's crazy. If I piss her off, she could give us a bad name … or burn down the clinic.'

Anna frowned. 'Why didn't you just mention Julia?'

'I did! I'd talk about Julia the whole time. I'd get so inventive of ways to emphasise how *not* single I was to this woman, but she doesn't stop. I see her around from time to time and she's almost impossible to shake off.' Justin signed, batting his lashes with a laugh, 'I'm not intimidating enough.'

He wasn't sure if Anna could possibly understand—Julia never did; or the rest of the staff.

'So, essentially, you have a stalker.'

'No. Not a stalker,' he shook his head.

'Had any underwear go missing lately?'

Justin, regretting that he'd told her, shovelled more food into his mouth to comfort himself. He was starting to feel full and could see Anna only pick at her food, so when the waitress came back to their table with the extra spring rolls he'd ordered, he knew it had been a bad decision to ask for them. In saying that, he had one dipped in sweet-and-sour sauce before the plate even hit the table.

'Geez, you really like your spring rolls,' she laughed, adding thoughtfully, 'Leo loves them too. Always makes us order them, even if no-one else wants them.'

Leo? Justin felt his body straighten against his will as he bit into the roll. Hadn't Jane mentioned a Leo? He thought maybe she had and wondered who this Leo guy was. Maybe he was the speed-date Justin recalled Anna having. This may have been Anna's way of saying she had a Leo—likely.

So, she had a Leo, it made no difference. Anna was merely a friend. A friend who just happened to have amazing eyes and (from clear memory) amazing talent when it came to kissing.

'So …' he began to fish nevertheless, 'Leo doesn't care what you want?' He smiled to take the edge off his question. Justin had gone to school with a Leo. He hadn't liked him either.

Anna smiled. 'I think I'm just a pushover, to be honest.'

'I wouldn't have picked you as a pushover, Anna.'

She laughed in surprise. 'What do you mean?'

'You seem to have a stubborn streak,' he openly observed, finishing his second spring roll and resisting reaching for another.

'Gee, thanks,' she replied wryly. 'Well, you would be wrong.' She folded her arms, stubbornly declaring she wasn't stubborn. 'I cave easily.'

'Hmm …' He looked over her thoughtfully. 'I don't believe you. I *have* seen the wrath of Anna remember. Get this Leo on the phone!' he demanded.

'Leo won't talk to you,' she teased. 'And what's this about the wrath of Anna?'

Her phone started ringing, saving him from responding, and she fumbled in her bag to find it, looking at Justin apologetically as she answered it.

'Is it Leo?' he mouthed, reaching for the phone. She held her finger to her lips, while making a series of 'ah huhs'. After hanging up, she told his curious face it was her work phone.

'Work?' he queried; eyebrow raised as he checked his watch. 'It's almost ten-thirty. You're a stripper aren't you?' He shook his head while granting an impressed grin and she laughed briefly, but gave no further clues.

'No, no. Not a stripper *Doctor Owens*,' she drew out. 'It was my work asking me to start at *stupid* o'clock tomorrow.'

'Do you go home tomorrow?' he asked, confused and surprised this hadn't come up already over dinner. He felt the clouds that had been hanging over him all day return at the idea she was leaving, and he had a random flash of the Luna Park clown laughing at him.

'No. I'm working in Sydney.' She told Justin this like it was obvious, and he felt the brief grey cloud lift and float away as he held back his smile.

'Ah, the plot thickens,' he tapped his fingers on his chin. 'You're a pilot!' he proclaimed with confidence that he had finally nailed it.

'No.' She rolled her eyes with a smile before offering to reveal her mystery career.

Justin looked aghast. 'And ruin the game? Are you crazy?'

'I can't believe they let you put a 'D' and an 'R' in front of your name, and you are a complete loon. I have grave concerns for Claude right now.'

'You and me, both,' he sighed. 'Now, if you have to get up at *stupid o'clock* as you put it, then we should go.'

Anna agreed and obediently went to the counter to pay. Justin, laughing that she was going ahead with the deal and feeling particularly ungentlemanly, filled his mouth with two more mouthfuls of food and watched her as he dunked another spring roll in sauce. On recalling it was the same food that Anna's Leo loved, he involuntarily frowned and shifted in his seat as he chewed. Watching Anna leaning down to sign the receipt, Justin held onto his frown — because now he simply felt guilty. Anna had pulled her hair behind her ear and revealed her profile clearly. The friendly smile she had offered the waitress was now gone, with no-one to see but Justin. She looked exhausted and he felt bad taking up her time.

When Anna turned back to face him, a blanket smile thrown over her tiredness, Justin quickly threw on his own and stepped to meet her halfway.

'Ready?' she asked.

'Yup.'

'I'm assuming you need a lift home too?' Anna smiled, but Justin could not now miss the truth beneath it.

'Oh, ah … no. I'm just going to walk,' he said, feeling embarrassment creep over his face and down his neck, with an unstoppable objective of causing further embarrassment.

He could only hope that she hadn't noticed. Though, after stepping out into the cooler night air, Anna insisted that she'd drive him home. Justin felt what small shine of masculinity he had left be tarnished further by his lack of licence.

'I can walk, it's not far,' he assured her. After so many years of depending on no-one, it made him feel pathetic having to get rides, catch the bus or ask for favours.

'Not far? It is too, and it's late and dark and cold. Justin, let's not forget that you have a stalker. The streets aren't safe for you, buddy,' she frowned.

'Okay, for that, you can drive me home,' he pushed her shoulder and climbed into her car without further protest.

By the time she'd pulled up to his grey house, with the help of his directions, they were laughing loudly. The feeling felt foreign to Justin, his lungs felt out of shape for the task, and his cheeks hurt from being stretched so wide.

'Well, thanks for dinner,' he said, patting his hands on his thighs silently, the laughter suddenly spent.

'Thanks for Claude, more,' she corrected.

'Not a problem. I guess I'll see you tomorrow then.'

'Yes,' she said, experiencing an abrupt loss of words and seemingly perturbed to where they could have gone to so quickly. Justin felt the discomfort on both their parts. He suddenly wished to be inside his house already, because in truth he felt like he was doing something wrong. That by sitting in the car with Anna, Julia would bust him — forgetting it was too late and that she already had.

'Okay,' Justin eventually said. 'Well, thanks again. Catch you later.' He climbed out of the car, possibly a little too quickly, and cringed, hoping he didn't appear too keen to get away. He paused before closing the door completely and leant his head back in.

'Hey Anna, I really am sorry about what happened in Melbourne.' He spoke before he could stop himself and wanted to slap his good intentions away instantly; but when she smiled, all the way to her eyes, he relaxed.

'Me too.'

Waving her off as she drove away, Justin climbed the steps slowly to his door. He took a breath in, as if to re-set his mind, and went inside to a very excited and very hungry scruffy dog.

chapter twenty-nine

Justin was delivering puppies. He alternated handing them to the young vet nurse and Mrs Henderson, the owner, as he pulled each one of the seven out. The labrador, who had unwittingly been stuck with these mad breeders, had needed an emergency caesarean and Justin had just declared this her last pregnancy. He even hinted to Mrs Henderson that she retire herself. Only time would tell, but he hoped that this time next year she wouldn't be on the phone to him, sapping his time and will to live.

By the time she left, sure to return the next day for her meal tickets, Justin wanted to high-five every staff member and client in the clinic.

'My god, she is hard work,' Justin told Sandra, who agreed wholeheartedly, while zipping over to look at the puppies. 'Oh, they are so adorable.'

Together they admired the new arrivals. Eric poked his head over the top to get a brief view, sighed and then totted off. Justin, sighing too, went back to the front counter to update the Hendersons' file. He heard Sandra approach from behind not long after—her sigh always the loudest.

'So-o, Justin … did you get home okay last night?' She sung his name with a hint of mockery and Justin looked at her suspiciously.

'Y-e-s,' he sang back, attempting to match her tone. 'Why do you ask?'

'Anna tells me you met in Melbourne,' she started, and he knew at once that this woman was treading where he didn't want her to. He suspected that even she knew this, but Sandra proceeded anyway. 'She doesn't happen to be the reason behind Julia leaving now, does she?'

Justin looked across at her quickly, taking his eyes from the computer screen to face her. He hadn't expected her to tread *there* exactly.

'N-No … why would you say that?' Justin felt his face heat up and tension fill his head as he quickly turned defensive — there was much more to the story. But Sandra just smiled her knowing smile.

'What makes you say that?' he asked again, trying to keep his desperation at bay and attempting to sound uber-casual.

'Relax. Just something your sister mentioned.' Sandra smiled and patted him on the shoulder. The phone rang and before Justin could demand more information from her, she took the call.

'Hills Veterinary Clinic,' Sandra answered and listened to the caller while Justin impatiently scribbled a note demanding which sister. Sandra shook her head and rolled her eyes. Taking the pen from his hand, she wrote 'Lesley' and continued to listen to the caller on the other end of the phone, content in going about her job when she hung up.

'When did Lesley *mention* that?' Justin probed, much louder than he'd intended. Sandra, glancing around the waiting-room, shushed him. 'When did you talk to Lesley?' he whispered coarsely. He'd spoken to her that morning, and she hadn't mentioned anything about her unveiling his life to his receptionist.

'Calm down,' she smirked, enjoying his discomfort. 'She'd called for you the other day and you were busy. We were chatting about that gorgeous little boy of hers, but I was worried about you,' she explained kindly, 'and she gave me a bit more information than *you* did.'

That was her justification?

Her supposed concern was no validation to pry into his life and discuss his problems. He felt humiliated that they had spoken about him, that Sandra knew more than he'd wanted anyone to know—that she'd spoken to Anna.

'Oh god, what did you say to Anna?' he rushed out; his heart pounding at the thought that Anna knew what was not for her to know.

'Justin, really?' she quipped, so clearly disappointed and sounding like his mother. In fact, he often felt that with Sandra around he had two mothers; two women to make proud, two to disappoint. And, even harder, two, to keep his life from.

'Gosh, I'm not senile. I didn't say anything to her. I wasn't even sure it was true. Well, until your face turned that lovely shade of pink that is. You should really work on that my dear,' she told him graciously before walking out the back to give the phone message to Eric.

Justin sat processing the conversation, the relief washing over him—the frustration cancelling it out; the guilt from the pettiness of his worries shaming him.

He was forced to get up when an owner needed help convincing their nervous shepherd through the doors, then spent the rest of the day trying not to think about Anna—what she knew; what she thought. Until Justin remembered that he'd see her again that night when she came to collect Claude. Then he smiled.

He'd get to see Anna.

Anna had a happy fluttering feeling in her belly all day—even when she had to navigate her way to a very well-hidden company as the sun came up. Admittedly, Wednesday had gotten the better of her, but seeing Justin, and clearing the air, had made her feel so much more normal. Plus, she had simply had a good time—a rare event of late. She did, however, hold strong concerns that the Chinese food from their dinner was making her body protrude a stench of garlic that could undoubtedly ward off the flu for the rest of her life. No-one had commented so far, so she could only assume she was safe—or that her new workmates were incredibly polite.

Now, back at her desk and in too much of a good mood to concentrate, Anna saved the file she had been working on and headed to the kitchen.

'You seem chirpy today,' Sally, the junior technician, observed. Anna gave a private smile to the wall as she made a cup of tea.

'Do I?'

She hadn't realised the difference holding a grudge against a person could make. Anna contemplated ringing the receptionists in Melbourne to better that relationship too. She even half-thought of calling Kyle—the date that had rejected her in a heartbeat. She didn't call either. But the mere idea was enough to make her feel like she was a better person for it.

Anna floated back to her desk and carefully planted her mug within easy reach. The task list looming in front of her was monstrous, her good mood unfortunately doing nothing to benefit that, but she couldn't avoid it any longer. Her new team had already been extremely accommodating and willing to give Anna plenty of time to familiarise herself with their projects and programs. Though what was even more appreciated was that they approached her personally with open arms. Anna was surprised by this because in her first two days she had completely lost the ability to converse. Social skills had become foreign to her. Asking questions, nodding, listening … it had all seemed too much. She had craved Mel's presence at work. Craved not having to think about what to say, not having to impress. Yet, thankfully, when her confidence progressed, so too had her personality. It now appeared to be behaving much more to her normal (granted, sometimes scatty) ways and her new colleagues took to her even more, not holding her lifeless arrival against her.

As nice as everyone was though, this hadn't stopped her from feeling lonely when she drove out of the car park each evening towards an empty home or to the hospital. Both of which were wearing thin on her—the lines under her eyes testimony to the fact. Old school friends were nothing more than a hazy memory to her, scattered across towns around the state. The only people she really knew in Sydney were her mother and Jane. The fact that she was enjoying work simply for the company, told Anna that she needed to do more with her time, so work wouldn't be her day's highlight. Anna had decided to take a day or two a week off from visiting the hospital. She hated admitting it, but she needed a break. Jane had been on Anna's case about putting too much pressure on herself. Jessica, the perky counsellor, had also urged her to take some respite after Anna had shrugged to the question of when she had last done something for herself. The previous night with Justin, and having actual real-life fun, only gave the idea more clout.

Tonight was going to be her first night off. The relief of knowing she wouldn't be fighting traffic to get to the hospital was welcome. A whole night to do as she pleased awaited her. Anna texted Jane to see if she was keen to meet up. When her phone eventually beeped a response, Anna leapt at it with hope and excitement that she had actual plans, imagining it to be like old times—old times being only weeks ago.

But it wasn't to be.

Hi hon, sorry can't do. Dad and Sarah moving stuff into new place. Stay away, it's getting ugly!

Anna had completely forgotten that Jane was moving. She felt a considerable stab of guilt that her new address, though closer to her work, wasn't anywhere near as nice as Justin's home—or as cheap—but it was a granny flat that she wouldn't have to share. She also wasn't sure how Jane would react to the idea that Anna and Justin were now on speaking terms, let alone eating terms. She shrunk at the thought of Jane's reaction, and then buried the thought for another day.

Anna left work at six, breathing into her hand to make sure she didn't smell, and headed in a different direction to her usual hospital route. It gave her a feeling of rebellion and freedom, followed quickly by guilt. Guilt—her constant companion.

Anna thought of her life in Melbourne, the one where she did something fun after work (or nothing at all), and quickly pushed it away. She'd be back soon enough.

Anna drove on, mixing up her life by heading to an animal hospital instead.

When Anna pulled up outside Justin's practice, she saw the oversized paw-print on the window. She shook her head before climbing out of the car. 'He's a *vet*,' she muttered, as if it had just dawned on her.

She felt embarrassed to have thought he would ever have been interested in a girl like herself; she felt like an underachiever in comparison. Justin had probably laughed at the moronic things she had said—or maybe she wasn't even worth talking about. Anna frowned at her vanity to think she was worth further reflection, even if it was to laugh at her.

The door chimed as she walked through. Anna saw the top of Sandra's head; her short hair styled smartly, her face glued to the computer screen, which was receiving a stern glare.

Looking up at the door's sound, Sandra smiled through her grimace. 'Evening, Anna. Here for Claude?'

'Hi. Yes,' Anna smiled back, noting the strong sterile smell of the room that she hadn't noticed the night before, and wiping her clammy hands against her skirt. 'You're looking like you want a brick,' she joked nervously, and Sandra nodded in agreement.

'I hate computers,' she sighed and slid the mouse across her desk in defeat before examining Anna over her glasses. 'I'll go get him.'

She disappeared into the depths of the clinic where Anna could hear animals voicing their want to go home. Anna wondered if by 'him' Sandra had meant Claude or Justin. When she returned holding her mother's grey cat, Anna couldn't help but feel disappointed.

'Hi Claude,' she whispered affectionately. 'How are you feeling, buddy?'

Sandra held Claude firmly and Anna could see his shaved ear was stitched neatly back together. His paw was now hidden by the white bandage wound almost all the way up his leg. His eye was less swollen, as was the anxiety Anna had been experiencing.

Anna was sure she could hear Justin laugh from out the back and, while straining to confirm, she struggled to also hear what Sandra was saying to her. Embarrassingly, Sandra seemed to realise this.

'Would you like me to see if Jay wanted to tell you anything?' she suggested politely, and Anna casually accepted the offer, absently fixing her hair. Sandra, watching Anna carefully, rolled Claude into Anna's arms and stepped towards the back again.

'*Doctor* Owens!' she called, sweetly. Anna sensed that Sandra didn't usually refer to Justin by his title.

'Yo,' he called back, and Anna giggled for no reason other than having heard his voice. The giggle, simply a release of nervous tension, sounded like no normal sound that Anna would usually make. She felt like an idiot, unable to stop herself performing so pathetically and had to remind herself (yet again) that Justin was taken — and out of her league, especially now that she knew he was a doctor. The list was growing against her. Even if she could scrape in on the looks department, she could never match him in brains. She wondered what his girlfriend did. Maybe she was a vet too and they'd have brainy children together; while Anna leapt from bad relationship to no relationship, for the rest of her life …

'Hi, Anna.' A voice broke her from her self-deprecation.

'Hi, Justin,' Anna smiled widely.

'Hi,' he said, smiling back.

'Hi,' Anna said again, forgetting she had already said that.

'*Hi,*' interrupted Sandra, stopping Justin from greeting Anna again. 'Justin, could you explain to Anna how to look after Claude's injuries?' She sounded more than slightly exasperated and excused herself to answer a call, leaving Justin to tell Anna what to do so that Claude didn't chew off his bandage or tear out his stitches — the mere idea sending a revolted shiver down Anna's spine.

'And you'll need to bring him back in about a week.'

'Okay,' she smiled stupidly. His face was unshaven and he looked scruffy; surprisingly good, but scruffy. His white coat had a claw mark just beneath the words of the clinic and fur clung to the belly of his navy polo shirt. Anna went to brush at it and stopped herself just in time. *Must keep both hands on cat. Do not touch the vet.*

'I'll, um, see you then, then.' Anna was raking her brain to try to think of something else to say. Weather, traffic, sport, hunger, the fur on his belly — all these options, yet no sentence could be articulated in time.

'Okay, Anna,' he told her, and hearing her name come out his mouth felt strangely intimate. Anna blushed and quickly excused herself, unable to cope with any further embarrassment. She drove home reprimanding herself every time a potential conversation starter occurred to her. The sensation to turn around and go back was fought over by her commonsense that it would only be more embarrassing to turn up and say any of the material she had come up with. 'So, how was that sunshine today?'

Home, and out of sorts, Anna laid a quiet Claude on her mother's worn lounge. She watched him lie awkwardly, unsure what to do with her time. Jane was busy unpacking and there was nothing she wanted to watch on TV. She skimmed over the latest Facebook feeds, while she ate a microwave meal, but was bored within moments. Instagram wasn't any better. The only worthwhile idea she came up with was sleep, an idea seemingly supported by her body. Her muscles suddenly felt weary as if to add further persuasion to the proposal; and Anna didn't protest. Putting herself to bed, she curled up under the faded covers, hugging herself tightly to warm up, and allowed herself to think of Justin—because no-one else was to know any different.

chapter thirty

It was Tuesday and Mel felt impatient that three-and-a-half more days had to finish before she could sleep-in again. Feeling far from energetic, she was having lunch with a group from the office, including Anna's replacement: a temp backpacking from Ireland with his thick northern accent. Consequently, her colleagues were making him repeat words. 'Say rubbish, say rubbish!' one demanded. 'Now say potato.' It was childish and pointless—albeit, amusing.

Mel didn't know his real name because the office had affectionately (and unoriginally) named him *Paddy*. Paddy had accepted this and therefore his true name was now lost on everyone.

Her phone beeped and her weariness was replaced swiftly with a feeling that wobbled her insides. Mel read the message and grinned.

Call me.

Her teeth gleamed to everyone around her.

'I'll meet you back at the office,' she told the group as she stood to leave. She hadn't told anyone about Tom. She knew the distance issue was big enough to make it seem stupid. She didn't want people to laugh, and she didn't want anyone to tell her not to bother. Worse, she didn't want people to give her hope.

Picking up her bag and swinging it over her shoulder, Mel pressed the call button.

'What took you so long?' he asked.

She grinned at his now familiar voice. 'Well, you could very well have just called *me*,' she rebutted.

'Well—I was trying to get out of a meeting,' he spoke sheepishly. 'Plus, I don't know how good my phone plan is.' He was referring to their long and frequent nightly calls.

'Fair enough,' she smiled. 'How's your day been?'

'Okay. Good, actually. Apart from that meeting. I, ah … managed to get a booking for a restaurant that I heard was pretty good.'

He sounded hesitant. It took her a moment to repeat Tom's words in her head. When she did, her smile struggled to hold the weight.

'For work?' she asked, trying her best not to sound testy—her feet slowing on the pavement.

'No. For a … um, date, actually.'

'Oh. Right.' She felt foolish. So, so foolish. The conversation stopped with a grinding halt and her feet did the same, a cloud of dust should have grown in front of her as her feet pulled up short.

He had a date. That was that.

'Aren't you going to ask me where?' Tom asked, bold and ignorant to the sharp pain in Mel's chest. Was this his way to tell her that nothing would come of them?

'Where?' she mumbled irately, no part of her wanting to know. She hardly knew Sydney to know any restaurant he'd booked anyway. Feeling her eyes burn, Mel bit her lip, hoping it would keep tears at bay.

'*Rush,*' he told her proudly. She didn't respond, she barely heard him—she could taste blood in her mouth as it swelled from her lip. 'Remember, you told me about it?' Tom urged, and Mel nodded. On remembering he couldn't hear a nod, and her pride not wanting him to know her shame, she gathered words together and spoke.

'Right, yeah. Didn't know it was a chain,' she managed, wanting to hang up. She heard him laugh and she *really* wanted to hang up. Her handbag slipped from her shoulder, it felt heavier than it had a minute ago, and she struggled to put it back in place, coordination now gone.

'*Melissa!*' he exclaimed, still laughing. 'It's not a chain. At least, I don't think it is.' Mel assumed her silence told Tom that she didn't understand because he continued. 'I hung up last night and thought, 'This is crazy'.'

Way to sock it to me.

Mel felt her hands shake. She looked behind her, grateful her colleagues were out of view.

'It's too hard being away from you … and you said you had nothing planned for the weekend … so I, um, booked a restaurant … and a flight. Mel, would you like to have dinner with me on Saturday night?'

Mel took in his words, careful to not misunderstand them. 'You're coming here?'

'Yes.'

'*We're* going to *Rush*?'

'Yes. If you want to that is.'

'You're coming here!' she laughed in relief and pure happiness.

'If that's okay,' he laughed back, relieved at her response.

'What about your soccer? Isn't it finals?'

'Soccer,' he scoffed. 'We're losing anyway. We're playing for fourth place. I'd much rather see you.'

'Really?' she grinned.

'Really.'

Justin was craving a burger, one with the lot: beef, bacon, egg, beetroot, and all the other regulars that hang out on a burger. Anna was due to pick him up in an hour and Justin planned to push the burger idea on her then.

Justin had rung Anna the day after she had picked up Claude, just to see how the cat was going. He'd reasoned that sometimes animals chewed at the bandage and he just wanted to check that wasn't the case for Claude. She hadn't answered the call and when he left a message to call him back, he'd left his personal mobile number — just in case she was too busy in business hours. It was a common problem for clients and he still didn't know what Anna did for a living, so really, it was just for her convenience. Customer service was very important; Sandra had told them this time and time again.

When Anna did call back, conveniently while he was on his lunch break, she had chosen to ring his mobile.

They'd talked for what Justin thought was only a little while, but when Sandra had to come and fetch him, he realised they had talked about nothing for his entire break; not her mum, not his deteriorating niece, and definitely not politics. Having hung up suddenly, he texted Anna later that night to apologise for cutting their conversation short. The one text led to a night's distraction, his phone's incoming message beep the theme song as he went about his usual routine. Mostly, he smiled at her words, but sometimes Justin had thought Anna sounded sad. Considering her quick move and mother's circumstances, he also thought she had a right to be.

Wanting to help, Justin suggested that they get a bite to eat when she brought Claude back in. He needed some distraction from his own life changes and the worries his whole family had for his niece. Bianca's condition, Biliary Atresia, was a huge weight of concern for everyone except her sisters, who had taken to calling her *Carrot*, completely unaware how serious her orange-looking skin was.

That morning, when Justin had told Sandra that he was getting picked up and wouldn't need a lift that night, she had smiled at him like she would a child, making a long 'hmm' sound. It had echoed in Justin's head, demanding attention.

'What does that mean?' he'd asked her cautiously.

'I was just thinking how well you've bounced back from Julia.' Sandra smiled genuinely. 'I'm happy for you. Anna seems *lovely*. Really adorable.'

'What do you mean? I'm not *with* her,' he shook his head, not sure how she had become so confused.

'Who aren't you with?' Eric asked, as he'd come past to grab a new box of latex gloves.

'Anna,' Sandra told him, looking to the box in Eric's hands. 'I *must* put that order in. We're low on gloves,' she murmured to herself while her fingers searched for a pen.

'Who's Anna?' Eric asked, stopping to find out, not one to pass on any gossip.

'Justin's new girlfriend,' Sandra told Eric as she wrote down a note reminding herself to place an order.

'Whoa, that was quick mate. That's great.' Eric slapped Justin on the back and returned to his client.

'She's not my girlfriend!' Justin called after him. 'Sandra, what are you doing?'

'She's lovely, Jay. If she's not your girlfriend, she should be. That's all I'm saying. I mean you *are* going on another date with her,' she informed him, her eyes peering over her glasses.

'It's dinner, not a contract of marriage. We're just friends,' Justin told her firmly. He didn't want rumors starting and definitely didn't want Anna to think that he had the wrong idea. 'Anyway, she's seeing someone.'

He was hoping this would be the end of the discussion. Anna and he were purely friends. They were barely even that really. They'd only met a handful of times and even then, it had always been by accident. In fact, he realised tonight would be the first time they actually intended meeting. But that didn't make it a date. It wasn't a date. Just a burger—hopefully.

At 7.45 p.m. Anna came through the door holding Claude. The door chimed and Justin stood at the desk like he had been waiting for them to arrive. Anna hoped they hadn't kept him. She'd been to see the counsellor again that day and had rushed home to avoid being late.

He welcomed them both with a big smile. If they had kept him waiting, he didn't seem to mind.

Anna was surprised by her reaction at the sight of Justin. She had thought the way her body reacted other times she'd seen him was purely her surprise, but now she was thinking it was actually the Justin effect. She returned his smile, feeling a little stupid that she couldn't control the extent of her grin and that she had just referred to his presence as having the *Justin Effect*—like he was a scientific theory. Nonetheless, she was sure her dimples collided with her ears and there was nothing she could do about it, short of inflicting pain on herself, and that would have just looked odd.

'Hi,' she said tightly, trying hard to control the giggle that threatened to escape her throat for no logical reason what-so-ever. Obligingly, Claude became restless and Anna appreciated the distraction. Justin offered to take him, leading them past the display of squeaky toys and into the clinic room. He held Claude's grey whiskered face to his and asked how he was feeling. Anna chuckled and noticed his receptionist standing next to the desk smiling at her. Anna wondered where Sandra had come from as she said hello, the wonder dissipating once Justin closed the door.

'How have you been?' Justin asked Anna this time as he put the cat down. Claude stood hesitant on the stainless-steel table, much more alert than his previous visit and undoubtedly preparing his escape.

'Good. You?' she replied, unsure why she felt so nervous. She didn't know whether to keep her hands in her pockets, on her hips, hold onto them or hang them.

She hung them.

'Good.' Justin smiled at her some more, containing Claude easily. Anna felt her face flush—as well as a now-familiar pang of envy for Julia.

Anna watched as he expertly checked Claude's injuries. Claude didn't even resist and Anna was impressed. She'd never seen a guy handle a cat, or any animal, so calmly and gently. It made her feel a little mushy and Anna wondered what Julia was like—until Justin began removing the stitches, and then that mushy feeling changed to a queasy feeling rather quickly. She made a small gagging sound and Justin turned his amused eyes to her.

'You okay?'

'Uh huh,' she lied.

'Just close your eyes, I'll tell you when I'm done. It'll only take a second.' Anna appreciated him not making fun of her and closed her eyes. She didn't know how Justin could stand all the things he had to see and do as a vet. Needles, scalpels, blood, poop—all those rating high on her list of things that would make her pass out.

'Hey, how do you feel about getting a burger tonight?' Justin asked as he worked.

'Is this payment again?' she smiled, eyes remaining firmly closed. She heard his small snips end, but he hadn't replied.

Anna crept one eye open, careful not to see anything gross. Justin stood tall, smiling at her.

Embarrassed, Anna worried she had something on her face causing him to smile like that. Paranoid, she wanted to brush at her face as a precaution but didn't want to look too obvious or bothered.

Justin gave a crooked, hopeful grin. 'I'll shout the burgers, if you drive?'

'Sounds okay to me,' Anna laughed, casually brushing her hands over her face, hoping she'd removed any mysterious unwanted items.

'Where is this car of yours anyway?' she asked curiously, as Justin paused to unwind the now battered bandage on Claude's leg.

Anna wondered what Julia thought of her hanging out with her boyfriend. If she had a boyfriend that was eating out with random girls, she wouldn't want to share him. Julia was obviously a much better woman.

'Ah …' he looked up at her briefly, then back to Claude, checking leg movement. 'It was hit by a car, so it's in getting repaired.'

Anna felt his frustration. 'Oh really? How annoying,' she empathised, remembering the rainy day when someone had run up the back of her car.

'How long until you get it back? A friend of mine had to wait months.'

'Yeah, I'm not sure. I've heard stories like that too. I think my car may be one of those cases.'

'Oh, no,' she sympathised, but Justin dismissed it and left her to fetch some ointment for Claude's paw while Anna commended him on his patience.

When Justin was finished only Eric was left in the clinic and he winked when he saw Anna—much to Justin's annoyance. Eric, who was unhappily married not ten years into the vows, was often living through Justin.

Justin discreetly shook his head at Eric to persuade him to stop.

'Hi, I'm *Doctor* Sidorvoski,' he told Anna, holding his hand out and bobbling his head like he was Brad Pitt, feigning modesty. Justin hung his head at the shiny linoleum floor, ashamed on behalf of his partner. Pulling out the doctor title was a big obtuse no-no in his book.

'Anna.' She shook Eric's hand reluctantly.

'Nice to meet you Anna.' Eric winked at Justin again and Justin felt his eyes bulge.

'Anna, this is Eric,' Justin interrupted. 'Don't refer to him as Doctor, you'll only encourage him and we're still looking into it.'

Anna smiled politely at Eric, but Justin noticed her retract her hand quickly, also uncomfortable with Eric's staring. She was no fool—not that Justin had thought otherwise.

Eric lacked certain social skills that most people possessed. Granted, he was a nice enough guy, and a good vet, but when you got right down to it—he was dull. Justin thought this dullness was the catalyst behind Eric's failing marriage. His idea of foreplay was most probably brushing his teeth. His wife, Paula, lovely and bubbly, seemed to be compensating for her husband's personality with cake—and a lot of it.

Looking at Eric with Anna now, Justin wondered if Eric had used the doctor line when he'd pulled Paula, because charm would certainly not have been a factor. Poor Paula, Justin mused.

They dropped Claude at Anna's mother's place, a fifteen-minute journey away, and Justin felt bad as he realised his plan was making Anna do so much extra driving.

'Burger time?' she asked, jumping back in the car.

'Burger time,' he confirmed. 'Know of any good take-away places around here?'

'Nope. I don't even know any bad ones.'

'Okay, then allow me to direct you.' Anna obligingly zig-zagged the streets until Justin pointed out their destination. A little place called *Jimmy's* shone out from between a bakery and hairdressers.

Justin cheered that they were open and jumped out of the car.

'Hey, wait for me.' Anna called, doing a poor job of being annoyed as she laughed at him standing in front of the counter ready to order.

'With the lot?' he smiled encouragingly.

'No,' she screwed her nose up. 'Just a plain burger. Oh, but with beetroot. It has to have beetroot.' He took the demand seriously; his own concoction was not to be messed with either.

While Justin placed their orders, repeating his barbeque-to-mato-mustard sauce request, Anna fetched drinks from the back fridge. The glass bottles made a brief clinking tune as she closed the heavy door, the sound somehow reminding him of his childhood and his whole body lifted.

They waited against the red laminate counter listening to the patties sizzle and the bacon pop, the smell only making Justin hungrier. He leant against the countertop while Anna hoisted herself on a stool and swung her legs. Outside, Justin could see her silver Mazda parked in front of the shop.

'Are you going to change your plates over?' he asked, want-ing to suss out her intentions with Sydney, in lieu of just asking her straight out.

'No point, I'll be going back to Victoria—once Mum's home.'

'Sydney doesn't tempt you?'

Anna looked at her car thoughtfully. 'A little, I admit,' she grinned. 'But Melbourne feels like home now. It's the longest I've ever stayed in one place,' she confided.

'You moved a lot?' He'd noticed that she never mentioned her dad and was curious as to why. Anna nodded as she sipped an apple juice.

'All the time. This is actually the longest my mum has been in the same spot as well.'

'How long?'

'Three years in the place she is at now. But she was not that far away for the two years before that, closer to your clinic. All over the place when I was growing up though,' she explained. Justin didn't respond, just nodded. He had no idea what it would have been like to have moved so often. He had only moved away to study and had otherwise been in the same area his whole life. But moving as a kid, saying goodbye to your friends time and time again, never knowing who you could trust … that would have been tough.

'What about your family?' Anna asked, legs continuing to swing.

'They have always been in the same house. They aren't going anywhere.' Anna smiled her awe at that concept and he actually felt sorry for her. Meanwhile, Jimmy—if that was his real name—signaled that their burgers were ready. Anna fetched the two fat paper bags, holding them up proudly as she bounced back. She perched herself back in place and he joined her on the next stool, unsure of the appropriateness of their proximity, but his hunger pushed any fleeting concerns aside.

'So, did your mum just like change?' he continued as he ripped open the paper bag, tore through the inner lining, and attempted to grip a tower of burger mastery in his hands.

'Um … no,' Anna hesitated at the question and frowned as she sized up her own burger. 'I don't think she necessarily *liked* the change. I think she just didn't know what else to do. Like when she grew sick of her job or a, very rare, relationship ended, it became more of a *coincidence* that we moved. Sometimes it was because of money too. We never had much. Had to be *thrifty*, I guess you could say.'

Anna shrugged and Justin nodded. With three kids, his family had had to be fairly thrifty themselves. He smiled. 'I have a *thrifty* story for you.'

Anna was grateful to have her childhood re-runs stop.

'Do tell,' she mused, struggling to bite her burger, sauce drooping onto her chin, beetroot sliding out, full cheeks grinning.

Justin watched with a smile as she mopped the sauce up and stuffed a flimsy napkin down her shirt like a baby's bib, gesturing for him to begin his story.

'A soccer mate—'

'You play soccer?'

Justin nodded and kept talking, 'is quite into saving his money. He was showing me his new wallet and was a little too excited that he had found it at a garage sale. For a *dollar*. The thing is, he was so happy about his bargain find, he failed to notice that it was a girl's wallet! A fully-grown, working adult man, with a *girl's* wallet.'

Anna chewed on her burger and his story. Justin could still smell the fat burning on the grill and tried not to associate it with his meal.

'By girl's wallet do you mean it was pink and had Barbie on it? Or do you mean, in your boy lingo, that he had a woman's purse?'

'He had a *woman's purse*. He said it was a steal, and he loved it because it had a metal clip for his coins. You know the metal snap-lock thingy?' he asked, chuckling. Anna nodded, laughing too. 'He was stoked he bought it so cheap.'

'Poor guy, that is thrifty,' she agreed. 'A bit too thrifty. Is he single? Because a little quirk like that will taint his relationship hopes.'

'He's married actually.'

'Well,' she warned. 'First stop women's accessories, next thing he'll be wearing his wife's dresses.'

They chuckled for the time it was worth and continued to eat—Justin commenting how slow Anna was, while his food was almost gone.

'You know,' she replied as she watched him eat, 'and this is just a suggestion, but you may actually taste something if you slowed down.'

Justin, looking at her aghast, finished his burger and wiped his face with the crinkled serviette. He glanced at Anna, who'd put her burger back down. She was half laughing at him and there was no denying that it made him feel good. Every time he made her smile, his ego was stroked—right now he was purring like ol' Claude on the inside.

Over the last couple of months, since Julia left, since the accident and everything that had come with it, he felt the difference in himself. He was shy when he wouldn't normally be. He walked with heavy shoulders and spoke less. He'd been placed on the bench at soccer more often and no longer played with any faith. Even when his phone rang, sometimes he didn't have the drive to answer it. But in his handful of moments with Anna, he felt laidback, and the closest to being his real self than he had been in a long time, maybe even years.

'Do you know what I feel like?' Anna interrupted his thoughts, and he looked on expectantly, hoping she'd say ice-cream. 'Wine. I'd love a glass of wine right now,' she fantasised, as she poked her half-eaten burger.

'Are you going to eat that?'

'No. Do you want it?' she asked, surprised, pushing it towards him. 'Do you think they'd sell a nice moscato here?' she joked, as Justin began reassembling her burger.

'Not a chance. But you have to drive anyway, my little delusional friend.'

'I could still have a glass … I haven't seen a wine glass in weeks,' she moaned, lamely thumping the bench. 'Just one.' And then, in a beat, her face hardened. 'I'm not an idiot.'

Justin was thrown off-guard, unsure of her sudden change and cautious to proceed. 'I don't think that,' Justin looked at her, confused. 'I'm sorry. Some people just don't realise that a small amount can push them over is all. I didn't mean anything by it,' he said delicately, thinking of what he'd learnt at his course.

'Yeah, well I'm not one of them,' Anna defended. 'Jerks.'

It was muttered, and almost inaudible under her breath. Justin wasn't sure he'd even heard right. 'Sorry?'

'Nothing.' She paused, uncertain to continue. 'Just, my mum …'

Justin was nervous, fearing where the clues may be leading. 'Your mum?' he prodded. Anna had never brought up her mother beyond the point that she was in hospital and she'd had an accident. All of his attempts to know more had been masterfully deflected.

'She was hit by a drunk driver.'

Justin felt like someone had pushed really hard on his chest.

'Oh,' he replied. He'd never felt so uncomfortable.

'They hit her and left her fighting for her life.'

Anna was barely looking at him, but Justin could see her eyes glisten. He slid a serviette across the counter, which she subtly picked up and pressed under her eyes.

'Arsehole,' Justin affirmed, his heart still out of rhythm.

She nodded, and when an overly loud woman walked into the takeaway joint, Anna gazed at the distraction, putting an immense amount of energy into watching her. Justin let her recoup and looked back at the burger. He'd lost his appetite at 'drunk driver' and now just pushed the bun around.

'Sorry,' she apologised quietly, coming back to face him, forcing Justin back from his own overcrowded brain.

'Don't be,' he smiled and tapped her foot with his. 'I'm sorry about your mum Anna. How is she?' He thought of Bernadette O'Donnell, the person he'd hurt, the name etched in his memory. Justin thought of her injuries and wondered how much her family must resent him. It made him feel sick. He wrapped the food remains in the paper and pushed them out of sight.

'She's doing better,' Anna offered, obviously regretting her breach on revealing such insight into her life and retreated back to her own thoughts. Justin let her. After all, though she had been making him feel happier, that didn't mean he was helping her in anyway. He wasn't going to push her.

'It's good you have Jane, then.'

Anna nodded, then smiled. 'The forever sensible Jane? Definitely. She's my rock. I'd be lost without her. I think, in truth, I've probably relied too much on her. Jane probably moved all the way up here just to get away from me,' she laughed lightly, attempting to conceal an obvious concern.

'I doubt that. I'm sure she's relied on you too.'

Anna shrugged. 'Maybe. I hope so. Then I won't have to feel bad.'

'I wouldn't feel bad. It's a fair compliment really. I mean, if you think about it.'

'Not a burden?' she asked, squinting her eyes together.

'Not at all,' he assured her and thought some more, smiling before he continued. 'My parents have been married thirty-nine years.' Anna repeated the number with wide eyes and Justin appreciated her amazement because he felt the same. 'I know. Imagine *thirty-nine* years with someone. One person!'

'I haven't even lasted thirty-nine weeks!' she laughed. Justin stored this information with curiosity and resumed his story.

'Obviously they didn't find it all easy,' he told her. 'My mum told me once that she didn't know how they survived the first ten years. But she said they relied on each other. They each had their bad days and supported the other through them. So, I know you're not married to Jane, but you both would have relied on the other. That's what husbands and wives are for, that's what friends are for.' He shrugged in conclusion.

Anna wiggled her mouth from side to side and, almost in a whisper, thanked him. She sat quietly, staring at the menu board, before eventually turning his way again. 'So, who do you rely on?'

Justin stopped and considered the question. 'I don't know.'

'You don't know? You must have a Rock? Who do you go to when life deals you a bad hand? Who do you trust most in the whole world?' she burst, astonished that it wasn't obvious to him. 'Julia?'

Justin shook his head, trying not to laugh at the idea, because he didn't want to discuss Julia, the fights and, more so, the reasons for the fights. Not now and preferably not ever.

'Adam?' she suggested, and Justin shook his head again. He considered Tom, and then his dad.

'I guess … my family. My dad. My sister, Jo.' He looked up at her face, which had changed to an expression he hadn't seen her wear before.

'Your dad?'

'Yeah.' Justin couldn't decipher her thoughts, much to his annoyance. 'Are you laughing at me?'

She shook her head kindly and waved her hands in front of her to assure him. 'No, no. Not at all.' She leant forward. 'I think that is pretty cool actually.' She sat on her hands and watched him, waiting to hear more.

'What do you mean?' Justin laughed. He didn't think his family was too out of the ordinary. 'You don't go to your family I gather?' he laughed, moving some crumbs around with his finger.

'Me? No. It's only Mum really, and we are just very different people—we don't think the same.'

'Does anyone?'

She looked at him, silently shrugging, and then back at the menu board.

'No,' she confessed. 'You're right. Don't get me wrong, Mum and I are close, but I guess she just never quite understood me,' she tried to explain, looking at him to see if she'd made any sense.

'In what way?' he examined her face.

She took her time coming up with an answer, her face a mix of expressions while he waited; they made him more curious about the girl who seemed so elusive to him.

'Lots of things. Our logic is different. Our priorities in life. Our sense of humor ...' she trailed off. 'I don't know if you've noticed *Doctor* Owens, but I tend to be a little sarcastic sometimes,' she pinched her fingers together to indicate a teeny amount and held them in front of her face.

'No,' he said in amazement. 'I do *not* believe you. Did she tell you that? Your *mother?*'

'I know, the nerve!' Anna smirked. 'Anyway, sarcasm was just my way of dealing with stuff, I think. But Mum took offence to it. I never seemed to make sense to her, and I always felt like she was looking for the bad in people. Me, in particular.'

'You said she was strict?'

She smiled at him, as if considering whether to comment.

'She was. Very protective; never wanting me to get hurt. Never trusting anyone — boyfriends especially.'

'Is that why you moved to Melbourne?'

'Yeah,' she admitted. 'I searched for jobs far away. I went to Brisbane first, but ended up in Melbourne. I love her — but I didn't know how to justify moving out unless it was far away. I felt unbelievably guilty leaving her, I still do. Especially ...'

'Now,' he finished for her, Anna's eyes falling back on the list of fast food options that Jimmy had chalked on the board. 'She's getting better though?' he reminded her kindly and she nodded, reset, smiled, and steered the conversation away from her life and back to his.

'Tell me more about this family of yours.'

Justin commended her efforts silently. 'Ah, the *Owens*,' he exclaimed in a Scottish accent, making her laugh out loud.

'My father is Welsh, but grew up in Scotland,' he explained, still using the accent. 'My mum is born and bred here in Sydney. Mum found Dad sitting on a gutter, drunk off his scone, outside a pub. He'd been visiting relatives here back in the seventies, and she gave him a lift home.'

'To Scotland!' Anna exclaimed.

'Yes. She found a little rowboat and paddled him home,' he remarked, proud at his mother's imaginary feat.

'Wow, she sounds like a true athlete,' Anna said appreciatively.

'Well, it's a genetic thing really,' Justin replied, as he casually kissed his bicep with mock arrogance.

'Obviously,' she obliged.

'My dad was too drunk to go anywhere and so my mum offered him a lift to his cousins' house where he was staying. Turned out she actually worked with his cousin and it all started from there,' Justin finished.

'Nice. A small world story. I like it,' she gave a goofy grin. 'So, are they still in love?' Her eyes rolled at the mention of the notorious 'L' word.

Justin thought back to things his parents had said to him over the years. He had always watched them carefully. As friends' parents' marriages ended, he'd worried his parents' marriage would eventually too. Yet, it never did.

Only a year or so ago, his mother had confided to Justin that after all the years she'd been married to his father, sometimes when she heard his car pull into the driveway, she still felt the butterflies she used to feel when they'd first started dating.

Justin hadn't believed her at first, thinking it sounded corny, but his father walked into the room on cue that day, and his mother's face changed instantly. He'd never noticed it before.

Justin began to pay attention to his father. He didn't know how he'd missed the fact that his dad's eyes followed his mum. When his mother left the room, his father was the one to see. When she came back in, he was the first to notice.

'Yes,' he replied firmly and smiled at Anna. She didn't look convinced. In fact, Justin thought Anna's smile was nothing short of patronising. 'You don't believe me?' he asked surprised.

'Oh, it's not that. I just don't know if anyone could *really* know,' she explained skeptically.

'So why did you ask?' Justin cried incredulously. 'Sounds like you're a non-believer,' he told her regretfully, truly feeling sorry for her attitude.

She retorted kindly, rolling her head onto her shoulder. 'Sounds like you're a dreamer.'

He stared at her, taking in the childlike face which housed such harsh opinions, unsure what he wanted to say. Anna smiled across at him, but he couldn't miss the cynicism and sadness in her eyes. Justin thought that with all the pieces he had gathered about her, Anna was possibly the most lost person he had ever met. Like she'd been thrown in the air so many times, she didn't know where to land. Didn't know she was supposed to. He felt almost angry at her as well, frustrated at her view on his parents' marriage. A marriage she had never lived — two people she had never met.

'You sound like a person who has never been in love,' he finally replied, with a tight smile on his face to try and tone the accusation down, not truly committed to hurting her feelings. Anna's reaction told Justin that not only had he hit the nail on the head, but that it was a sensitive issue.

A flight of fury whipped through her eyes and it jerked her head up. He watched as she chose her words hastily. Her face had flushed, and Justin considered whether to start doing damage control.

'How can you say that? My love life is none of your business!' she cried, ignoring that she was in a greasy take-away joint with public viewing.

'What!' he threw back, struggling to hold onto his smile, still hoping it alone would defuse the situation. 'This coming from the person who quizzed me on *my* love life mercilessly?'

Anna stuttered for words that wouldn't contradict her; knowing full well she had, in fact, done just that the night they sat on the beach.

'Well, *I* didn't go around making assumptions.'

'No? You mean you didn't just *assume* that my parents' marriage was a farce?' he said calmly, but now with disregard for her feelings, as he saw Jimmy flee to the back kitchen.

Anna's face remained hard as she stared at him, breathing through her nose and withholding all her words. Justin returned her stare; certain the pixie was not going to triumph.

'Well?' he asked calmly. He went to say more in the absence of her response but stopped when he felt his mobile ringing in his pocket. He fumbled for it before the person could hang up.

'Hello,' he spoke into the phone to no reply. 'Hello,' he said again as Anna watched on, shamelessly overlooking any of his rights to privacy. The screen read one missed call and his phone beeped with a message. Anna's eyes followed his every move.

'Was it Julia?' she asked innocently. He shook his head and gave her an impatient scowl.

'Anna, Julia and I broke up.'

She looked taken aback. Granted, he had snapped at her. Justin almost felt bad, but he was annoyed enough to not really care. Besides, the number he was looking at gave him an uneasy feeling. He turned away and listened to the message, feeling his heart thump.

'Do you mind if we get going?' he spoke to the counter as he put his phone back in his pocket.

Anna nodded cautiously. 'Is everything okay?' she asked, briefly overcoming her anger and defiance and showing mercy at the sight of his expression.

'Sure. Something's just come up,' he told her, not meeting her eyes.

They walked to the car and drove to his house in silence. Justin had felt her eyes drift over to him every few minutes, but he continued to stare straight ahead, wishing he was alone.

chapter thirty-one

Justin lay in bed, another night free of sleep, knowing today would be a significant day. His mind drifted across the faces of his family and he wondered how they were feeling at that point; whether they were looking at the glass half empty, or half full.

He had rung his father the moment Anna's taillights were out of sight. His news was only bad, not detailed. Bad news didn't need detail.

The next day at work seemed pointless. It was spent rushing from one client to another, squeezing family phone calls in-between. His parents kept asking questions which he was ill-equipped to answer, and it was all they asked of him, thinking a 'Doctor' would know.

Eric tried his best to pick up the slack and Sandra kept clients' frustrations at bay. Justin knew it wasn't doing their reputation any good, but it just wasn't his priority to worry about it.

Earlier that night Justin had Sandra drop him at the hospital. It took him an hour to make it to the special care nursery and when he finally stepped into the room where his young niece lay, he saw his two sisters by her side.

'Hi,' Justin offered, and they gave a grey hello in return. 'How is she?'

Bianca had been admitted unexpectedly while he was out fulfilling his burger quest the night before, her tiny body subject to even more tests.

'She's okay. Quiet and sleepy.' Jo spoke quietly from the chair closest to her daughter, her finger stroked Bianca's soft hair as she made a small moan in her sleep.

'Need me to get you anything?' Justin asked quietly, and both Jo and Lesley shook their heads. Lesley had it in her to smile, but Jo looked too stressed to try. She and Dave would have been there all day; Dave now at home putting their other two daughters to bed. Their grandmother, having had them all day, no doubt exhausted with their energy and her own worries, would be in bed too.

Justin thought of his own childhood and how lucky his parents had been to have had three healthy kids. He looked down at Bianca's still body, yellowed skin and swollen belly. It wasn't fair they couldn't protect her.

'When are they going to operate?' Justin asked, the words carefully spoken. Jo nodded her head and swallowed.

'Tomorrow.'

Justin nodded stiffly. The wait was like sitting on the bench. The surgical procedure proposed would reconstruct Bianca's bile ducts. They had been warned that though it was a relatively straightforward operation in most cases, it had a series of possible complications. Bianca's whole family felt shocked in knowing she could be suddenly snatched away, and they'd need to find out how strong they could be.

'How did your tests go?' Justin asked. The tests would determine whether Jo and Dave could donate a portion of their own livers to Bianca, a procedure that brought a whole other twinset of fear and hope.

Jo leant back in her chair. Lesley watched on uneasily and Justin guessed that she had been too nervous to ask the question herself. Jo looked from Justin to her newest daughter — who only weeks earlier was a nameless and growing bump of anticipation and wonder inside her body.

'Bianca's blood type is O Positive,' she laughed softly with derision. 'And Dave and I are A Positive. We don't match.'

Lesley opened her mouth to speak, but Jo spoke again, as if reading her mind.

'The girls are too young,' she said, ashamed that they had considered farming their other daughters' organs in aid of their sister.

'What about us?' Justin was furiously trying to recall his family's blood types, hope failing as he mentally crossed out options. 'Dave's family?'

'They've had blood tests to find out. His brother thinks he is O, maybe.' She shook her head with frustration. 'For now, all we can do is wait until they look inside and, if they find what they think it is, that the operation works … that it happens.'

Lesley and Justin both watched as Jo shook her head. Every website Justin had read had emphasised that the longer they waited, the more the operation's success rate decreased. He hadn't thought the mood could fall further, but a darkness had slithered in the room and had seeped deeper into their thoughts. The big pink balloon that floated a 'Get Well' message was the only thing that stood tall.

Without noticing, a serene nurse approached the colourful curtain, reminding Jo that only two visitors were allowed. Lesley, regretfully, stood to leave. She kissed them both goodbye, her eyes giving her away. Justin saw the guilt she felt for going home to hold her husband, knowing that her own child lay in his cot, healthy and happy in the next room. Justin wanted to reassure her but didn't know how.

When the last bus was due, he too bid Jo farewell. She would sleep the night by Bianca's side, while Dave would lie in their otherwise empty bed, nervous for the next day to reveal their future.

Life, simply, wasn't fair. There wasn't any other way to put it. It just wasn't, and never would be.

chapter thirty-two

Mel drove away from the airport on Sunday night feeling ambivalent. So happy; so sad.

She'd had almost two full days with Tom. One weekend, one night, many phones calls, hundreds of text messages and emails—and she was in love. She was sure of it. So sure, she'd told him.

They were at a café and he'd come back with an extra sugar for her coffee, impressively remembering she used more than a normal amount, and she had grabbed the sugar sachet and cried, 'You remembered! I love you!'

Tom had laughed, unaware the outburst was replaying at speed in Mel's head. She put the words in the context of actually loving him, realised it still applied, and—without thought—this realisation came out of her mouth.

'Oh wow, I really do love you.'

In the instant that she understood that it could all go horribly wrong and utterly embarrassing; he threw her a lifeline. Shaking his own sugar and ripping it open, he looked up at her blankly.

'Well, that's a relief. I was worried I was making a fool of myself. Because I can't *believe* how much I love you.' He broke his straight face with a laugh, she laughed, they laughed; and then she almost threw herself over the tiny table to kiss him.

'And it's not just the hair?' she checked.

'It's not just the hair.'

'I could shave my head and you'd still feel the same?'

'Shave away,' he'd grinned, his eyes waltzing around her face. 'Mel, I love you.'

He said it so simply, so matter of fact. She'd made a weird noise with her throat which let the moment down on its complete perfectness; she had to hope that Tom didn't hear it, but, apart from that, perfect.

That was only seven hours and forty minutes ago. Everything else was fairly elusive to her after that, except the fact that he'd just boarded a plane bound for Sydney and she'd be unable to hold him that night or the next.

When Mel arrived home, she ignored the ironing she'd originally intended to do and looked up flights instead. Before Tom had even landed, she had a return flight booked to Sydney for two weeks' time … it seemed like a lifetime away.

Justin came inside through the back door. Hamlet looked in at him with drool dangling from his wiry beard and pink tongue panting out from between his teeth. His furry face trying to coax Justin into coming back out to play.

'Wasn't a run enough for you?' he demanded from the dog. Hamlet tweaked his head to the side and Justin laughed. Outside, the sun was setting in an impressive display of orange that could do nothing but lift spirits. He opened the door hastily and gave Hamlet one last pat. After neglecting his most loyal pal since Bianca's sudden admittance, Justin had made a promise that he'd give Hamlet the attention he deserved before he went out that night. Which he had; only now his skin was slimy with sweat.

Justin pulled his shoes off as he trod towards the shower. He was having dinner with his family, celebrating the week's wins, and Lesley was giving him a lift to their parents in half an hour. Tardiness was her pet hate and Justin was faced with another pitfall of being dependent on others; big-sister crabbiness. He thought he'd done his time with it already as a kid and now, in his thirties, he was being punished all over again.

He slid his damp shirt off as the water heated up. His run had been fueled purely by his thoughts. Thoughts about Bianca, work, the accident, and, admittedly, about Anna.

They hadn't spoken since she'd dropped him home a week ago. The journey to Justin's had been silent, but he'd been too much in his own thoughts to note anything else. After Anna had left him at his doorstep, he'd called his family, and it was all he was thinking about at the time, or the last week.

But Bianca's operation went well and, though she was recovering slower than hoped, she was due to come home over the weekend. The intensity of the last month had simmered to a bearable level. And so, with a fresh perspective on family and priorities, Justin had told himself that it didn't matter that Anna and he hadn't spoken—that they barely even knew each other.

But no matter how much convincing Justin tried to do, the fact was he'd enjoyed having Anna around. He couldn't help but admire her, even her impulsive comments, and it somehow did matter that they hadn't spoken.

He was annoyed at what she'd said at the time, but now he just wanted to know they were okay. That he could run into her again (which seemed to be a strong likelihood) and it wouldn't be uncomfortable.

Justin showered quickly, not wanting to face Lesley's mood otherwise. When he was dry and ready to go, there was still time up his sleeve. He considered his options: dishes to put away, laundry, the latest *Veterinary Journal* to be read, a pile of printouts on Biliary Atresia disease, liver failure, liver transplants, survival rates … the phone. Justin picked it up confidently, slid his thumb over the smooth screen, looked thoughtfully at the picture of Hamlet hiding under the apps, found Anna's number … and then placed the phone back down on the bench. Justin stood staring at it for a moment longer before walking to the lounge.

Lying down, he picked up a bike magazine, flicked through some pages, skimmed an article on muscle fatigue and then wondered if Anna was into riding.

Justin glanced at the phone only three more times before he wandered casually back over and picked it up again.

He tapped on Anna's number and was just about to connect when he paused and cancelled the call. He didn't even know why he was calling her. Shouldn't she be calling him? She was the one out of line.

He went back to the lounge and turned the television on. The phone began ringing moments later and, with Anna in his thoughts, Justin leapt to it.

'Hello,' he unintentionally bellowed, expecting to hear her voice.

'Hi. *What* are you doing?' exclaimed Lesley, surprised at the gusto in his voice. He loved his sister, but his smile fell at the sound of her voice.

'Oh, hi.' He felt his neck and cheeks warm. 'Just, um … watching TV.'

'Ri-ight. Well, we're on our way now. Are you ready?'

'Yup. I'll wait out front.'

Justin locked up and waited by the kerb, folding into the back seat when they arrived. He was relieved to have dodged another speech about how people without kids don't understand the importance of punctuality.

'Hi guys,' he said to his sister and brother-in-law, Tim. 'Hi buddy,' he whispered as he shook his nephew's teeny hand. Josh clasped his finger and gurgled.

'Did you tell Uncle Jay you had your first hair cut today?' Lesley turned her head over the seat and spoke to her son. His, now shorter, fair hair matching his mother's and grandmother's. Baby talk proceeded for the remainder of the journey, all of them including Josh in their conversations. Justin often felt that after being an uncle fourfold, he knew more about babies than most childless males his age. He often wondered if his now natural progression in making baby talk to his sisters' kids was more embarrassing than he even realised.

Arriving at their parents' house, the mood wobbled with uncertainty. Reminiscing the week that had passed was about to begin, apprehension not even close to being lost amongst the celebration.

Jane had ventured to Anna's mother's place for a night of unnecessary eating and irrelevant discussion. It was the most useful thing either had done all week.

Anna was desperate for the company. She felt heavy with thoughts because beside her mother (with a pincushion for a hand and a leg hovering in the air all day), Anna had been feeling awful knowing Justin was mad at her. She hated the feeling that tainted her already depressing daily thoughts. Clearly, Justin thought highly of not only his parents' marriage and his family, but the concept of family in general — and so he should. She didn't even know why she had said what she did. She hadn't thought of the ramifications of casting her own skeptical thoughts out and about in public.

Each morning when she woke, for an instant she'd feel good ... a brief hazy instant. Then it passed, leaving a feeling she likened to having set cement in her stomach. Her face would pull the same confused expression as to why and then it'd hit her with a *Ka-thump. Bam. Crash.*

Her mum, Sydney, her job, the flat … and now Justin.

Thinking about it all made her feel downright dreadful, but she couldn't escape any of them. Her subconscious just flittered from one problem to another throughout the day, like a bird unable to decide which branch was the least uncomfortable.

Jane looked on at the old photos of Anna with amusement. She'd already cringed with disapproval at her mother's hectic garden.

'Nice hair,' she chimed ironically, and Anna acted stung by the comment.

'It was the fashion!' she retorted, laughing. She was eternally grateful that the hair industry had created anti-frizz products. 'At least I didn't have a perm,' she pointed out, thinking back to early photos she had seen of Jane.

'Touché,' Jane chuckled, leaving Anna's photos without further comment.

They had the television on but had plenty to talk about while they waited for a pizza to arrive at the door.

'How's that Vice-Principal going?'

'She's evil. There's nothing else I can say there. She is just good old-fashioned evil. Like Lex Luther, but with boobs.'

'Wow,' Anna smiled. 'She sounds delightful. How's Year Two then?'

'Ugh,' Jane moaned.

'That good, huh?' Anna grinned.

'The class is fine, it's their parents. Nightmares.'

'Well, raising kids is hard,' Anna rationalised. Jane raised her eyebrows with a laugh that Anna chimed in on. 'Well, you know, in all *my* experience.'

Jane, kicking her foot about in the air to an unheard beat in her head, sighed hopelessly. 'I want a kid.'

'I know … me too.'

They both sighed.

'You heard from your dad yet?'

'Speaking of parenting?' Anna smirked ironically. 'He called at about ten the other night, with no mention of the lack of contact mind you, and suggested I go visit him for a holiday so he can show me this great fishing spot he's found.'

'What did you say?' Jane grimaced at the idea of touching a fish.

'I said, 'great idea' and forgave him instantly. He barely even asked about Mum.'

'Did you speak to your mum today?' Jane asked, shaking her head at Anna's dad's ignorance, having witnessed its presence through Anna for years.

'Briefly.'

Brian was visiting tonight, and Anna preferred to give them their space. Even with her leg in traction and nurses having to change catheter bags for her immobile body, her mother and Brian behaved like love-sick teenagers. She was happy for them; Brian, widowed for nearly a decade, and her mother, historically single. But it made Anna ashamed for not ever having felt those sentiments. So, she'd concluded that letting them be alone suited everyone.

'I think I need to make a change,' Anna declared. 'I might cut my hair off.'

'Dye it blonde.'

'I am not going to dye my hair blonde.'

'Why not? Blondes have more fun … or so I've heard,' Jane said as she played with the tips of her own blonde hair. 'Complete bullshit if you ask me.'

'I'm not dying it blonde. Should I cut it? Leo cut hers and look what happened.'

'True. Cut it!' cried Jane, referring to Ioulia's third successful date with one of their neighbours and grinning about the two new-age personalities that had hooked up.

'Wait, didn't *you* have a date the other night?' Anna exclaimed in the moment she remembered. 'I'm so sorry, I totally forgot!'

The pit of guilt in her belly grew as she realised that not only was she lagging at work, not seeing her mum every day like she'd planned, and angering perfectly nice vets, she was also forgetting her best friend.

Jane shooed her away. 'Please, I'm glad you forgot. Saved me telling you how awful it was when he stood me up.' Jane nodded at Anna's wide eyes.

'He stood you up!' Anna was ready to hunt the guy down. He, whoever the jerk was, could be so lucky to have a date with Jane. 'How dare he? Did he even call?'

'No. He left a text message on my phone the next day.'

'And what did it say?' Anna burst, curious and fuming.

'*Sorry Jane. Was sent away for work. Talk later,*' she quoted.

'And did he?'

'Call? Or be sent away?'

'Both!'

'No and, don't know. I haven't heard from him since, so either way, I guess it doesn't really matter.'

'Bastard,' Anna offered, protective of Jane's heart like it were her own.

'I know,' she agreed, trying not to look too upset about it. 'I just …' Jane hovered over her words as she searched her brain for what she was trying to say. 'I'm just feeling tired. I'm tired of looking. I'm tired of caring what I look like every time I walk out the door, *just in case* I meet a potential guy. *My guy.* I'm so sick and tired of the effort involved in just thinking about how single I am. How I am nowhere near a relationship, let alone marriage … or kids. What if I can't fall pregnant, but I find out when I'm forty? What if I meet *my* guy and I can't have children and he leaves me because of it, all because I was too old? My eggs are shriveling up as we speak!' she cried, pointing at her ovaries and then taking a breath.

'I have a Halloween Party on tomorrow night—Halloween Anna! It is the last place on earth I want to go to. I just want to be home relaxing. But if I stayed in all the times I didn't want to go out, I will never meet anyone. Anna … I'm just so *tired*.'

Anna listened patiently, but she didn't have anything to say. No hope to give, because Anna was sitting in the same boat. Single, lonely, tired, and in a boat with no paddles or clue of where to go.

Anna was letting her guilt about her mother, living in Sydney, fear, and just her own lack of energy stop her from having hope. After Kyle hadn't even bothered with her, she wanted to give up. But Anna had come to realise during Jane's monologue, that she had better do something about it before her friend's fears became her own reality. It was time she stopped pitying herself and take control, and one little idea was propelling her forward. Justin, it seemed, was single after all. The fact that Justin had showed no further sign of being interested in her in that way kept it a little idea, but it gave her a fantasy to wonder about and wander about in. He *had* kissed her once and that fact fed her hopes.

'Let's go out,' she told Jane as a plan hatched in her head.

'What, now?' Jane sat up, alarmed.

'No, silly. If we're going to be single, let's go and enjoy it. Let's go out! *This* weekend.' Anna was decided. She felt in control like she was grabbing the bull by the horns, horse by the reins. She was ready to go, ready to let her hair down. She was pumped and set on the idea. Dancing, laughing, a few drinks. They'd eat out, get dressed up—

'Oh, I'm busy this weekend. Halloween,' Jane made a gag face. 'Plans with my sister …'

'Oh'. Fantasy Party-Anna fell flat on her face, sober.

'Next weekend?' hope building in her voice again.

'It's a date,' Jane grinned, and for once they had a sure thing for a date in their diaries.

After everyone had stopped bothering to poke at their food, Justin and Dave offered to wash up. They used to do the dishes and talk sport, but those conversations of late were rare, replaced more often by an exhausted silence.

Dinner had been cheerful, with sporadic moments of pessimism, followed by joy again. The kids made the only reliable sound of life in the room and were the sole source of entertainment, while the fear of Bianca's ongoing health was a constant.

Outside in the warm air, Justin gave a moulting Dolly a bowl of scraps (after taking away the potato bake and strawberry ice-cream his dad had insisted was the dog's favourite). He frowned as she limped to her dinner, but she looked content as she feverishly gulped down the food that no-one else could stomach. Back inside, Dave and he tackled the clean-up at the kitchen sink, Jo coming in to join them not long after.

'Dave, Sammy is requesting your help with a monkey face,' she smiled lamely. It was a smile that said a million things. The notion of bringing her baby home was driving her, but Justin could tell the family dinner was a source of stress for them. To be away from the hospital that night was nice; but the shame it brought them to not be by Bianca's side, even if it were only this one last time, was immense. Justin's parents insisted that it was for the best. 'Keep some sense of normalcy for Samantha and Olivia,' they'd say. 'Celebrate,' they'd grin encouragingly.

Justin wasn't so sure. He could see the anxiety splayed across their faces, even if it was for only a couple of hours before Jo replaced the post of Bianca's other grandmother, and rejoined her daughter's side, whispering promises of home.

Dave retreated back to the lounge room, ready to contort his face for the amusement of his second daughter. Jo substituted for him by picking up a tea towel.

'How are *you* going Jay?' she asked. 'I'm so sick of hearing that question, so I'm turning the tables.'

'Okay,' he replied vaguely, denying himself any right to complain to her.

'Have you seen much of Adam lately?' she raised her eyebrows. Justin hadn't told her anything about Adam, so felt sure that she had been talking to Lesley.

'Um, no. Not really … why?'

'No reason,' she replied, lying terribly.

They worked together quietly, Justin wiping down the sink, and Jo putting the dishes away in their respective homes. The downside of such a large family was the number of dishes they could dirty.

'Hey Jo, what do you think of that saying, 'You can tell a lot about a person by the company they keep'?' Justin was unsure of his own opinion, though he'd been considering it frequently.

'I think there is a lot of truth in it,' Jo told him. 'I *also* think it came from left field. Why do you ask?' she asked curiously, an actual smile twitching on her lips.

'Someone just said it to me is all,' he replied, busying himself at the sink again.

'Who?' Jo smiled innocently, but he suspected she may have already guessed.

'Um, Anna,' he said casually and smiled against his will. He quickly hid it, though not quickly enough, judging by the smile that grew on his sister's face.

'Anna, huh? We still care what Anna thinks do we?' She asked like a big sister that had just found out her little brother had a crush on a girl. He could see her eyes laughing at him and he felt exposed.

'No, no, I was just … wondering.'

'Well, if you were just wondering,' she smiled. 'I'd have to agree with Anna. Scum usually hangs with scum.'

'So, what do you think of Adam?'

'Honestly?' she asked, raising her eyebrows high and he shrugged. 'I think he can be a charmer, but I wouldn't trust him as far as I could throw him.' Her face grew serious, about to offer something more, then stopped.

'I wouldn't trust him if I were you Jay,' she said quietly. Justin soaked it in as he scrubbed a forgotten saucepan.

'So … what does that say about me?' he asked, embarrassed.

Jo looked at him and searched his face. Justin had been judging himself cruelly of late and he'd been having thoughts run through his head that he'd probably denied access to previously. He was wondering what he'd been doing with his life. Why he had called Adam a friend for so long? Why had he allowed himself to believe that he was in love with Julia? That she was in love with him? He'd cursed himself numerous times for letting himself be fooled by both.

Adam had left no void in his life, and, surprisingly, Justin didn't seem to miss Julia either. He noticed not having that person to call, he definitely noticed not having sex, and he noticed not having a person to go out with; but he didn't actually miss *Julia*. It sent a chill through him to think that he had been considering marriage. Justin wondered if he had just settled. And if he had, then where else in his life had he succumbed to satisfaction through mere laziness? He hated to think, yet by pulling his life apart as if he were spring cleaning his brain, thinking was precisely what he had been doing. His past hopes and dreams now seemed foreign to him. Then Anna turning up again, and again, caused thoughts to move around in his head that he didn't know what to do with.

Justin looked to Jo with hope.

'It says … that you are an exception,' she smiled, squeezing his arm. 'Now stop being so darn hard on yourself.'

They'd finished the dishes and were leaning on the bench when Lesley walked in. 'You mind if we get going soon Jay?' she asked, and Justin felt it was like the old days, she'd always avoided the dishes somehow then too.

'And …' Lesley came close to them both and hushed her voice. 'Next Friday is *Dad's birthday*,' she lowered it more. 'I got the present, but I just need to confirm numbers. Jay will you be bringing anyone to dinner?' Jo turned to Justin, eyes lit.

With all that was happening, their dad's sixtieth had arrived. When life blew up, it was hard to imagine that normal things still happened—bills, supermarket queues and, of course, birthdays. Their dad had insisted they do nothing. Lesley, the key instigator for the event, had planned to cancel it, but Jo and their mum had insisted it go ahead as planned.

'It's your birthday Dad. We're not going to miss it,' Jo had urged him, though later stated that Dave would stay home with Bianca.

'We need happy things too, love,' his mother had reminded him, and so the night was still going ahead.

'Bring someone? No. Should I be?' Justin asked, wondering if Lesley had forgotten his single status. Lesley shrugged, and Jo piped up mischievously.

'Aren't you going to bring *Anna*?'

Justin wasn't sure how he felt with the knowledge that Jo poking fun at his life was the thing that made her smile.

'We're *just* friends!' he moaned in exasperation, causing Jo to smirk and Lesley to look between them for more information. She faced Jo to find out.

'Are they finally together?' she squeaked.

'What? What do you mean *finally together*? We're just friends,' he assured them. 'She has a boyfriend. Leo!' he exclaimed, as if knowing the guy's name proved a point. 'And I'm not telling either of you anything about my private life ever again. You can't be trusted. Anyway, it's weird. Telling my sisters things … it's not normal,' he huffed.

Lesley slapped him on the chest.

'Oi!' he cried, exaggerating the pain. When he was younger that would have sent his mother running in to defend her youngest.

'*You're* not normal,' she retorted. 'Now, just call me if Anna will be there okay. I need to tell the restaurant,' she told him firmly, and he could see Jo grinning wickedly.

'*We are just friends!*'

'Who?' they heard his mother cry out from the lounge room. 'Oh, are you talking about Anne?'

His sisters began laughing as they heard Dave and Tim correct her in unison.

'*Anna.*'

Which only made the girls laugh louder.

Justin looked at them both, alarmed.

'Do you just tell *everyone*?' he demanded, keeping his voice as low as possible. But, and much to his dislike, they simply shrugged and began their goodbyes, ignoring his gaping mouth.

Jo hugged him goodbye with a fading smile. The seriousness of her life having reappeared in a flash and she was forgiven. She held him longer than her usual goodbye hug and he wrapped his arms around her.

'If you need anything, just call,' he told her as she released him.

'Thanks Jay. Now I better round up these girls.' Discreetly wiping her eyes, she swung a happier mask over her face and headed back to the front of the house, where giggles were being emitted louder with each moment that passed. Jo called to them as she approached, and Justin followed to finish his goodbyes. He hoped to leave without further Anna-based questions, and he succeeded—a small reprieve for himself.

Justin unlocked the front door and felt his mobile buzz against his thigh, telling him he'd received a message. He opened it as he kicked his shoes off.

Hi Justin. How r u? Anna

Justin stared down at the words in his hands, a surprised smile creeping slowly across his face as he read them and then hit reply.

Hi Anna. I'm good. How are you?

He brushed his teeth, waiting for a response. His eyes only leaving the phone's screen so he could spit out toothpaste. It beeped again before he was finished. Hanging the brush out his mouth, so as to give the message his full attention, he opened the next message.

I'm OK … I'm sorry about the other night. I was a negative cow. I'm really sorry.

He read it. Re-read it. Again surprised. He wasn't used to apologies.

He continued cleaning his teeth while he thought of a response.

It's ok. I've missed you, he typed, before deleting it with a frown.

It's ok. Thanks.

Justin washed his face, thinking that he should have added more to his message — the notion to just call was simply out of the question.

I'm sure they r in love.

Justin wasn't expecting that either. It took him a moment to put the words in context. His whole annoyance at her felt petty and childish to him now.

Thanks …

He wrote, unsure where to go from there. His tiredness from the day was decreasing with the thrill of hearing from her. He had begun to think she had returned to Melbourne and her life there — presumably selfish boyfriend included — and he'd never get to see her pixie face again.

So you'll still talk to me?

For his own childish amusement, he let her sit on that one for an extra minute while he climbed into bed.

Well u may have to feed me again, but I'll consider it :)

As he set the alarm for the next morning the phone beeped again, and he jumped to it like a kid on Christmas morning.

How about a drink instead? Jane and I are going out next weekend. Can you make it?

What day?

His dad's sixtieth looming in his head.

Saturday.

'Saturday,' he grinned to himself.

Free as a bird.

He smiled in anticipation of her next message.

Can u bring some friends? Preferably single ones!

Confused, he sent another text.

Sure. What about Leo?

He waited, puzzled.

Melbourne … and taken!?

Disappointment reined his body. He knew that Leo was *taken*, but her message requesting single men made him hope they'd broken up. Distance could do that.

Right. See you then.

Justin closed his eyes and put his phone down, only to be beeped at again.

Will talk before then. Night Justin.

He wasn't sure why his head felt so dreary. They were just friends.

Nite x

chapter thirty-three

Nite x

She stared at it for longer then she needed to.

x

Who wrote just one little 'x'? When did they write it? What did it mean? Did it mean *anything*?

Did *she* mean anything?

She'd be happy just not to mean 'nothing', but could she mean more?

Justin talking to her again, or texting rather, made Anna happy and she was happy with just that. She was.

But people didn't send an 'x' to someone who meant nothing, did they? And why hadn't he told her that he was single earlier? Why had he let her think he was in a relationship? When had he and Julia broken up anyway, she mused, because he didn't seem too upset about it.

Unless, it was his way of keeping her away.

'Boys, nothing but trouble,' she grumbled to herself, before taking one last quick look at the final message and drifting off to sleep.

Justin visited Jo, Dave and his nieces every other day for the next week. They all tried to do the same, lending a hand wherever they could. He didn't go the night of his course, he learnt about vehicle maintenance instead. The relevance was minimal to him, but he reminded himself he only had three classes left.

Jo and Dave were both mentally and physically exhausted, and Justin found himself thinking of Anna and what she was going through. By Thursday Justin realised he had little time left to find someone to drag out with him on Saturday night. After the buzz of Anna inviting him had subsided, the idea of having to convince someone to come along dawned on Justin unwelcomingly. He didn't have many single friends, or ones he'd want leering at pixie smiles. After the last few times he'd headed out with those guys, he'd ended up in a hospital, a strip club and car accident respectively, so he'd been steering clear of them. Having hardly bothered to turn up to training now that the soccer season was over, they may not care for him anyway.

He reached for his phone, calling the only bachelor he'd want to see.

'Tom, what are you up to?'

'Hey, Doc. I'm, ah … don't laugh, but I'm cleaning,' Tom told him, and Justin laughed.

'That's not like you, is your mum visiting?'

'Ha-ha, no … my, ah, girlfriend actually.'

'Since when? How did I not know this?'

'Well, we kind of met because of you,' Tom enlightened him, but Justin was lost and bummed because Tom was his one sure hope for Saturday night. 'In Melbourne,' Tom continued, and Justin's head quickly worked out who he was referring to.

'Anna's friend?' his voice did nothing to conceal his surprise. 'Mel?'

'The one and only,' Tom answered with adoration coming through the phone. Justin knew that sound. He'd known Tom a long time and knew that sound to mean one thing. 'Mate, I am gone. Completely love her,' Tom laughed. And there it was. Justin smiled genuinely, but the call had taken a completely unexpected direction.

'That's great mate … feeling a little lost though. When did all this happen?'

Tom laughed, and Justin could hear how happy the guy was in that sound. Hearing Tom's story, Justin felt bad that he hadn't seen Tom in weeks, and he only lived around the corner. Granted a rather big corner, but definitely a corner. Neither had turned up to soccer, or training, on the same days for weeks, work stopped them meeting, family had consumed Justin's time—and a girl, it seemed, had been taking up Tom's. They *had* spoken, briefly, but not about Mel; nor Anna.

'So, she's coming up this weekend,' Tom concluded with an exhale. If he had to be honest, Justin felt jealous that that night hadn't put the same positive spin on his own life.

'Wow. You certainly kept that quiet.'

'Felt less foolish that way.'

'Did Mel?' he asked with curiosity. Anna hadn't mentioned anything about this match either and Justin suspected she'd been kept in the dark also.

'Um … yeah.' Tom sounded momentarily embarrassed. 'Hey, did her friend call you about that spare room of yours?' And things started to make sense.

'Jane?'

'Yeah, that's her … I think.'

Justin thought back to the afternoon where Anna's eyes shone red rather than green and he laughed to himself. He'd thought it was too much of a coincidence.

'Yes, but she didn't take it in the end, it's still empty. I'm thinking of keeping it that way. I had another guy call, but I'm pretty sure he was stoned.'

'At least you don't have to clean up for anyone then,' Tom reminded him pointedly and Justin laughed at the mess he could imagine was before him. Tom and his housemate were grots.

'Ah, I'm sure she'd be worth it,' to which Tom agreed. 'So, the whole point of my phone call was actually to invite you out on Saturday night because, and this seems just weird now, Mel's friends, Jane and Anna, wanted single men to go out with … but that wipes you out.'

'Mel's friends? Whoa, we do have some catching up to do. There's always Adam?' Tom suggested.

'Yeah, yeah, right.' Justin had already called him an arse that day; he figured that would be enough.

'Well, Mel hasn't told anyone she's coming up yet, but I'm sure she'll want to see them. So, we may be there … just not quite single,' he laughed. 'Do you think you can handle two girls.'

'Tom, I can't even handle one,' Justin told him truthfully.

Tom hung up to be a domestic goddess, he even intended on cleaning his usually green swimming pool, which was a huge statement of affection, and Justin thought he'd better do some work himself. The usual family dinner was shifted to Friday for his dad's sixtieth and he had no excuse to ignore his lounge room any longer. It housed an assortment of painting accessories and he was beginning to suspect that if he didn't put the paint on the walls soon, the tins would rust shut.

An hour later, with his furniture pushed to the centre of the room, he'd almost finished one wall when a knock came from the front door. Justin froze to hear the sound again and sure enough he heard a small rhythmic tap. Justin looked out at an excited Hamlet through the back door, his paws marching up and down on the spot.

'Who is it Hamlet?' he asked, but the wag of the tail didn't provide any clear answers.

Justin put the paintbrush down, wiped his slightly painted hands on a towel and stepped to the front door. The glass, creating a kaleidoscope of the visitor's shape, gave no clues as to who was on the other side. He unclicked the door and opened it to see Anna's face, and Anna's uncertain smile.

'Hi,' she said quickly, arms crossed around her body. 'Is this a bad time?'

Justin looked behind him, down the hallway and then down to his hands, before looking back at Anna—and smiling his smile.

He had paint on his fingers and a small streak across his forehead, just near the scar that split his eyebrow. He was wearing a faded black shirt decorated with small flecks of paint and Anna thought he looked good. So good, she felt her cheeks burn and she cursed herself for showing up unannounced.

She'd been at the hospital and her mother had been exceptionally quiet. The doctors suspected she had a blood infection and were investigating further. Anna had thought that explained her mother's quiet exhaustion, but whilst out of earshot, Brian had told Anna that there had been a visitor that afternoon that she wouldn't elaborate on. Almost instantly, Anna had wondered if it were her father. She hoped she was being paranoid, but when he did reappear in their lives it was always at the most inopportune time: late at night, busy at work, or when her mother was happy. Not that being in a hospital bed was happy. But having Brian by her side had made her the happiest Anna had seen her in years and Anna hoped—as did her mother—that her next move into Brian's house would be her last.

Anna was so suspicious that her father had returned, randomly stealing himself away from his great fishing spot, that she questioned her mother—who only clamped up more. Anna eventually gave up and, though still full of questions, had left. The entire drive towards her mother's home was just a blur of memories. A blur of childhood hopes and dreams. She'd called Jane, but her phone was off and the next person that occurred to her was Justin.

Without thinking clearly, Anna had steered the car towards his house and walked herself up the path to his door. She'd knocked and said hello, without even considering the implications of being there. She didn't consider that it may seem bizarre or too forward. She didn't think that turning up to practically a stranger's house with a head full of issues was inappropriate. But there she was, saying hello to a guy in a faded black t-shirt and a friendly smile, and she began to cry.

chapter thirty-four

'Anna, what's wrong?' Justin's smile fell as soon as her tears did. 'What's happened? Is it your mum?'

He guided her inside and Anna apologised as he walked her into the lounge room, only to be halted by the furniture congregating in the centre of the room. They could have sat there but she'd have to sit on his lap, not that he would have minded, but he suspected Anna, or her boyfriend, may have. Justin apologised and steered her to the kitchen instead. Having no tissues, he tore off sheets of paper towel, which she accepted and he apologised once more as he handed them over. Anna wiped her face, blew her nose and apologised.

'Okay, we have to both stop,' he said, and she looked up in confusion—her demeanor even smaller as she sat with remains of tears in her eyes.

'Apologising,' he explained. 'We have to stop apologising.' He offered a small laugh in exchange for her small smile.

'Sorry Justin,' she said, and then laughed, embarrassed at herself as Justin shook his head at her.

'What am I going to do with you? Do you want a drink?' she shook her head, but he poured her one anyway and another for himself. 'Do you want to talk?'

She scrunched her face and shook her head, nodded and then shook her head again.

'Sorry I —' she put her fingers to her lips. 'Oh, sorry, I said sorry. Crap, I said it again. Sorry. Crap!' she growled at herself and he laughed at her fit of apologies.

'I'm not really sure why I'm here. I … um, sorry. Oh, shoot!'

'It's okay Anna. Really,' Justin assured her. 'I'm glad you're here.'

'You are?' Anna looked at him intensely and it made Justin think of their night on the beach. It made him remember how she'd traced his face with her fingertips and kissed him like he was breakable. It had sent goosebumps over his body then, and every time he'd thought about it since.

'Yeah, I could do with some company,' he confided in her, absently rubbing his arms. 'But, more importantly, how are you at painting?'

She sat up. The freckle above her lip moved when she smiled, and he wondered if Leo loved her. They couldn't have been together long, but she spoke so comfortably about him, it must be serious. He thought of Tom and Mel, which was just as quick. Leo was a lucky guy, Justin thought regretfully, as he watched Anna perk up.

'I *like* painting. Not sure how good I am, but anything is better than sitting in an empty house again and feeling sorry for myself.'

'True,' Justin agreed and smiled widely. 'Follow me.'

Via the lounge room, Anna was momentarily distracted by Hamlet. She let herself outside and ruffled his head as he scrambled up the leg of her jeans. Justin listened to her ask how his day had been and who did his hair. She reminded him of his nieces; childish and uncontrolled, but completely adorable.

Anna was completely lost in her thoughts, stroking blue paint on Justin's lounge room wall, when she was guided back to reality by his voice.

'Um … Anna? Anna!' He was laughing at her and she came to, peering down at him from her position on the ladder, oblivious to what he wanted.

'Anna, you just leant on the wall.' Her otherwise clean top now displayed blue paint across her chest, and he laughed as she realised it.

'Well that's subtle,' she frowned, after her initial cry of annoyance, turning to face Justin so he could clearly see the image she had unintentionally created.

'It might wash out,' he reassured her. 'Just go rinse it,' he nodded his head to the laundry and kept painting.

'And wear what?' she croaked. 'My bra?'

'Well, if you want to …' She climbed down the ladder and dabbed his cheek with the brush.

'Hey!' he cried, wiping at his face with the bottom of his shirt.

'No thank you,' she told him curtly before giggling at her shirt again. 'I'm such an idiot. *Leo* will enjoy this story,' she said to her chest.

Justin smiled falsely at the mention of Anna's other life and wondered why she didn't call him tonight instead of turning up at his place.

'I'll get you one of my shirts,' he told her, leaving the room, grateful his mood change was noticeable only to himself; frustrated that Anna affected him so easily. Why couldn't he just treat her like any other friend?

When he returned, Anna had disappeared from the ladder's side. He found her at the laundry sink, trying to scrub the shirt with it still on her body.

'Why didn't you just wait?' he exclaimed, while trying to ignore the fact that her shirt not only had paint highlighting her breasts, but now was very wet and stuck to her body even more, each curve obvious to him.

Justin had to force himself to think of something else. *Work*, he thought hastily, think of that.

'Impatient I guess,' she shrugged. 'Didn't want it to dry?'

He shook his head at her, still thinking intensely of work.

'Here, wear this one,' he handed her his shirt and turned away to leave. 'I'll leave you to it.'

'Thanks Justin,' he heard her mumble as he reached the edge of the kitchen.

'S'ok,' he called over his shoulder, accidently catching sight of her back as she pulled her shirt off. He froze. The view of her pale pink bra strap and smooth skin stopping him from turning his head back faster than he should have. Quickly, he stepped into the safety of the lounge room. He found his paint brush again and thought determinedly about Eric and Sandra.

Anna walked back in, his shirt falling to her thighs. 'I should probably go,' she told him sheepishly. 'I didn't realise it was after midnight.'

'What?' Justin looked at the clock to confirm. 'When did that happen?' he put his paintbrush down and wiped his hands.

'Hmm, somewhere between you having to listen about my childhood and me painting my body I think.'

'Neither a problem,' he grinned. 'Thanks for painting my house at the same time.'

'Anytime,' she smiled and fumbled with her keys—it was all she had brought inside. 'Thanks for listening Jay.'

Justin couldn't be sure, but thought it was the first time she'd called him 'Jay' instead of Justin, and he liked it. 'We can do a shirt swap next time,' she suggested, and he nodded.

'I'll try not to stretch yours,' he promised. 'And I'll see you Saturday.'

He wondered if he should mention Mel and Tom, but decided it wasn't his place.

'See you Saturday,' she smiled, and Justin led her out, waving her off at the curb. He went inside and painted for another hour. He couldn't stop thinking about work.

chapter thirty-five

Anna woke in the early hours. She'd considered getting up and going for a run, or a walk at the very least, but felt so warm in bed; snug in the shirt she'd worn the night before, too tired to remove it when she'd reached home.

She thought briefly of Justin, grateful for his kindness and his listening ears—then her thoughts fell to her father. Concern rising again that he had returned to her mother's life. Yet, she also thought how nice it would be to see her dad again if he were in town. The longing she felt for him made her feel confused and disloyal towards her mother. Anna's mind settled on a memory that had been etched into her mind many years ago, during the era of her parents' divorce.

Her father had picked her up early one Saturday and had agreed to take her wherever she had wanted to go.

'Tap dancing!' she'd cried. Anna could clearly remember her excitement. Her friends at school had dance classes and she had desperately wanted to join, though her mother had told Anna repeatedly that they couldn't afford the same for her.

Obligingly, her dad took her to a dance class, regardless of what he knew Anna's mother would say. Anna didn't realise he was softening the blow for her, trying to make divorce a treat. But tap dancing they went.

Her dad walked behind Anna as she ran ahead, past the aging commemorative plaques and perfunctory photo of the Queen, and inside the local hall. The teacher, tall and slender and with her hair pulled tight, had brought over spare shoes. Anna was already on the scratched wooden floor trying them on for size when her father made it to her side. Anna remembered the anxiety she'd felt when the other girls had begun to tap their soles on the ground; each click making her hands search more frantically for a pair that fit her. 'Your feet are too small for these ones,' she shook her head down at Anna. Anna had watched sadly as the teacher told her father where he could buy tap shoes for the next week's class. But Anna knew it was an offer valid only for that day. She knew that she wasn't going to get tap shoes of her very own that day, or any other day. She just wasn't that lucky.

After her father declined the offer for her to join the class shoe-less, they left, her head hung low. She'd strapped her seat belt on in the back seat as her dad started the engine and called over to her, 'Where to now my *Tiny Dancer*?'

He'd winked. She never forgot that wink.

They drove to the beach where they skimmed stones on the wave-less water and dug the biggest hole they'd ever dug in the sand—it had covered her whole body. He'd called her his *Tiny Dancer* for the entire day, before forgetting the nickname forever.

Anna, however, remembered it; always yearning to be called by it affectionately by her father, just like he had that day. When she heard *Tiny Dancer* played, she never knew how to feel. The chorus threw the memory in her face, bringing with it a trail of fondness and disappointment. She wanted her father to remember it too—wanted it to be their thing, their memory. But it was hers alone.

That same afternoon, all those years ago, he dropped her back home without getting out of the car. With sand in her hair and salt on her skin, Anna hoped he'd come inside and stay forever.

But he didn't.

He waved her off from the driveway. Her mother stood at the front door waiting for her, almost as if Anna had had to choose. Her dad drove down their road and it was the first time he was gone for weeks. The end of her dancing dream was the setting for the rest of her childhood. When she heard that song, she saw her father driving away from them. Even now he turned up only when he wanted; caused them heartbreak whenever he wanted. And then he'd leave.

The knot in her stomach swelled.

chapter thirty-six

Justin felt worn out. His father's sixtieth birthday dinner had followed Bianca's first smooth week at home, calling for an even bigger celebration. The doctor's belief that the surgery was successful had finally gained some trust by her family. It was what they'd hoped and prayed for but hadn't dared expect.

'Where's Anna?' his mother had asked genuinely when he'd arrived. 'Jo and Lesley said Anna would be coming,' she sounded disappointed as she looked around him, seeing if this 'Anna' she'd heard of was maybe coming up behind him.

As Justin explained to his mother that her daughters were in fact horrible people, he suspected it may be a long night. It wasn't; just the opposite. But as he stood at the harbourside bar on Saturday night he knew without a doubt that he was well out of experience at going out two nights in a row.

He'd had dinner with Tom and Mel earlier at another nearby bar, feeling completely and utterly like the third wheel that he was, but relieved that they had come at all.

Justin had offered to meet up with them later, but Mel had insisted they eat together, claiming that she wanted to get to know him better. She hadn't told Anna or Jane of her arrival in Sydney, or that she was seeing Tom. Consequently, they had no idea a very anxious Mel would be joining them out in Sydney that night.

'Why didn't you just tell them?' Tom asked, amused at her nerves. The warmer days brought longer days and, as they sat outside watching the sun setting over the Harbour Bridge, Justin could see that Tom and Mel fit. He wondered whether that would be affecting their address status or their frequent flyer balance.

'I know, I know. I thought this would be fun,' Mel explained hopelessly as she poked an unwanted salad. 'I was wrong.'

'It will be fun,' Tom assured her and looked to Justin for support. 'Right?'

'Sure,' Justin smiled tightly, because Mel wasn't the only one feeling nervous. He'd eaten almost as little as Mel.

When the three of them turned up to the agreed upon open-air Opera Bar that Tom had suggested with Justin's approval, Anna and Jane were already there. Justin spotted them first, followed anxiously by Mel. They were on a narrow, elevated level that looked out over the water and up to the famed white sails of the Sydney Opera House. They stood amongst a small group that they seemed to have befriended whilst under the evening sky. Both did a double take upon seeing Mel when she walked up the cascading steps to join them. Amongst the squeals of delight and confusion, there were brief introductions. When Anna stood in front of Justin to say hello, the ease from their painting session was somehow erased and Justin didn't understand why. They did an awkward shuffle to kiss the other's cheek. Both went to the left, then the right, before finally coordinating. Their lips barely grazed the other's skin and Justin was confident that she had shared the same memory of their not-so-brief kiss in Melbourne.

Anna hastily turned to greet Tom and Justin's skin clung to the faint touch of her lips as he watched on. Her green dress revealed her bare legs and the sight etched into his mind for future reflection.

The next hour was spent in a strictly female huddle, Mel answering question after question, their heads randomly popping up and looking at Tom, and then Justin; but mostly Tom. The huddle shuffled to the bar, the bathroom and back to the table before it dissolved.

Tom and Justin, trying not to feel self-conscious, took the opportunity to catch up themselves — which wasn't such a thorough process.

'So, how's it going?' Justin asked Tom, calling over the live band below them and referring to Mel's arrival.

'Good.' Even his teeth gleamed. 'Really good.' That covered it all really and they headed to the bar that bustled with Sydneysiders moving uncontrollably to the music; embracing the feeling that summer was on its way by drinking faster than recommended. Their group to be no exception.

Justin really wanted to ask Tom if he'd told Mel about his accident, concerned that Mel already knew, more so, that she'd tell Anna. But he was too ashamed to tell Tom he hadn't been honest about it. He knew it was something he had to tell Anna about, but hadn't seemed to find a safe moment. She was so angry about her mother that he knew it wouldn't be received well. He was also certain that if she found out any other way, that it would be worse. He didn't want to lose her trust, but he thought telling her held a greater risk of losing her altogether. He'd call Tom after Mel went home, he decided; gambling that his secret was safe until then.

By their second return from the lengthy drinks queue, the girls had long disappeared to the mock dance floor.

It wasn't how Justin had imagined the night.

Tom and he sat watching the harbour that bobbed and twinkled beside them, their eyes falling on the girls intermittently.

Justin was experiencing a strong sense of déjà vu. He never would have thought that the same girls his eyes had randomly fallen upon almost three months ago in Melbourne, would now be so entwined in his life. He never would have thought that some random girl, at some seedy bar, would now rule an increasing amount of his thoughts—and be taking her shirt off in his laundry.

Mel returned to drag Tom off to dance—the same Tom who didn't dance, yet was too new in the relationship to blatantly refuse. From his perch, Justin cringed with sympathy as Tom struggled to coordinate his body. He briefly watched Jane and Mel try to instruct him, but it was Anna, who was dancing with a complete stranger, that had his attention. He watched their every move, though could hardly stand to. The guy looked like a slime ball.

Justin went back to the bar, preparing for the next round, and returned to find Anna and Jane sitting at their acquired bench, waving like tourists at a ferry that motored past. He passed them their drinks while they promised the next round, before sliding in next to Anna on the long seat. He couldn't deny how glad he was that she was now dance-partner free.

'Hi there, Doctor Jay,' Anna sung, grinning up at him, and pinched his cheek. Again, her calling him *Jay*, or *Doctor Jay* for that matter, made him feel like she'd just called him 'oh thee wonderful man that walks the earth'—it basically had the same effect.

'Found any *ladies*?' she asked, pronouncing ladies suggestively and laughing, alcohol having blanketed any awkwardness from earlier.

He shook his head. He hadn't been looking at any other lady, bar the one that had just pinched him.

'Where's the single men you promised?' she pouted, and the effect of *Doctor Jay* wore off instantly.

'Sorry, no luck. Jane will have to find her own guy,' he told her unenthusiastically, bringing a cool cider to his lips. Jane was taking photos for the next table with at least two men eyeing her optimistically—Jane would be fine.

Anna looked at him with a raised eyebrow, just one; he didn't know she could do that. He liked that she could do that, and he wondered if he were odd for finding it an absolute turn on.

'That guy seems to be getting pretty friendly out there,' he said, indicating the slime ball on the dance floor who was grinding up beside her only moments before.

'Yeah, I know,' she giggled. 'He was kinda cute though,' she nodded excitedly and squished her face.

Cute? He looked like a wanker and besides, he thought, wouldn't Leo care about this? He sure as hell would.

'He's still looking at you,' Justin told her, not even bothering to smile. He was not impressed—more so when Anna looked over to confirm. He watched as her smile broadened at the sight of the slime ball staring at her, and Justin felt his body stiffen.

'Hey, I think *he* thinks I'm with you!' she cried, realising that her catch was looking between her and Justin. She shoved him playfully and laughed again. 'I'll be single forever with you around!'

Justin felt his forehead wrinkle.

'Anna, what about Leo?' Was she that drunk? He was beginning to lose his patience.

'Leo?'

'Yeah, *Leo?* Wouldn't he care?'

'She,' Anna corrected him absently, completely missing the whole tone of the conversation that Justin was having with her, and now he really was confused. It had been a long week and his brain had taken it upon itself to clock off already.

'She?' he asked, looking down at her face, her cheeks still flushed from her recent and lengthy set of dance routines.

'Yeah, *she* wouldn't care. She'd be happy for me. That way she wouldn't have to hear me whine about being single all the time,' she laughed, looking out onto the dance floor and searching for the guy again. Not that it was too difficult; he was still watching Justin and Anna like a beady hawk about to snatch its prey.

Justin shook his head in an attempt to make all the information meet up and make sense.

'Anna, who is Leo?' he spoke as cool as he could.

'My flatmate. You know that. She helped you with Jane, remember?' she spoke so flippantly while watching the others on the dance floor, completely missing the stunned look on Justin's face. 'What is this fascination with Leo that you have anyway?' she asked, distracted this time by the cheers from another nearby table.

The slime ball was focusing just on Anna now. Justin began to wonder if he would come and pee on her leg and mark his territory. He turned back to Anna.

'You're single?' he asked, but she heard it as a statement.

'No need to rub it in, Justin. I'm fully aware that *no-one* wants me.' She rolled her eyes and playfully nudged him, the nudge almost pushing him off the bench. Justin saw Anna's dance partner straighten his back in the instant body contact was made — completely aware of every inch of space between Justin and her, mentally calculating how close they were each moment they sat next to each other, and figuring out how close he should allow them to get before intervening.

Justin was in a daze.

Anna was single. She'd been single all this time. Hope rose in him and a smile splayed across his face. Flashes of possibility reeled through his brain.

Then it hit him. Harder than he would have expected. He hadn't known Anna was single, but she, obviously, had.

Had Anna been remotely interested in him, she would have done something about it. If Anna had wanted to be with him, she wouldn't be dancing with a slime ball.

Realising this, Justin felt even further away from her. He was hopeful that the buzz of the crowd would conceal his disappointment. Before, only moments ago, he had thought only a boyfriend to be in the way of them being more than friends. Now it was the fact that she didn't want him. He felt like an idiot.

Anna, unaware of the realisation Justin's head had just made, laid her head on his shoulder. 'I'm *so* drunk,' she groaned.

He foolishly looked at her profile; her perfect and freckled nose, her soft lips and pink cheeks, her shiny hair falling on his chest.

He wanted to stroke her head, hug her … take her home and keep her forever. But he couldn't do that. She didn't want that.

He felt his breath catch in his throat and coughed. As her head slowly lifted off his shoulder, he saw her dance partner approaching. Fast.

'Oh look,' she sung. 'My knight is coming. He'll look after me,' her head bobbled on her neck happily and she smiled up at Justin, who couldn't manage to return it.

Anna slid off the seat and stood as the guy reached her side. He snaked his arm around her waist and pulled her towards him.

'Smooth,' Justin muttered nastily under his breath, before standing and extending his hand. 'Justin. Nice to meet you,' he smiled down at him.

'Brett,' Slime Ball replied, cautiously looking Justin up and down as if to figure out if he could take him on.

'C'mon babe,' he yelled into Anna's ear, loud so Justin could hear. 'Let's go dance.'

Anna giggled and slinked off behind him. Justin watched her go but couldn't stomach the guy, Brett, as he called himself, as he pushed himself up against Anna. Jane had followed too and joined Mel dancing around Tom—who was loving the attention.

Justin took his seat again and looked out across the harbour, appreciating the view and trying to deny his mind of thoughts about Anna, or the right to feel bothered. Then his eyes fell on another familiar face. Luna Park twinkled from under the bridge, its bright lights reflected in the water. The clown's face continuing to laugh at his situation, taunting that time and distance hadn't done him any favours.

Justin glanced down at his drink and finished it off. He went to the bathroom so he didn't have to watch Anna, or the clown. When he returned, the group sat back at the table with no Anna in sight.

He scanned the bodies in front of the band, asking Jane where Anna had gone. But he spotted her green dress before Jane could even point her out. She was in the middle of the crowd, arms wrapped around Brett's neck and Brett wrapped around her tonsils.

'Whoa,' screamed Mel. 'Go Anna!' Jane and Tom laughed along. All three stared on shamelessly. Mel began commentating on the kiss like it was a horse race, to the hysterics of Jane. Tom laughing too. Justin strained a smile and tried to focus on his next drink that Tom had placed in front of him, while he, the designated driver, drank lemonade.

Too much alcohol flooded his body as Jane's shoulder nudged his.

'Hi Justin,' she smiled.

'Hi Jane,' he called out over the music and smiled good-naturedly. 'How's Sydney treating you?'

'Good. Okay. Still deciding,' she nodded and glanced over at Tom and Mel, then briefly over at Brett and Anna, both couples engrossed in each other. 'How's Melbourne treating you?'

'What do you mean?'

'Anna, Justin. I'm talking about Anna,' she told him with an exasperated smile.

'Anna?'

'Yeah, *Anna*,' she repeated and shook her head. Justin, not knowing how to respond, didn't.

'Did you know she leaves her hair in the drain?' He looked at Jane, baffled. 'If it helps, she could be bald by the time she's forty. It really is a lot of hair.'

'What are you talking about?' Justin laughed, careful of his voice.

'Nothing,' Jane sighed. 'Hey, wanna dance?'

Justin went to say no but reconsidered.

'Sure.' He stood up to even Jane's surprise and they left Tom and Mel for the band.

They were a safe distance from Anna when Jane found two other women she'd met in the bathroom queue, and they amalgamated their dance group to one. Justin found himself as the token male and the girls lavished all their attention on him.

He twirled and dipped them. They shimmied against him. One grabbed his arse. Another stepped on his foot. They sung to him, and Jane laughed when one tried to suck his ear. His nerves were so slow that he didn't even realise what she was doing until Jane was grimacing at him.

Justin completely forgot about Anna being in the same space, until he saw her unmistakable eyes through the crowd.

She was only three bodies away. Her body obediently dancing, her eyes fixed — on him. Justin stopped moving altogether and held her gaze.

Jane and the girls continued to bounce around him, and when one bumped into his shoulder with too much enthusiasm, Justin lost his balance. He stumbled, and when he composed himself, smiling at the others briefly, Anna's face was gone. He searched the crowd but couldn't see her anywhere. One of the girls grabbed his hands and began to twist with him. He laughed politely and moved along. But his eyes scanned the bar constantly, searching for dark wavy hair, pale green eyes and a pixie face. But she was gone.

chapter thirty-seven

Jane dialed Anna's number grudgingly, too determined not to try again.

'What happened to you last night?' she demanded when Anna finally decided to answer her phone, unquestionably annoyed at her friend.

'What do you mean?' Anna asked obliviously.

'Are you kidding? You disappeared! You didn't even say goodbye,' Jane cried, her voice finding a whole new octave.

'Hey, whoa. Ears,' moaned Anna over the phone, but she was getting no sympathy from Jane.

'Anna!' she cried again. 'I was worried. You run off with a total stranger. You don't answer your phone ...' her voice lowered, but her temper didn't.

'I didn't run off with some stranger. I just ... went,' she cut in defensively. 'And I texted you.'

'You texted, 'I'm going. Will call tomorrow'—which you didn't.'

'I was just about to.'

'You didn't go with that sleaze, Brett?' she confirmed.

'No. I didn't,' Anna assured her, offended, and Jane felt relieved. 'But I'm so glad you thought to tell me he was a sleaze after he left Pash-Rash on my face.' Jane almost let a laugh escape but wanted to make sure Anna knew how upset she was.

'Well, you should know better Anna,' she told her sternly.

'Thanks Mum,' Anna told her. 'Should I have known better to not kiss him or to leave?'

'Both!' Jane's voice rose again against her control. 'Where did you go anyway?'

There was some silence on the other end, but Anna eventually answered.

'I just went home. I had a cab charge from work, so I caught a taxi.' She sounded odd, making Jane even more concerned for her stupid friend.

'Home? Taxi? An, are you okay? It's not like you to not say goodbye,' her voice soothed.

'Sorry. I'm sorry Jane. I wasn't thinking. It was dumb to go. I'm really sorry,' then added as an afterthought, 'Did you all get home safely?'

'Yeah. Tom drove me home.'

'Good,' she sounded relieved and guilty.

'Hey, maybe you could call Justin today. Before you bothered to text, he was freaking out a bit when we couldn't find you,' Jane suggested.

'Justin?'

'Yeah—Justin. Remember that guy you've spent the last couple of months drooling over.' Jane was beginning to think that due to their mutual level of blindness that the two were truly made for each other.

'What! I have not,' she denied.

'Anna, I love you. But forgive me when I say you are stupid. You both are,' she sighed sleepily, her head still thumping.

'Thanks. I feel *so* much better about myself. Excuse me while I go write a motivational book to inspire others.'

'Anna, seriously, why did you spend the night all over that Brett guy when you have Justin sitting there, madly in love with you?' Jane was almost begging for an answer.

'I'm sorry? Jane, I am not interested in Justin,' she denied. 'Furthermore, Justin is not interested in me, least of all in love with me. How much did *you* drink last night?'

Jane didn't believe a single word and wanted to laugh at Anna's defiance. 'Right. Anna, the tension between you two needs a government warning.'

'Jane, if Justin was interested in me, he would have made some kind of move. I'm not his type, trust me. We are just friends. Simple.'

'Friends? What about that night on the beach? What about all this time you spend together?' she raised her most valid points to the case.

'Convenient friends,' Anna declared, frustrated.

'What about the beach?' Jane pressed.

'We were drunk.'

'Helping your mum's cat?'

'He's a vet!' Anna justified, her voice rising. 'And he's a nice guy.'

'What about him watching you all night?'

Silence.

'Just friends huh?' Jane smiled ironically. 'Wish I had a friend like that.'

Justin ran to the soccer fields in an attempt to make up for an otherwise unhealthy weekend. He passed a few other runners and wondered if they were fuelled by shame as well. He'd gone to bed a dreary sod and woke up much the same, until his mother called, on Jo's behalf, asking if he could mind his nieces that afternoon while Dave and Jo caught up on sleep; offering to cancel her plans otherwise.

Being reminded of the bigger picture gave Justin the perspective he needed. He had a life to live and it was officially time to take control of it. If Anna wasn't interested, then it was time to accept it and move on. Anna was something that wasn't meant to have happened. She'd crept in when he was unsuspecting and he didn't know how to shake her from his daily thoughts, but he'd have to. He also had to start looking after himself. No more Uber rides and take-away.

Determined, Justin committed himself to soccer that day. He'd missed their semi-final and many other games over the last weeks. So, when he'd miraculously turned up to a post-season game the week before, they left him on the bench for the bulk of the game. Today, he promised himself he'd play at his best and start to earn his team's respect back for next season.

Justin reached the fields in record time, the heat not the deterrent he'd expected. Walking through the car park, he saw a familiar red car and took a moment to recognise it as Julia's. Confused, Justin slowed his walk, squinting to see her.

He could only see the back of her, but it was without a doubt her blonde hair. Her actual face obstructed by the one she was kissing. Justin felt his face bend into a fusion of bewilderment and curiosity. This look altered sharply when Adam stepped out of the car, tapped the bonnet and strutted towards the team.

Justin's eyes followed Adam, whose back was slapped by teammates on his arrival, then returned his gaze back to Julia, who was reversing her car out of the space. She drove slowly so the gravel didn't flick at the red paint and she spotted Justin as she turned the car to face him. He watched for her reaction, searching for guilt, but she ignored him completely and drove on.

Justin felt somewhat disorientated, a mix of feelings ambushing him. He waited a moment for them to settle and the feeling that stayed was simply anger. It wasn't about him wanting Julia, loving Julia or missing Julia, because none of those things would have been true. It was about respect — or lack of.

He walked stiffly up to his team. Adam sat on the grass lacing his boots and grinned up at Justin.

'Decided to show up did ya mate?' Adam cried, loud so the team would hear.

'Yeah,' Justin said, softly. He smelt the familiar smells of sunscreen, Deep Heat and meat pies, but felt like he was in an alternate place to anywhere he'd been before. Justin looked around at the field. Few were warming up. No-one looked stressed; the game result didn't affect any tally this time of year. Tom wasn't even playing. Justin saw a group of women perched on picnic chairs, stretching their legs in the November sun and ready to watch their partners play, remembering how Julia had never joined them. He looked back at Adam.

'How's Julia?' he asked, controlled, and Adam looked momentarily thrown. 'I gather you're together now?'

Adam gawked at him and chuckled. 'Mate, you know me. I don't *do* together.' He jumped up and took a swig of Gatorade.

'So, you're just sleeping together?' Justin asked, ignoring those brave enough to look on.

'Bud, don't take it personal.' He slapped Justin on the back and went to walk on the field.

'Nah, why would I do that?' Justin smiled sharply. 'How long Ad? How long after we broke up did you wait?'

'Mate ...' Adam started in defence. But Justin was distracted by the jeering from his team.

'Wait? Ha! Didn't bloody wait at all,' Shane laughed, and Adam glared over at him.

'What is he talking about, Ad?'

Adam shrugged his shoulders and then unashamedly admitted to 'hooking up' once or twice with Julia. Anger boiled inside

Justin and he struggled to control it. His whole new-life philosophy was being shrouded by a dark and menacing cloud.

'When I was in Melbourne?' he forced out of clenched teeth.

'Sure,' Adam shrugged again, as he stretched his calf.

'After you spiked my drink?'

Adam rubbed the back of his neck with a chuckle, 'I don't know what you're talking about.'

'You don't know what I'm talking about?' forced Justin. 'You slept with my girlfriend and you fuck. Up. My. Life … Are you a *complete* arsehole?'

'Hey bud, what can I say,' he smirked.

Justin, whose rage had been impressively managed, knew he was slipping. He looked at the faces of his team. They stood quietly, watching the scene with interest, waiting for Justin's reaction. He knew what they were really waiting for was a fight, but Justin wasn't going to deliver, they didn't deserve the show. Adam kept talking.

'It's not like you can talk Jay. You fucked around with some tramp down there. Don't act all better than—'

And Justin delivered.

He stayed for the game. Justin had too much anger not to play and he scored more goals in one day than he had in the season—they still lost. Adam stayed as well, too proud not to. He tried to trip Justin up whenever given the chance, attempting to make up for losing face over the hit Justin had given him. It mostly backfired and so, though Justin went home with more bruises than he was due, Adam went home with a swollen face, a twisted ankle and a skin-less knee.

Justin was offered a lift home, drinks out, dinner … but he needed to think. He jogged home, his muscles eventually giving up halfway and he had to resort to a slow walk. As he rounded the corner that showed him the length of his street, his phone rang; the ringtone muffled by the contents of his pack. It required too much effort to find, so he let it go to voice mail as his skin, after the day's preview of summer, welcomed the shade of his street.

Walking up his front steps, and opening the door, Justin could smell the strong fumes of fresh paint and he instinctively thought of Anna. He ignored the image, along with Hamlet's pleading face, his throbbing hand and the insistent ring of his mobile, and opted for a shower.

Once clean, he'd thrown himself on the lounge and was moments from drifting off to sleep when he heard his mobile again, followed by his house phone, and then a knock at the door and voices of little girls.

Justin cursed.

He'd completely forgotten he was on uncle duties. He slowly approached the front door, preparing his best welcome smile.

'Uncle Jay!' they squealed as his mother held her ears.

'Sammy! Livy!' he squealed back and threw his arms in the air, much to their delight. 'Hi Mum,' he said more quietly and kissed her on the cheek. 'Were you trying to call?'

'I did, but figured you mustn't have been home yet,' she smiled and guided the girls inside. 'Have fun girls. Make sure you ask for lots of piggyback rides.' They squealed again.

'Thanks,' muttered Justin.

'No problem darling. How was football?'

'Yeah. Good,' Justin nodded, concealing the truth.

'Good, good. Well, I best be going, I told Dad I'd be back to collect him in fifteen minutes. Dave's going to collect them once they get Bianca settled and have a rest, or once you've had enough.'

'No worries,' he laughed. 'Have fun tonight.'

She kissed him goodbye and tottered off down the walkway in her heels. His mother was always quick to get ready; his dad was surely still fixing his tartan tie to perfection.

'Ye got te wear it proud son,' he'd boom in his thick accent, then chuckle like Santa. Forty years in Australia and he still sounded like he'd just stepped off the boat.

His parents had another birthday engagement with simply each other—an annual tradition that Justin was sure was part of their marriage success. Not the one dinner of course, but his mother's birthday, the anniversary of the day they met, their wedding anniversary, a New Year's date. His parents always made sure, amongst all the hurdles, they celebrated the anniversaries. This year would bear no exception.

'Uncle Jay,' the chirping began, 'Nanny said you would make us dinner. Can we have pizza? Can we?'

His insides groaned in sheer exhaustion and his head questioned the noise that two little mouths could create.

'Sure,' he smiled, hoping he had enough ingredients to pull off something that resembled a pizza. 'How about we watch a movie first?' He suggested it like it was the most fun thing they could ever do, and they nodded along eagerly.

Thank god for Disney, he thought, as he selected a movie and the girls glued themselves to the spot, chattering excitedly about their cushion options. Justin reached for his bag, digging inside for the phone and finding he'd had an unusual seven missed calls.

Standing in the doorway, he listened to the messages.

The first two were hang-ups, followed by his mother, whose call was followed by Jo. Another hang-up, and then Julia.

'You're a petty arsehole Justin. How dare you do that! Call me back.'

Justin pressed the button to hear it again, maybe his ears deceived him. But no, that was Julia, clearly calling him an arsehole. Justin shook his head and chuckled to himself. It was a laugh of relief that Julia dumped him. Only weeks ago, he'd thought he'd lost a loving girlfriend, now he knew he was blessed. As for Adam, now there was an arsehole. Justin felt liberated that he no longer cared about Adam's opinion. Justin had no need to entertain him and didn't know why he ever had — he should have been done with him when he was at school. He listened to the message one more time before realising there was another. Tom.

'Just heard you smacked Adam out. Call me back.'

The girls were singing along to a genie — not knowing the words only made them cuter. Justin moved from the doorway and slumped himself on the lounge, refraining from singing himself, and definitely not dancing like Samantha was. He was frowning at a paint run he'd noticed when his phone rang again. Julia.

'Hello,' he exhaled, as he stood up to leave the room, the girls looking on.

'Who is it? Is it Mummy, is it Mummy?' cried Olivia.

'No Livy,' he told her, but Olivia, steadfast, watched on. 'Hello,' he said into the phone again.

'Who is it?' Olivia persisted, determined it really was her mum.

'It's Julia,' he said as he put the phone to his chest, smiling as Olivia's face fell and she retreated back to the movie while he stepped into the hallway. How had he not noticed that before?

'Hello?' he repeated into the phone for the third time and could hear Julia sigh in frustration.

'You're an arsehole.'

'Nice to hear from you Julia. Was there anything else you wanted to tell me?'

'You're an arsehole,' she repeated. She never did know what to do with sarcasm.

'*I'm* an arsehole?' he clarified.

'Yes. Who does that? You are so pathetic. What, do you think pulling a stunt like that will win me back? Because Justin, you are sadly mistaken.' She'd spat the words through the phone and Justin almost felt the need to wipe his face.

'Well, no Julia. I didn't think it would win you back. If I thought that was the case, I wouldn't have done it.' She was silent; too cryptic for the likes of Julia. 'Julia, what are you even doing with him?' Justin asked, resignation clear in his voice.

'He's fun,' she told him callously.

And I wasn't? He knew this would play on his mind. Maybe that's why Anna went for the slime balls of the world, he wasn't fun enough.

'Right. Well, good luck with that. If that was all you wanted to tell me, that I'm a boring arsehole, then I need to get going.'

Silence again.

'We're finished Justin,' Julia declared, like Justin had just begged her to return to him.

'Thanks for the heads up. Enjoy the herpes.'

Justin hung up with a shake of his head. Hearing her voice after so long made him feel odd. He was glad she was out of his life, but the betrayal was a jolt to his system — and if he were an arsehole he could think of a few descriptive words that would describe her.

He looked at his newly painted walls, now a dull blue, feeling relieved he hadn't painted the room the khaki colour that Julia had pushed for.

Justin lay his limp body on the lounge again and as soon as his head hit the armrest the phone, cruelly, rung again. Justin let out a loud groan and both his nieces turned to look at him in wonder.

'What's wrong Uncle Jay?' asked Samantha in her concerned three-year-old voice.

'Nothing Sammy, I'm just old.'

She nodded with understanding and Justin rejected the call, choosing to lay quiet instead, only for it to ring again minutes later. Giving in, he pressed the phone to his ear and didn't bother to get up. 'Julia?' he said quietly, not wanting to disturb the girls and too tired to speak louder.

The voice on the other end stuttered.

'Hello?' he said impatiently. '*Hello*, Julia is that you?'

'Um, no. It's ah … Anna.'

His head felt like a fat chicken trying to take off. Low, slight rise, then a thud.

'Oh.' *Oh*. 'Hi.'

'Were you expecting another call? I can go,' she offered and was ready to hang up. He briefly considered letting her.

'No, not really. How are you?' he asked, trying his best to conceal his disapproval and annoyance, but knew it was a prickly response. Anna made no sound and he thought maybe the signal cut out. 'Anna?'

'Yes, sorry,' she piped in slowly. 'I was just calling … Jane suggested I call you. Just wanted to say, um, sorry I left without saying goodbye.'

But what was he to do with that? It wasn't really the fact that she didn't say goodbye that had bothered him. It was why she had left—who she had left with.

'No need to apologise. It's your life,' he told her, faking indifference and rolling his eyes.

'Oh, okay. Sure. I guess I should let you get back to it then,' she said meekly—but he wasn't falling for her innocence this time.

'Okay.'

'Is that Mummy?' cried Olivia in the moment when Justin thought he could hang up and move on. He shook his head at her.

'Who is it? Is it *Julia?*' she crunched her face up and he laughed despite his not wanting to. He shook his head again and held his finger to his lips to shush her.

'Is it Daddy?' she squealed, unable to contain herself and running to his side. He heard Anna laugh softly and it had an uncontrollable effect on him.

'Is that your niece?' she asked kindly.

'Ah, huh.' Olivia was practically holding her breath with anticipation and Samantha had now joined her, both waiting expectantly to know who their uncle was talking to.

'It's Anna.'

'Who's Anna?' Samantha asked, trying to figure out if this was good for her.

'My … friend.'

'Can we talk to her?' Olivia enquired.

'No,' he told them flatly. 'Sorry Anna, I should probably go.'

'Why not? I want to say hello.'

'*I* want to say hello,' chimed in Samantha.

'No,' he laughed, unable to contain it any longer, and heard Anna laugh too. The girls began begging and Justin, unable to convince them with pleading eyes alone, gave in. 'Anna, would you mind saying hello to two crazy little girls?'

'Sure,' she laughed lightly, and Justin felt his reluctance towards her lessen.

Then he thought of her with Brett.

He warily passed the phone on and watched as his nieces spoke to Anna with their sweetest voices—they knew how to work the masses. When Olivia asked Anna if she was her new Aunty, Justin snatched the phone back.

'Sorry about that,' he rushed out and covered the mouthpiece while he answered Samantha with a firm no.

Anna excused it with an awkward laugh. 'You have your hands full I think.' She sounded tired and he didn't want to imagine what had prevented her from sleep that morning. 'I'll ah … talk to you later?'

It was a clear question of his forgiveness and part of him thought he shouldn't answer; that it'd only bruise his ego further. But somehow, between believing Anna was a friend by coincidence and seeing her on his doorstep in tears, he knew he wanted to speak to her every day and later wasn't soon enough.

'Sure Anna. Talk to you later.'

They hung up and before Justin could finish his exhale, he was on duty again.

'Can we have pizza now?' moaned Olivia, quickly moving forward while Justin's head was still rewinding and playing back the recent calls. He swung from being called an arsehole and Anna's laugh.

He'd wanted to enjoy the latter for a little longer, but they made pizza instead. The girls, helping to decorate, successfully made as much mess as they possibly could in his normally tidy kitchen. The room looked like an explosion and when they'd finished eating their faces looked equally chaotic. They then continued the frenzied theme in his bathroom, where their splashes covered all previously dry surfaces, before snuggling into the spare bed together; a text from Jo indicating they'd be later than planned.

'Can we have a story Uncle Jay?' Olivia asked, unconcerned of her parents' whereabouts. 'The one you told us last time, about the mushrooms?'

'Yeah, I like that one,' Samantha whispered, quiet now that the lights were off.

He told them their story in a whisper and they drifted off to sleep, leaving Justin to tackle the disaster area that was his kitchen. Dave arrived not long after and Justin helped him put the two sleeping bodies into the car without stirring them. Back inside his house, he felt his hand ache, but it was the first time he thought to do something about it. Finding some ice, he thought how the last time he needed ice was from Adam hitting *him*. Then he remembered Anna handing it to him on the first night they'd met, and he fell asleep on the lounge feeling miserable.

Tomorrow, he'd move on. Tomorrow he'd take life by the horns. Tonight … not so much.

Sunday night was Tom's turn to drive Mel to the airport. Waiting at the boarding gates, they weren't saying much. Mel played with his fingers and he watched on quietly, both afraid to ask the unspoken questions.

Tom took in a firm breath as her departure time approached faster than felt fair. 'So, where to from here?' he braved, much to Mel's relief and fear, for now it was her that had to answer the question.

'I don't know,' she said sadly, looking at his face reluctantly.

'I don't want you to go. Stay the week. We'll call in sick,' he suggested. Mel shook her head and smiled faintly.

'We can't do that Tom.'

'We can't afford to keep flying up and down either.'

She didn't reply, he was right, but the other answer was too huge a step to grasp or too sad to suggest. Her flight was called before she had any words to say.

They waited until nearly everyone had boarded before they both stood and embraced each other. Tom kissed her on the forehead and murmured into her head to have a good flight. She mumbled into his chest to drive home safely. Stepping away was the hardest part and once she'd done that, she handed over her ticket and then allowed her wobbly legs to walk towards the plane, tears threatening to come. Finding her seat, her phone beeped as she reached to switch it off.

I love you.

chapter thirty-eight

Anna was driving towards Justin's house. She had come straight from the hospital and when Anna explained why she needed to leave, her mother's eyebrows had risen at the mention of Justin's name. Anna had to brush it off and hope she would remember not to talk about Justin for a while. She didn't want her mother getting ideas.

She was almost at Justin's now—the nerves told her this more than her location. Anna made what she hoped was a nerve cancelling noise to relax, and failed. She and Jane had both discovered they had no plans for Saturday night and decided to avoid feeling tired and lonely on their own, by going to the movies; where they could feel tired and lonely together.

Anna had invited Justin with a huge degree of hesitation and only because Jane had suggested it might break the tension that Anna had described from their phone call. Anna hadn't told Jane that Justin had been expecting a call from Julia at the time, nor did she tell her that she suspected they were back together. She should have. She had wanted to. But talking about Justin after *that* night just seemed awkward.

Anna didn't want Jane thinking anything of her and Justin being friends (or more than friends in this case) any more than she wanted her mother to—even if both were in fact right about her feelings for him. In fact, especially because they were.

She was particularly worried how she'd handle the situation of the three of them at the movies together, until a bigger hurdle presented itself … how she would manage with the *two* of them. Jane had rung that afternoon, begging to be forgiven for cancelling. The guy, who had stood her up because he was sent away for work, had in fact stood her up to fly to Beijing. He was now back on home turf and ready as ever to wine and dine Jane and make it up to her. And who was Anna to say no—though she did. Jane then ignored her and threatened to make up rumours on Facebook if Anna even thought about cancelling on Justin.

So, Jane wasn't going, and Justin was.

Anna *was* looking forward to Jane's phone call the next morning. A date tradition they'd shared for years in their quest for a suitable boyfriend, with the dissection of possibilities usually done in their flat. But that future conversation didn't detract from the butterflies taking flight in Anna's belly as she pulled into Justin's empty driveway and honked the horn. His car was still missing, and she wondered briefly when he was getting it back.

He didn't come outside immediately (which, quite frankly, provided firm opposition to Jane's claims of Justin's feelings), so she honked again—rhythmically. It amused her and squished some of her worry. Justin came outside frowning. As he closed the glossy front door he mouthed, 'What are you doing?'

He looked disturbingly good in a bright blue t-shirt and shorts. One of the benefits of Sydney was that one didn't have to dress for every weather condition that the sky could throw at them. Looking down at her own summer attire of shorts and sleeveless top, she frowned, wondering at what stage in their lives had they stopped—as a rule—getting dressed up on Saturday nights.

I'm getting old, she groaned inwardly, but smiled as Justin pulled open the door and climbed in—convincing herself that her outfit, though casual, really was cute.

'What are you doing you nut?' he asked. 'My neighbours are old. They'll complain.'

'Give them my number,' she told him unconcerned.

'Maybe I will,' he warned. He looked like a giant in her car and fidgeted with the seat, trying to move it back so his knees weren't up around his ears.

Justin spoke as Anna reversed the car out onto the leafy street. 'So how come Jane piked on us?'

'She has a date.'

'Oh, a date. Gossip,' he rubbed his hands together.

She looked at him with an arched brow. 'Gossip?' She laughed as he shrugged unapologetically, happy that awkwardness wasn't joining them for the ride.

By the time they reached the theatre, with Anna claiming Justin's instructions were too delayed, they were running late. Justin jumped out to buy the tickets while Anna parked the car. After a near collision with a newly-licenced teen, she found him lining up at the Candy Bar.

'Tickets?' she asked, concerned they'd end up having to see an action movie instead of the comedy they'd agreed on. He flashed two tickets to her and asked if she wanted anything to eat.

'No, I ate already,' she told him.

'Where's the fun in that?' And told her he was getting a jumbo popcorn, Coke and a bag of Maltesers.

'Watching your weight?' She was actually quite jealous she couldn't get away with that kind of diet.

'You sure you don't want anything?' he checked, for the sake of preserving his own order, and as she shook her head to firmly decline, she saw Justin's face visibly pale. His mouth gaped slightly, stupefied.

'What? What's wrong?' Anna looked into the crowd, thinking maybe it was Julia. After Justin had asked if she were Julia on the phone the other night, Anna wondered if they really were getting back together. She was curious as to what kind of person Justin went for, if not girls who sucked his ears.

'Remember me telling you about that woman who kept hitting on me at work?' he asked from the corner of his mouth.

'The stalker?'

Justin nodded — reluctantly.

'Well, she's heading this way.'

Anna watched as a voluptuous woman with platinum-blonde hair walked in their direction. She was tucking her mobile into her bra as she approached.

'Quick. Act like you're with me,' he pleaded as his eyes skittered from the woman and then back to Anna.

Anna shrugged and did the first thing she could think of to suggest she was *with* Justin. She reached for Justin's head and kissed him. She let her lips linger for an exquisite moment before she pushed him away and smiled up at him.

Justin's face was one of wholesome good-looking-ness — and shock. He went to speak but checked where his stalker was first. Evidently, a foot away and glaring.

'Hey … Vanessa,' he exclaimed, like he'd genuinely just noticed her. Anna could hear the slight wobble in Justin's voice and found it hilarious that he was disturbed by this woman.

'How have you been? How's Fluffy?' Justin asked with a false keenness.

'Very well thank you, Justin,' she spoke to Justin curtly and glanced up and down at Anna before deciding to just ignore her. Anna almost laughed. She had to hide her smirk by looking away and when she thought she had it under control she snuggled into Justin and put his arm over her shoulder pointedly. At such proximity she enjoyed the faint smell of his aftershave and the weight of his arm over her body.

'Babe, aren't you going to introduce us?' Anna asked sweetly and saw Justin hide his own smirk.

'Yes … Honey,' he told her slowly. 'Vanessa this is my, ah … girlfriend.'

Vanessa looked at Anna with contempt.

'Hi,' Vanessa smiled unconvincingly. 'It's nice to meet you Julia. I was beginning to think you didn't exist.' She flicked her platinum hair extensions over her shoulder and her face twisted into a nasty smile; Anna had to fight the grimace.

'Actually, it's Anna,' she corrected, and Vanessa glared at Justin. Clearly, she had assumed she was next in line. A flicker of fear appeared on Justin's face before he composed himself.

'Julia and I aren't together anymore,' he responded carefully. As Vanessa went to speak Justin was tapped on the shoulder.

'I think you're next,' said a lanky teenager with braces. Justin smiled his apology at Vanessa and ordered. Anna smiled amusingly at Vanessa, who was staring her down; her overly-plucked eyebrows narrowing in.

'I need to go, my movie's starting,' she snarled at Anna, the stale smell of cigarette smoke hung on her breath and Anna wiggled her nose to comfort her senses. When Justin turned back with full hands, Vanessa, The Stalker, was gone—nicotine and her exotic perfume were all that remained.

'Thank God for that,' he muttered as he sipped his drink and then snapped his head up. 'Hey, what was with you kissing me?' he demanded.

'You said to act like your girlfriend!' Anna croaked back.

'You could have just held my hand,' he reminded her as he re-gripped his drink.

'Oh, yeah.' She grinned, stealing a piece of popcorn. 'Didn't think of that.'

'Yeah, yeah. Just couldn't help yourself. I know.' She wanted to comment but figured that anything truthful would only place their friendship in a whole new level of weird, and it was weird enough as it was.

They took their seats and as they waited for the previews to end Anna suddenly jumped to the edge of her seat.

'Justin,' she grabbed his arm. 'Look!' Three rows in front, Anna could work out Vanessa's blonde bombshell. Justin turned back to Anna and pulled a face, making her giggle more than was called for.

'You know for someone who didn't want anything, you did a pretty good job of eating my popcorn *and* my chocolate,' Justin told Anna, rattling his empty popcorn box at her as they walked out of the cinema.

'I was hypoglycemic?' she tried, and he raised his eyebrows. 'It was an accident?' she tried again, holding her hands up.

'You freaking girls,' he rolled his eyes, tossing the box in the bin. 'You say you don't want anything and then eat ours! Thank goodness Jane couldn't come or I'd have had nothing.'

'Well, it doesn't count when it's not yours,' she told him seriously. '*Everyone* knows that.'

'Is that right?' he asked, as he shook his head. 'Women.'

She grabbed the bag of Malteasers off him and dug to the bottom to pull out the last few. She was expecting Justin to stop her and when he didn't, she glanced across at him. His face was strained, and Anna followed his line of sight to see Vanessa. She was talking to another equally bold woman and Justin looked back from Vanessa to Anna. Anna wondered if he was going to bolt or hide behind her. When Vanessa's head began to turn,

Justin pounced. His hands abducted Anna's face and he kissed her. Passionately.

Anna almost choked on the chocolate that had been in her mouth. It was now lodged somewhere between her tonsils and her heart, an organ which had suddenly leapt to attention. Justin pulled away and looked at her anxiously.

'Do you think she saw that?' he whispered.

'Wha-huh. What was that? You just *kissed* me,' she informed him, coughing slightly.

'You started it,' he shrugged. She wanted to grab him and make it happen again.

'Now hold my hand, *sweetie*,' he grinned and walked her past Vanessa who clearly *had* seen the kiss. He gave her a friendly wave and led Anna out the doors. Anna was grateful for the assistance because she felt like she could very well have passed out back there.

'You just kissed me!' she cried again. He kept walking, pulling her along a step behind.

'Well, I won't tell anyone if you don't,' he said flatly and dragged her towards the car park.

She wondered what he meant by that. Maybe he wouldn't want anyone to know. Maybe he'd be embarrassed if people knew they'd kissed. Maybe he really was getting back with Julia.

Oh.

Anna drove Justin to his grey home. They chatted about the movie, but overall, they didn't say much. Her brain was preoccupied. As a reaction to Justin's lips, she was swept away by how lonely she actually felt and wondered if she'd ever find anyone who'd want to be with her — really want to be with her. Then she started thinking of her mother, her mother's empty home, Melbourne, and her flat.

Home.

It was a vicious cycle of thought patterns and it made for bad company.

She pulled up to Justin's house. It looked hidden in the dark street and this time she didn't even notice that his car was absent.

'You okay?'

'Yeah, I'm fine,' she smiled reassuringly across at Justin. 'Hey, do you mind if I just use your bathroom?' She meant to go at the cinema but was led away too quickly.

Justin opened the door for her and she stepped quietly down the hallway. When she came back out, she found him sitting on the edge of the lounge flicking through his phone.

'Hi,' he smiled up at her. It made her insides squirm—his face made for a great smile.

'Hi,' she replied with a forced lightness. 'What'cha doing?'

'Just reading the headlines,' he showed her the Facebook screen he was scrolling through.

'Anything interesting?'

'Yup. Nick Napoli has just begun his fifth weights session for the week,' he shared as he flicked to another post without even looking up. 'And Amanda McKay has been vomiting for three days.'

'Good to know,' she nodded earnestly, and he looked up.

'You okay, Anna?' She nodded, poorly, to his concerned look. 'You sure?'

'Yeah. Fine.' But Justin didn't look like he was going to back off that easily.

'Just a bit stressed I guess.' She felt her face redden slightly and tried to think where she'd left her keys when she walked in.

'How come? Come sit.' He patted the lounge, but she shook her head, knowing she should get home.

'Just Mum and work and being here,' she said, quickly adding, 'In Sydney that is.' He nodded and patted the lounge again, but she shook her head. 'No, I should get going.'

'Oh. Okay then.' He pushed himself up off the lounge, but when Anna stood motionless, Justin looked on with growing confusion. 'Um …'

'I just don't want to go back there Justin,' she admitted and looked away, avoiding his eyes. She felt a bit shaky admitting that to someone, let alone herself.

'Hey, it's okay Anna.' He held her shoulders and bent down to talk into her eyes. 'You can stay here,' he offered simply. He smelt like popcorn and aftershave.

She smiled gratefully but shook her head. 'Thanks, but no. I have to go.'

'You don't. Just stay here. I can make up the spare bed, or you can take mine. I'll crash on the lounge,' he pointed behind him.

'No,' she laughed quietly. 'Thanks Justin, but I need to go.' She took a breath in to motivate herself to leave. She could very happily have crashed on his lounge. She loved being in his house more than she was sure was acceptable. She felt safe there, where at her mum's she felt anxious and trapped.

'Why?' he pushed. 'Just stay. It's really no problem.'

'I can't. Jane's going to call first thing and my phone's almost flat.'

'So, call her from here,' he suggested, not understanding.

'I'd never hear the end of it if she knew I was here.'

Anna hoped Justin didn't look too far into what she had said. The words were out of her mouth before she thought about it and when he looked at her puzzled, she knew that it was an odd thing to say.

'Why? What does Jane have to do with it?' Justin looked completely stumped—and amazing in that darn blue shirt. She hugged her bare arms for want of something to do with them.

'Oh, it's nothing. It's just that … after last week, at the bar, when I, ah … left,' she was watching his face and it seemed to dawn on him.

'You're worried she'd tell him?' he said, tagging Anna with the confused role.

'Tell who what?' She scrunched her face trying to figure out the puzzle.

'That guy. Sleaze Ball, or Brett … whatever you want to call him.'

'What has Sleaze Ba— I mean, Brett, have to do with it?'

'Well, are you seeing him? I guess he'd have a problem with you being here?' Justin asked, cold all of a sudden.

'I'm not with him! What made you think I was with him?' she demanded feeling disgusted that he had thought that.

'You left with him.'

'No I didn't. You think I'd just leave with a total stranger like that?' Anna was appalled and embarrassed. Is that what he thought of her? That she'd go home with anybody who'd have her.

'No. I didn't. That's why I was surprised,' he calmed down and sighed. 'I'm sorry. So why did you go?'

Anna hesitated, hoping to stop the words from coming out, but they fell out anyway.

'Because I saw you with some girl sucking on your face.' She felt mortified that she had admitted it—annoyed she couldn't stop herself. Justin was silent for a moment and Anna watched as his face changed. His eyes were now squinting.

'What?' he breathed stiffly. 'Are you kidding? I had to watch that greasy slime ball suck your whole face all night, and you walk out because some girl with a wax fetish sucked my ear for two seconds?'

Anna regarded him sharply. Her body reacting to so many different elements of what she had heard. She wanted to raise her voice back and she wanted to defend herself for leaving that night. She wanted to defend that maybe the girl didn't have a wax fetish, and that the reference to sucking her face was quite unattractive. But the part her brain had stalled on was the part where he sounded jealous of the sleaze ball, or Brett rather — whoever he was.

Justin was breathing harder and Anna was sure that he hadn't intended to say so much.

'Why would you care if he was kissing me?' she asked nervously.

Justin stepped forward, frowning at her.

'What do I care? Anna, are you being serious?' he asked incredulously and when she nodded, she felt almost afraid of what he'd say next. 'I care because my life has been *awful* this year and then you walk in and make it good. You spend all this time with me, you show *no* interest in me, but you were all over that moron in *one* night?'

She stood still. Not really sure to believe her own ears. Maybe she misunderstood; she was having trouble comprehending the situation.

'You look confused,' he told her. Anna nodded obediently, unsure what the rest of her face was doing. 'Let me make it clear then … and please, stop me if I'm only embarrassing myself.'

She nodded again, stupidly, and let him speak.

'I am crazy about you,' he spoke slowly, walking the words over the border of friendship to a place that offered more; simultaneously, a place of no return.

'But …'

'Anna, *I. Want. You.*' He emphasised each word. Nothing confusing there.

She blinked.

Breathed.

'You want *me*? You're not back with Julia?'

'God no,' he spoke, appalled. 'Anna, I can't get you out of my head.'

'But … I thought … how come I didn't know that,' she spoke very slowly like she was trying to work out a quiz that exceeded her IQ.

'I have no idea!' he breathed out in exasperation. 'I thought *you* were seeing someone. Leo! Slime Ball! You seemed totally uninterested, so I tried not to be blatantly obvious,' he exclaimed.

'Leo's a girl,' Anna said blankly.

'I know!' he cried, and she found herself unable to focus.

'And I'm …' her body was buzzing, 'not with Slime Ball.'

'No,' he shook his head and spoke quietly. 'I know this now.'

'I thought you weren't, um …' she didn't know what to do with her hands, they seemed so foreign to her, and she was trying so hard to look calm and in control.

'I wasn't what?' Justin asked delicately.

'Interested,' she admitted softly, her face burning. Justin smiled at her and a nervous laugh escaped his body for a brief moment. He shook his head.

'Wrong,' he smiled. '*So* wrong.'

He stood for a moment looking at her and Anna had nowhere else to look but back. They both seemed to be assessing what had been said. Both marginally amused.

Anna was the first to react and took a shy step forward. Justin's cool hands found her face halfway and he pulled their faces together for the third time that night, though this time it wasn't hasty, and it wasn't a farce.

He held her neck with both his hands and kissed her softly. It was the kiss that replaced all past kisses in her memory bank and she didn't want it to end. When he pulled away, Anna pulled him back and kissed his smiling lips.

'So, where are you on the staying over thing?' he slipped in eventually. 'I don't think we got to the bottom of that.'

'Oh … is that offer still open?' she asked between kisses.

'Definitely,' he murmured as he kissed her neck.

'Where am I on it?' she asked as her lips rested on his Adam's apple.

'Yeah?'

'I'm *all* over it,' she said in the sexiest voice she thought she had ever pulled off. Anna would have praised herself some more; but her efforts were going in to relishing the thrill of being lifted and carried down the hall, without even a hint of being dropped. She didn't even have time to worry that her choice of underwear that day brazenly displayed Tickle-Me Elmo.

Justin tapped the bedroom door open with his foot and she pulled his shirt over his head as soon as her toes touched the ground, running her fingers down his firm chest and resting them on his stomach.

'You sure?' Justin asked quietly. 'Tell me to stop and I will,' he promised.

'Don't you dare,' she warned with a whisper.

And he didn't.

chapter thirty-nine

'Anna?' Justin nudged her gently.

'Hmm?' she murmured sleepily, waiting for him to continue.

'Are you a serial killer?' he whispered.

She hesitated.

'You mean, by profession?'

'Yeah.'

Silence filled the room once more while he waited.

'No.'

Justin smiled to the ceiling in the dark, he kissed her bare shoulder, before drifting back to sleep.

chapter forty

Justin lay in his bed watching Anna.

He ran his fingers through the brown waves of her hair and a small smile rose to her cheeks briefly. Justin felt like he'd been drifting through life all this time and hadn't even realised it. But with Anna in his thoughts, in his space, in his bed … he felt like he'd collided with happiness. Like she was the missing piece of a puzzle, which snapped perfectly into place. And with that click, his life made so much more sense. He finally felt like he was going in the right direction, and after spinning around for so long looking for it, he felt dizzy. He simply loved her. He suspected it before, but knew it now—allowed it now. He loved her in every way he couldn't even think to say. It was more than the sum of her quirks, ways, brains and beauty. And for the first time in his life, he felt like someone else completely carried his heart.

Justin gulped at this thought, quickly realising that if Anna went away, if she moved back, no, *when* she moved back, she'd have his heart still. Suddenly his pulse quickened. She had him. She had complete control over him. She had his complete devotion. And he was sure, she didn't even know it.

Anna lay with her eyes closed. She was mostly asleep, but aware she was in Justin's bed, in Justin's arms, and happy. His arm, entwined around her arm, lay across her chest and moved with her breath. She could feel the soft hairs underneath her hand and the muscles of his forearm. She could not remember ever feeling that happy. Ever. She was simply serene.

Her skin tingled as he traced his fingers through her hair and Anna wished she could make time stop so she could just lie there and enjoy the ride.

She wondered for a moment what the feeling reminded her of, but she couldn't place it. She was just happy. Anna kept her eyes closed but felt her smile remain.

The ring of the phone woke them. Justin groaned inwardly, while Anna groaned outwardly. Neither of which did anything to make the ringing stop.

Justin reached for his phone while Anna poorly wrestled his arm to leave it. 'Hello,' he said gruffly, his voice box not yet receiving the wakeup call that had been reserved for his heart that morning.

'Justin!'

'Speaking,' he replied, unperturbed, closing his eyes again and using his spare hand to trace Anna's hand.

'Justin, it's Jane!' Her panicked voice officially woke him and forced his eyes open.

'What's wrong?'

Anna, eyes also cast open, watched him with concern. Jane spoke again, rushing all her words. 'I-can't-get-a-hold-of-Anna! I've tried her mobile, the house phone, her mum. I figured you saw her last—I'm just worried Justin. Did she say anything about today?'

Justin was momentarily thrown. His brain, after the quick hit of adrenaline fuelled from Jane's panic, was now trying to regain control.

'Hey, it's okay. She's here,' he soothed. 'I'll put her on.'

Anna looked at Justin perplexed, and accepted the phone while he settled back into the pillow with closed eyes. Feeling Anna's eyes remain on him, he crept an eyelid open.

'You need to talk into the phone,' he murmured.

'Hello?' he heard her say distractedly and could hear Jane exclaim her name, which made him smile. He could only work out snippets of Jane's words after that, but Anna's were clear.

'I'm sorry,' followed by a long pause while she listened.

'I, um, stayed at Justin's.'

'Yeah …'

'Listen, I'll call you later.'

'I'll tell you later.'

'Yes, I promise.'

Anna continued to promise to call and Justin continued to smile at the conversation.

'Okay, bye,' Anna said as she cancelled the call and then tossed the phone at Justin.

'Yeow,' he complained when it landed on his belly, eyes officially open. 'What'd you do that for?'

'You know why,' she laughed at him, against her intentions.

'Sorry. I didn't think,' he admitted, rolling over and hanging his face over hers. 'I guess Jane knows now.' They smiled at each other stupidly and Justin leaned down to kiss her.

'Good morning,' he told her, twisting a strand of her hair around his finger and then behind her ear.

'Good mor—' she began, before Justin's phone began again. He hung his head before looking over at the phone. The screen read *Mum* and he briefly considered leaving it. He did have a girl in his bed and that girl was Anna. But with Bianca a constant worry looming in his mind, he apologised and took the call.

'Hel-lo,' he said, much clearer than the last time, and hopeful that the universe was not about to burst his bubble. Anna mouthed 'shower' and Justin watched as she slinked out of his bed. Pulling her shirt on, she collected her bra and shorts from the floor where he'd removed them, and tip-toed her way out of the room — Elmo etched in his sight.

'Jus-tin!' Anna sung out.

'Ye-es!'

'Do you have any moisturiser?' She winced her dry, make-up-less face into the mirror in hope. There was a silent pause before he called out.

'Bottom drawer.'

Anna did a silent cheer, pulled open the drawer, and frowned.

'There's only shaving cream in here,' she yelled, confused, shuffling the contents of the drawer to check and hearing footsteps head in her direction, before Justin stuck his head around the door.

'Anna,' he looked at her seriously, 'What would ever make you think that I would have moisturiser?' Before she could reply, his head was gone.

'Smart-arse,' she muttered. 'I hope you get wrinkly.'

'I heard that,' he informed her from the next room.

'Damn,' she said, frowning at her reflection. 'I guess you don't have mascara either?' she called louder and heard him scoff.

'Hey, you found the towels okay?'

'No, I just used yours,' she replied absently as she patted her hair dry with Justin's oversized towel.

His head was back around the door. 'You used my towel? That's gross.'

'Well, it's your body,' she reminded him and resumed drying her hair. Justin laughed, the sound thrilling to Anna's ears, and then, at a sound from outside, he disappeared again.

Anna pulled open more drawers to find some toothpaste and rubbed her teeth with her finger. It didn't really suffice, but she figured using his brush would have grossed him out more than her. She sprayed his deodorant on and smelt like a man; Justin in particular. She'd found his aftershave in her searches and spent a lengthy moment with her nose hovering over the bottle, greedily breathing in the scent she'd been rationed over the recent months.

When she felt satisfied, Anna hung up his towel and looked in the mirror. She gave herself a wide grin, one that she thought would be planted there for at least the next week and padded down the floorboards in search of him.

'Hey, what's your problem anyway?' she called. 'You'll *sleep* with me—but won't share a *towel*? I mean if ge—' her brain tried to stop the words, but they only stalled momentarily before being able to cease completely, '—erms are your prob—'

Anna's feet ground to a halt.

An awkward smile froze on her face as she desperately tried to work out how embarrassed she should be. For she had found Justin in the hallway, but he wasn't alone.

An older woman with fair hair stood staring in wide-eyed astonishment at Anna. Two little girls stood at her side, smiling intently, their eyes bouncing in excitement to see a new face—or familiar face.

'Ah … hi,' Anna stuttered, cringing. She looked at Justin for help, but he only shook his head, smirking. 'Um, sorry about that,' she tried.

'Anna, this is my *mum*, Katherine,' he gestured to his mother. 'Mum, this is Anna,' he told her with resigned amusement.

His mother offered a kind smile, which Anna snatched up gratefully. Though, as Anna repeated in her mind what she had just loudly proclaimed, she cringed again.

'Nice to meet you Anna,' Katherine said. 'It's nice to have a face to the name at last,' she smiled at her son. Anna smiled politely, fearing his mother had heard her as clearly as she imagined and was forming horrible opinions of her.

'It's nice to meet you too. I've heard a lot about you all.' She hoped her genuine interest was compensating for her lack of modesty.

'I'm Samantha!' cried Justin's smallest niece.

'Me, me! I'm Olivia,' cried the eldest.

'I think we met a little while ago,' Anna spoke to them. 'But, how are you today?' She leant lower for them, shrinking away from Katherine's (seemingly) friendly stare.

'We had a sleepover at Nanny's!' Their excitement equalled their sweetness and Anna grinned with them, overhearing Justin's mother suggest that a little more sleeping would have been preferred.

'Mum's just dropping the girls off,' Justin told a grateful Anna, as if reading her thoughts.

'You look like a fairy,' sung Samantha as she swung her body and stared up at Anna. Justin and his mother laughed.

'Oh, why thank you,' Anna laughed too. 'I think *you* look like an angel.' Samantha's face glowed with pride.

'Don't be fooled Anna,' warned Katherine as she winked at Samantha. 'Right. Well, I should get going.' She bent down to kiss the girls and Anna took the opportunity to look back at Justin. His eyes were still laughing at her.

'Anna it was lovely to meet you,' Katherine spoke sincerely.

'Yes,' Anna agreed. 'And, ah, sorry … about, um … that,' she spoke awkwardly, waving her hand behind her to indicate where her blurted words lay.

'Oh, please love,' she laughed and held Anna's arm. 'I think I needed that. And it's good to know …' she patted Justin's chest, 'that my son still tells me lies,' she smiled warmly at them both.

Justin cleared his throat to stifle his laugh.

'Bye darling,' she told him and kissed him on the cheek. 'Have a good day kids,' she sung as she left, and Justin closed the front door. Anna got the feeling that when Katherine said 'kids', she was referring to Justin and herself more than the two girls who stood in the doorway looking up at their uncle expectantly.

'I think Hamlet had something to show you,' he told them, and they shrieked off towards the backyard.

Anna groaned shamefully once they were alone, partially relieved (but mostly mortified) to hear him laugh. 'You could have warned me you know.'

'Sorry, it was a last minute favour. You seriously suffer from Foot-in-Mouth disease, don't you?' he shook his smiling head and pulled her to his chest. Her head nestled there and he rested his chin on her damp hair as his arms held her. She breathed in the smell of his shirt which still smelt of popcorn.

'Hey?' she asked, remembering what his mother had said before she left. 'What did you lie to your mother about?'

'She asked whose car was here and I told her a friend was keeping it here for a while,' he said simply.

'Why didn't you just say it was mine?'

'I don't know. Because you were in the bathroom, she was in a hurry, and I figured I could skip all the questions and assumptions,' he lamely tried to justify.

'What questions? What assumptions?' she asked playfully, stepping back to watch him search for the right answer, thinking this guy was as adorable as his nieces.

'That you stayed here … that we slept together. But you took care of that anyway. So, thanks.'

'But that *is* what happened!' she cried while grinning at him and having too much fun.

'But she didn't need to know that! I don't need my mother knowing everything about my life, alright,' he laughed in exasperation.

'Is it because you're embarrassed by me?' Anna blinked her eyelashes.

'Wha — No!'

He looked at her sad, rosy face and sighed.

'Okay. You got me,' he frowned. 'The truth is, I just didn't want her to meet you when you didn't have any mascara on. Or moisturiser.' He smiled at her helplessly and shrugged. 'Kind of embarrassing for me, you know?' He walked away, calling over his shoulder, 'You want breakfast?'

Anna stood staring at his broad back and went to say something, something witty and bright, but she had nothing. Her brain had stalled again on where she was, and a bubble of happiness made her want to do a little scream. She refrained and followed Justin.

The girls were still in the backyard, Hamlet being agreeable to whatever they wanted to do to him. Justin stood with his head in the fridge, frowning.

'I don't have much, I'm afraid. Unless you like oranges,' he nodded towards the bowl of oranges on his kitchen table. 'You're not a chef by any chance, are you?' he winked.

'No,' she laughed, finding it ridiculous that he still didn't know what she did. 'I should probably get going anyway,' she told him with regret and he looked up with disappointment. 'I need to do laundry. Dull, I know, but I haven't many clothes. Then see Mum. *And* Jane,' she rolled her eyes. Justin smiled and nodded.

'So, I can't tempt you to a day with a three and six-year-old?' He had stepped closer and squeezed her waist in such a way that would have made her drop all her clothes to the ground in an instant if asked.

He kept looking at her and Anna mentally redressed herself; the buzz of his touch careening around her body like a child running through rooms and yelling out, *'Santa's been'.* The buzz ricocheted off cells in her body, causing the word to spread, making her grin stupidly.

'Well, you could …' Anna started, rejoining reality. 'But I should get other things done. Maybe I could see you later?' she suggested, feeling bold in saying it, because she was nervous he'd not want that. But Justin smiled, and her slight fear did a pirouette and landed back in her belly as a feeling of exhilaration again.

'I'm all yours,' he told her, a grin momentarily owning his face before he squished his eyes together. 'Crap, I promised I'd turn up to training later today. And I told Eric we could go over some paperwork tonight. But I can cancel.'

Anna persuaded him not to; assuring him it didn't matter, while convincing herself the same.

'Oh hey, did you want to have a shower? I can watch the girls if you want,' she offered, but he declined. Suspecting it was only out of politeness, she forced him to the bathroom.

'You sure you're okay with them?'

'Yes. I could be a nanny for all you know.' He looked at her, questioning the idea. She could see him trying to put her, and everything he knew about her, in the context of being a nanny.

'Are you?' his voice high that he may have finally found the answer.

'No,' she told him earnestly, 'but we'll be fine. Now go shower, you smell,' and walked off with a smile he'd never see.

Anna found the girls brushing Hamlet's tail and settled herself down on the grass with them. The sky was a clear blue and the sun was welcomed on her skin. Hamlet lay like a toy as the girls poked and prodded him and Anna was impressed by his tolerance.

'Where's Uncle Jay?' Olivia asked, Samantha still focusing on the dog, her pudgy hands patting him roughly.

'He's having a shower.'

'I'm not allowed to have a shower by myself,' Samantha informed the whole backyard. 'Mummy says I make too much mess.' She seemed quite proud of this achievement and looked at Anna for a response. 'Do you have to watch Uncle Jay shower, too?' she continued, and Anna laughed despite her attempts to answer seriously.

'Ah … I'm sure he'll be fine,' but she enjoyed the mental image and wondered if his ears were burning.

'Are you going to play with us today?' Olivia asked, visibly excited at the prospect of a new play friend. Anna shook her head and smiled.

'No, just till Justin gets back,' she explained.

'I have a baby sister,' Olivia boasted. 'But Mummy says Uncle Jay can't look after her.'

'Is that right?' Anna laughed.

'He looks after baby animals,' Samantha informed her as she threw herself on poor Hamlet like a sumo wrestler. She then proceeded to chase him around the backyard, Olivia in tow, back and forth like it was an infinite source of entertainment. Anna watched on, equally amused and impressed by their endurance, before the three finally collapsed at Anna's feet again. In a heap, they panted together, their long blonde hair tangled with Hamlet's grey coat.

'Are you Uncle Jay's girlfriend?' was the next question and Anna went to shake her head, before she wondered if it were true. She froze. *Was she?* Recent antics aside, it seemed too soon to assume the title.

The girls watched her, waiting for an answer, their steady eyes focused on her face which had blushed uncontrollably.

'Well?' came a voice from behind her. The girls looked up at their uncle, who had appeared unexpectedly, and shrieked with delight. He scooped up Samantha, who giggled loudly, and spoke to Olivia.

'Livy, are you tormenting Anna with questions?'

Anna could feel her blush darkening and cursed her body's inability to keep the blood away from her cheeks at crucial moments such as these.

'No,' Olivia smiled sweetly and patted Hamlet. Her eyelashes fluttering like a butterfly. Justin looked at Anna and rolled his eyes at Olivia's brilliant acting skills.

Anna reluctantly stood and dusted herself off. Justin — understanding what that meant — told the girls to say goodbye to Anna.

'Bye An-na,' Olivia cried.

'Bye Anna,' whispered Samantha and reached to give her a hug from Justin's arms. Anna took her and felt her heart melt when Samantha clung to her body. Anna kissed her soft cheek adoringly and put her back on the ground.

'Bye sweetie,' she told her, and Justin walked her back inside the house, first telling Hamlet that he was in charge.

'Cute kids,' Anna told him as they approached his front door. She thought briefly of all that had happened since she'd first stood on its other side.

'That they are,' he grinned.

'You seem to have them a bit. Is this because you're the best brother ever, or did you lose a bet?'

'Neither,' Justin laughed, finding Anna's keys in the lounge room where they'd been abandoned the night before. 'Their sister's been giving them a run for their money, so it's an all-hands-on-deck kind of situation. Sorry if they pestered you,' he offered, aware that their last question still hung in the air unanswered.

What determined a girlfriend anyway, Anna wondered?

'No, they were fine. I answered their questions the best I could,' she laughed. She didn't want to leave just yet, just knew that she should.

'Yeah?' he grinned. 'I noticed you stumbled on one.'

She gave him credit for his boldness and blushed, not possessing the same confidence to know what to say.

'Yes, well … See ya,' was all that squeaked out of her mouth.

'See ya,' he returned, laughing at her side-step of the still-unanswered question, before kissing her with a kiss to knock the socks, that she wasn't even wearing, clear off her feet.

'See ya,' she said again, not yet letting go.

'I'll call you later,' he told her, and she believed without a doubt that he would.

They both heard a sudden tearful cry of 'Olivia!' and Anna promptly left to let Justin deal with the accused.

Anna was happy. He was calling her later. *Justin* was calling her later. Her *boyfriend* was calling her later?

She toyed with the beautiful notion for hours.

chapter forty-one

Tuesday night, Justin's most disliked night of the week, blew his expectations.

It was the sixth night of the course, but the first he'd had to lie to Anna. The lie felt awful and devious, but he hadn't yet figured out how to voice the truth. Especially now.

He hadn't seen Anna since she had left his house Sunday morning, but they had spoken into the morning for the last two nights and his thumb was feeling the strain from texting her at every moment he found.

He had learnt a lot though; like that Anna had attended seven different schools across three states. That she had never owned a pet. That apart from her parents, her only other family were some older and distant cousins. That she hated peanut butter but loved peanut M&M's; and that a SEGA rocked her world and was her most loyal friend in the nineties.

Much of their phone calls were also filled with silence, too tired to talk, but not wanting to hang up — merely content with the other's company.

Anna suggested that she come over after she finished work that night and Justin was anxious for the course to begin so it could end. In all that he had learnt about Anna, he still had no

idea what she did for a living and was questioning his determination to play the game. How was he to have known that
the stranger he had a random conversation with, in a hospital
in a complete other state, would be the girl he'd go and fall
in love with? Though, in retrospect, her eyes should have been
clue enough.

He was determined that when she came over that night, he
was going to figure it out or admit defeat. Justin had hinted for
a clue from Tom, but Tom had already been sworn to secrecy by
Mel. So, Justin sat in the classroom, wishing the next two hours
away, brainstorming possible careers.

The program itself was surprisingly interesting. Had it been
personal choice that brought him to the room each week, Justin
doubted he would have begrudged the time spent. What he
hated was the principle of having to go by court order. That he
was judged for something he unknowingly did and had to sit in
a room every week and be classed as someone who didn't know
better. The long bus trip, the late hour getting home; that was
tolerable in comparison to what it did to his pride.

The facilitator for the week, Angela, introduced herself as a
former paramedic. She spoke enthusiastically about the YouTube
clips about to be shown, but when she struggled to make them
run it gave Justin hope that the clips would be omitted from
the night's presentation. That maybe they could go home early.
With Anna in his sights, Justin was already figuring out the next
bus out of there.

After a silent curse, Angela apologised to the class and busied herself trying to fix the problem. No-one offered to help,
because no-one cared to see it work.

Justin checked the time on his phone for the fifth time since
the session began and messaged his sister to see how she was. Jo
replied promptly, letting him know Bianca would be readmitted
to hospital if her weight didn't improve. His heart sank at the

news. Feeling useless, he searched Google for Bianca's condition again, searching for hope, and paid vague attention to Angela's increasing stress—eventually feeling bad for her, but clueless to offer help. Heart surgery on a dog? Sure. Buttons and cords? No chance.

Angela had picked up the internal class phone, too preoccupied to control the group from getting loud and restless. Justin watched for a chance of the class's cancellation as she nodded into the receiver, glaring at the projector screen which relayed the computer's desktop. Then, without any assistance from Angela, the cursor zoomed around the screen at high speed. Icons were clicked, tabs opened; all so quickly that the class as a whole began to pay attention. Their heads following it like a game of tennis.

'Hey, how's it doing that?' one guy called out, his mouth hanging open. Angela shared their awe.

'All the computers are hooked up to the same network,' she explained. 'They can fix the problem remotely.'

'Huh? What?' the same guy called.

'IT,' she told him, pleased her computer now seemed to be cooperating. 'Amazing, huh?' and the class nodded appreciatively. To Justin it looked like the computer had a mind of its own. Craig seemed to be the only one unimpressed, but Justin reasoned that he was an office guy.

A relieved Angela began her video presentation and the class's mood dropped again, hope only rising halfway through the second clip when the computer froze. Justin felt Angela's frustration, amid the refreshed hope that he could leave early. They heard her curse, not so silently this time, before heading for the phone. She hung it up much faster and everyone watched, waiting for the cursor to zip around.

'They're coming down,' Angela told them, looking resigned to an unsuccessful night.

Anna was tired. She'd started work at seven that morning and then someone had called in sick. At midday, when she'd agreed to cover an off-site evening shift that wasn't far from home, it hadn't seemed like such a bad idea. At six, she hated herself for being so keen. She had no idea what she had been thinking. Actually, that wasn't true. She was thinking of Justin. Her mood, even when at the hospital, had been entirely happy. She knew Justin had to work late and knew her mother had visitors for the day, so she had no reason not to take the extra work. Plus, it was Jane's birthday on the weekend and she could do with the overtime, given all the expenses her bank account had seen of late.

Anna was about to text Justin when the phone started ringing and she had to dash downstairs to fix another problem. Her company had been working on the server for the college for the last month. They had hired a company who had done a very bad job and so This is IT staff had been sent all over Sydney to isolate the glitches. She comforted herself with the knowledge that in just three more hours she would be at Justin's and it wouldn't even matter if the other company were in fact run by monkeys. Her body, fingers to her toes, tingled with excitement.

Anna jogged down the stairs, her ID tag flipping around her neck as she went.

'Hi Angela, I'm Anna,' she smiled as she walked into the room and towards the computer, briefly noticing the small group that were chatting loudly.

'Hi. Sorry Anna, it just won't seem to work.'

Anna assured her it would be fine, undid all the cables and put them back together like a basic puzzle. She walked around the computer and felt eyes on her. Self-conscious, she glanced at the class to see Justin sitting amongst the group.

Her face broke into a grin and she mouthed a very surprised hello. He gave a faint wave back and Anna noticed how pale he looked, just before she felt confused. She gave him a quizzical look—wasn't he meant to be at work? Then, figuring it must have been a veterinary course, was impressed that the college attended to such a broad range of vocations.

With a racing heart, Anna had to force herself to focus, but kept thinking of Justin, and Justin watching her. When she'd found the problem, Angela thanked her profusely and Anna beamed at her—giddy that her guy was only metres away and wanting to laugh that he knew her job and the game was finally over.

Angela asked the whole class to thank Anna and Anna bowed her head with an embarrassed chuckle and turned to leave, giving Justin a slight wink on her way out. He definitely looked pale, she hoped he wasn't sick.

'Oh, Anna! You forgot this,' Angela stood, holding out Anna's ID tag. As Anna reached to take it, she saw what Angela had since clicked onto the screen. Now in black and white, Anna saw the words *Traffic Offenders Program: Drink Driving Rescue.*

Anna read it again. She felt her head fall to the side, not knowing what to make of what she was reading. Confused, she turned her head to Justin, hoping he would bring some clarity. Not just clarity, but some source of information that would reassure her. Some sign that what she was reading, and him being in that room, meant something other than what it seemed to mean.

But the look in his eyes gave her no comfort. The look on his face told her what she didn't want to know—or be.

'Thanks Anna,' Angela told her again, but it was more of a friendly hint to now leave so she could restart her session.

'No problem,' Anna muttered and left, her body moving by some unknown means. Surely it wasn't herself that could be making movement happen. Breathing and walking at the same time suddenly seemed impossible.

Anna had walked halfway up the hallway before she realised that she was going in the wrong direction. She turned back and when she neared the now offensive door, she slowed. It was closed, they couldn't see her. But she now knew that behind it was a group of people who had been caught for drink driving. A group of people like the guy who'd hit her mother's car. Inside that room could be the person who'd almost killed her mother. She felt vengeful. Her face burned with rage.

Inside that room, was Justin.

chapter forty-two

Mel marched into a travel agent early Thursday morning, flat white in hand and determined.

'I'd like to book a trip to Europe please,' Mel replied clearly, when asked how she could be helped. She told the woman precisely what she wanted, never one for diversion, and just before eleven, walked out feeling somewhat disturbed by the amount of her savings she had just committed. One phone call later and that feeling transformed.

'Is this stupid?' she asked Tom.

'Yes,' he laughed. 'I don't know about you, but this is possibly the stupidest thing I've ever done. But it was about time I think,' and Mel laughed too. She wasn't normally one to take risks. Ioulia would take risks. Anna would take risks—often unknowingly. Mel, however, was always skeptical. Until now.

'So … we're really going?' She could hear the happiness in his voice and it made her feel sure.

'Yup. In four weeks and five days we will be shivering in Paris.'

Tom had been in town for a business meeting and, preparing for another regretful goodbye, the two had seriously discussed their options. Break up or move was all that Mel could see; both seeming far too extreme. Then Tom suggested travel—find out how well they could handle each other every day. Both had talked about an unrealised dream of Europe and so, after some research, that is what they decided to do. Four weeks of Europe. Four weeks of each other. And then they'd decide what to do.

Mel thrived on pressure, but she had huge concerns whether her love could. Going away seemed like the most romantic way to find out.

They had yet to tell anyone but their bosses their plans. She knew her family, the forum from which her sensibility stemmed, would not approve. But she knew that if anyone would support her, it would be her friends, which was exactly why she hadn't quite mentioned it to them yet. Just in case they didn't.

Walking home after work, Justin dialled Anna's number for what felt like the millionth time to no avail. He'd stopped leaving voice messages because he was sure Anna was deleting them before even listening to what he had to say. He had learnt the name of the company she worked for but was given such bad service when he called that he doubted his messages even made it past the narky receptionist who had answered. He'd texted countless times, begging Anna to accept his calls or respond. But she didn't.

It was perfectly clear that Anna wanted nothing to do with him, regardless of the fact that he still very much wanted everything to do with her.

For three days he had walked around, deliriously happy, like she was his. He'd let himself think that what they had was set in stone; had arrogantly dreamt of their future. He hated himself for running ahead with it, but there was no denying that he had—he'd already grown old with her.

A week ago, he'd had it all. He knew the touch of her skin. Yet something so perfect and so recent in time was so unreachable; so frustratingly irreversible. He cursed himself; the stupid course. Adam. Julia. And then himself, again. He'd woken from an amazing dream into a bleak reality.

Justin's phone beeped and he jumped, not expecting a response. His heart beat wildly as he opened his messages, bracing himself.

Mel and I going to Europe! BBQ Sat before xmas. C u there!

Justin read it three more times before he realised it wasn't Anna who had sent the message. Once he made sense of it, he didn't know if the relief he felt was because he hadn't just been served a message of hate, or because Anna wasn't the one about to leave the country. Both, Justin realised, though it was with a side of disappointment that Anna still had no desire to talk to him in any capacity. He didn't have to be a doctor to figure out she still didn't want to be with him either.

He should have told her about the accident. He should have told her the day she turned up at the clinic. He'd been gutless and now he had no hope.

It was at least another block before Justin even processed what the message had actually said and reached for his phone to call Tom.

'Are you crazy? What if you realise you hate each other and you're stuck in Belgium?' Justin's laugh sounded like a lie to his ears.

'I know. We have both said that, not Belgium exactly, but we realise it's crazy. But better we find out in Belgium than giving up, right?'

'True,' Justin admitted, swatting at a fly that was determined to camp on his cheek. 'Nah, it will be great. I'm impressed.'

'Thanks mate. Guess time will tell,' Tom chuckled. 'Oh, hey, how's your niece?'

Justin frowned. The weight Bianca had gained since her operation was still declining. She was at the hospital every other day and the worry had crept back now that it was obvious that the surgery was not the success they'd celebrated.

'She's okay,' Justin said what he wanted to be true. 'She's having pretty regular checkups … she'll be okay.'

'That's great.' Justin could hear Tom hesitate before continuing. 'So … Anna found out, eh?'

Justin paused and frowned miserably. He was really beginning to despise himself but was too frustrated to snap out of it.

'Yeah. She did,' he admitted sombrely. 'Mel tell you?'

'Yeah. We fought. Apparently, I should have told her.'

'Well, thanks for not. So, first fight? I'm honoured,' Justin smiled forcefully and heard Tom grunt a, 'You're welcome.'

'Did she forgive you?'

'Yeah, yeah, she did … I think. What about Anna?'

Before he even answered, Justin suspected Tom already knew that she hadn't and didn't plan to. He looked up the street ahead of him and sighed.

'Tom, how did I get here?'

Tom didn't reply. Justin could hear him tapping keys, still at his desk.

'You've just had a shit run. She'll get over it.' It was said so simply that Justin scowled at him for making it seem so straightforward.

'Yeah … sure,' Justin lied. 'Hey, I better go. I have a hill coming up. See you Sunday?'

He hung up to tackle the remainder of his walk home for another day. He really missed his car. The workshop had rung to say it was ready for pickup two weeks ago. But he didn't have the logistics to get it and didn't see the point, partly worried he'd be tempted to drive it. A risk he would consider taking, but given his recent luck, knew he'd be a fool to take it.

chapter forty-three

'Are you going to call him?' Jane broke into Anna's thoughts as they sat on the new couch in her tiny granny flat. Earlier they'd been out for Jane's birthday along with her sister, Sarah. While Anna had been in the ladies', Jane had felt obliged to tell Sarah that Anna was not her usual self and swore she had never seen her like this. Even after one of Anna's more promising boyfriends had admitted to impregnating another woman during his four-month relationship with Anna—but had still hoped they could stay together—had she reacted this fiercely.

Sarah had offered to set Anna up with her husband's friend, but Jane refused. Besides being too soon, and despite the claim he had his own business and was very attractive, the 'just out of a relationship' fact was a deal breaker and Jane refused on Anna's behalf, and then her own.

Anna had returned to the table mute, furiously knifing her food with a sad scowl on her face that was yet to fade.

'Well?' demanded Jane, trying again to break into Anna's reverie. The hum of the air conditioner filled the otherwise quiet room as the November temperatures soared outside. She'd already shared a one-way conversation with herself about Mel's Europe trip—with an actual boy—and was losing patience.

And though the shirt Anna had given her for her birthday had been lovely, she had been the worst company all week and Jane felt slightly peeved at her for being so moody on her birthday.

'What?' Anna asked vaguely. 'Sorry, did you say something?'

'Anna! Snap out of it. Just for today at least. *Please*.'

'I'm sorry Jane. Really, I am,' she spoke genuinely, her big eyes pleading Jane's.

'It's okay. I understand,' Jane sighed. 'Are you going to call him?'

Anna looked at her, stunned, like Jane had just suggested she walk down the street naked, do a cartwheel and then give birth.

'No! Why would I?' she said incredulously, and Jane shook her head.

'Um, maybe because it's doing your head in *not* talking to him. Maybe you could hear him out?' Jane suggested and really wished that Anna would take her up on the advice.

'I know everything I need to know Jane,' Anna spat at her.

'Fine. Call, don't call. But don't be a bitch to me, I didn't do anything,' she snapped back, and the pleading look returned to Anna's face.

'Crap. I'm sorry. I'm sorry. Let's just not talk about him.'

'Okay, fine.'

'I'm just so angry with him.'

'I know,' Jane soothed.

'He *lied* to me.'

'I know.'

'I slept with him,' Anna moaned.

'I know.'

'*Really* slept with him.'

'You mentioned.'

'I miss him.'

'I know.'

'I'm sorry,' Anna apologised, dejected.

'I know.'

Anna sighed loudly, and Jane copied.

'Let me make it up to you. What can we do for your birthday that's fun?'

Jane beamed.

'Red wine or white?'

'White.' Anna smiled appreciatively; her mood more than marginally improved already.

chapter forty-four

Justin sat in the classroom waiting for the seventh and final week of the traffic offenders program to begin and then, finally, end.

If he was bitter at week one, he was livid at week seven — now that his presence there had lost him Anna. Knowing there was a possibility of Anna being in the same building and not being able to talk to her made him irritable and restless.

To add insult, his niece had been readmitted to hospital, too weak to be at home. Her family felt teased by the initial operation, and now awaited another.

The final course topic was *Insurance and the Law*. The screen was lit by a bright white light and they waited for the presentation to begin, everyone keen to 'graduate'. The facilitator that week, a lawyer named Ian, looked at the same screen mystified. Justin watched as Ian pressed buttons making nothing appear, and his body began to tense. He could sense what was about to happen like it was a movie he'd seen a hundred times. When Ian made a joke about hating technology, Justin felt his heart quicken. If he had a chance of knowing what to do, he would have done it for Ian in an instant. Instead, Ian picked up the phone to call for assistance and life began showing in slow motion. Frame by frame.

Justin's palms sweated. His heart worked faster as he pulled at the shirt around his neck and shifted in his seat, but she appeared before he felt prepared.

Seeing Anna walk in was the height of his shame. He wished he could hide. Unfortunately, being one of the tallest people in the class, there was no chance of hiding behind anyone.

As she walked in, her head high, determined not to look in his direction, his whole body reacted. He wanted to hug her and shake the rigidness out. Every move she made was under his watchful eye. He thought that with all the hardness she was trying to emulate, that she actually looked smaller and more fragile. How much he missed her was even clearer to Justin and he was baffled at how, in such little time, he could feel like he needed her so much. When she wasn't making his heart race, she steadied him.

The others talked while they waited. Ian was trying to assist Anna, but Anna was ripping out cords and pressing buttons so fast that Ian had to step back, rendering himself useless. Justin watched as he attempted a joke, but Anna barely returned a tight smile and kept working. Her speed clearly indicating just how much she wanted to be out of that room.

He could see Craig off to his right, still in his suit and tie, eyes fixed on Anna admiringly. Justin wondered if she'd noticed. He had to resist throwing a pen at Craig and succumbed to a glare, that Craig noticed, but mistook for a shared appreciation of a good-looking woman. He gave Justin a knowing nod and turned his eyes back to Anna's backside. Justin was reeling. He liked Craig, he really did, but he was willing to change his opinion if he didn't stop looking at Anna like that. He felt protective of something that wasn't his to protect.

Once Anna had left the room and the slide show had begun, Justin's head was too preoccupied to concentrate. His heart rate had only just begun to slow to a normal beat when the session came to an end for the final time. It was all over, but he hadn't heard a thing about legalities, duty of care, or court hearings.

The others scraped back their chairs to leave, giving brief farewells. Justin vaguely copied, noticing Ian pick up the phone. He watched on as Ian lightly hit his forehead with his hand and laughed a jolly laugh.

Justin nodded a goodbye to Craig and returned a goodbye to one of the girls heading out the door. As he waved her off, Anna marched briskly past her into the room.

Justin's heart was off again, like a horse out of the gates.

He considered leaving, but he missed her too much. Hoping he had a chance to be alone with her, Justin wasted time re-tying his shoelace as the remaining few people dawdled from the class. The instant Ian excused himself to Anna, Justin timed his approach like a martyr.

He knew that she had seen him, but Anna occupied herself fully with the computer, pretending she hadn't. Justin didn't let this sway him.

'Anna?' he was standing right by her side now. She fiddled with cords and ignored him. 'Anna, I need to talk to you.'

She stopped and looked up. The expression she wore made his insides shrink and he wondered how such a sweet person could make him feel like a child.

'Why?' she asked, her voice so cold he almost backed down. Almost, but a surge of anger and frustration rose inside him and pushed him on.

'Why?' he exclaimed, before forcing his voice down.

'Yes. Why? There isn't anything to talk about.'

She spoke with such finality as she pushed a cord into place; about to make her getaway.

'Yes. There. Is,' he said slowly in an attempt to stay calm. 'Anna, what are you doing?'

'I'm working,' she replied simply, stepping towards the door.

He grabbed her arm roughly and she spun around, shooting him a potent look. Justin flinched, composed himself, and pressed on.

'Anna. We could be happy. You and me. I know it,' he pleaded. 'Just let it happen. Give me a chance.'

'Let go of me,' she demanded softly.

'I can't,' he replied sadly. 'Give us a chance Anna. Please.'

'No,' she said with clear determination. 'I can't.'

'Yes you can Anna, you can.'

'No, I can't. I can't be happy knowing what you've done,' she spoke softly. 'You lied to me. I know nothing about you. You and me wasn't real and I can't put all my faith into a lie like you can. There is no 'us'.'

'It was real,' he assured her, hurt by her words and the want to make it better. 'Listen, I'm sorry I didn't tell you. Believe me, I am so sorry. But I just didn't know how.' He was pleading and he felt pathetic and desperate. 'Just talk to me.' He took a breath and waited.

She stared back, offering nothing.

He understood that Anna didn't know anything about what had landed him in that room each week and, rationally, he'd thought of that a lot over the last week. He'd believed that if Anna did know his story, she'd feel differently. But he also believed that if she cared enough, she'd at least ask questions for herself and hear the facts — she'd give him the benefit of the doubt. But there weren't any signs of doubt as she spoke.

'You need to go.'

Justin felt any hope he'd held on to vanish.

'You know what Anna?' he asked, patience following in hope's path. 'This is bullshit. I know it, and I think if you gave yourself some credit, you'd know it too.' His breath was storming in his chest and his brain was drowning in all the words he wanted to offload. She was only a foot in front of him, but it may as well have been miles from where he was because he couldn't reach her. He felt like nothing he could say would make a difference. Angry or nice, nothing seemed to be heard or wanted to be heard. He took in her fury-filled green eyes, which were usually his favourite feature. They glared into him like an animal. Her arm hung stiffly by her side and her mouth was hard. He braced himself.

'Is everything okay in here?' A voice cut in from the doorway. 'Anna? What's going on?' Ian demanded, eyeing Justin suspiciously.

Justin was still trying to recover from his own words and his thoughts were now in overdrive at being overheard. He imagined how bad it looked.

'Hi!' squeaked Anna in an unusually high voice. She looked at Justin and back to Ian, who waited for an answer.

'Everything is fine,' she eventually responded, not convincing Ian.

'I think it's time for you to leave,' he announced firmly to Justin, who felt frustrated at being interrupted and being in possibly a worse position from where he'd started.

He looked at Anna, her stance firm.

'Right,' he said to the room. 'Bye, Anna,' he added softly and walked towards the door. Ian turned sideways to let him pass, giving him an authoritative look that spoke a million words of warning. Justin wondered what Anna would tell him, but didn't look back. He just kept walking; his steps echoing down the empty corridor as they took him further and further away from her.

chapter forty-five

Mel sighed over the phone. Loudly, so that Tom knew he wasn't totally forgiven (out of solidarity mostly). She'd spoken to Anna earlier, who seemed just as angry as she had a week ago when she'd furiously accused Mel of holding out on inside information about Justin.

'Did you invite your friends to the barbie?' he sighed, and Mel was giddy again at the idea that they were soon leaving for their Winter Wonderland tour, annoyed for Anna, but happy to separate the situation from her and Tom.

'You mean, my *two* friends in Sydney?' she reminded him, her voice vaguely sarcastic.

'Um … yeah,' he laughed. 'Are they coming?'

'Yeah. Jane promised to invite her sister as well,' she trailed off, her finger tracing the pictures in the magazine in front of her.

'Oh … good,' Tom replied, sounding strained. Mel, noting this, confirmed why after one key question.

'Is Justin coming?'

'Ah … yeah. He is,' Tom admitted and neither said anything. Mel felt her face frown. According to Anna's earlier attack, Justin was still the scum that walked the earth. Tom's laugher crashed into her concerns. She eventually joined in, given no better option.

'Wow,' he chuckled. 'This is going to be entertaining.' Mel snorted, making Tom laugh louder, taunting Mel for her snort.

'Stop it!' she cried, involuntarily snorting again. It sent him into another round of laughter. Mel soaked the sound in. She loved his laugh and she smiled at where she had arrived in such a short time.

The weather was a complete paradox to the season as Anna drove to the hospital that night. Rain splashed drearily on her windscreen as she battled the traffic. Parking was just as hectic, forcing her to park at the furthest parking station and run through the rain to dry ground. It made the visit even more wearing, but she had worked late the last three nights in an attempt to avoid her restless mind, so was determined to visit her mother.

A Friday night at the hospital was sadly also her best offer. Not that she was fussed; her body ached from its inability to sleep and her head felt too cramped with sheer disappointment to do anything else.

She forced her lips to move in an upwards direction for her mother, hoping the disguise worked.

'Good news,' her mother beamed, and Anna brightened from the sound in her voice. 'My lung is almost strong enough; my blood is clear, and my leg has aligned *sufficiently*. They think early next week I can go home.'

'Aw, Mum, that's fantastic. Have you told Brian?' she asked, laying her handbag on top of the pile of books and magazines her mother had stashed beside her bed to keep her occupied. She had whispered on many occasions that the other 'inmates' weren't that chatty.

'Yes.' Her mother felt for Anna's hand and squeezed it. 'Anna he's insisting I move in with him straight away,' she laughed, delighted that someone wanted to take care of her. They were so in love it made Anna as green with envy as it made her happy.

'So that means … that you are completely free,' she sung.

'Mum!' Anna cut her off, then lowered her voice. 'I have never seen it that way.'

'I know dear. But you have given up so much—and I appreciate it—but you don't need to stay up here. You never did; though I am eternally grateful. Anna, your life is in Melbourne.' She smiled and Anna, unable to return it, felt a hint of sadness sweep through her as she envisioned where this life of hers was meant to be; the finality which her return would bring. Her mother noticed the change.

'That is, if you want to go back to Melbourne. I'd love you to live up here of course,' she smiled enthusiastically. 'And you do have some nice friends up here,' she continued, before adding slyly, 'Jane. Justin …' Anna knew she mentioned Justin as a means to source information and Anna shook her head, staring at her mother's cast as a diversion. She kicked herself for ever mentioning him to her in the first place.

'Justin,' she started. 'Isn't such a good friend.' Her mother looked on eagerly. Nine weeks trapped in a hospital bed and any source of gossip was entertaining. Anna could relay a story of what colour socks she was wearing and her mother would have listened intently.

Anna didn't know quite how to back pedal from Justin, for the sake of the conversation as well as her heart.

'Oh? What happened?'

'He lied to me.' *Simple, leave me alone.*

'Was it a bad lie?' her mother searched, and after much self-debate Anna surrendered a brief version of the story. A part of her knew she'd probably regret it, but it spilled out regardless.

Her mother made noises at all the right moments, acknowledging the information, and when Anna was finished, looked at her daughter and smiled.

'Anna, I understand that must have been hard. It's your choice not to see him anymore, and if you go home then maybe it won't matter …' Anna agreed hungrily, wanting her choice to be the right one. 'But … he clearly wants to talk to you about it. Maybe just hear him out?'

'I don't want to,' Anna protested in frustration.

Her mother smiled. 'Okay, then don't. Like I said, it's your choice. Your life.'

A silent moment hung in the air before Anna spoke a grateful thank you. Her mother, however, mistook the sound of Anna's voice as a green light to speak further.

'You do seem to like him though. Brian and I thought—'

'You spoke to Brian about him?' Anna was appalled.

'We thought you may end up together, the way you spoke so highly of him,' she admitted, only marginally uncomfortable with the admission. Anna felt embarrassed and angry to be the topic of conversation, let alone her supposed feelings for Justin. She should never have mentioned him.

'No!' yelped Anna, mortified. '*Not* ending up together,' she said firmly, and her mother shrugged her acceptance. But it didn't deter Anna's response. 'You don't even know him anyway! Since when did you like a complete stranger? You don't trust anyone. My whole life you told me not to trust anyone and you were right.'

'Anna,' she tried to calm her daughter with her tone. 'I was wrong.'

Anna stared wide and wild eyed.

'I was. I was probably *too* careful with you. I didn't want you to get hurt like I did. I couldn't believe that not everyone would let you down.'

Anna, ignoring her mother's newfound rational thinking, powered on — the need to vent overwhelming her. 'Mum, he's as bad as the stupid drunk teenager that did this to you. I could have lost you!'

'Now, now,' she hushed, as if Anna were a child still. 'You can't blame one person for something someone else has done. And he wasn't a stupid teenager. He was a much older man and he seemed wise enough when I spoke to him. We're all human Anna, we all do stupid things that we don't know how to admit to,' her mother added softly, sadly.

Anna nodded obediently, though not relinquishing her anger at Justin. Her body, calming, nestled into the too-familiar chair. She was growing more tired but felt her head tilt to the side. Something was echoing in her head that didn't make sense.

'Wait, what are you talking about? When did you speak to the driver?'

A look of caution took its cue on her mother's face while she spoke. 'I'm sorry, Anna. I hadn't told you. I knew what you would think. But he turned up when I was in ICU. I didn't see him,' she rushed as if to extinguish Anna's reaction. 'He wasn't allowed in, but the nurses told me he'd been. When I was moved here, he turned up again and … we spoke.'

'You spoke!' Anna cried. She wasn't sure what angered her more; that her mother hadn't told her, that this guy had such a nerve to turn up, or the fact that her mother was actually okay with it.

'Did you tell Brian that too?' she bit sarcastically, and her mother gave Anna the look that mothers have, the disappointed and unimpressed one that makes you feel two-feet tall.

'Yes. Brian was arriving as he was leaving one day. They met.'

'They met … how many times has this guy come?'

'A few times. I'm sorry Anna. But my point is, maybe don't judge Justin so harshly if he's a good person in all other respects.'

'They let him in here!'

'Anna, yes, I said it was okay.'

'Why?' She really did not understand any of this; she wanted to throttle the guy more than ever. She wanted a voodoo doll, and lots and lots of pins. Her mother seemed lost for reasons and stumbled on her words. Anna watched as she took a breath in and exhaled.

'Anna, there comes a point where you have to learn to trust people … forgive people. I know I haven't always done this, I'm trying though, and I hope you can too.' She looked at her daughter while she spoke, spoon feeding the words like she was a baby. 'Anna, there's something else.'

'Anna!' a voice exclaimed pleasantly from the door and she turned to see Brian; still in his pinstripe trousers, tie neatly around his neck.

'Hi Brian,' she muttered, distracted by the unfinished conversation. Anna had so many questions, but the look her mother gave told Anna to save them for another time.

At least now she knew who the mystery visitor had been from weeks ago. A part of her was relieved it wasn't her dad, the other was mind-blowingly annoyed by the audacity of the drunk driver for visiting her mother.

'Boy, is it raining hard out there,' Brian exclaimed. Anna's hair was testament to that, having had curled up to half its usual length. They laughed at her when she pointed this out.

'I'm a walking barometer,' she told them miserably.

After an hour or so of useless banter, Anna excused herself to battle the wet roads, eager to call Jane. If her mother would be moving soon, she had some decisions to make.

Stepping outside, she frowned as she was struck by cold fat drops on her way to the parking station. Her stomach was demanding attention and she realised she hadn't properly eaten since breakfast. Avoiding the rain and the roads for a little longer,

Anna ran into the Children's Hospital that sat next to the main building her mother was being treated in. Bright red and green tinsel decorated the much warmer hospital in sporadic scenes of festivities. It reminded Anna of different times. Christmas was less than a month away and it seemed to have crept up while Anna had turned her back on life.

A coffee shop, also decorated in Christmas cheer, was brewing at the entrance and she joined its small queue.

Catching her reflection in the cake display window, Anna's hair gave her a fright. She tried to smooth it and frowned at the lack of cooperation or improvement. Tucking it into a ponytail just as she was served, she ordered a toasted sandwich after very little procrastination, and wished Mel had been there to see it.

The coffee's strong perfume relaxed her, and she flicked through a communal magazine while waiting for her order. It was good to know that Miley was in trouble again. However, seeing Jennifer Aniston without make-up only made her feel worse about herself and she put the magazine down. She felt eyes on her and subtly looked up to see if she were right, or simply paranoid. But they were still watching, and she wasn't being paranoid at all. The eyes on her were Justin's and her whole body froze.

Immediately, she wanted to smile at him. But then the pain he'd caused set in.

He was wearing the same blue shirt that she could remember clear as day removing from his body. Though now it was wet, and she assumed he must have recently arrived from the downpour outside.

Justin looked unsure of what to do and her mother's words were still resonating inside her sleep-deprived head, making Anna uncertain what to do herself. Jane's urges floated in next, so too did Justin's own words from the other night in the classroom.

She was so mad at him she didn't know what to do and she was using vast quantities of mental strength not to recall the body that was within the blue shirt, while also dulling the mortification that images of her own body could also be under review at any time, by him.

Justin walked slowly up to her side, staying a reasonably safe distance away, and said hello.

Anna wanted to be cold, but she was also very much aware of where they were, and she didn't want to be insensitive to that—even if he was a lying, sneaky, drunk.

'Hello,' she said icily, though she didn't mean it to sound so harsh. 'What are you doing here?' she added more softly, curiously. Only a small part of her wanted to ask if someone needed an arsehole transplant and he was offering his. *Arsehole.* Then she reprimanded herself for being so immature. She was a child; almost thirty and the mentality of a child. It was ridiculous.

His hair was almost black from the rain's input, and his weary eyes looked red. Lost for words momentarily, Justin didn't notice his mother walk briskly up to the shop towards him. Anna barely recognised her. Her face looked as drawn as Justin's and Anna felt bad for the whole arsehole comment, even though it had only been in her head.

Katherine smiled when she recognised Anna. Anna, meanwhile, felt even more uncomfortable and wondered what his mother knew about their situation. She also wondered if Justin's mother could read minds, like her own mother, and knew that Anna had just mentally called her son an arsehole.

'Anna! Hello,' his mother sang happily when she was closer to the counter where they stood. 'What brings you here?' Justin flinched at the sound of his mother's voice.

'Ah … my mum,' Anna stuttered. 'Next door, that is.' Anna wondered again what Katherine knew, especially when confusion flickered over her face and towards her son.

'Oh. I hope she's okay?'

'Yes. Yes, she'll be okay …' Anna nodded politely, aware of Justin's heavy gaze.

'Good to hear.' She smiled genuinely and touched Justin's arm gently as she turned to him. 'Justin love, sorry to interrupt, but could we make that two flat whites, one hot chocolate, and two muffins?' He nodded, and Katherine smiled at the two of them.

'Would you like me to help carry it?' she asked meaningfully, and Anna shifted even more uncomfortably in her spot — praying they would call her order so she could make a speedy getaway.

'No, I'll be right,' Justin assured his mother. Katherine smiled and reached for Anna's hand, commenting on how nice it was to see her again and wishing her mother well, before saying good-bye and leaving. Part of Anna wanted to grab at her cardigan to stay. The rational side of her brain begged her to refrain.

'Why are you here? What's happened?' Anna asked quickly. His family being at the hospital highlighted the gravity and possibilities of why he was in front of her; his nieces' beautiful little faces flashed through her head. Justin stumbled again and Anna's worry heightened. 'Justin?'

'Um, my niece is still sick. Bianca.' He admitted uneasily.

'What's wrong with her?' Anna asked with concern, expecting a broken bone; the flu.

'Um …' He clearly didn't want to talk about it with her and it hurt. She was being a hypocrite, she knew, but she wanted him to be able to tell her everything. 'Her liver is failing her. They operated but her body hasn't responded as well as they'd hoped.' Justin avoided eye contact and Anna automatically reached for his arm, stopping herself just short of contact.

'Oh Justin, I'm so sorry. When did they find out?' She heard her order being called and was now ignoring it.

'She's been sick since she was born, they only confirmed why six or seven weeks ago.' He was playing it calm; she could tell he wasn't.

An inkling of hurt echoed and spread throughout her body because he had never told her, had never let on what was happening. She had always just thought Bianca had a runny nose when he said she was sick. Okay, inkling was an understatement, she felt lied to, again, and wasn't even sure if it were justified.

'When did they bring her in?' Anna asked, trying not to display her disappointment, genuinely feeling both sympathetic and empathetic for the whole family. As a veteran, she knew hospital visits were not easy. Justin searched the counter, delaying his answer.

'She was readmitted this week, but she came in a while ago. Maybe a month now,' he confessed. Then added, as it came to him, 'The night Claude had his stitches out.'

Anna felt shocked. All this time she had been visiting her mother. All the times they had spent together. All the times she had dumped her life on him, and he'd never once hinted his family had their own hell going on. She'd bared her body for this guy and he hadn't even bared his life.

'I was trying not to burden you,' he sighed in response to her thoughts, stepping away from the counter so those around couldn't hear so easily.

'Justin,' she shook her head firmly, 'that is not a burden. Not one that I wouldn't have wanted at least,' she added, trying to keep her voice low. 'People want to help when things like this happen. People care,' she looked at him sincerely. *I care,* she thought, but didn't quite know how to say that over her pride.

She felt torn between the compassion she felt for him and his family, her own anger at him, and him being a complete lying arsehole. She should probably stop calling him an arsehole, however. He really wasn't one.

'Sorry,' he mumbled and shrugged.

'Wow,' she said, and he nodded. A silence hung between them as her dinner went cold. 'You're really one for secrets, aren't you?' she added flatly, numbed by reality and the screens he had put up to protect his. His vague clues to his life, his family and his problems, made her feel sidelined. Made the friendship they had seem false.

His face darkened. 'It wasn't a secret,' he said delicately.

'Then why did you go to so much effort not to tell me?' Anna retorted, uncertain. 'Why would you bother to contact me so much? Beg me to forgive you? When you were being so elusive about yourself anyway?' she asked, angry now and simply flabbergasted.

'Some things aren't easy to say,' he told her, louder than the vast hospital foyer needed. They seemed to have an audience. Albeit it consisted of two older ladies, with at least one wearing a hearing aid; a mother trying to wrangle two energetic little boys, and a guy that was hopefully busy keeping her sandwich warm — but an audience nonetheless.

Anna glanced around and hushed her voice when she spoke next.

'You think I don't know that?'

He didn't reply.

'Justin, this is big stuff you've kept from me. How can you spend so much time with a person, how could you want to spend *more* time with that person and not tell them something like this? How could you be so … so … vague?' She said 'vague' like the word was offensive and took a breath in, completely failing at composing herself.

'How could you not tell me about your accident?' she threw in, because that was the part that she couldn't get past and had kept her up at night.

'I didn't want to lose you!' he threw back. Again, way too loudly, and two families walking by turned their heads to the noise with disapproving eyes.

Anna stood still, staring at his face—his red eyes. She felt regretful and spoke quietly. 'Well … you did.'

He nodded regretfully, hung his head and exhaled. 'I wasn't being vague. I wasn't meaning to anyway.'

Anna didn't reply straightaway. She was trying to be wise and let herself calm down. 'I guess it doesn't really matter now anyway.' She twined a defiant strand of hair back behind her ear and excused herself to collect her order. Justin gave a remorseful look, but she didn't want to see it.

He'd stepped up to make his family's order and she waited while he paid, wanting to walk away but not quite knowing how to.

Justin smiled politely at the barista and Anna could see how embarrassed he was to have caused a scene. She didn't understand how a guy who felt causing a scene was wrong, a guy who was so smart he was a doctor, a guy who was so quick witted it exasperated her … how could this same guy be so stupid to drink, and then get in a car to drive?

Anna watched his long fingers run through his dark hair as he turned back to her.

'Listen Anna, I'm sorry. I don't know what else I can say. Not telling you this stuff meant I was free from it all with you. I'm sorry if that makes me a bastard. If you want to hate me, then hate me. But I can't change anything.'

He sounded resigned to the fact and Anna realised sadly, and with consequence, that he was right. There was nothing he could do.

They called his order much quicker than hers and Justin retrieved it with another polite smile. He stowed the smile away in the instant he faced Anna.

She didn't know how to respond. She wanted more time to process the words; wasn't she entitled to more time? Here he was, the guy who represented the person she despised most in the world, also being the best part of her world.

'Are you catching the bus home tonight?' she asked, trying to show mercy, thinking of the rain outside. He looked mystified for a moment and then smiled slightly.

'No. My parents are giving me a lift.' He looked at the coffees in his hand with discomfort. 'I should probably get these back before I have a riot on my hands.'

'Right. Yes. Go.' She stepped out of his way and extended her arm for him to pass.

'Thanks. I'll see … talk … um … take care,' he said shyly and walked past. It made her sad. Knife-in-the-heart kind of sad.

'Justin!' she called out as he was almost out of earshot. He stopped and turned, careful not to drop anything, and waited—hopeful. The old ladies at the table watched on with interest. Anna didn't clearly know what she wanted to say and meekly offered, 'I hope they can help Bianca.'

Justin studied her face before speaking.

'Thanks, Anna. Me too.' He smiled a sombre smile and walked away.

Anna climbed into her mother's bed that night wondering what a simple life would feel like. She couldn't sleep, and she thought of Bianca. Wondered what she looked like, if she was like Olivia or little Samantha, or dark like their mother. Anna wondered just how sick she was and was angry at herself for focusing on Justin not telling her anything, when she should have asked more about the little girl that lay in hospital. How he and the rest of his family must be feeling, she could only imagine.

Before seeing Justin, Anna had intended to call Jane. Post-Justin, she didn't know how to phrase the collection of feelings inside her. They all made sense, until she tried to put them together; until she imagined saying them out loud. She needed more time to make sense of things before she could talk about them.

When she eventually fell asleep, the rain soothing her from outside, she dreamt of Justin. It seemed she couldn't control him entering her dreams, as well as her life.

chapter forty-six

Sunday night, before the sun retired, Anna roamed the streets. They were getting more and more familiar each day and she found it a retreat from her mother's ever empty house. She had to admit that though the beach may not have been her neighbour, it was still a nice place to live. The trees, so old and seemingly wise; she imagined that they had witnessed a lot in their years and she enjoyed strolling under them, loving the smells they brought.

She climbed the steep footpath that would take her to the park, the cicadas singing loudly. Sweat slid down her back, but as she took in the feel of the evening, she felt energised. The sky was an eerie yellow and gave the impression that something grand was happening, somewhere.

She passed a group of teenagers sitting on the park swings. Anna tried not to stare, but took in their smiles, their awkwardness and their laughter.

She wondered what life was going to bring them. What treat? What hell? Anna wasn't sure if she felt envious of them, and their ignorance, or if she felt sorry for them. For, right now, at an age that Anna guessed was about fifteen, they were probably thinking how much life sucked. They probably dreamed of being older, imagining it to be so much better and having so much freedom. And maybe it was better, but Anna had never felt more confined.

As she walked to a cushy patch of grass, Anna thought of Justin and felt her heart zip down to her belly and back again. It was confusing. She was angry, there was no denying it. But the secrets he'd kept from her, his ability to keep her out, actually made her curious to know more, not less—regardless of what she told her friends. Anna had finally accepted that maybe there was more to his story that was worth hearing, but really, when she boiled it all down and was the most honest, she simply missed him. She thought now that that was the feeling she hadn't been able to pinpoint.

Anna had found herself practising what she would say if she called him, and rehearsals were daily. A part of her hoped he would call her, though since the night he'd approached her at work, he hadn't made one attempt to contact her. Even after the run-in at the hospital, when she'd most expected a follow-up call or message, there was nothing.

He finally listened and Anna wasn't too sure how she felt about it.

Justin sat at his kitchen table. He was finishing his fifth of the seven worksheets he had to complete for the Traffic Offenders Program. Now that the course was over, he was eager to send them off, leaving room in his brain to procrastinate about other things.

Feeling his enthusiasm wane, Justin's eyes drifted across to his phone. He was still accepting that Anna wasn't going to call, but it also held too many other entertaining options to not be tempting.

As he reigned in his self-control, focusing harder on the assignment at hand, a beep alerted the arrival of a message. Justin dutifully finished his sentence and reached over for the phone. Always relieved when it wasn't from his family, he slouched back in the chair and opened the message.

You going to Tommo's BBQ? We'll give you a lift mate.

Failing to get old, Justin hated his inability to drive.

Yeah, that'd be great. Otherwise I'll walk.

He really didn't want to walk. He was nervous at the idea that Anna may be there, and walking would only prolong an already anxious journey. The reply came through quickly.

It's cool. The mrs and I will pick u up.

Justin, wondering if Smitty's wife liked being referred to as his 'Mrs', opened the next message as his phone beeped again.

How is Bianca? Anna

Justin almost fell off the chair. He stood up. Sat down. Stood again; wishing he knew how to react.

At work, he had made Sandra confiscate his phone, just so he didn't succumb to temptation when he needed to be concentrating. Sandra took it quietly, asking too few questions for his liking. It only meant she found the rest of her information elsewhere, which disturbed him.

Before he'd given it to Sandra, his hands would reach for it compulsively. He'd texted Anna many times, deleting each one before he could press send. He'd called a hundred times, always quitting before it rung through. But outside of work the phone was in his possession full time and he looked at it like it was a doughnut and he was the guy on a diet. Now, he had reason to text, and while knowing he shouldn't, he held his breath as he replied.

She is doing her best. How is your mum?

Bianca was not good. But he didn't want to say that. He didn't want to add life to that idea. Dave's brother was under heavy medical assessment to be a potential live donor and the whole situation felt so incomprehensible, that it just didn't feel real.

Anna didn't reply straightaway and Justin felt certain she had her own hesitation to continue.

Good. She goes home soon.

Justin instantly feared what that meant.

That's great. Will you be living with her then?

Justin didn't take his eyes off the screen while waiting for the next reply.

Yeah it is. I'll be moving back to Melbourne

Justin felt his heart fall and tossed the phone onto the table. He had nothing to reply with.

Anna sent the last message, wondering what Justin would say. A part of her — most of her entire body makeup — wanted him to say, 'Don't go'.

It was an ego thing. She knew that. She wanted to feel wanted. But he didn't reply, and she wasn't sure what that meant, so she continued to sit on the hill.

The yellow sky was turning a darkening grey as Anna laid her head back on the ground and looked up at the leaves above her. Small bits of sky peaked through and she watched a bird flip around a branch.

She knew she should turn back but felt too heavy-hearted to move her feet. Her blood was being pushed around her body by the adrenaline of texting Justin and it was making her muscles shake. Maybe contacting him was a mistake, she thought, cursing retrospect.

She slowly sat up, beginning the journey home, and rested again. An ant was crawling down her bare leg and Anna watched it, mesmerised by how simple it made walking look. Then it bit her.

'Yeoch,' she whined, pressing her nail into the bite and shooing the bug away, wondering how something so small, hurt so much.

Anna sulked home, her feet scuffing the ground as she went. She didn't want to be at her mother's musty home that made her feel ten years old; but she felt apprehensive facing her altered life in Melbourne. She didn't know where she wanted to be anymore and resented the decision looming in front of her.

chapter forty-seven

Jane went to work in a bad mood. Her students looked on cautiously, seeing that their beautiful Miss Vadam wasn't smiling that morning like she usually did; her blue eyes undeniably flat.

Anna had called on her way to work to announce that she had given her notice at work and was moving back home—in two weeks.

Three things annoyed Jane about that call. Firstly, Anna would be far away, again. Secondly, Mel had invited them to a barbeque send-off, set for the day after Anna was now leaving. Mel would literally be flying over Anna as she drove south, which meant Jane would be attending the event on her own. Mel, who Jane had called as soon as she ended the call with Anna, was also annoyed at Anna, and had suggested Jane bring her sister and her husband. They refused. In their defense, they already had plans. Jane knew this because she called Sarah as soon as she had rung off from Mel, begging her to come. Sarah promised she'd try and in turn called her husband, Matt, to convince him to cancel their original plans, but Jane didn't think she could count on that. She wanted Anna there.

Anna hadn't even come up with a good reason to be leaving so suddenly. She had no reason not to wait at least another day, or until after Christmas, and Jane suspected her urgency to leave had everything to do with her not wanting to see Justin.

'It's not that,' Anna had persisted. 'I just want to go home.'

Pfft, Jane thought. Her second graders lied better than that.

The third, and actual, reason for her annoyance was that Anna was moving back to Melbourne … and she wasn't.

She gave her class Christmas craft to start the day, reminding herself not to take her mood out on eight-year-olds; Anna being selfish, or her own envy, had nothing to do with them.

There was a buzz of excitement in the fourth room of her mother's ward. After weeks of waiting, her mother was going home. Anna parked her car, mentally ticking off the final time that she would need to battle the hospital car park.

She had spent the last couple of nights cleaning her mother's house and packing some essentials to begin the move for both of them. Over at his house, Brian had been busy making room and modifications to accommodate his new roomie for weeks, in anticipation of her release. Anna had driven a carload over and was taken aback by what would be her mother's new home. Not one brown cupboard or mouldy ceiling in sight. She'd finally live in a place she deserved and Anna felt at ease.

Ioulia, who had been enjoying the flat to herself, was also busy removing incense smell, as promised, for Anna's return to Elwood. At work, Anna knew that the person who replaced her was keen to stay and she felt guilty that they would soon be out of a job—though there was talk he'd be filling in for Mel while she was away. If she were honest, Anna wasn't looking forward to exchanging her new, reliably air-conditioned office, for the dingy old one at the start of summer. Mel wouldn't even be there for four weeks to make it worthwhile and she hardly thought a postcard from Paris would fill the gap.

Anna walked along the hospital hallways, vaguely looking into the other rooms. Happy faces, sad faces, blank faces. She couldn't wait to no longer be another face of the hospital.

She stepped off the lift and headed straight to her mother's room, almost walking into a man wheeling his IV drip beside him.

'Oh, I'm so sorry,' she apologised, embarrassed at her clumsiness, glad he wasn't fazed.

'See you, Bernadette,' she heard a voice say kindly nearby. The sound of her mother's name brought Anna's attention back, just as she walked into another person, this time the one leaving Room Four.

'Excuse me,' he apologised, although it was Anna's fault completely. He stepped back and held his hands in front of him. Anna looked towards her mother's room, confirming it was still number four, and turned back feeling more than mildly dazed.

'What are you doing here?' she asked Justin. He didn't reply instantly, like the dread inside of her was requesting, and his whitening face was making her nauseous. He looked into the room and Anna knew he saw her mother's, shorter, dark hair, and her short frame.

'Justin, what are you doing here?' she swallowed, her voice threatening to rise higher as the stress rose in her body. *Don't let it be,* she prayed silently.

'Anna?' she heard her mother call from the custody of her bed, still needing help to get out of it. Anna ignored her.

Justin had hung his head, shaking it in disbelief, and she knew without a doubt that he had been playing two roles in her life.

'I'm sorry,' he mumbled. 'I didn't know,' he offered weakly.

'You didn't know,' Anna repeated, her eyes searching for a chair. Because the man with no face, that smashed into her mother's car and into their lives, was Justin.

His hand reached for her arm and Anna shook him away sharply. 'Don't,' she said sternly, the harshness echoing between them.

'Anna …' He began, but had nowhere else to go from there.

'Jay?' she heard her mother call to Justin this time, and Anna's head fell to her shoulder.

'Jay?' she repeated. He nodded again. Apologised again. Anna walked around him; tears were bracing themselves for free fall. Every part of her body had just been assaulted by truth and her cells quivered with the information, her legs wilting beneath her. Her heart sat in her throat.

'Anna,' Justin pleaded again, quietly and without hope.

'Please go,' she asked of him, urging, begging even, that he would walk away as she stepped into the room and closed the curtain behind her.

Her mother looked up at her and Anna fought to hold on to her sense of self. She pulled at the neck of her blouse, trying to shift the feeling that was beginning to suffocate her. She began collecting the remaining get-well cards.

'Did you meet Jay, Anna?' her mother asked innocently, knowing perfectly well that they were outside the room together. A concerned look took over Bernadette's face. 'You weren't rude I hope Anna. He really is a nice fellow,' she urged, trying her best to assure Anna of something that she already once knew.

'Mum,' she said, stopping her from going on. 'Mum, please.' Anna tried to focus on the ground; the cards, the sheets … breathing. But her mother continued, showing no mercy.

'You know it takes a lot of guts to visit like he does,' she continued to defend Justin and it rattled Anna more.

'Mum, stop,' she said firmly. 'I know him already okay … we've met.'

Anna could feel her mother's surprised eyes bore into her. 'Mum, *Jay* is Justin. Justin was the person who put you here,' she told her mum. The words repeated in her own head, trying to make sense of something that was nonsensical.

It was *Justin* that did this.

Justin had had to sit outside to compose himself. The shock of seeing Anna, of being caught coming from her mother's room, of knowing who he had hurt, was immense. He had never visited so late before and wondered if that was how he'd missed her other times. He hated that he had come tonight. If she hadn't forgiven him before, he knew that his hope for Anna was completely wasted now. He'd lost her so many times, but this was surely the last time. Even he wouldn't forgive himself in her shoes.

He sat on a bench, the air easing the muscles on his face, but not the hurt in his heart. He loved her, and he'd lost her. He'd lost her, and he didn't want to accept it.

Numb, he walked the distance to the Children's Hospital and into its colourful foyer. He trod quickly past the coffee shop and continued on to the corridors of the infants' unit. His legs felt hollow, but his steps felt heavy. Justin reached the room and inhaled deeply. He moved past the first family, with their drawn curtains, to Bianca, with Jo and his mother by her side. The room stunk of fear and he felt useless being in there. It sapped his soul; and his soul, having already been sapped that night, was not taking to it lightly.

'Justin.' His mother said his name like she had been waiting on his arrival.

'Mum. Jo … Bianca,' he greeted them all solemnly and smiled faintly down at his niece. Her face was an unnatural colour, worse than two days ago when he'd visited last. Her little belly swollen and her breathing shallow. Justin stopped when he heard his mother say his name again, her tone undeniably grave.

'Justin,' she swallowed and looked across at Jo for encouragement. Jo nodded but refused to look at Justin. He saw her tears fall from sore eyes. A tissue, already lived and crumpled in her hand, wiped them away only for more to replace them.

'The doctors are concerned about Bianca.' His mother paused and cautiously looked at Jo again before continuing. 'Her condition is getting … worse.'

Justin nodded. He knew this. He could see this.

'I know Mum.'

'No,' she shook her head, speaking her next words slowly, walking him through. 'It's putting too much strain on her kidneys; they're worried it could result in renal failure. Dave's brother was cleared today, to … donate. They are performing an emergency transplant first thing tomorrow.'

Justin breathed in, and out; knowing he was unable to fully appreciate what this news felt like for his sister, but knowing it made he himself feel sick.

'And … are they confident?'

'Justin …' Katherine looked down and shook her head gently. Her face didn't return, but her shoulders shook. Her worn hands went to her face and Justin pulled her to him. He looked at Jo, whose tears were now heavy, but whose eyes still refused to meet his, her hand at her mouth. His own mouth felt dry as he hushed them both, hugging his mother till she was able to continue. No part of him wanted her to continue.

When she cleared her congested throat, he braced himself.

'They have told us to prepare for …' she didn't go on. Justin knew what she was unable to say — *the worst.*

He felt like he'd been hit. What his mother was suggesting seemed unreal. Justin felt his mouth hang to say something, but he had nothing worth saying. He looked at Bianca in disbelief and felt his eyes sting, her body blurring in front of him.

Justin nodded. He didn't know how he was allowed to react as the uncle, the brother; an 'Owens' man. He bit on his lip, paced the crib, nodded again, and then left, absently excusing himself.

How could this happen? Why? He didn't understand it. He saw bad things happen every day; bad things to good people. And he always knew it was awful, had always known it wasn't fair. Was empathetic, was sympathetic. But something hitting *his* family? That didn't make sense. Understanding felt out of his reach, even though a part of him felt like he was moments from grasping it.

He didn't even have the right to say, 'It'll all be okay,' because he didn't know that it would be. He was removed enough to not feel the magnitude of pain that Jo and Dave would be experiencing, but too close and involved to be able to step back and even consider that everything might be okay.

Justin walked heavily through the hospital. He felt weak; weaker than he had only moments before when he didn't think he could feel any lower.

He steered his body in the direction of the toilets. Leaning against the gents' door, he almost fell into the small room. It was lit up by fluorescent blue lights and his eyes adjusted badly. Justin stumbled into a cubicle and his body weight collapsed on to the seat. He didn't notice hitting his thigh on the toilet roll holder. His head was in his hands and he was sobbing. Huge sobs that made him gasp for breath and made the floor blur under the blue safety lights. Everything was blurry, except the pain in his chest; the piercing sharp pain that made the tears fall. The pain was the only thing that made this feel real.

Death could ride by at any moment and kidnap Bianca in its path. It was no longer a ridiculous notion to consider, it was no longer something to deny. His niece was dying, and tomorrow would undeniably change his family and their lives.

chapter forty-eight

Anna lay on the edge of Thursday morning. Her eyes, red and aching, were wide to the darkness around her. Her head thumped like a marching band had inhabited her brain. Each thought was like a bang of a drum or blow of a horn. It was too much thinking.

Thinking, thinking, thinking.

She was tired of it. And all the thinking did was take her in an endless parade of circles.

It reminded her of that game when she was little, where you hit a tennis ball around a pole. Except now that was her head. Round and round. Knotted to the very tip, and just like that freaking ball, she felt at the end of her rope. She felt like the pole was actually jammed in her head—or maybe it was her heart. Her head and her heart hurt so much she didn't know what was normal anymore, didn't know what was what.

She saw the photos of herself around the house; the ones with her mother twenty years ago. Ten years ago. Twelve months ago. It was Anna in a whole different place, yet the same place at the same time—lost. She hadn't realised quite how much until now.

When Anna had accepted the call from the hospital all those weeks ago, she had unknowingly and unwittingly exchanged one set of fears for another. She went from fretting about loneliness, to fretting about living. Specifically, her mother living. She had had to suddenly face living life without a net to catch her.

And that was hard. It undid her and taught the word 'perspective' in a way she'd never had to know before.

But now, with faith her mum was safe, she had built up her foundations again. Thinking loneliness was also cured, only made them stronger. Then they were shaken, badly, by Justin being in that damned classroom. Justin being in Room Four however, astronomically ripped them away. She'd thought life had decided to give her a break and was unprepared for its meanness to continue.

In short, Anna was a mess.

She didn't know which piece of her life to pick up first, and she didn't want to burden her friends with asking. But trying to figure it all out was exhausting and she couldn't take anymore. There had been too many blows in too short a time.

She felt angry; violently angry. Angry at Justin, angry her mother had been hurt, angry to leave the life she had, angry to be pitied, for being lied to — for being alone.

Angry at the words on that classroom's screen; angrier to know it was Justin that broke her mother.

Old fury built in her for not getting the childhood she had thought she deserved — the father she wanted, the mother she'd needed.

She was angry that she felt so angry; and finally, admittedly, unfairly, she was angry at her mother — for not being stronger.

And all that anger, all that fury, it made her sad; unbelievably sad. Tears heaved from her body. Breaths rasped in as callously as her thoughts and fears.

She'd called in sick to work and hidden inside, avoiding life. Work, people, talking, making decisions; it felt like too much now that the final straw had fallen. She wanted to sleep all day, and not think, but as she lay exhausted in bed, that was all she was able to do. Hours stretched in front of her and denied any mercy from her thoughts.

When the sun went down, the darkness brought even more light to her feelings. The shadows taunted her, and she had no-one to make it brighter.

chapter forty-nine

It was almost closing time and for the second day in a row Justin waited for the phone to ring; for Sandra to come and tell him that the call was for him. It didn't help that he worked in an environment where the phone rang all day long. Each time, his ears pricked up at the sound and to the conversation that followed. He'd freeze, mid movement or sentence, and wait. His clients looked at him oddly, though that could also have been due to his appearance. His bloodshot eyes were testament to his sleepless night, his clothes crumpled from their stay on the floor the night before. Bianca's new liver was transplanted the day before, and though the operation didn't go badly, the twenty-four, and then forty-eight, hours that followed were critical. Yesterday he waited painfully to hear from his family to know it was over and that she had coped. Today he waited with growing faith she was safe.

Justin thought the day's steady run of appointments would allow him to be too busy to think—but was wrong. Justin felt confused each time someone commented on the festive foyer, which Sandra had overly decorated in reindeers and fake snow, because it felt six months too early.

Increasing the difficulty of the day, Justin was faced with a cat that needed to be euthanised.

Justin guessed that the owners already knew their cat's fate before Justin did, before they even closed their front door, and before they reversed out of their driveway. Nevertheless, that didn't take away his task of actually needing to voice it. He'd watched them nod to his diagnosis, taking in all the facts they needed to comfort themselves for the decision that was about to come … and he thought of Bianca.

He'd gone to reception and let Sandra know what was happening. She made a sympathetic sound and organised the invoice quietly, asking kindly if *he* were okay, the concern all too clear on her face and Justin wished she hadn't asked.

Though he hated that particular part of the job, it *was* his job. He had done it countless times and never with such concern from his receptionist. Admittedly, on this day it had shaken him, but he hadn't thought it was enough for Sandra to notice. Her asking was only shaking him more.

'Sure. Fine,' he replied and turned away quickly, walking into tears and mutterings of goodbye.

Afterwards, Justin told them how sorry he was for their loss and the cat's owner, Mr Pao, shook his hand. Justin frowned at the paradox of the gesture. *Thanks for killing my cat.* He thought of his brother-in-law shaking Bianca's doctor's hand …

Late that afternoon, when most people counted the minutes till the dawn of the weekend, Justin heard a knock on the clinic door that showed mercy to his hours of anxiety.

'Justin?' Sandra stepped in the room as he tried to brace an angry rabbit. 'There's a call for you, when you're ready.'

He knew it was *the* call. Her voice told him it was *the* call.

Justin was mid-examination and while he finished up, he wondered which family member had rung. His mother? His father? Jo? Dave? It may have mattered which person spoke, to what the outcome was.

He took the call in the back office and faced the wall. Fleetingly, he thought of the Pao's cat.

'Hello?' he spoke into the phone. He didn't know whether to sit or stand. But he stood while he came to a decision, peeling his gloves off and tossing them in the bin, wiping his sweaty hands awkwardly on his pants.

'Justin,' his father spoke. His father, the authority of their family sent to do the hard work? The man who could control his emotions like no-one Justin had ever met. The man with a Scottish boom.

'Justin,' he boomed now. 'She's doing well.'

Justin exhaled and sat down.

'Oh, thank God,' he breathed, running foreign fingers through his hair. Tension from making his face move all day erased. His heart pounded, relief making his body want to do cartwheels and sleep all at the same time.

'She's alert and well. The doctor said she's accepted the liver fantastically. Only time can really tell, but they are confident, so it's a great start, eh?' His dad chuckled, undoubtedly relieved. 'She is one lucky lassie.'

'How's Dave's brother?' Yesterday he was feeling sore but claimed to be more alive than he ever had, to be able to help.

'Good, good.' His dad laughed. 'Says he's secured the 'Favourite Uncle' title for life.'

'It's all his,' Justin agreed. 'How are the others?' Justin asked more seriously, and his dad exhaled loudly.

'Aye, I don't think it has set in yet,' he sighed.

'What else did they say?' Justin asked, needing more medical points of reference to ease his mind further. The day before, the information was too vague, the hours too precarious to verbalise details.

'She has a lot of medication, but nothing more than before,' his dad offered and thought some more. 'The doctors say the liver is functioning as best they'd hoped. Her colour is much better, though they're keeping close watch on her immune system and kidneys.' Justin worried with the risks still to come but rejoiced in the happier news.

'How's Mum?' he asked after a silence and heard his dad find the kindest answer.

'Tired. I need to take her home.' The worry in his voice was evident. They said goodbye and Justin hung up, momentarily letting the news sink in until his mobile rang from across the room, bringing him back to work. He let it ring out and walked back through reception. Sandra, swiping a client's credit card, looked at him intently, desperate to know the news. As Justin happily welcomed Harry the poodle into the clinic for his checkup, he smiled widely at Sandra to let her know Bianca was safe for now. Her face flooded with relief and she held her heart. Justin laughed, and it felt amazing.

Justin fished his phone out of his bag after Sandra had dropped him home that night. He listened to the voice messages while searching the fridge for food. He'd had no time to shop, so his options were limited.

Cutting up an orange, he heard the first message from Lesley, saying they'd see each other at the hospital the next day. Justin had considered trying to see if Bernadette was still there, though figured that now she knew who he was, it would be inappropriate for him to return; regardless of how badly he wanted to apologise for the latest situation.

Justin deleted another message and reached one from Tom.

Hey Doc, not sure if you've heard, want to hear or are even supposed to hear, but Anna's gone back to Melbourne. Mel thinks she's lost the plot—not her words. Thought maybe you'd want to know. See ya.

Justin listened to two more hang-up voice messages before he decided to make a call of his own.

chapter fifty

Anna woke up feeling disorientated.

It took her a moment to realise where she was and why she was there. The unexpected knock at her door, the arguing, the crying, it all met her consciousness swiftly and she yearned to be asleep again. It had been taking her so long to fall asleep, even in her missed bed, that she doubted her body could make it happen again. Grateful Ioulia was out for the night, she saw the clock on the new microwave, marking the minutes that had passed. She couldn't believe he had come. For her.

Exhausted, Anna leant her head on the door, daring not to breathe, just so she may hear his breath. She could feel Justin's weight on the other side of the door. Or maybe she could just sense that he was still there. Maybe, if she was completely honest, she just really wanted him to be. She didn't want to know that he, despite his efforts to see her, had now given up on her. That she wasn't worth the effort or the heartache after all. At the same time, and the reason why they sat on opposite sides of the door, she wished he *would* just walk away. She knew that it would be for the best that he did.

Anna shivered and was reminded of what she was wearing. She grabbed at his t-shirt and on recognition cried quietly. Why was she doing this? She loved him.

She knew she loved him like she knew the sky was blue, because what else could this feeling be? She physically ached to have him in her arms. To smell him. To kiss him. She knew she wanted him more than anything. But she also believed that it wouldn't work. It couldn't work. Not in the end.

She couldn't be with him and know what he had caused. It was all about self-preservation now.

So, Anna continued to sit there; too afraid to live life with him, and too afraid to live it without him. Too attached to stand up and walk away.

Justin sat by Anna's front door, frowning as the wall pressed relentlessly through his shirt, and staring at the Christmas star that hung on the chipped door; their words had only chipped at it further.

He'd been sitting there far too long for comfort and Justin had begun to wish he'd better planned this.

After he had heard Tom's message, Justin called Jane, who had reluctantly verified that Anna's mother had been released from hospital, that Anna had taken off for Melbourne, and that she had seemed to have lost the plot (not Jane's words). He had then taken his car—the one his father had picked up only a week before and he'd obediently not touched—and driven to Tom's house, demanding he drive him to the airport.

Justin, nervously biting his thumbnail for the duration of the drive, committed Tom to getting Anna's address, and called in a favour from the recently married Paul, to drive him to it. He secured a ticket for an eight-twenty-five flight and arrived to the white apartment building in Elwood close to eleven p.m. He stood at its steps, praying for a chance, and waved Paul off.

But when he tapped at her door, Anna had refused to open it, and Justin had refused to go away. And it wasn't about the distance he'd come, he simply couldn't leave knowing she wasn't okay, he couldn't be away from her anymore, and he refused to believe her when she begged him to go. And maybe that is what every stalker claimed, but he didn't want to leave, and he couldn't.

Everything that had happened to keep them apart aside, Justin wanted Anna more than anything. He didn't think it'd be too hard to communicate this, but what began with a simple knock at her door, asking to come in, continued as a heated and fuelled battle of wills. He had tried to talk over her with his explanations and she copied; each one speaking louder in an attempt to be heard. It was a tug of war where both had finished shrunken on the ground, defeated and spent, with nothing of use being heard at all.

Now, hours later, his back ached and his tired eyes burned; the events of the week having completely depleted his energy. Justin almost reasoned that he should go and try again in the morning — the success of Bianca's operation being enough celebration for one day. But he felt greedy for more.

Justin knew what he felt for Anna wasn't something he had ever felt for anyone he had ever met. He doubted he could feel like this for any other person that walked the earth, and he didn't want to have to prove it to be so. What's more, he believed, right to his very core, that she felt the same — though she'd never said anything to make that real.

How he felt with Anna was not something he would give up on, not yet, and definitely not for comfort or pride's sake. Justin held his heavy head in his hands. He could hear Anna sniff on the other side of the door and his heart sank.

At almost two a.m., it was well and truly Saturday. Her neighbour had arrived home an hour ago. Thankfully, after the yelling. He had given Justin an awkward look, unsure if he were homeless, a menace or simply pathetic, as he let himself inside across the hall. Justin decided not to care unless the police were called.

There was a soft thud on the door, right near his ear and he realised her head must be right next to his. He gently placed his head where the noise came from. If he could will the door away, he'd be exactly where he wanted. Not on a floor in a doorway, the spiky hairs of the worn carpet prickling his skin; but just to have her next to him. Justin thought he could smell her perfume and it was a cruel trick to his senses. He slid his fingers under the door, they could only just wedge under, but it was all he had left to reach her.

In the dark entry, a scrap of yellow light from the hallway crept in from under the door, though it failed to let in any other clues from the outside.

Hugging her knees, Anna wondered if Justin was cold too. If he'd eaten? How angry he was; how tired? He must be tired, she thought. She herself felt intoxicated from exhaustion: hastily packing, the long drive, the protests of her decision, work, insomnia; Justin. Prior to Justin's arrival, she had revelled in the fact she was home and could start putting Sydney behind her — at least until her promised Christmas return. She shuddered at the thought of returning, curling up even more and thinking of Justin just centimetres away.

His eyes, his smile — his beautiful, big smile. His hands, his jaw, his voice …

Part of her felt like it was in an argument with itself, warning of the consequences of her thinking such thoughts. But her sense of rationality was as impaired as her heart and she continued on.

His eyes, his smile, his hands, his jaw, his laugh—his big, beautiful laugh.

With each thought Anna felt sadder. She could feel her brain surging with various feelings. More tears began to slide, but too tired to wipe them, and knowing her efforts would be fruitless, she let them track down her face, down her neck and onto his shirt. Something dark appeared under the door and Anna blinked to clear her eyes. She ran her finger slowly along the rough carpet until it collided, and a small noise came from her throat.

He was still there.

She stroked his fingertip and, in her state, didn't consider the fact that he'd know about it. The idea of touching him had taken over her logic and the effect it had made her silent tears fall faster.

'Anna, please let me in,' she heard him quietly say. She could hear him shuffle on the other side of the door, and the light from below moved. His fingers remained under the door and Anna looked down to see that her own fingers were still touching them.

She unlatched the lock and his hand slid away.

Without thinking of the hours of effort she had put in to not opening the door, Anna opened the door.

Justin scrambled from his knees to his feet. He was undoubtedly surprised that, after so long, she was facing him. He stood, staring at her anxiously. Unshaven, with dark messy hair, Anna saw how worn-out he was, and guilt nudged her to open the door further.

Justin's fingers felt a jolt of surprise when her cool fingers began to circle his. It sent a shiver down his spine and he whispered for her to let him in. He didn't think for a second that she would, but when he heard the lock click, he bolted to his knees.

As the door opened, he thought his startled legs may give out as he clamored to his feet. Anna opened the door halfway and he noticed she was wearing only a shirt; incidentally, *his* shirt—which did nothing to hinder his wanting for her.

She looked up at him with a face so scared and so wounded that it hurt him to see. Her cheeks were wet. Her red eyes had mascara smudged under them. Her hair was falling out of place. She looked awful. The worst he had ever seen her. And he had never wanted her more.

In one swoop he stepped inside and closed the door with his elbow. He grabbed her face with both hands and pressed her into the wall, kissing her fiercely. There was no tenderness, just sheer desperation. Her wet face was pressed into his and she kissed him back like she'd been starved of breath.

She felt nearly frantic to have him; frantic, crazy, irrational, wild and hopeless.

She folded her legs around his waist. One at a time, gradually around him, until her whole body was hugging his; their mouths never losing touch, desperate to be as close as they humanly could.

She could feel his muscles tense as he pressed her more firmly into the wall, her shoulder bumped the mirror that hung there and, in that moment, Anna sobered.

'No,' she mumbled, but he didn't seem to hear, only kissing her harder.

'Stop. Justin, stop.' She'd dropped her feet back to the ground, annoyed at herself. 'Justin, we can't … I can't.' She shook her head, tears falling involuntarily, and Justin stood very still. 'I can't be with you. This can't happen.'

Silence hung in the dark, surrounding them in vain. It was as if someone turned the music off. Anna felt guilty that it was her.

'I'm sorry,' she murmured, too tired to offer more explanation as she swiped at the tears with her palms. It was nothing different to what she had already said, and yet he waited for more. Anna stood there in his quiet, going over in her head what she could say. What she wanted to say. Thinking what would make him understand, without resistance, and leave. But words were twisting and turning, and she didn't think it was anything she could rehearse, not with her heart pumping as hard as it was. Everything seemed so complicated and unfair.

Anna tried to transfix herself on the notion she could be asleep soon, calming her slightly, but the idea fled at the unexpected volume of Justin's words.

'Anna, for crying out loud, *say* something! Anything!' Justin begged of her and she felt like he was pushing her off a ledge.

'I don't know what to say … I don't know what I want.'

His head hung for a moment and she wondered if he'd let it be easy.

'I've heard you say that you wanted … someone. You complained about being alone,' he reminded her quietly, before gaining more confidence to proceed. 'But here I am. Here's what you said you wanted, and you say it's nothing. I mean *nothing*? I'm sorry, I'm not trying to sound conceited, but Anna, I think we have something that is pretty fucking great. You say you want love, but then you don't seem to believe in it. You don't even recognise it when it's staring you in the face.'

He stood taller than she had ever seen him, so sure of himself. Anna could barely tolerate it, because he was wrong. He had it wrong. With every word that he spoke, her face rose higher. Her eyes locked in, never looking away—though every part of her wanted to run and cry her heart out. Anna shook her head at him once he was silent. His poor assumptions made her angry and she forced herself not to correct him, because it wasn't just about love.

'I do want those things Justin. But not with you,' she told him harshly and felt his recoil. 'I just want normal! A normal life, in a normal relationship, with a normal person.'

Justin looked at her for a moment, taken aback. 'Yeah? Well, Anna, a normal person is just someone you don't know very well.'

She felt outraged and didn't know why. Flustered and confused she blurted out words like a child in a playground. 'Yeah, well you're pretty good at keeping things that way, aren't you?'

He laughed an ironic laugh and it egged her on.

'This isn't the life I wanted! *This* isn't what I want. This here …' she pointed between the two of them, 'is *too* complicated. I don't want complicated. I —'

'*This* is life!' Anger took up any space in the cramped doorway as he cut her off. 'This is the stuff that shapes our lives. Bills, work … accidents. Anna, this *is* life, and *life* is complicated. You can't run away thinking it's not right, that it's not normal. Anywhere you go, anyone you are with, there will be arguments Anna. No-one plans for bad stuff when they dream up their life, but that doesn't mean it won't happen, and it doesn't mean it's wrong. Stop running. Let's just work it out.'

Anna shook her head, sure. She wasn't going to fall for him any deeper, only to be hurt again. She wasn't going to fall for him, only to wait out their end.

'Anna, I don't want to be eighty and still trying to convince you of how I feel. And how I feel isn't going to change.'

'You don't know that,' she shook her head.

'Yes, I do. You are wasting the time we can have together. Take a risk. Living life avoiding problems is only going to keep you lonely. You're doing what your mother did,' he added softly.

'What is that supposed to mean?' Anna demanded; her defenses high.

'Look at her Anna. You said yourself that she hardly stepped out. Your dad left and she avoided pain by avoiding life. Locking herself up, moving all the time, never settling—not trusting anyone. You're doing the same thing. A problem happens, and you run away.'

'That's not true. She has someone now. She's happy now. Don't you dare compare me to my mother. You don't know her,' she replied icily. Anna didn't understand why *he* didn't just walk away, give up and move on.

'I think I know you though,' he said quietly. 'Are you happy now?'

His words hit her like he'd sent a foot into her belly, and though Anna felt impressed he'd been paying attention, she was also disturbed by his analysis, and angry at his boldness.

Feeling suffocated, Anna desperately wanted to be by herself and have the whole situation out of her life. She hated herself for opening the door and she wanted Justin gone so she could get on with getting over him.

'You don't know me,' she told him, the coldness remaining in her small voice. 'And clearly, from what I've learnt about you lately, I don't know you either. Quite frankly Justin, I don't want to.'

As her last words fell on his ears, only his eyes reacted. She stepped back slightly, anticipating that her wish was about to come true.

'Right,' he told her, nodding his head, his brown eyes the most vacant she had ever seen them. 'Right, of course. I'm just some guy you met at a bar.'

'Who then drives home,' she reminded him like the bitch she felt like. Justin smiled, a sad ironic smile, which allowed Anna to see just how far she had stepped over the line.

'Right. The guy who drives home.'

With that he walked past her, out the doorway he had haunted for the night, and was gone.

chapter fifty-one

Sandra had hung the Christmas cards, sent from their grateful clients, around the clinic and played her *Christmas Classics Album* (continuously) from her desktop; murmuring the lyrics happily as she worked. She negotiated the requests to turn it off by leaving a constant supply of slices in the kitchenette. Justin, however, didn't feel festive in the slightest, and no amount of Sandra's famed lemon slice altered that—though he had tried. Meanwhile, his mother, amongst all the drama, already had an oversized tree arranged in her lounge room, complete with wrapped presents for everyone. Olivia and Samantha shrieked when they saw them, squealed when they recognised their own names, and cried when they were told they couldn't open them for three more weeks. Now, with a week to go, their anticipation was at breaking point.

Even Jo and Dave looked happy about Christmas. Bianca had arrived home and that was a lifetime of Christmas wishes all wrapped up for them. Lesley and Tim were excited that it was their son's first Christmas. And Justin's dad had already made sure his Santa suit fit and his wine collection was stocked.

In the Owens family, it was all about Christmas—except when it came to Justin. Justin was too busy acting busy to even acknowledge it. So busy trying to avoid people that he'd accidently included life as well.

Unintentionally, Justin had spoken to Tom. He'd rung Justin with his number withheld, and the conversation only encouraged him to remain a recluse. Justin had felt duped when he recognised the voice and even more duped when he heard what Tom had to say—who was oblivious to the impact his words had.

Justin, whose pride was still recovering from his whirlwind trip to Melbourne, and not wanting to look any less masculine than he already felt, shrugged off Tom's update. Though, he genuinely felt bad for Julia when he heard that she had caught Adam cheating on her. Not surprised—this *was* Adam—but definitely some empathy. Admittedly, the vindictive part of him also enjoyed the story.

It was the news that Mel had seen Anna—who apparently was fine and had returned back at work in Melbourne—which affected him. He had known it was just an eventuality, but it made her move official. Knowing his visit only drew the nail further into the coffin, didn't help. He hated that she left Sydney, and him, in such circumstances—and so soon. He was still stunned she'd left so quickly, and before Christmas, and he knew that was his fault too. He'd had a pipe dream that she'd fall in love with him and stay. Stay long enough to be friends (if not marry him and have his children) so he felt like he had something to cling to.

But it didn't work out that way.

And, truth be told, he was angry at her. When he left her apartment that morning, he found the beach she loved and sat on the rough sand. He watched the flat water while thinking over the situation in his head; the anger building as the sea came in. He accepted Anna was angry at him too, that she had some right to be, but he couldn't accept that she wasn't willing to talk to him and give him a chance to explain. If she'd listened to the whole story, he was sure he wouldn't have been sitting on the sand waiting for the sun to come up, alone. But the fact that Anna had never asked for it, or given him the slightest opportunity to tell her, made Justin think maybe it wasn't worth it. He didn't like to think it, but maybe she wasn't worth it.

chapter fifty-two

Wednesday had included a lengthy lunch with Mel. Even though (after running out on her Sydney role, claiming over a week of sick leave, and having only just returned to work) she had a lot of work that should have been a priority. Furthermore, though Anna was worried her recent lack of attendance had damaged her reputation, management had chosen her to present their services to a potential new client who she had been corresponding with while in Sydney—flying her in business class and providing a company car for her to do so. They felt sympathetic towards her unexpected departure and, knowing she was returning for Christmas, felt it would serve everyone if she returned to Sydney a little earlier to run the presentation, finalise her work there, and say goodbye properly. Anna, flattered, felt horribly guilty and rejected the invitation instantly. She wasn't keen to be in Sydney any longer than was required, especially when the offer followed on from her own unprofessionalism. But they insisted, and when Mel heard she had declined, had guilted and begged for Anna to take the offer. It would mean Anna would be in town for Mel and Tom's get-together. Anna refused again and when Mel's face threatened to turn nasty,

Anna approached management and sheepishly told them she'd love the opportunity.

All of this meant that Anna now had only one more day to get her work (and herself) organised and she was under the pump to do so.

Regardless, the time with Mel was wonderful, and helped ease Anna's concerns that she'd made a mistake returning to Melbourne. Mel seemed equally relieved to have her friend back and as she spoke of her impending European holiday, Anna felt green with envy. She also felt green with anxiety of returning to Sydney and turning up at Mel's send-off party—which she'd only ever seen as a 'we're going overseas and you're not' celebration. But as Anna listened to Mel, she realised that she hadn't even stopped to consider how her friend would be feeling; besides excited.

In fact, Mel was terrified of having to meet all of Tom's friends and family, was stressing that she couldn't fit enough jackets into her bag and she'd freeze to death in Switzerland; and, although Anna had thought Mel had worked past this, was still concerned she and Tom would find themselves hating each other a week into their trip.

Her final concern, however, was that they wouldn't break up at all, but that they'd come home still in love, and one of them would need to make the sacrificial move. Anna, guiltily, also worried about this as it would mean Justin would not be shaken from her life as easily as she'd hoped.

Pushing the thought aside, besides trying to redeem herself for her recent selfishness, Anna was relieved not to be dealing with her own life for once. She wondered if this was her counsellor's motives. Anna had had a final meeting with her only the day before she had run into Justin. She'd wanted some closure before she moved back to Melbourne—not intending at the time to do so quite so prematurely. Maybe Jessica chose that career as a way to avoid her own problems.

Mel, using her vulnerability well, and having already won the battle of wills for Anna to even attend the bloody party, had also begged Anna to be at Tom's house early to help set up. Anna, not understanding what set-up was needed for a barbeque, had awkwardly declined, claiming she should visit her mum that day, hating that she was actually worried Tom had asked the same favour of Justin.

By the time Anna left for home that night, the anxiety she was already feeling about what was a basic barbeque to the other guests, had increased significantly. By that stage she was thinking of sticking to her original plan and not leaving for Sydney until Christmas Eve. She was desperate to keep the distance between her thoughts and Sydney's attractions for as long as she could—each step south of the border could only offer her more protection.

And then, after Christmas, she could return home. A home that now smelt of incense, but home nonetheless. And free from the drama she'd found in Sydney.

As she drove through the peak-hour traffic, Anna imagined telling Jane and Mel, again, that she wouldn't be at the barbeque and wondered if she'd come out of the conversation unharmed. An even more extravagant idea was not returning for Christmas either. Two risks she'd have to lend more time to considering later.

chapter fifty-three

'I love this song.' Anna's voice hit a high note as she cried out to Jane. They'd been to Jane's new gym in a conscious effort to become healthier before all the Christmas parties made a noticeable impact. Undisputedly, it was Jane's idea. As was returning to Sydney.

Jane had rationalised to Anna that if she was going to be miserable romantically, she should at least maintain positive relationships with her work ... and her friends. So Anna had taken her seat in business class on Friday morning (feeling reluctant, but admittedly also exceptionally accomplished and smug), arrived at the Sydney This is IT office via taxi, and by lunch time had been congratulated on an impressive presentation of the company's newest capabilities. She was welcomed back enthusiastically and was grateful when she ran into John Chan that she could apologise properly for leaving so unexpectedly. He had been surprisingly kind about her sudden departure, surprising her further with a lavish and belated farewell cake in the tearoom — complete with fond speech. Afterwards (and almost every week she had been there) he had suggested she consider a permanent, and more senior position with them in the future. Weeks ago, Anna had thoughtlessly told Brian this and it was the very next day that her mother, a little too coincidently, began her 'Bring Anna Home' campaign. She had asked her to first stay for Christmas, then hinting at the idea of making Sydney home — an idea that, in certain moments, Anna had entertained with lopsided interest.

Leaving the office later that afternoon, even after such a long day, and even with Tom and Mel's party looming only one sleep away, Anna felt positive and in control again. So, when Jane had counter offered Anna's suggestion of Friday night pizza with exercise, Anna had agreed enthusiastically.

Since leaving Melbourne, both had admitted to physical laziness due to mental exhaustion. Tonight, they drove home with muscles quaking and brains firing, determined to continue with their gym attendance when they parted ways after the holidays.

Anna, singing duet with one of Mariah Carey's Christmas classics, easily dismissed Jane, who claimed that Anna loved *every* song.

'Yeah, well, it's not a person. I don't need to have monogamous relationships with my song choices. I love it and you can't help love.' Anna smiled brazenly.

Jane rolled her eyes. 'What would you know? You say you've never been in love,' she teased.

Anna hesitated before growing defensive, 'Well … I still *love*. I love you.' She fluttered her eyelashes sweetly as Jane pulled up to a red light, which seemed to be as frequent as Anna's favourite songs that night.

'I'm *so* lucky,' Jane droned.

'The point, my little lovebird,' smiled Anna, 'is that I love this song,' she declared, singing louder.

Jane raised a brow at Anna's mistaken lyrics, feeling glad to have her back. They drove along the main road, Jane searching for more songs as Anna's 'favourite' ended. Every station seemed to be running ads.

'Why do they always do this? Put a song on!' Jane growled at the radio, frowning at it until, finally, a song played. 'Where've you been?' she spoke to the song crossly.

'What and you're happy with this song?' Anna enquired with amusement. '*Love Really Hurts?* It's inappropriate. And crap.'

'What, you don't *lurve* this one?' Jane remarked, poking fun at Anna further; happy to see her more like the Anna they all knew. The Anna who was also trying to deny the fact that her heart was broken, that her mother's near miss had terrified her; and the Anna that was refusing to admit she actually missed Sydney.

'Ha, ha, smarty. No, it's a silly song. It's way too boppy for its message. How can they sing 'Love really hurts without you. You're breaking my heart but what can I do',' she sang—badly. 'How can they sing that and sound so darn chirpy?'

'Fine,' Jane laughed, defeated. 'You find a better song then.'

Anna fiddled with the stations and found another FM station that had remembered to put a song on. She leant back in her chair.

'There,' she smiled, satisfied.

'What do you mean?' giggled Jane. 'It's the same song!'

Anna listened and frowned. She must have hit the same button. She changed it back to hear the exact words being repeated on the other station. The girls looked at each other. Jane laughed. Anna frowned.

'That's hilarious. What are the chances that this old thing would be on two stations at the same time?' Jane chuckled. 'Try again!'

'I can't,' Anna shook her head meekly. 'The universe must want us to listen to this song.'

Jane looked at her friend, ready to laugh again, but saw she was serious. Anna had spent way too much time with Ioulia, Jane conceded, to consider the universe's part in an FM line up.

Anna had settled back into the seat, soaking up every word as if it was a poem being recited specifically for her. Jane stifled a laugh, refraining from teasing like she most wanted to.

'Do you think I'm being an idiot Jane?'

'Yes.'

'I mean about Justin?' Anna asked sadly and Jane was caught offguard, not knowing the right thing to say. She assumed that saying 'yes' again wouldn't help.

'Well …' she stretched out. 'I can understand where you're coming from. He lied to you. Okay, he didn't lie,' she thought out loud, 'But he hid something that was pretty important. Especially in your circumstance …' Anna nodded appreciatively. 'All that aside, he seems like a great guy and I thought you both had something,' she admitted openly.

Anna nodded some more and chewed on Jane's words.

'We had something,' Anna agreed. 'But we only had the beginning of something, you know? The *very* beginning at that. And the beginning is always good. That's the whole point of the beginning, right? There wouldn't be a place to start if it wasn't great, right?' Anna managed to rule out the entire relationship and justify her decision with her own questions.

'Well … that's not exactly true,' Jane interjected. 'You kind of started angry, remember?' Jane, feeding the truth tentatively, felt relieved when Anna took that truth well.

Jane drove on while Anna sunk lower in her seat, deep in thought.

'I just don't know how I could forgive him,' she eventually spoke. 'I know he didn't purposely hurt my mum. I know that. But he did do it and he did drive drunk. How can I pretend that didn't happen? I know he's angry at me for not getting past it. I get that. But how can I, Jane?' she begged, completely perplexed at the concept. Jane didn't respond, as lost for answers as Anna.

'I've never fought with someone so much in my life,' Anna exhaled. 'It really wasn't meant to be. And I moved anyway …' she concluded. The song ended, and Jane spoke her next words carefully.

'Did you ever think, maybe, that you just never found anyone worth fighting with? Or worth fighting for?'

Anna looked at Jane, who kept her eyes on the road, her hair escaping from its ponytail. She looked unusually frazzled, but she spoke sense.

'Maybe Anna, you just couldn't be bothered before. Maybe *they* couldn't be bothered because, and no offence, it wasn't worth the effort,' Jane looked across kindly, she'd slowed for another red light and Anna looked back away, the idea a tad too confronting.

'He wasn't my type,' she muttered defensively.

'You're right, he wasn't,' Jane agreed, and Anna stared at her in surprise, not expecting Jane to agree. 'For once you picked someone decent.'

Anna sat quietly, waiting for the wheels to move along from under her again. Her fingers fidgeted with the hair elastic on her wrist, twirling it around and around, her eyes refusing to look up.

'Even if I could forgive him, it's ruined. I … I just want him to think the world of me,' she said and then laughed at the vainness of it. Jane laughed too. 'Is that really as bad as it sounds?'

'No. It's not,' Jane admitted, a hint of sadness in her voice.

'I want him to think I'm perfect, and I hate that he doesn't think that. That he already knows, very well, how *not* perfect I am, and I know how *not* perfect he is … I really thought he was perfect,' she added, quieter still.

Another car honked its horn for them to move, but Jane chose to ignore it and it sped off around her as the light turned red again.

'Anna, don't you think he's thinking the same thing?' she suggested. 'And anyway, he may know you are not perfect, but I think he already thinks the world of you.'

Anna shrugged a grateful smile. 'But you're just saying that. You don't know that,' she dismissed her.

'No, I do know that.'

Anna looked up, with hope that maybe Jane had spoken to Justin, that she knew it for a fact. 'I know, because *I know* you are far from perfect, but I think the world of you too.'

Anna smiled, touched. 'You have to say that, I depend on you to.'

Jane shook her head. 'Anna, he loves you. I'm sure of it. He wouldn't have gone to Melbourne if he didn't. Perfect or not, it doesn't really matter does it?'

After a restless night and fruitless Saturday morning sleep-in, Anna packed up more of her mother's belongings, losing hours in the old photo albums, and eventually drove them to their new address. Wincing, her exercise efforts from the night before made themselves known as she climbed out of the loaned company car and into the sticky heat.

Anna knocked on Brian's front door, rearranging her enthusiasm. Jane's words had plagued her all night. The word 'love' considered painfully so. The thought that Justin could be at Tom's that night made her want to vomit. The only thing that eased her anxiety was telling herself that no-one could make her go to the party. Not Jane, not Mel — even if she had sworn her attendance to both of them.

She quickly smiled as Brian welcomed her in and out of the sun. When she followed him down the airy hall, Anna felt grateful he thought her mother was worth all his effort. His commitment through the long weeks her mother had spent at the hospital seemed mammoth to her. All the tests, fears, infections, injections, and waiting—he'd stood by her.

'Hi Mum,' she tried to sing, but it came out as more of a croak.

'Hi love.' Her mother, now perched on an expensive cream lounge, Claude by her side, and with an impressive six-foot pine tree presented beautifully behind her, smiled so wide that one wouldn't be a fool for not knowing the pins in her leg were a constant discomfort. Her arms were now bandage free, her hair had re-grown enough to cover the scar on her head and the shadow of her chin hid the other. Looking at her now, one would think her mother simply a little tired. She had months of physiotherapy ahead of her, monthly check-ups on her lungs, a careful diet and various pills, but the fact that it was all ahead of her was something grand.

Brian politely excused himself and Anna sat down opposite her mother's outstretched leg where they could both enjoy the beautiful view of the bush land beyond the picture window; the summer heat muted by a canopy of branches.

'How are you doing?' At the sound of Anna's voice, Claude looked up, glanced at her with indifference, and then settled his face away, showing no signs of gratitude for the care she had recently provided.

'Good,' her mum smiled again as she stroked his fur. 'How are *you* doing? How was the trip up?'

'I'm fine. It was fine.'

'And your presentation?'

'It went really well. Thanks.' Anna was so distracted by her impending night that she couldn't come up with enough words. Preempting her mother's thoughts, she willed her to have some useless gossip to impart rather than talk about Anna. What colour towels Brian used, perhaps.

'Have you spoken to Justin?' she asked, straight off the bat, and Anna wanted to reply that it was none of her business. She had no intention of sharing that Justin had arrived at her door in Melbourne. The scene from his visit was all too raw in her mind; the truth of his character all too confusing. What it meant and how perfect she thought he was otherwise, fought to override all the other senses in her head.

Anna lied and shook her head, trying to restrain herself from reacting in any form. 'Have you?' she asked sarcastically, failing to hold back and hating the unluckiness of it all — and her behaviour in Brian's house. Her mother shook her head.

'No, Anna,' she sighed. 'I haven't.' She kept her voice low. 'But I've been doing a lot of thinking and I think … we need to talk.'

Anna, feeling worry swirl, watched as her mother shook her head with embarrassment. 'I don't know where to start,' she admitted uneasily, and Anna sat patiently. 'I need to be honest with you Anna, but first I need to ask you to forgive me for not being honest to begin with. I was … scared.' Her mother looked away and Anna felt herself sit forward.

'The police have spoken to me about the accident. I had assumed that Jay – Justin, sorry — would have told you this already. But, Anna, Justin was actually the one who *saved* my life … the accident was not his fault,' she stated. 'It was mine.'

Tom's barbeque was kicking off in almost three hours. Justin had three more hours to decide what to do. Three hours to add to almost three months of simply not knowing what to do. He didn't know why he thought it'd be any different after tonight; in all honesty it would only be worse, because as frustrating as it was, chasing Anna had become all he knew. Once this night was over, once he decided to be in the company of her best friends, or not; or be in the company of his once friends, or not; he'd have to find a way past it all. Justin was curious to know how that was going to work out for him.

He wondered briefly if he should do what Tom and Mel were doing and go overseas. Maybe work in a practice in Scotland and stay with relatives. This plan crashed quietly when he recalled his financial situation. It was officially extinguished when he remembered that he had a business to run. It was only half-hearted anyway because how could he leave his family? After almost losing her, why choose to miss seeing his niece grow up?

Justin sat on his back porch, feet up on a paint tin, throwing a ball against the grey wall — thinking. He held a bottle of beer in his hand and drank from it only when he thought he'd come to a decision. Needless to say, the beer was warm.

Thump.

Hamlet sat on the grass, panting in the heat. His black eyes followed the ball, anxiously waiting for Justin to command him to fetch. But he didn't. He just kept throwing the ball — missing a catch nearly as often as he drank the beer. Justin had found a rhythm and the consistency brought him peace of mind; he finally had control of something.

Tom would forgive him if he didn't go to the barbeque. Justin had already preempted not going by suggesting he take Tom and Mel to dinner on the Sunday night. He'd texted that it would be a better way to get to know Mel and give them a chance to talk. Not that he actually wanted to talk or get to know Mel any better, and not because he didn't like her or approve of her or their plans, but for the simple fact that she was Anna's friend and Justin didn't want to tip-toe around that little pearl with them. But he would, if that meant getting out of tonight.

Thump.

'Hamlet,' he declared, and the dog threw his head up, thinking this was his moment. 'I'm not going.'

Justin sipped his beer and Hamlet cocked his head to the side. Justin threw the ball.

Thump.

He wondered if Anna was happy; if she missed Sydney. If flying down again to ask her would be considered a good way to get over her.

Justin had avoided Tom's calls but knew from a voicemail that Mel had arrived safely and agreed to have dinner on Sunday. Justin felt bad knowing that it was his fault one of her closest friends wouldn't be there tonight. He then experienced a rare moment of understanding female logic that this would mean that Mel was also, in fact, annoyed with him. And not just as a supportive friend.

Justin held the ball in his hands for a moment longer, gazed at the wall, and threw it again.

Thump.

If he didn't go, he would be encouraging Mel to think even less of him. If Mel thought less of him, Anna would too.

Justin sipped his beer and frowned.

He was going to the party.

Thump.

Justin had managed to turn up to soccer training that week and learnt that most of the team would be turning up to Tom's as a pre-Christmas-drinks opportunity. It made him edgy. He'd even considered quitting the team, for about a second, before acknowledging that it was a stupid idea. Quitting would only take more life from his life. Adam made no more effort than usual, and his initial surprise at Justin turning up to training had shifted to a general indifference. Adam played harder next to Justin, and Justin played better next to Adam.

Thump.

Would Adam be there tonight?

He sipped his beer.

Anna sat up in shock, the low lounge barely defeating her efforts. Claude stirred at her movement and darted off the lounge in a flurry.

'You were on the phone while driving? Who were you on the phone to?' she quizzed her with a peculiar interest. It wasn't particularly relevant, but she was curious. Her mother looked away again and Anna's senses pricked up.

'Your father,' she admitted, her face an expression of guilt.

Anna felt annoyance more than surprise. She had had concerns he would reappear but wasn't happy that he had a presence in her mother's life already.

'Dad?' she asked the room. 'Why were you talking to Dad? Was he here?' Anna shook her head and felt her brow furrow, feeling uncomfortable with how she felt, recognising jealousy growing in her like an ambitious weed.

Her mother stalled again and looked at Anna pleadingly to lower her voice.

'Anna, your father … has issues,' she spoke tactfully, ignoring part of the question, and Anna could see she was being kind. 'He's not good with money, I guess you could say.'

'Like, gambling?' Anna gasped.

'No, no. Not a gambler exactly, just terrible with money —really terrible. Buying things we never needed, getting involved in hare-brained money-making schemes that always failed, maxing out credit cards. He was, and still is it seems, terrible with money. Always has been. Anyway, he needed some help and he called me that night,' she admitted shamefully.

Anna took in the information, matching it to her memories, checking it over to verify; frowned when it did all fit.

'Had you leant him money before?' she pried and hated it when her mother nodded. 'Often?' and her mother nodded again.

Anna recounted moments in her childhood that she couldn't do the things her friends could because they had no money. Thought of the dresses her mother had stitched to save the funds for something more necessary, like rent. Anna thought back to the last time she'd seen her dad and had shouted him dinner as he'd claimed to have forgotten his wallet.

'Is that why you broke up?' Anna asked guiltily, knowing she had often blamed her mother's character for her parents' breakup. That it was her fault they weren't granted the regular life she had so hopelessly craved. She'd let her father's clues be deciphered to mean that her mother was cruel and irrational, when in fact she was protecting herself and her ignorant and thankless daughter.

'Yes. We were about to lose the house. We fought every day about it. I asked him to leave,' her mother confessed, making Anna's guilt official. She let that sink in before she asked her next question, noticing Claude approach them cautiously.

'Why did you lend him the money then?'

'I loved him.'

Anna didn't like that answer. In truth it disgusted her to know what stupid things people could do and claim love as the reason.

'Did you give him money this time?' Anna asked warily and was relieved when her mother shook her head, Claude wilting back by her side.

'No. That's why we were arguing.' Her mother took in a breath. 'Anna, I hadn't told Brian, or you for that matter, that I had contact with him. I guess I didn't want you to have contact with him because I didn't want you to be caught up in his problems. And I'm sorry. As for Brian, I guess I didn't want him to leave me. I knew he didn't want me talking to him. So, when I lost control of the car, and I remembered why, I didn't know how to tell you,' she confessed, moving her body uncomfortably.

'But you told the police?'

'Yes … and Justin,' she added reluctantly. 'I'm sorry Anna.'

'Justin knows about Dad?' she demanded, utterly appalled. Claude cowered and fled again at the sudden jump of her voice.

'No,' her mum hushed. 'Just that the accident wasn't his fault,' she amended, and Anna felt a small amount of relief amongst the feelings of humiliation that were resonating in her body.

'But he *was* drunk?' Anna needed to verify, and her mother conceded with a shrug.

chapter fifty-four

There was a warm breeze from the summer sky as Anna arrived at Tom's house. She was in Justin's neighbourhood now and the proximity to his home had an unusual effect on her—its presence radiated from only streets away.

Anna was late, she couldn't decide on the right clothes, and that would be her excuse. Not the nausea that had swept through her body as the waves of fear hit her increasingly throughout the afternoon. She wanted an outfit that said 'ignore me' and 'unforgettable' simultaneously. But every concoction she came up with had a missing piece that was awaiting her arrival back in Melbourne. She bleakly wished she were with those pieces now.

For the party, she had eventually settled on a loose white dress, teamed with the slides she had bought while braving the Christmas crowds on Chapel Street that week.

Anna approached the house slowly. Another couple were also arriving as she walked up the drive. She smiled a hello, testing her social skills were in operation.

Anna didn't want to be there; had no desire to be around people she didn't even know, or to participate in useless banter. Pretending she cared about the latest blockbuster, news head-lines, the humidity, the Prime Minister's latest blunder or the day's crickets scores were of no interest or concern to her. She was hanging out for the New Year, so she could start afresh.

Anna took a breath and stepped inside, and almost straight into Tom.

'Thank you!' he shook his hands in prayer position and turned his face skyward. 'You are late young lady … but Mel is going to be very glad to see you,' he grinned. 'Agh!' he gasped. 'You need a drink. Quick … to the bar,' he yelped and pushed her towards the kitchen.

Anna was grateful for the task, dodging the first hurdle of arriving solo. Hating again that she had conceded to come, Anna really wished she could have just been busy, really sick … or in Melbourne.

She should have stayed in Melbourne.

Sure, Mel would never have forgiven her, but maybe it would have been worth the trade-off. If Supportive-Anna hadn't encouraged Mel in believing how great this darn barbeque was going to be when Mel revealed her blind panic, it may have been easier. Now, not coming would have been mean, and, closer to Anna's fears, would have revealed her true weakness.

Really Anna came for the chance to see Justin, she knew that. She knew that while she tried on her entire, though small, supply of clothes, and she knew that when her body shook with anticipation. Whether to talk to him, apologise, or just to say goodbye; she wasn't sure. She didn't want Justin to think she wasn't brave enough to show her face, or that he was right, and she ran away from her problems.

She walked into the kitchen where two much younger girls were pouring a row of shots.

'You want one?' they giggled, and Anna declined responsibly, though tempted; it would take the edge off her nerves.

She watched as they clinked glasses and downed a drink. Giggling into one another, they reached for another. Anna, partially envious of their state, reached for a wine glass and an open bottle of red she saw on the bench, adding another from her bag to the collection.

She moved slowly, delaying being a part of the crowd, but with drink in hand she had nothing else to do but take a deep breath and hope for the best.

Outside, Anna stood next to Mel and Jane, critiquing Tom's fake Christmas tree which stood pride of place in the middle of the yard, when she spotted a familiar face. She'd been there long enough now to relax, the wine having reached her nerves, and she was beginning to enjoy herself.

'Hey, how do I know that guy?'

All three pairs of eyes looked in the direction Anna had indicated.

'Never seen him,' Mel stated with disinterest, swaying as she searched the yard unsuccessfully for Tom, her eyes almost useless without her glasses, moreso with an empty wine glass in her hand. Anna could see Tom clearly. He was not that far away from the mystery face.

'Sorry, me either,' Jane piped in, eyes fixed on his firm tanned body. 'Hot,' she admired, before adding bluntly. 'Looks like a wanker though.'

Unusually for Anna, she agreed, somewhat put off by the guy's mannerisms, but she couldn't look away either. The answer was creeping up on her, she could feel it. She watched Tom approach him and shake his hand, holding on to it as they spoke.

'He doesn't look happy, does he?' asked a squinting Mel, having now found Tom.

They all watched as what seemed like a tame conversation, became a scene of interest that many other eyes watched. Not that it was loud; Anna couldn't hear a word they were saying, but Tom seemed to be warning his friend, who in turn acted unconcerned. Their body language drew attention and Anna was curious why other people were watching with such interest. When Tom finally walked away, heading towards Mel, those paying attention waited for the other man to react. Instead, he brazenly left the yard to go inside and Anna turned her attention back to Tom, who was now at his girlfriend's side.

'Having fun?' he asked them, making a clear attempt at brushing off the confrontation, unaware they too had witnessed it.

'Who was that?' Mel and Anna asked simultaneously, and Tom rolled his eyes.

'That was Adam.'

'Adam!' Anna slapped her thigh, 'I knew I knew him.'

'You know Adam?' asked Tom, crinkling his brow. Then, 'Melbourne! Of course!'

Jane and Mel watched the conversation, their heads turning back and forth like they were at an ABBA reunion show, the name being only vague in their memories. Tom could see Mel's eyes furrow trying to work it all out.

'I'll explain later,' he told her, squeezing her waist. 'Hey, anyone want any drinks?' And a moment later he was gone. Mel followed and Jane, receiving a message from her sister to say she'd arrived, went searching for her. Anna wasted half an hour talking to the shot girls from the kitchen, learning that they were Tom's much younger cousins, before she saw another familiar face sitting beside her on a green plastic chair, biting into a sausage sandwich with gusto.

'Hey, Sarah's husband … Matt!' she called boldly, recognising Jane's brother-in-law. Wine, and having accepted that Justin would not be coming, had relaxed her, stripping her brain of etiquette. 'How are you going?'

'Hi, Anna, right? I didn't see you there,' he spoke, revealing the contents of his mouth.

'I thought you guys had other plans tonight?' The shot girls bopped off for another drink and left Anna and Matt to chat.

'Nah, we are just good old-fashioned late.' He laughed, and a piece of bread flew from his mouth and landed just short of Anna's new shoes. 'We thought we had two do's on tonight, but turns out they were one and the same,' he grinned.

'How do you mean?' Anna felt confused.

'Tom's a mate of mine,' he explained. 'So, this was actually where we were going when Sarah said we had plans.'

It all clicked, and Anna laughed with him at the teeny tiny small world that they lived in. They chatted about work, Sydney, and Melbourne perks.

'We'll have to go again,' he told Anna with that assurance that married people have, that they still had other years together — a notion that was foreign to Anna. She encouraged that they should travel down, wondering what it'd be like to know you always had someone to do stuff with, someone to go places with and make plans with. Her thoughts were interrupted by Sarah, who had saddled up next to Matt giggling.

'Hi Anna,' she sung happily, smacking a kiss on her husband's cheek and then Anna's. Anna laughed a hello in return, blushing slightly. She hadn't seen her since Jane's birthday, and she still felt embarrassed by her mood that day. But Sarah didn't seem offended, in fact, Anna had never seen her so cheerful and wondered what her secret was, unless of course that secret involved a fermentation process, because *that* secret was no secret to Anna.

'Hey ba-be,' she drew out as she wriggled onto her husband's lap and wiped the tomato sauce off his chin. 'Tom told me to ask if you've been wearing my dresses … I don't get it. Something about you stole my purse. But why would you steal my purse? I don't get it?'

Matt looked at Sarah in confusion, he seemed just as perplexed as his wife and Anna held concerns for the two of them—and Tom. Matt reached into his back pocket, pulling out his wallet. He showed it to Sarah, confused, and when Anna noted the shiny metal clasp on his purse, an odd feeling came over her.

'Oh, hey,' Sarah slurred on; Anna figured she must have run into Tom's cousins in the kitchen. 'You didn't tell me that Julia and Jay broke up,' she hit him playfully.

'Sure I did,' he defended. 'Didn't he tell you that when we picked him up?'

'Nope,' she shook her head and lost her balance. 'And you didn't tell me that Julia slept with *Adam*, or that Jay broke his nose!' she continued, laughing now, holding her hand over her mouth. Matt tried to balance his wife, assuring her that no nose was broken, and Anna tried not to feel as sick as she did. The incident with Tom and Adam was rapidly making sense. Anna scanned the yard for Adam now, she hadn't seen him since.

'You guys know Justin?' Anna asked as casually as she could, looking around again, confirming that Justin still hadn't arrived, regardless of the clues that now told her otherwise.

'Jay?' sung Sarah. 'Yeah, he's great. Poor guy,' she shook her head sadly and then grinned happily a moment later. Matt, noting Anna's interest, and Sarah's vagueness, continued for her.

'You know Jay?' he asked, and Anna nodded, smiling faintly. 'Poor guy's been totally gipped this year, hey?' he told her with pity. 'We haven't really seen him much since the accident,' he confessed and Anna nodded again, glad Matt was so chatty because her own tongue felt tied. Tom joined them loudly at that moment.

'Anna!' he cried. 'Sarah! Smitty! Woooo,' he threw his hands in the air and they all laughed happily—Anna's more than mildly forced.

'So, how do you know Jay?' Matt asked her and Tom looked on expectantly. Anna didn't know what version to give and swirled her wine absentmindedly as she considered an appropriate answer.

'Mel and I met through Jay and Anna,' Tom offered kindly, intoxicated, but with good intentions nonetheless. Sarah and Matt reacted to the news happily. 'This is Doc's true love,' he then added, much to Anna's astonishment and embarrassment. Sarah cooed and Matt bobbed his head happily. Anna excused herself.

The group wasn't very loud for the amount of people that filled the yard, but it was too loud for Anna's thoughts, which suddenly seemed to be screaming inside her head, and she needed to be alone.

Hoping no-one would notice her departure, she slowly wandered down the steps that led to the pool, which lay ignored and silent at the bottom of the yard. Looking behind her as she went, she glimpsed couples leaning into one another, a group huddling over a phone screen; women gossiping. She saw all these people, but not the one person she almost hurt to see, even though the mere idea terrified her.

Deflated and confused, Anna quietly opened and then closed the gate against the festivities and stepped down towards the pool. Its coolness eased her instantly and the smell of jasmine brought back old memories which she wasn't even clear on. She felt a feeling of safety. Mel had warned them of the mosquitoes it bred, but Anna was willing to risk it as she carefully stepped out of her shoes to sway her toes in the water.

Strung high over the pool were rows of tiny fairy lights. Little white bulbs twinkling like stars in the summer night sky. It was simply beautiful. She stepped deeper into the water, only briefly taking her eyes off the lights around her, careful not to spill her wine. She felt like she was in some magical place; far, far away from her life that was sending her brain into orbit.

She began to wonder why everyone was not in the prettiest part of the garden, when she heard someone clear their throat from the back of the decked pool area. Simultaneously, she was bitten by two mosquitoes, lost balance, and stumbled with a clumsy splash, only just avoiding falling dramatically into the pool. The magical moment she was enjoying dissolved along with her Sauvignon Blanc into the water.

Anna's face reddened as she strained her eyes to make out the person in her company. She quickly stepped out of the pool and self-consciously sunk her wet feet back into her shoes. She felt an instant anger towards them: for ruining her moment, for ruining her new shoes, for finding the space first … for seeing her stumble like a drunk and lose her drink.

Totally valid points, she thought.

'Are you alright?' the voice asked, and at the sound of his voice she knew that she was not.

'Sorry,' Anna replied. 'I didn't know you were down here. I didn't know that you were here,' she motioned weakly towards the crowded yard above. Just his voice, his presence, was making her emotions skew. She felt tears brewing and felt angry that he could do that, and all he did was ask if she was alright.

Bastard.

'Don't be. I had a phone call I needed to take. I was about to go back.'

She didn't reply. She really couldn't. One word and she was sure she'd start crying. She bit her lip to give her brain some other hurt to deal with.

Justin, not knowing what to do, kept talking. 'I can go if you'd like Anna.'

She didn't reply.

'I didn't think you would be here.'

She couldn't speak.

'Anna, are you okay? Did you hurt yourself? Please … say something,' he pleaded gently, coming closer. But she simply stood there. She could almost reach him now, if she really wanted to. She knew what she wanted to say but had too much fear and too much pride to say it.

'Okay, well, I don't know what to do,' he confessed, quietly exasperated. 'I know what I want to—' he stalled on his words, getting quieter as he spoke, talking more to himself. 'I don't know what to do.'

With hesitation, she looked up at his face. His brown eyes looked concerned, tired, and sad; definitely sad. But mostly, Anna just thought they looked beautiful, and her heart threw in an extra kick for good measure. Justin took another small step forward and was now peering down at her. Her mind started reeling. She thought she could see his arm shaking, but it may have just been her that was shaking.

'How's your mum?' he asked gently.

'Good,' she squeaked. 'Bianca?' she managed to get out, hoping he'd work out the rest of the question.

'Better,' Justin said, shrugging the subject, his voice low. She felt desperate to touch him, to hold him, to be held by him, and was surprised when he reached for her.

Before she realised what was happening, he had brought his hand up towards her throat, glided his fingers under her ear and crept them through her hair. Little goosebumps sprouted across every inch of her body. It was like the power going back on after a blackout.

He pulled her right up to his mouth and spoke. 'Anna, I'm in love with you,' he apologised.

Her breath caught with her thoughts and everything seemed to stop. He brought her mouth to his and kissed her. His lips taking full command of hers for one brief, beautiful moment. 'And I'll want you for forever.'

He repeated the kiss, sending her heart into overdrive. If it gave an extra kick before, it was just throwing them away now, Cancan style.

'But Anna …' His hands rested on her shoulders, the 'but' he spoke of weighing on her more. 'Chasing you?' His lips, that only moments ago had loved her, squirmed to the side. His head shook, 'I know I have to stop.'

He looked into her eyes and took his hands back; the weight not lifting. She held her breath, not wanting to know what he was about to say, but praying he'd just hold her, kiss her; kidnap her.

'So … I'm going to go now.' He stepped away instead. 'Goodbye Anna,' he added quietly. And with that he turned, walked up the steps to the gate, opened it, and was gone and out of sight before Anna could comprehend what had happened.

She stood looking up at the fairy lights feeling paralysed.

With every moment that passed, a goosebump his kiss had brought sunk back into her skin—the power, gone again. As the last one disappeared, her head fell, and not long after, so did her tears. The blurry lights strung across the pool continued to twinkle down on her. Almost mocking that their life was so graceful, while Anna's was a mess. The warm air still embraced her skin, but now she felt cold. She felt alone too.

But she was alone.

chapter fifty-five

Jane clanged through the gate. Anna wasn't sure how long she'd been alone, but it ended loudly.

'There you are. I've been looking everywhere,' Jane exclaimed and then scoffed at the glass floating in the pool. 'You'd think people could pick up after themselves,' she complained, and Anna thought momentarily that she might be issued a detention.

As Jane fished the glass out of the pool, Anna almost laughed at the metaphor it brought — Jane, always picking up the pieces of her life. Anna looked on guiltily. She didn't want Jane doing that for her anymore.

By the time Jane had rescued the glass and reached Anna, Jane realised that she had been fussing over the wrong problem.

'Anna, what's wrong?' she asked in alarm. 'What's happened? Was it Justin? I saw him. He was saying goodbye?'

Anna gave a slight nod and Jane waited while she calmed and composed herself.

'He just … left.'

'You spoke?' Jane confirmed, and Anna nodded again. 'And he left? Oh, Anna, I'm sorry,' she hugged her friend, speaking over her shoulder. 'Well … I don't know if this is the right time, but I had something to tell you. It's why I was looking for you,' she began.

'What is it?' Anna stepped away, looking on vacantly as she swiped at another ruthless mosquito.

'Well, I was talking to Sarah?' Jane checked Anna was paying her full attention. 'She said you were talking to them earlier and for some reason she's under the impression you are Justin's new girlfriend … anyway; she said that Matt was there the night of Justin's accident. They'd gone out for drinks with their soccer team and that guy … Adam?'

'Yeah?'

'He was there. Apparently, he was joking around about adding a bit of 'spice' to Justin's life and not long after, Justin left.' She told Anna like it was vital, but it meant nothing to Anna.

'So?'

'So? Anna, Justin wasn't actually caught for drink driving, but DUI. *Driving Under the Influence.* Sarah said she heard they'd found ecstasy in his system.' She whispered ecstasy like the word itself was illegal.

'Great, so he takes drugs as well. Terrific,' Anna muttered.

'Anna! Think about it. What did you tell me about that night we first met Justin?'

Anna focused on a fairy light and wiped at her face. Jane was already nodding as Anna swung her head back with realisation.

'Adam spiked his drink?' exclaimed Anna.

'I asked Tom, had to force it out of him, but that's what they think happened.'

Anna sat down on a sun lounger, humiliated, relieved, and embarrassed beyond means.

'It was never his fault,' she managed, looking up at Jane; the lights making a halo behind Jane's head while she shook it.

'What happened out here tonight?' Jane asked soothingly, squatting down to Anna's level.

'He kissed me, told me he loved me … and left,' she admitted, crying again.

'Well, what are you still doing here?' Jane laughed softly. Anna looked behind her at the trees and the pretty lights.

'Jane,' she said, so quietly that Jane had to lean over to hear her. 'I love him.' Anna's shoulders shuddered, she was so tired of crying, but the tears grew bigger as she tried to swipe them with her hand.

'An, honey, it's about time,' she smiled kindly. 'You may want to tell *him* though.'

'Justin!' Anna's voice was hoarse as she wheezed from running. Consequently, his name didn't travel very far.

'Justin!' she tried again. But he continued to walk further away from her.

'Jay! Doc! Owens!' she stopped to cry out, at a loss of what else she could shout.

Justin looked over his shoulder momentarily and she waved for him to stop, but he didn't. Anna faltered. She was unsure if he'd actually seen her and wondered if she should just let him go.

She watched him walk. His tall body under the streetlights, his dark hair, his long arms. She took him all in, remembering the kiss he had just left on her lips.

Anna looked down at her feet, her new and impractical shoes almost daring her. In a flash, she kicked them off, apologised to them, and ran. Her dress flew around her as she moved, her necklace whipped her face, and her hair stuck to her lips, but her feet kept hitting the footpath.

She reached him just as he was about to turn up the next street. He didn't seem to hear her, and Anna was only a few feet behind. She grabbed his arm, pulling his hand out of his pocket. Justin twisted around sharply and, when he realised it was Anna, looked at her in surprise.

He pulled the earphones out of his ears, not breaking their eye contact, and waited for her to speak.

'Hi,' she gasped, her lungs hostile about having to now speak as well. She tried to control her breath and hold onto some dignity as he watched her. 'Hello,' she tried again.

'Hello,' he returned, looking on expectantly, not knowing what he should be thinking, but visibly noting her red eyes which still burned from her tears. He looked guarded and she didn't know where to start.

'Justin ...' Anna looked at her feet

'Yes?' he was watching her carefully, searching her face for clues.

'Um ...' she glanced across the road.

'Anna, just *say* it.' She looked up at him. Her heart was going wild. She could have been about to bungee jump she felt so nervous. She wanted to sit down. His eyes flickered, looking almost angry, and the fear of him walking away again flicked a switch inside her. Suddenly her adrenaline kicked in. She leapt.

'Justin, I love you,' she confessed. She thought his stance relaxed and his eyes softened, though to Anna's distress he didn't respond to confirm this. Her heart was hurtling to the ground and he didn't respond.

'I'm sorry. I'm sorry I didn't listen to you. I made assumptions that I based on ... on ... on ignorance, I guess. And I'm sorry. I shouldn't have done that, but I did, and I'm sorry. I should have heard you out.' She blurted it all out, the words racing from her lips before she could even edit them.

He watched her, silent and expressionless, as she spoke and then considered her carefully.

'Why?' he asked simply. 'Why now? Why not earlier?' he was cautious, and Anna was sure he'd walk.

'I know the truth now.'

'I could have told you the truth.'

She nodded. Her eyes stinging relentlessly. 'You're right, I know. I'm sorry.'

He shifted his weight and she breathed before tentatively continuing.

'You were right about other things,' she admitted slowly, and he listened. 'I'm not used to people hanging around and I was scared. I didn't want us, if there was an 'us' that is, to turn bad. I resented you for my mum and I didn't know how I could get past that. I just didn't know how Justin, and I-I guess I used it as an excuse. I felt things I didn't know what to do with and I pushed you away. You have every reason to be angry at me. I was a bitch and I'm sorry. I just want you to know that I'm very sorry,' she fiddled with her hands. 'And that I'm in love with you,' she finished.

She focused on the ground, her bare feet on the rough concrete. The space between them was excruciating and she wished she could just turn and run back now that she had said what she'd wanted to say. She curled her toes and saw another pair of feet in front of hers. Looking up, her nose was almost on his chest, which was rising slowly. Anna tilted her head to see his face.

'Anything else?' he asked calmly. She thought for a moment and nodded.

'Yeah. That kiss back there …' she motioned down the street. 'Uh-huh?'

'That was amazing,' she said quietly. Justin smiled a small smile and lifted her chin towards his face.

'*That?*' he asked, his brow crinkling with confusion. 'That was nothing.' He gave her the lightest of kisses on her forehead. 'Do you want to walk me home?'

Anna took in the sight of his face. Flashes of their history flicked through her head while she smiled with certainty.

'I do.'

With a smile, he slipped his hand into hers and they wandered down the street, grinning at each other every few moments. They'd rounded the corner and had said nothing more until Justin cleared his throat.

'Um … Anna?' She looked across at him expectantly, a docile grin on her face.

'Hmm?'

'Where are your shoes?'

epilogue

Justin sat on his sister's lounge, taunted by his brother-in-law over the Australian cricket team just losing the match. Tim didn't even like cricket, so the taunts were empty — Dave took them to heart though.

'Oh, Jay,' sung Jo from the kitchen. 'Favourite brother of mine?'

'Only brother,' Justin corrected her.

'Number One uncle …'

Justin smirked at Tim, holding his forefinger up and mouthing 'Number One.'

Tim flipped him off. 'As if. You didn't even give a liver.'

'Most adored vet …'

Dave sat back, relieved Jo wasn't asking for him and he could continue to dwell on the unexpected loss.

'Y-e-s?' Justin asked carefully.

'Sammy won't go to sleep,' she sighed, staggering into the room with her daughter wrapped around her leg, tactfully adding, 'And she just *loves* your storytelling.'

Justin laughed as he held his hands out and collected his niece, clasping her little hands in his, and raising her up onto his shoulders in one swift motion. 'Say no more.'

'She's demanding your mushroom story. What is this story anyway?' she asked Justin, who smiled elusively and ignored the question.

'Sammy are you going to say goodnight to everyone?' her dad suggested meaningfully.

From over Justin's head, Samantha squealed a goodnight and waved her hands to her mum, dad and uncle. As they passed the kitchen, she waved to her grandmother and aunty.

'Where's Anna?' she whispered down to him.

They found Anna and his dad in front of a laptop. Anna was trying to explain (to the man who struggled with everyday telephone operation) virus protection. She clicked buttons and maneuvered her way around like a true geek and Justin felt proud.

'Hi Jay,' welcomed his dad as he noticed them tower into the room. 'This is some brain ye have here,' he pointed to Anna with his thumb and she shooed him away modestly.

'I know. To think I'm only with her for her looks,' Justin grinned. 'Samantha here wanted to say goodnight.'

His dad scurried over and stretched up to give Samantha a loud raspberry on her cheek, which put her into hysterics, and they heard Jo call out to them.

'Dad! Don't excite her now!'

He rolled his eyes at Anna. 'Aye, now they tell *me* what to do,' he complained at the paradox. Anna tried not to laugh at him, but she shared a small smile with Justin. Justin knew she still found his accent hilarious.

'She had a special request for you,' he told Anna, who pressed her finger to her chest in surprise.

'Wow. Well then, goodnight Sweet-Sammy,' Anna told her and blew her a kiss. Samantha swiped at the air and clumsily pressed Anna's kiss to her lips. Justin took Samantha down the hallway, past Bianca's room — where she lay snoring gently in her cot, happy, healthy and oblivious to all—to the bedroom she shared with Olivia.

'Story, story,' she clapped her hands together as he laid her under the covers in the bed next to Olivia's, who lay waiting patiently.

'Shhh, we don't want to wake Bianca,' Olivia whispered, holding her finger to her lips to shush her sister, who mirrored her.

'Okay, which story would you like again?'

'The mushroom one,' Samantha whispered loudly and almost instantly. Justin couldn't help laughing, and began quietly, while sitting at the end of the bed.

'Once upon a time, far, far away, there was a farmer who lived near a forest. He lived on a farm that grew fairytales. Ones for little boys, ones for little girls, ones for dogs, and ones for cats—even ones for grown-ups.'

'What about birds? Are they for birds too?' Olivia asked and he nodded.

'Sure, even birds. The fairytales grew under mushrooms and he worked very hard in the fields to make them grow. But one day he went outside and was very sad. He found flowers beginning to grow on his farm instead. Now, *everyone* knows that fairytales can't grow under flowers, they need mushrooms …' he looked down at Samantha and her eyelids were closing, a small smile on her face. Justin continued on about the fairytale farmer, how the flowers were taking over his farm, how they made the fairies fly upside down, and the leprechauns sing backwards. He told them about the pixies whose wings wouldn't work, and about the one named Annabelle, who could stop the flowers growing, but had run away—and pixies were really hard to catch.

Justin saw their restless bodies rest. Their eyelids flickered closed and their chests rose and fell as he continued the story in his lowest voice.

'He searched *all* day and *all* night for Annabelle. He searched over the hills and down to the sea. The fairies even helped him look—but they were upside down and couldn't see. The farmer was so tired he almost gave up. Then, one day, as he walked home through the fields of flowers—where there should have been mushrooms—he heard someone laughing. The farmer crept towards the sound and found Annabelle playing with a ladybug behind the biggest mushroom left on the farm—the biggest he had ever seen. The farmer was over the moon, because *everyone* knows that to catch a pixie, a perfect pixie like Annabelle, is the trickiest thing to do of all.'

He took a final look at their faces and turned to leave.

'Uncle Jay?' whispered Olivia, who had fooled Justin into thinking she was asleep, and he'd completed his job. He looked at her with surprise and waited for her to go on.

'Do you love Annabelle?'

Justin smiled. He loved these kids.

'Yes. I do.'

'Why?'

Justin thought about it for the briefest moment before answering, sure Olivia wouldn't understand.

'She's my rock.'

She seemed satisfied with this answer and Justin went to leave again.

'Uncle Jay?'

'Yes, Livy?'

'That's what she said.'

www.ingramcontent.com/pod-product-compliance
Lightning Source LLC
Chambersburg PA
CBHW060939190726
48286CB00005B/1342